Fierce Passion

Look for these titles by *Phoebe Conn*

Now Available:

Fierce Passion

Phoebe Conn

PUBLISHING

Samhain Publishing, Ltd.
11821 Mason Montgomery Road, 4B
Cincinnati, OH 45249
www.samhainpublishing.com

Fierce Passion
Copyright © 2013 by Phoebe Conn
Print ISBN: 978-1-61922-200-7
Digital ISBN: 978-1-61921-840-6

Editing by Linda Ingmanson
Cover by Kanaxa

First Samhain Publishing, Ltd. electronic publication: November 2013
First Samhain Publishing, Ltd. print publication: November 2014

Dedication

Fierce Passion is dedicated to my wonderful family and dear friends who are always there when I need them. I love you all dearly.

Chapter One

Barcelona, Spain

The exquisite orchid corsage lay beside Ana Santillan's place card. It was whiter than snow and tied with a fiery red satin ribbon. She made a yearly donation to the children's charity benefiting from tonight's gala dinner, but she wouldn't have been singled out with such a lovely corsage. There was no card, and that week beautiful rose bouquets had also arrived at her condo without a sender's name.

She'd assumed her mystery admirer might be too shy to sign a card, but if he'd left the orchid at her place, he must be there and hope to meet her tonight. Anticipating an awkward introduction to a man she'd rather not know, she spread the starched linen napkin over her lap and left the orchid untouched.

Seated with advertising personnel she knew from modeling, she smiled at their spouses and partners. Armand Leyva, one of her favorite photographers, gave her a welcoming grin. She enjoyed her companions' decidedly ribald humor, although as the evening progressed, she grew increasingly uncomfortable. The eerie sensation of being watched created an itching ball of heat between her shoulder blades. She made her living with her face and figure, but being slyly observed unnerved her.

The popular benefit drew a wealthy crowd, and she recognized most faces but knew no one well. Turning to see who sat nearby, she found Santos Aragon with his American fiancée. Although she and Santos were through months ago, she didn't envy his latest willowy blonde. Someday soon he'd shatter the poor kid's heart and leave it scattered like glass at an accident scene.

She scanned the tables seated closer to the orchestra, but no one gazed her way. The hairs on the back of her neck continued to twitch. Someone stared at her even if she couldn't catch him. He hadn't approached her during the cocktail hour, but she'd arrived only a few minutes before everyone had been ushered into the ballroom.

The dinner had been quite good, even if she hadn't eaten more than a mouthful or two, and the auction would soon begin. She excused herself to beat the rush to the restroom. The hotel's newly remodeled lounge was decorated in ivory and gold with comfortable padded chairs, and rather than return to her table, she sat to rest and ripped her fingers through her gently curled hair.

Leaving early would make it far too easy for an adoring fan to follow her home. She yawned, kicked off her silver heels and rested her feet on a bench facing the long mirror. If she'd come with one of the brawny men she'd posed with last week, maybe being watched wouldn't be so unsettling. Unfortunately, she wasn't particularly fond of any of them.

She looked up as the door opened, and nearly hissed as Santos's fiancée entered with Maggie Mondragon. She nodded to Maggie and forced a smile. After posing her whole life, she easily summoned a pleasant expression.

"Ana, I haven't seen you since, well, it's been a while," Maggie greeted her. "I framed all the beautiful photos you took of Rafael and me. I believe you've met my sister, Libby."

"Yes, at the photo shoot for the Aragon cologne ad," Ana replied. "Santos and you are spectacular on the billboards, although I prefer the intimacy of the magazine ads."

"They're my favorites too," Libby replied. "That's the last time I'll say yes to modeling. It's much harder work than people imagine."

Ana eyed Libby with a sudden inspiration and stood to study their side-by-side reflections in the mirror. Santos had a weakness for leggy blondes, and she'd be a fool not to use their remarkable resemblance to her own advantage. "We have the same coloring, the same height and size. Would you do me a favor?"

Surprised, Libby turned cautious. "What sort of favor?"

"Someone's been sending me roses, red one day, yellow the next, and this morning, a flaming orange. There aren't any cards. There's an orchid corsage at my place, and I'd rather not stay if my mystery admirer hopes to meet me tonight. If we exchanged gowns and you went back to my table for a few minutes, I could slip out without being followed."

"Wait," Maggie warned, her voice full of concern. "If someone is stalking you, we should notify the hotel security."

Ana laughed. "Spanish men shower women with flowers every day. If I complained someone's been sending roses, I'd look ridiculous."

"The magazines with your fashion spreads have excellent relationship articles. Don't you read them?" Libby asked. "Controlling men often begin with flowers and gifts, and their true nature doesn't emerge until the woman attempts to break it off."

"That's why I'm very careful about the men I date," Ana countered. She congratulated herself silently for keeping Santos's name out it. "All I want to do is go home. Will you help me?"

Libby and Maggie exchanged perplexed glances. "Why not?" Libby answered. Ana's gown shimmered with silver threads while Libby wore a long, dusty-rose sheath. She'd also worn her long hair down and softly curled. Once they'd switched gowns, all she had to do was bend over to fluff her hair, and when she stood, she could easily pass for Ana at a casual glance.

"We do know an excellent private detective, if you'd like a reference," Libby offered.

Ana gave Libby's arm a fond squeeze. "Thank you, but no. I'll send your gown to the beach house Monday, and the deliveryman can pick up mine. Give me five minutes to find a taxi before you return to your own table."

"I saw where you were seated," Libby replied. "Maggie, we came in together. Why don't you walk Ana out, and she'll be mistaken for me."

Maggie sent a quick glance at the mirror and curled her long pageboy behind her ear. "Fine, let's go."

Ana took a deep breath. "You keep talking, Maggie, and I'll keep my head down as though I were following closely."

Libby let them go, counted to ten and left the restroom as several women entered. She raised her hand to shade her face as she made her way through the maze of tables and slid into Ana's place. Dessert had just been served, and her companions were exclaiming over the raspberry mousse cupped in a chocolate shell. She took a bite.

"Oh, this is good."

Armand's brows shot to an extraordinary height.

Thinking he'd recognized her from the Aragon cologne ads, Libby raised a finger to her lips. She'd pushed her hair forward so those seated beside her couldn't see her face clearly. She picked up the orchid corsage and buried her nose in it while Armand continued to stare. Ana had only asked for five minutes, and when Libby saw Maggie rejoin Rafael at Santos's table, she assumed Ana must have already left in a taxi.

She sat up and smiled. "How silly of me. I seem to be at the wrong table. Please excuse me." The orchid corsage remained in her hand as she left.

Santos stood as she came to the table, and he swept her with a puzzled glance. "I'd swear you were wearing pink when we arrived."

Libby gave him a light kiss and returned to her place. "How perceptive of you. Ana Santillan and I swapped gowns."

Maggie touched Santos's sleeve. "I know your opinion of Ana, but she needed a favor, and we were glad to help."

"Why would she need another gown?" Santos asked incredulously.

Rafael, Maggie's husband, leaned forward. "Women think in an untranslatable language. Don't try to understand them."

"Save your advice for a man who needs it," Santos shot back.

"Fine, because it doesn't come cheap."

"Gentlemen, please," Libby scolded. "This dessert is incredibly good. Let's enjoy it in a peaceful silence. I'll answer all your questions later, Santos. I promise." She gave her lips a saucy lick, and as expected, Santos's dark gaze lightened to a sexy smolder.

The Aragon beach house was designed by a protégé of Antonio Gaudí and was a stunning example of surrealist architecture. With curves rather than sterile straight lines, the home had the perfection of a seashell nestled along the shore of the Mediterranean. Libby and Santos went back and forth between her room and his so often they had to sit up and look around in the morning to discover whose bed they'd chosen.

She turned her back to him and lifted her hair in an invitation to unzip Ana's gown. "Thank you." She stepped out of the slinky silver dress and folded it over her arm. "Someone has been sending Ana roses without including a card. She thought he might be there tonight and wanted to leave before he approached her."

Santos responded with a rude snort. "She has very low standards.

I can't believe she'd shun a man who'd send flowers."

She poked him in the chest. "Don't insult her. We have the same taste in men."

He caught her hand and pulled her close. "Avoid her. Tonight she wanted your dress. Who knows what she'll ask for next time you meet?"

She rubbed her hips against his. "I love it when you go all macho. I won't let her have another chance at you, and that's all that matters."

He growled against her throat. "Macho I can do."

Her man was so easy to distract, and she was far too curious about Ana Santillan to avoid her indefinitely.

Maggie sat on the side of their bed and kicked off her heels. Rafael studied her wistful expression. "Didn't you have a good time tonight? Should I have bid on something in the auction?"

Everything about the black-eyed gypsy fascinated her. His hands were as handsome as the rest of him, and she watched him unbutton his shirt. "It was a lovely evening, but we shouldn't bid on expensive things we don't need."

He shrugged off his shirt. "It was a very good cause."

"True, and I'm happy to help all the children's charities, but I really thought we'd be on our way to having our own family by now."

He took her hands to coax her up and helped her out of her fluid pale peach gown. The luscious color complemented her hazel eyes and hair, and her lingerie was a dreamy lavender with a smooth satiny feel. "The two of us are a family," he insisted. "We were only married last summer, after you'd nearly bled to death." He kissed the scars on her wrists. "You can't rush nature. The babies will come in time."

She swayed against him. "I hope so."

He pulled her close and fondled her hair. "We'll have all the babies you want, even if we have to rely on science to become parents."

Her smile turned slyly seductive. "I prefer the old-fashioned method."

"So do I, so let's not waste any more of tonight." He overwhelmed her with affection, and they were swiftly lost in love.

Ana made it home without being followed, but her mystery lover already knew her address. She paused at the security guard's desk. "If someone arrives claiming I'm expecting him, please send him away. I don't care who he is or how magnificently he's dressed."

"Yes, Miss Santillan. Has someone been bothering you?"

"I attended a large party tonight, and I'm being cautious. Thank you, Jacob, good night."

Rather than walk into a dark room, she always left the lights on in her condo. Nothing was out of place, although the fragrant roses on the coffee table were a colorful warning something was definitely amiss. She wouldn't toss them until their blooms began to droop. She went into her bedroom and carefully slipped out of Libby's dress. It was scented with the haunting Aragon cologne. Maybe Santos splashed it on her for fun.

She yanked off the pink diamond ring Santos's father had left her in his will. Miguel had died much too young, and while Santos resembled him, she longed for the original Aragon man.

Ana was so easily recognized on the street she seldom left home without a large hat and dark glasses, or her favorite disguise, a straight black wig with bangs that brushed her eyelashes, generous Goth eyeliner and baggy black clothes. She'd always tip the security guard before she left so he'd recognize her and allow her back in, but she loved being able to go for long walks on Sunday afternoons and not draw more than an occasional idle glance. Slumping along rather than walking with her usual regal grace, she felt exhilarated the whole way.

El Gato Café off Las Ramblas was a favorite place to order tea and bite-size nut cakes and sit on the patio to read. When a young man carrying a bulging backpack asked to join her, she nodded and remained focused on her book.

"Thank you. This place has become so popular there aren't any empty tables or I'd not have bothered you."

A good-looking guy with glossy black hair and eyes the color of dark smoke, he was so tall he couldn't fit his knees under the table and had to sit sideways. When after a few minutes of scanning one of his books he cradled his head on his backpack and closed his eyes,

Ana reached into her bag for her camera.

From the day her mother had first pushed her in front of a camera, she'd known models had very short careers. Growing up, she'd spent so much time in photographers' studios she'd developed a real talent with a camera. She eased out of her chair and knelt to photograph the student from several angles. With no plans to sell the photos, she didn't need a release, but she hurried to return to her chair and hide her camera before he woke.

When he sat up, he brushed back his hair and checked his watch. "It's too beautiful a day to study architecture anyway. I like your Goth look. There's something primal about it."

Relieved not to be recognized under such a thoughtful stare, she offered him a cake. He took it off the plate before she'd finished asking.

"I forgot to eat breakfast," he explained between bites. "I need to order something. Would you like anything more?"

"No, thank you, I'm fine."

He stood but took only a single step. "Will you watch my books?"

"Yes, they'll be safe." She watched him duck to enter the café. She spoke to few people outside of her modeling jobs, and he was a refreshing change. There was no harm in letting him believe she was an ordinary girl who enjoyed wearing black.

He returned with a thick roast beef sandwich and a beer. "I study here for the sandwiches. What are you reading?"

"*The Prisoner of Heaven*, Carlos Ruiz Zafón's latest."

"Great writer. He spends part of the year here, but I've never met him. Have you?"

"No, not yet." He was concentrating on his sandwich, rather than on her, which was a glorious relief. There had been no rose bouquet that morning, perhaps because florists were closed on Sunday, or leaving early last night had discouraged her mystery fan.

She marked her place and closed her book. "I need to go. Good luck with your studies."

"Wait a minute, I don't know your name. I'm Alejandro Vasquez."

"Ana," she replied.

"Maybe I'll see you here next Sunday, Ana."

His warm smile made her long to come back and step into his

world, if only for an afternoon. "I'm not here often."

"You could try." He reopened the thick textbook and looked very serious as he turned the pages.

Relieved he hadn't recognized her, she nodded and walked away without making any promise she was unlikely to keep.

Larina Flores was a highly respected fashion photographer, but Ana hated working with her. The woman demanded poses that were nearly impossible to hold and then took her time photographing them. Ana studied ballet to have the supple grace of a prima ballerina, but it was lost on Larina.

"Try and look more like a man, Gian Carlo. Thrust out your chest and pull Ana closer."

"Did she just insult my manhood?" he whispered in Ana's ear.

She answered so softly her lips barely moved. "We're being paid too well to walk out."

"What do you want?" he called over his shoulder. "Am I to look like a rooster?"

"Yes!" Larina cried from behind her camera. "Channel a crowing rooster if you must, but I need more swagger."

"Think of a matador," Ana suggested.

"They do know how to strut." He stretched and threw back his shoulders. He was tall, sandy haired with blue eyes, and had a swimmer's sleek physique. He and Ana were posing for a Gucci cologne ad and had been working under the hot studio lights for two hours. "Why don't you spray us with a hose so there will be water dripping off me rather than sweat."

"Hush, Gian Carlo," Larina ordered. "We're nearly finished, and sweat gives you a virile edge."

"She insults me every time she opens her mouth. You do know I'm straight, don't you?"

Ana hadn't given his sexual orientation any thought. He was just another model to lean against. "Yes, of course," she assured him. He was more fun to work with than many men were, and she was sorry she hadn't thought to take him to the benefit Saturday night.

"That will have to do," Larina called. "Now I want a few shots with Ana alone and some with you by yourself, Gian Carlo. Your light eyes add some heat, but I don't want to print a stare-off between you and all the other men selling cologne. Aragon is outselling everything else on the market, and your Nordic look will counter Santos's dark glare."

Gian Carlo turned away from the lights and blew Ana a kiss. When they were finished for the day, he walked along with her out of the building. "I'm sorry I didn't have a chance to speak to you Saturday night. Why did you leave so early?"

Ana came to an abrupt halt. "Have you been sending me roses?"

He frowned, clearly perplexed. "No, should I have?"

She shifted her bag on her shoulder. "Of course not, but someone who wishes to remain anonymous has been. I left early to discourage him, if he was there."

"It must be difficult to avoid a man you can't name," he responded with a soft chuckle. "I often have to scrape off giggling women, but it's a hazard of our trade."

"Men don't scrape off as easily." With sunglasses and her long hair hidden beneath a floppy hat, she hoped no one would think her worth observing. In a loose brown shirt and jeans, she blended easily into the passersby. "I'm about to starve to death. Are you hungry?"

"Always. It'll give us a chance to talk, and there's something I need to ask you."

She took a deep breath. "Please wait until I've finished eating."

He took her hand, and they walked around the corner to a place they both liked. She lived on fruit and vegetables unless she was a guest at a private party where meat was served. The beef on the Aragon ranch had always been delicious, but she'd not be invited there again. She ordered a fruit salad and sat back in the booth.

"When you mentioned a matador," Gian Carlo said, "you must have been thinking of Miguel Aragon. How about Santos? Isn't he enough like his father to interest you?"

"There's no comparison between them. Santos plans to marry his American honey, and she can have him."

A smile skittered across his lips. "You ought to hide your hostility better. It makes you sound insincere."

Not caring, Ana shrugged. "You must know what it's like to be

17

done with someone."

He took a sip of water. "I'll admit to being done with the same woman multiple times. Sometimes it's easier to stay with someone who's all wrong than look for somebody right."

"That's certainly true, but what if you're not the right person for anyone else?"

"Are you that depressed?" He reached across the table to take her hand. "You shouldn't be alone with such dark thoughts."

She pulled her hand free. "I've said too much."

"You were being honest. Don't apologize. We should go out, be photographed by the paparazzi and make everyone jealous they aren't with us."

He was an appealing man, and a popular model, but she shook her head. "We'd just be pretending like we do all day, and I need a rest."

"That's why I wanted to talk with you." He waited until she'd finished the last grape on her plate and then chose his words with care. "I've always hoped modeling would lead to acting jobs. The woman who invited me Saturday night, Rachel Oliveras, is an attorney who handles my contracts. There's nothing between us, but she's more comfortable going out with an escort, and I do look great in a tux."

"You most certainly do." Her mood had lightened as they ate, and she tried not to laugh at his unending self-absorption.

"Rachel has a friend who does casting for Pedro Almodóvar, and he's looking for fresh faces for his next film. I have a script to practice. If you'll read it with me for the audition, it will help me get the part. I can't talk to a wall and be convincing. They want to see me tomorrow morning. Are you free to do it?"

"I don't have anything scheduled. Do you have the script with you?"

He patted the messenger bag beside him in the booth. "I do. Do you want to come to my place? Or we could go to yours."

"My place," she offered.

He had a red MG and drove them to her condo. When they came in, she saw the pink rose bouquet on the security guard's counter. "Are those for me?"

"Yes, Miss Santillan. The same chauffeur brought them. There's a long dress for you too."

"Thank you, Henry." The silvery gown was in a clear drycleaner's bag, and she folded it over her arm while Gian Carlo picked up the bouquet.

The roses held sparkles of dew as though they'd just been plucked from a well-tended garden. "You'd think a man who'd go to this expense would sign his name," Gian Carlo mused. When they reached the elevator, he pressed the button. "Could they be from a woman?"

"I hadn't thought of that. I suppose they could be, but whoever it is must expect something in return."

"Maybe they're simply dazzled by your beauty."

Ana stepped into the elevator, removed her hat and shook out her hair. "No one appreciates us for our intelligence and charm, though, do they?"

"I don't complain." When they reached her floor, he followed her down the hall to her door. "Let me go in first and make certain everything is all right."

"I'm sure it is. We have excellent security." She unlocked the door and gestured for him to precede her. Afternoon sunlight bounced off the living room's pale yellow walls, giving the pretty room a cozy warmth. The furniture was upholstered in a vivid blue and buttery yellow along with a wing chair covered in a complementing floral fabric. A thick cream-colored area rug softened Gian Carlo's footsteps as he carried the roses to the glass-topped coffee table.

"The yellow roses look the prettiest in here," he offered. "Do you want these in another room?"

Unwilling to give him a tour, she shook her head. "Leave them with the others." She hung the gown in the coat closet. Libby had attached a note with her cell phone number, and Ana slipped it into her pocket. "Would you like something to drink?"

"No, thank you, I'm fine." He sat on the couch and pulled the script from his bag. "This isn't a long scene. Come here so you can read it with me. I'm playing Guillermo, who's been hired by a man he's always admired. It means he'll be moving far away, and he's saying good-bye to his girlfriend. He's excited, and naturally, she's stunned that he's leaving her behind."

She took her place beside him and pulled a throw pillow onto her lap. "How does one portray stunned?" she asked.

"I'm the one trying out for the part, Ana. It doesn't matter what you do other than say your lines."

She finger-raked her hair off her forehead. "Fine, you start."

"Pretend I'm walking around the room, too excited to sit beside you."

"Fine, I'll use my imagination." When he rushed through his opening lines, she raised her hand. "You need to slow down. You can still sound thrilled with this unexpected opportunity, but the audience needs to be able to understand you."

He frowned and smoothed the page. "There won't be an audience, Ana. It will just be the casting director and us."

Gian Carlo's looks had made him a successful model, but he hadn't shown her even a shred of acting talent. "Take your time and give the casting director a longer opportunity to observe you."

"Oh, I see what you mean. Let's start again."

Ana had only a word here and there, but she soon got caught up in the emotion of the scene. She spoke her first line softly, the second a little louder, and when her character realized Guillermo was leaving her, she went way past stunned to a vivid heart-wrenching sob. She looked up at Gian Carlo. "How was that?"

"A little over the top, but the casting director will be looking at me, so it won't matter."

They ran through the scene a couple of more times, and when he was satisfied they could give it a professional reading, he stood, ready to go. "I hope the scene didn't depress you. I don't have the whole script, but your character probably appears at the end and spits in Guillermo's eye."

"I've never had an occasion to spit, so we're lucky it isn't in this scene." He'd pick her up in the morning, and she wished him good-bye at the door.

With time on her hands, she loaded the photos of Alejandro into her laptop. Asleep, he looked older, and she wondered if they weren't closer in age than she'd first thought. He had a lanky build. Maybe he jogged or played soccer. Whatever exercise he chose, he looked fit and damn good. Even if his age wasn't an issue, he had no idea who she was. If he had known, he would have bragged to his friends about meeting her, and she'd not have wanted to see him again. It was better to be a Goth girl who appeared occasionally on a Sunday afternoon.

They'd both have fun, and no one would be disappointed or hurt.

Ignacio Belmonte was a highly regarded casting director, but he looked startled when Ana and Gian Carlo were shown into his office. Ignacio was of medium height and build, with brown hair and a closely cropped beard. "We're looking for someone new, not models who are on every other billboard." He checked his calendar and found a reference to Rachel Oliveras. "Now I remember why you're here. Obviously a mistake on my part; let's get it over with quickly. We'll go into the studio and film it."

Ana had pulled her hair back and worn a minimum of makeup. She wouldn't stand out anywhere in her black pants and a tailored white shirt, but Ignacio apparently gawked at every billboard he passed, or he was overly fond of women's magazines.

The studio walls were painted black and held only a few risers and battered wooden chairs.

Ignacio moved behind the video camera. "Just sit there together. Do you know your lines?"

Ana had few to learn, and to his credit, Gian Carlo had memorized his. She sat forward on her chair, as though eager to hear what he had to say. When Belmonte waved for them to begin, Gian Carlo spoke his lines with a deliberate care as though he were struggling to find the proper way to break his girlfriend's heart. She gave it her best and sobbed on cue.

The casting director came around in front of the camera. "I might be able to use you as an extra, Gian Carlo, but I definitely want Ana."

Gian Carlo looked as deeply disappointed as could be expected, but Ana didn't know what to say. She stood and shrugged. "I wasn't the one auditioning."

"So what? You had more emotion in your face than any of the actresses who've auditioned for the part. I can't believe many men have walked out on you, but your anguish touched me. It's exactly what we want on the screen. We'll put you in a wig and cheap dress so no one will recognize you. We won't begin rehearsals for several weeks, but leave your contact information with my secretary, and we'll send your contract to your agent."

Gian Carlo was so angry he didn't speak to her on the way back to her place, and she made no excuses or apologies for the way the morning had gone. Belmonte was completely wrong, however. The only man she'd ever loved had bid her a final loving farewell and died.

Chapter Two

A white-rose bouquet sat on the security desk, and Ana wished she'd been there to receive it personally. "How long has this been here, Henry?"

He looked up at the wall clock. "Maybe half an hour. This time it was a florist's deliveryman. Their tag is on the roses."

There had been no tags on the other bouquets, and she hoped it would be a clue as to the sender. Unfortunately, the little envelope was empty, and she removed it from the bouquet. "Please take these home to your wife. My condo is beginning to resemble a wedding chapel, and I don't need more flowers."

"Thank you, Miss Santillan. She'll love them. I'll tell her they're from you."

She cocked her head slightly. "Are you a stickler for honesty, Henry?"

He leaned close to whisper, "I try to be, but if I say I bought the roses, she'll suspect I'm apologizing for something and demand to know what I've done wrong."

Ana laughed with him and went on up to her condo. She'd added water each day and the four bouquets on the coffee table still looked beautiful, but maybe she'd misunderstood why they'd been sent. She kicked off her flats, sat down at the dining room table and pulled out her phone. A quick review of messages revealed nothing she couldn't recall. If someone thought they owed her an apology, she'd surely remember why, but came up with a blank.

Maybe one of the ads she'd done had spurred sales and the roses were sent as a lavish thank-you. If that were the case, someone from the advertising agency would have signed the card. They always took credit whenever they could. She turned the small florist's envelope to read the name and number and called them.

"Hello, this is Ana Santillan. Your deliveryman brought me some beautiful white roses, but there's no card. Could you please tell me who sent them?"

"Oh, Miss Santillan, how nice to speak with you," a cheerful woman replied. "A very nice man, a chauffeur driving a limousine, but his employer didn't come inside."

"Did he use a credit card?"

"No, he paid in cash. Is there something the matter with your bouquet? We'll replace it immediately if there is."

"The roses are the most beautiful I've ever seen. Has the chauffeur visited your shop several times lately?"

"No, I'd not seen him before today. Is there something I should tell him if he returns?"

"Yes, please explain I no longer accept gifts without the sender's name. It's very important for security, you understand."

"Yes, Miss Santillan, I'll do that. Good-bye."

Ana bet wherever the chauffeur had bought the other roses, he'd paid in cash, so there was no point in calling around hoping to discover his employer's name. Perhaps he expected her to begin waiting for him in the foyer and had switched to the florist's delivery to keep his employer's identity hidden. Her admirer struck her as more of an ass than dangerous, and she forgot him to check her work calendar.

A job scheduled with Armand tomorrow for a jewelry line might be fun. A study of Renaissance paintings had provided her with a wealth of graceful gestures, and a ring always looked more beautiful on a carefully posed hand. She had a ballet barre in her second bedroom and traded her street clothes for a black leotard. Her mother had insisted she study ballet, and she'd loved it. At one time, she'd hoped to join a ballet company, but she'd grown too tall. There were some male dancers over six feet in height, but ballerinas were dainty creatures they could easily lift and turn, not striking women born with the height for haute couture.

She took an occasional ballet class and admired the way ballerinas kept their stately posture long past middle age. After warming up, she put on her favorite music and danced only to please herself.

Wednesday morning, Armand kissed both her cheeks. "What

game were you playing Saturday night? You were there, then you weren't, and Libby wandered into your place for a few minutes."

Ana debated telling him about the roses, but, sure it would sound silly, she shrugged off his question. "I wanted to leave early without being noticed, and Libby helped me escape. Now what are we doing today?"

"I want that sultry look you do so well. After Teresa does your hair and makeup, choose any of the black gowns on the rack. I'm creating a nighttime scene on a balcony. You'll play the confident woman waiting for what the night will bring."

"No man today?" she asked.

"No, I want you to fill the page, glancing over your shoulder. We'll leave the man to the viewer's imagination."

"Fine. That's the best place for them."

Armand rested his hands on his hips. "Oh, my dear, I expected to see you with a date Saturday night. Are you alone again?"

"I wish you wouldn't stress the word 'again'."

He bowed his head. "Forgive me."

"Of course."

Teresa had a small studio. An artist with hair and makeup, she had delicate features and tight gray curls that flopped about like a lion's mane. She'd been with the ad agency for many years, and she and Ana worked well together. She fluffed the model's hair. "You have such beautiful hair. Are you going to let it grow forever?"

Ana's soft curls touched her waist now, but she had no reason to cut it. "I may." She closed her eyes as Teresa worked to give her an elaborate upswept do, and followed the makeup artist's directions as she applied cosmetics to give her a sultry lavender-shaded eye.

Armand's assistants had set up the nighttime backdrop. Denise was a petite bundle of energy and Roberto a laidback, ponytailed man. The ad featured magnificent diamond jewelry, and when they'd finished shooting, Ana watched over Armand's shoulder as he put the photos on his computer. They had exactly what he'd been told to capture, but she wasn't satisfied.

"We've seen this same ad a million times. Why don't we try for something new?"

He turned to look up at her. "What do you have in mind?"

25

"What if we went with playful rather than sultry, and I posed in a towel with a shower in the background, or a waterfall, or a lush garden. Make it look as though diamonds are all a girl needs to wear."

Roberto nodded. "Let's use the green screen and fill in the background later. Maybe with a few fig leaves, we could set you in the garden of Eden."

"I won't pose in anything smaller than a bikini," Ana responded. "If you have a snake dangling from a tree, it will look as though diamonds are evil, so we shouldn't go there."

"A waterfall would be good," Denise offered. "We can spray Ana so it looks as though she's wet from standing so close to the water. Make her skin sparkle like the diamonds."

Ana turned and raised her hands as though blocking the spray. The diamond bracelet, necklace, ring and earrings all flashed their bright fire near her face. "How about this?"

"I like it," Roberto said.

Armand shrugged. "We can try it. Let's wrap you in a sarong so you'll look as though you're on an island vacation. Go see what Teresa has."

Teresa had yardage they used for a variety of purposes, and they chose a pale lavender silk that showed off Ana's slim figure and peach-toned skin. Once the photos were in the computer and the waterfall inserted into the background, they were all pleased they had something original and new. Ana went to change into her street clothes. When she came out, Armand was speaking with one of the ad executives who'd been at her table Saturday night. Rather than interrupt them, she waited to say good-bye.

"Good work," the executive complimented. "This will take the campaign in a fresh direction."

Armand shrugged. "I often have more ideas than those in your first sketches."

"Then stop hiding your talent and keep using them." He slapped Armand on the shoulder and walked away.

Denise came up behind Ana. "That wasn't right," she whispered. "You're the one who offered the new ideas."

"We all worked on it," Ana countered, but she gave Armand a hurried wave as she left. He'd not known she was standing close enough to overhear him take credit for her suggestions. Roberto and Denise had offered their ideas too, and Armand should have reported it as a joint effort, rather than solely his. He was a great photographer, but from now on in his studio, she'd keep her ideas to herself.

Ana used the alcove off her kitchen as an office rather than a pantry. She kept her work calendar on the wall and tracked her earnings and expenses on her laptop. She'd been doing more work with her favorite designers this year, but each new job brought the uncomfortable suspicion it might be her last.

That week, gorgeous potted plants began arriving for her, and rather than refuse them, Henry used them to decorate the building's foyer. Henry didn't work on the weekends, and she neglected to tell his substitute to refuse deliveries for her. When she came back from running errands Saturday morning, there was a large gold-wrapped box of expensive chocolates waiting for her.

"I love these, Juan, but please leave the box open here on the counter so anyone walking by can enjoy them." The candies were gone before noon.

With nothing planned for Sunday, she took a deep breath and fought not to feel pathetic for wanting to spend some time in an attractive student's world. Doubting he'd be at El Gato, she donned her Goth outfit and makeup and walked farther than she had last Sunday. It was a cool spring day, perfect for exercise, and when she reached the café, she was surprised, and more delighted than she'd care to admit, to find Alejandro there.

He leaped from his chair to wave. "I'm glad you came back. I wasn't certain what time you'd been here last week, and I was afraid I'd missed you."

She slid into the chair he pulled out for her. He'd rolled up the sleeves on his white dress shirt, and in neatly pressed jeans, he didn't look as young as he had last week. She'd been concentrating on not being recognized, however, so maybe her glances of him had been too brief.

"Thank you. I hadn't looked at the time either. I was out walking,

27

and this is a convenient place to stop."

He shoved his hair out of his eyes and regarded her with a wicked grin. "Then you didn't come just to see me?"

"I'm happy to see you, let's leave it at that," she replied, glad she'd made the effort. Models knew how to hold a static pose, but energy nearly rolled off him in waves.

"You didn't bring a book?" he asked.

"No, sometimes I like to just sit and watch people go by."

"You do that too? I pick out someone and imagine what their life might be. They could be on their way to meet their grandmother, or a lover. The possibilities are endless."

"You don't think about their houses?" she asked.

He flashed an amused grin. "No. I think about houses too much as it is. My father complains I spend far too much time playing with cardboard models and not nearly enough with pretty women. What can I get for you? Do you want those little cakes?"

"Yes, I love them, with tea, please." She sat back and tried not to smile too wide. Alejandro had a disarming charm, but she'd have to carefully manage her remarks to share what little truth she could. Perhaps that she was pretty and single would be all he cared to know.

He returned with two plates of cakes and tea for her. "I ate when I first got here."

She was sorry she'd deliberately taken her time arriving. "I didn't mean to keep you waiting."

"You told me you weren't here often, so I didn't count on seeing you today."

She took a cake and savored it in tiny bites. "Sometimes I work on the weekends."

He took a cake from his plate. "What kind of work do you do?"

A partial truth would do. "I'm a photographer."

"What do you do, weddings, babies?"

A heavy-set man strutted by with a bulldog, their rear ends bouncing in rhythm. She nodded so Alejandro would notice. They tried not to laugh, but couldn't help it. "I could sit here all day," she confided. "It's more entertaining than most films."

"It is, but tell me about your photography."

She'd hoped to skip over it. "I do freelance advertising work, print ads, that sort of thing."

"A cereal box on the table?"

"Sometimes. Now tell me why you're studying architecture." She held her breath, and relaxed when he took the bait.

"Barcelona is filled with the most extraordinary architecture in the world, but I plan to work on affordable housing, not mansions for the rich. I want to concentrate on the environment, use solar technology and keep the costs low. Cities shouldn't have overcrowded slums. Everyone needs a comfortable home."

When he'd grown serious, she saw him as an attractive man rather than a friendly kid. She hadn't wanted anything more than an entertaining hour, but there was a huge difference between harmless flirting with a student and playing with a grown man's emotions. She straightened up in her chair. "Are you considering individual homes rather than blocks of apartments?"

"High-rise slums? Yes. People should have a yard to grow vegetables and a safe place for their kids to play."

"Suburbs, then. I don't mean to be rude, but I thought you were younger than you probably are."

He had a deep, rolling chuckle. "I'm twenty-six. Is that too old for you? Architecture will be my second degree. My first is in business. I must not have impressed you last week. What did you think, that I'm seventeen or eighteen?"

Embarrassed, she licked her lips. "Yes, but if you hadn't impressed me, I wouldn't be here."

He leaned closer. "Whom do you usually hang out with, tattoo artists?"

Startled, she didn't immediately recall her Goth disguise. "I don't know a single one, but I'll bet they're fun."

"I doubt it. If you're not tired of walking, we could go down Las Ramblas to the port."

It was a casually made invitation, and Las Ramblas was a wide boulevard filled with shops and tourists, not a narrow dark alley. "It's one of my favorite walks. Give me a minute to finish my tea. Didn't you bring your books?"

"No, I'm taking the afternoon off." He leaned back and rested his hands behind his head. "I'll be finished in June. Then I hope to find work with an established firm for experience before I go out on my own."

He was such a charming man, she doubted he'd have much trouble finding a job. "It must be wonderful to be able to design a building that could last for centuries. My work is ephemeral, and I capture only moments."

"All I build now are models. We aren't too far from my apartment. Do you have your camera? I'd like to have some good photos of my models. In my shots, they look like overturned shoeboxes. I'll pay you whatever you usually charge."

Men often offered invitations to their homes, but for the illusion she created, not for the woman she actually was. Alejandro was so unabashedly sincere, however, and she was a spectacular fake. She looked down at her beautifully manicured nails and scooped up the last cake. "I'd love to see your models, but I haven't done any architecture, and I'd hate to disappoint you."

"All I have are models, I'm not asking you to photograph La Sagrada Familia."

She laughed with him. "I love the cathedral, but I've not taken my camera there. Maybe I should."

He ate another cake. "Once you begin looking at buildings, you'll see them in a whole new way. Details you've never noticed will pop out. Can you describe the front of El Gato without looking?"

She closed her eyes. "It's painted a pale yellow with green woodwork. There are windows across the front, one over the door. There's the most wonderful aroma coming from inside, baked goods mixed with tangy spices." She opened her eyes and looked toward the building. "I forgot the sign."

"I asked about the building, and you got most of it. There's tile work beneath the windows, but if you're always seated out here, maybe you've missed it."

She sat forward to look. "I must have seen it when I went in to order but didn't remember."

"But you would if you'd photographed the café."

The bright spark of intelligence made his gray eyes attractive rather than too pale for his dark hair and tanned skin. He'd make a handsome model, she thought and quickly dismissed the idea. "It

30

sounds as though you've done some photography yourself."

He brushed sugar from his hands. "Just for my classes. It's another thing to get the right light and angle. I'm not any good at it."

Her tea was already cold, which surprised her. Cold tea was good too, but she hadn't realized they'd been talking so long. He was so easy to talk to. Too many men spoke only about themselves, as though pretty women couldn't possibly have interesting ideas of their own. "Maybe I can give you some tips, and I don't charge for work on Sundays."

He saw her check her watch, leaned forward and lowered his voice. "Is there someone waiting for you at home?"

"A man, you mean? No, and my housekeeper doesn't come home from vacation until tomorrow."

Apparently relieved, he sat back and studied her expression with renewed interest. "You have a housekeeper, what's her name?"

"Fatima." She was afraid she'd admitted too much. Models made a far better living than freelance photographers, but Fatima was real.

"Fatima. That's perfect. Let me guess, is she a petite woman who wears black uniforms with frilly white aprons?"

"No, she's more generously proportioned, and frilly aprons don't suit her."

"So you're a freelance photographer who lives alone with a housekeeper?"

"No, she doesn't live-in. She has her own home and family."

He ate the last cake on his plate. "What about you? Where's your family?"

The truth wouldn't hurt. "My father died when I was small, and a few years ago my mother married a French chef. They make their home in Rouen."

"Do you visit them often?"

"When I can. Now tell me about your family and your father who fears you don't meet enough women."

He slumped in his chair and shrugged. "The story is too common to repeat. My father wants me to follow him into the family business, and I worked with him for a while, but my heart wasn't in it. Architecture is my real passion. My parents are divorced. My mother lives in Greece with her new husband, and my father and his second wife are here and have two young sons. One of them will probably go into the business while I build low-income homes."

"It's a noble calling."

"Thank you for seeing it that way. Do you love photography?"

"Yes, I do, and I understand why you'd not want to continue with work you don't love. Parents can demand too much from their children, and it's important to break free."

"Like your Goth pursuit. Do you wear it in Paris?"

She wore it only on Sunday afternoons. "No one notices what I wear in Paris. Are you ready to go?"

He rose, helped her from her chair and took her hand. "Tell me if I'm walking too fast. Most girls have to run to keep up with me."

Their hands fit together comfortably, and she squeezed his fingers. "My legs are almost as long as yours."

He stopped to look and nodded. "You're almost all legs, aren't you? I like that in a woman."

"Most men do."

Las Ramblas followed a centuries-old pathway along a dry riverbed to the sea. In the eighteenth century, the wide boulevard had been bordered with monasteries and convents. Universities had followed. Now it was home to an opera house, luxury hotels, and a remarkable palace designed by Antonio Gaudí. Expensive boutiques, flower stands and an outdoor market at Plaça de la Boqueria drew tourists as well as locals and created a lively mix of the past and present.

He led her down a side street to a four-story building that was more than a century old. "It's divided into studios for artists. There are benefits to living in my office. I never have to put anything away before I go home."

The elevator was framed by a gilded cage and creaked as it rose slowly to the top floor. He unlocked his door and gestured for her to precede him. The high-ceilinged room had a bath and kitchen at the far end. Three large windows faced south and provided spectacular light. There was a drawing table placed beneath one window and a computer and printer beneath another. Two long tables filled the center of the room, and the loft overhead held his bed. A futon sat against the wall along with a sleek racing bicycle that looked expensive.

Ana walked around the tables slowly. One was stacked with his working materials; his finished models sat in the center of the other. The tiny houses were perhaps six inches square with beautifully painted windows and doors. Solar panels rested on the slanted roofs. "You've built a whole town here. I love it." She bent down to study the row of houses resting on painted gardens.

"You don't have to pretend to be more excited than you really are. I can take a noncommittal shrug."

He had no idea how greatly she was pretending, although not about his models. "I like your work, or I wouldn't say so. Your craftsmanship is superb. These don't look like overturned boxes at all."

She pulled up a chair and drew her camera from her bag. "What are you doing, taking photos while you're standing looking down?"

"Sometimes. I either get too close or stand too far back. Whatever you do will be an improvement. The houses are built of modules that can be combined to create larger homes."

"I see." She worked until satisfied she'd caught the models in the best light and entered the photos in his Mac. "How do these look?"

He leaned over her shoulder. "You've made the little village look real. If all your work is this good, you ought to be photographing more than cereal boxes."

He was wearing the Gucci cologne from the ads she'd done with Gian Carlo. It held a hint of a shower-dripped forest while the more seductive Aragon had the darker essence of the restless sea. Disappointed in the direction of her thoughts, she took one of his business cards with his name and number stacked beside the computer. "May I?"

"Take two or three. You might meet someone looking for an architect. Do you have cards? I want to see you again."

She slipped out of her chair. "I'm sorry, I didn't bring any. But I want to see you again too." She raised her arms to encircle his neck and pulled him down for a good-bye kiss. He tasted of cinnamon, and one kiss wasn't nearly enough. She pressed closer. His first kisses were easy and sweet, and hers filled with a sad longing. She'd had such good intentions, but he was a man, not a boy who needed to be protected from the desire curling low in her belly.

He picked her up, swept the cardboard and glue off his worktable, sat her down on the end and stepped between her knees. She laughed with him and unbuttoned his shirt. Coarse black curls covered his chest and narrowed to a thin line toward his belt. She traced the path with her fingertips.

"You better have condoms," she whispered, "or I'm not going any lower."

He spread kisses along her jaw, drew a condom from his back pocket and laid it on the table within easy reach. "I hoped I could talk you into coming here." He fumbled with the buttons on her shapeless blouse, but her purple lace bra stopped him cold. "This is like unwrapping a present. Why do you wear such baggy clothes?"

She cupped him through his jeans and felt his heat. "I like being comfortable. Don't you?" She unfastened his belt.

"Comfort," he repeated hoarsely. "You're amazing."

In more ways than he knew. She kicked off her boots and slid her arms around his waist to pull him closer. She didn't want to think at all, but simply feel and forget. He was muscular and lean, fit as he'd claimed, and his solid warmth was so good to rest against. This wasn't a pose for a camera, but real, and she meant every tender caress.

He picked her up to slide her pants down over her hips and found her purple thong. "I swear I thought you'd wear black boxer shorts." He tugged her pants over her knees and let them drop on the floor.

"The Goth image needn't go that far." She nibbled his earlobe and kissed the smooth hollow behind his ear. She helped him peel off his shirt and licked his collarbone.

He shivered. "Where did you learn that?"

"Trial and error," she purred against his lips. She'd studied with a master, but clung to Alejandro rather than her memories. "Tell me what you like."

"Everything," he murmured. He unhooked her bra, tossed it over his shoulder and bent down to kiss her pale pink breasts. He sucked the rosy crests and rolled them between his fingertips. "You're so pretty."

She pinched his flat nipples and felt him flinch. "You're a very handsome man, tall enough for me, and you make me laugh." She wrapped her legs around his hips and squeezed tightly. They fit together remarkably well, like lost pieces of a puzzle found at last. He pushed down his jeans, pulled on the condom with shaky hands, and she drew her thong aside to welcome him.

He entered her with a slow push, and watched with a fascinated glance as he withdrew and surged into her again. He thumbed her clit. "You feel so hot and good."

She leaned into him, cupped his balls and stroked them gently with her thumb. "I can make it feel even better." She tightened her muscles to pull him deeper with every stroke. She rocked against him, savoring his touch as he slid on her wetness. She breathed deeply, floating on the growing pleasure until she felt him gasp. She pressed her knuckles against the smooth skin behind his balls to hold back his orgasm with a firm touch, and then raised her hand to let it rocket through him. His last thrust caught her too, and she hugged him tight to glory in it.

It took him a long while to form words. "That was..." he began.

She touched his lips. "You don't need to describe it. I felt it too."

He tossed the used condom in the wastebasket, hiked up his pants and picked her up. "Let's use the futon and rest a minute. I think I can walk that far."

He put her down on her feet, and she took his hand to pull him along. They nearly fell into the thick futon and snuggled together in a languid heap. She could have lain there forever, but she'd eventually have to tell him the truth. She rested her head on his shoulder and waited for his breathing to slow before she slipped from his embrace. His thick black hair fell in his eyes, a dreamy smile graced his lips, and he looked as though he might sleep until dawn. She wished she could stay, but couldn't. She went to the worktable to gather up her clothes, pulled on her pants, buttoned up her blouse, but left the lacy purple bra where it lay. She grabbed her bag and camera, and carried her boots out the door to pull them on outside in the hall.

She used the stairs rather than the moaning elevator. On the second floor, she passed a young man on his way up. She dipped her head as she passed him and mumbled a greeting. She looked as though she could have been visiting any artist in the building and hoped he wouldn't ask questions Alejandro would be embarrassed to answer.

Walking home at a near sprint, she didn't slow to a stately walk until she reached her condo. As she came through the door, she saw the pet carrier at the security desk. She blamed herself for not being empathic with Juan the day before, but if he'd accepted something for her, she wasn't going to be happy. "Please tell me whatever is in the pet carrier isn't for me."

Juan leaped to his feet. "The man who brought them said they'd been chosen especially for you. They came with everything, feeding bowls, cat box, litter, food, a little bed. They're a brother and sister. Don't you want them?"

Ana bent down to look into the kittens' sweet little faces. One was black and the other white. They were pressed close to the grid in the carrier door and begging for attention with faint high-pitched meows. Her heart fell. "Was there a note with them?"

"Instructions you mean? No, I guess he thought you'd know how to care for them."

"Can you describe the man?"

"He was just an ordinary sort of guy, not too tall, and had a few extra pounds. I thought you knew him. I should have asked him to sign in."

"Someone's been sending me gifts—roses, plants, the chocolates yesterday. Now kittens? I'm afraid he'll send me a horse tomorrow."

Juan panicked. "Don't you want the kittens? They're awfully cute."

"They're adorable, but I'm not always home and can't keep them." She leaned close and looked him in the eye. "You accepted the delivery of something I didn't order, so it looks as though you're the new owner of these delightful pets."

He swallowed hard. "Pets aren't allowed in my building, or I'd take them."

"Sure you would. Help me get everything into the elevator, and we'll worry about finding them a home tomorrow."

He came out from behind his post, grabbed the carrier and made a second trip for the bags of accessories. "Oh, I forgot to tell you they're named Romeo and Juliet."

"Perfect. I'll bet Juliet is the black one."

"How did you know?"

She shook her head. "Does it really matter? Thank you. If anyone brings anything else for me, tell them I am not accepting gifts unless I know the person, and they've called to let me know it's coming."

"Don't you think that's dangerous, Miss Santillan? They'd go out and come back the next day and say they'd called you."

"Fine. Just say I'm not accepting gifts period." She pressed the elevator button and rode up to her floor. "Come on, little darlings, there has to be someone who wants kittens." It took her three trips down the hall to carry everything inside. She didn't think it was a good idea to allow Romeo and Juliet to run free, but she didn't want to shut them in the bathroom, or her home dance studio either.

She sat down on the floor and unlatched the carrier door. The kittens bounded out and climbed into her lap. "Affection won't work. This is your home for a few days, not forever."

Romeo jumped off her knee and ran under the couch, but Juliet curled up and began to lick herself clean. "I should have showed you two the cat box first." She scratched Juliet's ears and wondered if Alejandro would like a pair of cats.

She'd left him in an exhausted dream and wouldn't disturb him now, but it was nice to think he'd welcome her call.

Libby had sent her number, and there was another good reason to call her. "Hi, this is Ana Santillan. Someone just gave me two really cute kittens, and I need to find them a home. Do you like cats?"

"I love them, but you know Santos's housekeeper, Mrs. Lopez. She'd toss them out in the sand and let them fend for themselves."

Ana tickled Juliet's rounded belly, and the kitten licked her fingers. "I'd forgotten about her. How about Maggie? Does she like cats?"

"Do you want her number?"

Ana bit her lip. "Will you please ask her?" She gave Libby her number. "While I have you on the phone, would you please give me the name of the detective you mentioned?"

"Javier Cazares. Let me get his number."

She came back with it quickly, and Ana wrote it down and said good-bye. "I really do need more friends, Juliet."

She'd call the detective tomorrow. Now she had to deal with the kittens. While she remained seated on the rug, Juliet stayed close. In a few minutes, Romeo came out from under the sofa to join them. She made a grab for him and put him back with his sister in the carrier while she made a home for them in the guest bathroom with their cat box, food and water dishes.

A bubble bath in her own bathroom followed, and she stayed in until her fingers wrinkled. She wrapped herself in a towel, stretched out on her bed and played over possible phone conversations with Alejandro until she was certain she could manage it.

She pressed in his number. Her number was blocked, so maybe he wouldn't answer, but he did on the second ring. He had a marvelous deep sexy voice, and she spoke softly. "Hi, this is Ana."

"Where did you go? I hadn't had nearly enough of you. You forgot your bra, so you'll have to come back."

She made her voice soft and low. "I didn't forget. I left it as a memento. You could bring it to El Gato next Sunday if it's cluttering up your place."

"It's not. I'll use it to create a shrine. I miss you already. I can't wait until next Sunday to see you. Let me take you to dinner tonight."

"Don't you study on Sunday nights?"

"I told you I'm taking the day off. We're both too thin. It's no fun to eat alone. Do you want me to come get you, or would you rather meet somewhere?"

She'd washed off his scent but could still feel his warmth deep inside. She'd already blown whatever good intentions she'd had, but a casual dinner wouldn't get her in any deeper. She coughed to clear her throat and named a place not too far from her condo. "I'll meet you there." She ended the call cradling Juliet on her shoulder. She'd completely forgotten to ask if he liked cats.

After she'd disappeared, Alejandro had been afraid he'd never hear from her again. He hadn't meant to fall asleep, but she'd given him the best orgasm of his life and he'd been lucky he hadn't passed out on the floor in front of her. He couldn't remember the last time he'd met a woman he'd wanted to see again and had to call his father to brag.

"Mark today on your calendar. I've met a girl I like, and you didn't have anything to do with it."

"I'll make a note of it right now. What's her name?"

"Ana."

"Ana what?"

"Do you plan to sic your detectives on her?"

"It's always wise to be careful."

"You've blamed me for being too careful, and now I'm not careful enough?"

"Do whatever you like. Does she know who you are?"

"No, but I'll tell her soon."

"You may think she doesn't know, but I'll bet she does. Women can smell money on a naked man."

"Good-bye." He hung up and left his cell phone on the table. His father's fortune had tainted every relationship he'd had. Ana was a sweet girl and not overeager to plant her hooks in him. He wished she'd given him her last name so he could do some detective work on his own and was immediately ashamed the thought had even crossed his mind.

Chapter Three

Ana had plenty of time to get ready for their date, but Goth Girl never went out at night, nor did she ever meet anyone for dinner. With the size of her wardrobe, she could pull something together. An architect who intended to build low-cost housing wouldn't want to date an haute couture model anyway. It was only a convenient rationalization, but so what? She hadn't wanted to see a man in months, and she definitely wanted to see Alejandro again and again.

A long-sleeved black dress from the back of her closet looked good with her flat-heeled boots. She wore red lingerie, black lace stockings and the pale lip gloss Goth Girl required. Her nails were a flame red, which she supposed was out of character, but Alejandro hadn't noticed that afternoon. She added onyx earrings and silver bracelets to complete the look. Fashion depended upon appropriate accessories, but she wasn't making a fashion statement tonight.

She draped a black cashmere shawl around her shoulders, picked up a small clutch bag and paused to glance at the full-length mirror. Disappointed she looked more like herself than a Goth devotee, she started over with slim-fit jeans, a snug black T-shirt and a black blazer. She searched her jewelry box for a clever steampunk fish pin made of brass gears and springs and pinned it on her lapel. She could have worn heels and not towered over Alejandro, but stuck with the flat-heeled boots.

She had a black bag with a shoulder strap and tossed the clutch back onto the closet shelf. She checked the mirror again, struck an aggressive pose and was satisfied she'd be fine, unless a real Goth group eating at the restaurant recognized her as a poser. Her Porsche was in the condo's underground garage, but no Goth fan would drive such an expensive car. She practiced walking with a jerky stride on her way there, but as she entered, she worried she might be recognized even in a black wig. Alejandro was waiting for her in the bar. She went straight to him rather than pause at the reservation desk.

Alejandro took her arm and led her to a small table. "When I didn't find you when I woke up, I was afraid you hadn't been real. You're definitely real tonight, but you look different somehow, more grown-up."

He'd added a jacket to his dress shirt and jeans and was the same man she'd seen earlier. She glanced down at her blazer and jeans. "I could go home and try again."

"No, you look beautiful. I didn't mean to insult you. What do you want to drink?"

She supposed she ought to order beer and drink it from the bottle, but her disguise didn't have to go that far. "White wine." She took a small sip when they were served. "You looked very different to me when I saw you this afternoon, so if I look different to you now, I understand." She dipped her head to let her wig swing forward to brush her cheeks. That afternoon, he'd been concentrating on more appealing parts of her body and hadn't discovered her wig. She'd known he wouldn't.

He reached for her hand. "Let's start again. I like the sultry artist look. I hope the rest of your afternoon was good."

She smiled and licked her lips. "It didn't compare." She pulled a photo from her purse. "Someone gave me a couple of kittens, and I need to find them a home. Here they are napping on the sofa."

"They are cute. Are you sure you want to give them away?"

"Positive. My mother never allowed me to have a pet, so I'm not used to having little creatures underfoot. I told you I travel for work, so I can't keep them." His gaze was so warm and sympathetic she was tempted to tell him about the cascades of roses and other gifts, but a freelance photographer wouldn't attract such devotion. Instead, she offered only a sweet smile.

"When are you leaving town?" he asked.

"Wednesday, I'm doing a fashion shoot in Mallorca."

"It sounds like fun, unless the models are all prima donnas and give you a hard time."

Feeling as though she'd stepped out of her life to commentate from the sidelines, she took another sip of wine. "The best are very considerate and fun. I enjoy working with them."

"Only the best?"

"That's all I'm willing to say. If word got around I'd bad-mouthed a model, I might find myself out of work."

"You're pretty enough to be a model yourself."

"Thank you, but I prefer staying behind the camera."

Their table was ready, and she insisted he take the seat facing the other diners, while she sat with her back to the room. She hid behind her menu. "Their filet mignon is excellent, as is everything I've tried."

"You come here often?"

"No, just once in a while."

"The way you stop by El Gato?"

He was teasing her, and she liked it. "I'm more often at El Gato than here. You must have favorite places too."

"I do, but last week I had to take my father's place at a charity auction, and I don't do well when I'm forced into a tux."

He had to be talking about the event she'd attended, but she hadn't seen him there. She wondered if he'd noticed her, or rather, Ana Santillan. "A tux is nothing compared to what women have to suffer through to look good for a black-tie event."

"It's not the tux that's the problem. It's having to sit with strangers and make idle conversation."

"That is a strain." She focused on the menu and then glanced over the top. "Couldn't you use some investors for your low-cost housing project?"

"I could, but an auction to benefit sick kids isn't the right place to pitch my ideas."

She rubbed her toe along his calf. "I understand. I'll bet you look very handsome in a tux."

He laughed and set his menu aside. "You are different tonight, and it's not just your clothes. You didn't say more than a couple of words the first time we met. This afternoon is an incredible blur, and tonight you sound as though we'd just met."

"I don't mean to disappoint you." She lowered her voice to a husky whisper. "The sex was great, but it takes a while to get to know someone, and I haven't been out on a date in a while."

"Bad breakup?"

She took a deep breath. Santos didn't deserve a comment, but his father did. "The man I loved died." She didn't confide that Miguel would undoubtedly be the love of her life.

He looked horribly embarrassed. "I'm sorry. I shouldn't have asked. It's just that we seemed so close this afternoon, and..."

She reached across the small table for his hand. "Don't apologize. We do get along well. The people who know me know, and it's no secret. He had a weak heart, and his death wasn't unexpected."

"I'm still sorry I asked. I ride in bike races—not the Tour de France, but amateur competitions—and I'm fit. I can give you a health certificate from my physician if you like."

"Thank you, but no." He was so sincere, and other than one overwhelming truth, she was giving him only a thin veneer of her life. She felt only a snippet of guilt and clung to the fun of the moment.

"We're supposed to be thinking about food." He gave the menu a quick glance, and when their waiter returned, he ordered the filet mignon, and she asked for a spring-vegetable-filled empanada. "Tell me about the chef your mother married."

Grateful for his curiosity, she sat back and relaxed. "Andre is short, round and makes the most delicious food I've ever tasted. If my mother hadn't seen him first, I might have married him myself."

"I could learn to cook."

He looked as though he'd make the effort, and he'd been such a giving lover, she wished they'd met while she was being herself. "I think you ought to focus on architecture."

"I'll be finished in June. I'll never be finished really, because there will always be something more, or new, to learn."

"Like photography, but the continuing challenge is good."

Their conversation flowed so smoothly she was surprised by how quickly the evening passed. She ordered a lemon tart for dessert as an excuse to stay longer. "I love these. They have the sweetest zing."

"So do you." He took a bite of an apple baked in a flakey crust. "This is good too. We could order after-dinner drinks and stay until this place closes. Or we could go to your place and check on the kittens."

Her home, with some of her magazine covers framed in her bedroom, was definitely off-limits until he knew who she was. "Not tonight. I have an early job, and..."

"I understand. I have an early class. But I could just look at the kittens. Then if you don't find someone to take them, maybe I could keep them at my place while you're on Mallorca."

His generosity made her feel all the worse. "Thank you. I've just realized Fatima will be back tomorrow, and she can care for them while I'm away."

"If you have her, then you can keep them," he suggested.

The man definitely had a point. "I don't really want to, Alejandro."

He nodded. "May I give you a ride home?"

"It isn't far."

Looking alarmed, he leaned forward. "You can't walk around the city alone at night. We'll either go in my car or I'll walk you."

She reached for his hand and gave him an affectionate squeeze. "There's usually a taxi out front. I'll take one."

"Is hiding where you live part of the Goth persona?"

"Mystery is part of my allure." She winked at him and finished her tart. There was a taxi available. He opened the door for her and handed the driver several bills. It was an awkward moment, and when he leaned close to kiss her, she grabbed his shoulders and kissed him with the same passion she'd shown that afternoon. "I'll call you as soon as I come home from Mallorca."

She entered the taxi and pulled the door closed before Alejandro could respond. "Please turn at the corner. I only live a few blocks away, but we can take the long way." She didn't know what type of car Alejandro owned, but no one followed. She'd definitely call him, although she was torn about what to say. He'd soon expect to learn her last name and where she lived. She couldn't blame him if he felt he'd been tricked. But if she hadn't been hiding her identity, they'd never have met, and it was so nice to escape the tedious fame that brought out all the paparazzi leeches. Maybe a trip to Mallorca would be all she'd need to find a way to set everything right.

Fatima let herself into Ana's condo on Monday morning. She went into the kitchen, set down her shopping bag and tied on her apron. "Are you here, Ana?"

Ana met her with the kittens in hand. "Good morning. Do you like cats?"

Fatima took a step back. "Not really, but it looks as though they're already here." She was old enough to be Ana's mother and behaved more like a favorite aunt than an employee.

Ana put the kittens down, and they raced away. "I put their cat box and food and water in the guest bathroom. I'll shut them in there so they won't be in your way. If I can catch them."

Fatima heated water for tea and opened the refrigerator to store the fresh fruits and vegetables she'd bought that morning. "That's a good idea. The vacuum cleaner will probably terrify them."

Ana tightened the belt on her robe and leaned back against the counter. "How was your vacation?"

"It was good. Bruno is happy as long as he can fish, but my sister and her family always have problems, and I can't help them when they ignore my advice. We stayed only a couple of days with them, thank goodness. It was a good trip though. I found some new ways to prepare fish."

Ana had always found Fatima's advice valuable, even if her own sister didn't. "I could use some advice too." She told her about the presents that kept arriving. "I can't imagine who it is."

"Sounds as though someone's fallen in love with you." Fatima took a new sponge from the drawer and wet it to wipe the tile counters.

"It would be nice if it were someone I'd met, rather than someone who's fixated on a cologne ad from a billboard."

"You meet people all the time. Maybe you quickly forgot him, and he's too shy to sign his name." She rinsed the sponge. "I don't see a single stray crumb. Didn't you cook anything for yourself while I was away?"

"Some soup, I think. I ate out and bought salads to bring home. Now I need to catch the cats and get dressed."

"Just leave them for now. They aren't causing any trouble yet."

"Not yet," Ana echoed. She needed a lot more advice on what she should do with Alejandro, but she hated to admit how much trouble she'd gotten herself into on her own.

Paul Perez had been Ana's agent for several years, and while he worked diligently to guide her career, she was often a step ahead of him, and his usual impish smile was absent that day. "You should have told me about Ignacio Belmonte's interest in you before the contract arrived in the mail."

She smoothed her short skirt over her knees. "I doubt anything will come of it."

"Well, I don't. Belmonte seems sincere. Do you realize what starring in an Almodóvar film would do for your career?"

"It's a small part with only a few lines, and Belmonte plans to hide who I am, so how's that going to help me?"

Paul left his desk to walk to the window flooding his handsomely furnished office with morning light. At five-seven, he had to look up at Ana, but he took care never to stand beside her. He was slim with curly dark brown hair, wide-set hazel eyes and a neatly trimmed mustache and goatee. He was always attractively dressed, today in a well-tailored gray suit. People understood he was serious when he spoke, but Ana continually caused him unnecessary stress.

"The part could lead to something more, another film, or a lucrative endorsement contract. You need to look past the present at what might come next. We're always building, Ana. You must remember that."

"Yes, Paul, always building, I understand. I'm doing the Galen Salazar's shoot on Mallorca this week. His last show won a lot of praise, and his new fashions should be equally good."

"That's just it!" Paul emphasized. "You can't rest on merely being 'equally good'. You must always be better than your last shoot. Acting brings a whole new dimension to your career. We should have pursued this ourselves. Please sign the contract, and I'll return a copy to Belmonte and keep yours here in our files."

He sat down and pushed the contract toward her. "You're twenty-four with maybe another ten years to model. What do you plan to do then, marry and have triplets?"

Ana signed the contract and handed it to him. "I never think about getting married, but I'll survive, Paul. You needn't worry about me."

"I'll worry anyway. Your affair with Miguel Aragon did wonders for your career."

Sickened he would put Miguel and her career in the same breath, Ana stood and took a step toward the door. "I was already well-known when I dated Miguel. He's dead, and I'll not date another matador simply for the publicity. I'll concentrate on Galen Salazar's work for the time being and nothing more."

"Enjoy Mallorca," he responded through clenched teeth.

That afternoon, a package arrived for Ana in the mail. It contained a pair of black velvet heels adorned with gold lace and braid. Sexy and feminine, they were some of the most beautiful shoes she'd ever seen. The designer's name, Lucien Lamoreaux, was on the box, but she'd never heard of him. They fit perfectly, and she walked up and down her marble tiled entryway. "What do you think, Fatima?"

"If you ever attend a coronation, those will be the heels to wear."

Fatima was always diplomatic with her opinions, but Ana already loved the shoes. There was no return address on the package and no letter inside. "These can't be from Lamoreaux, or he'd have included a note saying he hoped I'd love his shoes and wear them often."

"They must be from your shy boyfriend," Fatima mused aloud.

"At least it isn't anything alive, but I need to do something about this now." She sat down still wearing the gorgeous heels and called Javier Cazares. "Libby Gunderson gave me your name. I understand you've done some work for Santos Aragon."

His raspy voice was hushed as though he didn't wish to be overheard. "I never discuss my clients, Miss Santillan. How may I help you?"

"I hope this doesn't sound too absurd, but someone's been sending me gifts—bouquets of roses, potted plants, chocolates, kittens, now designer shoes. I don't know who it is, but it has to stop."

"You've absolutely no idea who it might be?"

"No. There are no gift cards with anything." She told him about the chauffeur. "He didn't visit the same florist twice, but I do have one florist's card."

"Do you have security cameras where you live?"

"Yes, we do." She gave him her address. "I'm going downstairs, Fatima. Maybe I should put the kittens in the bathroom so they won't get out when I leave or come back."

"I'll do it. Just give me a minute."

Ana changed into flats and left before the kittens could notice the open door. "Henry, I need to see the security footage when the chauffeur dropped off the roses. Can you access it?"

"Week before last, wasn't it?"

"I should have kept better track of this, but yes, it started then." They watched it several times, but the chauffeur's hat and rose bouquets hid his face.

Javier Cazares soon arrived. He was a slender man who wore his gray hair slicked back. His gold-rimmed glasses and serious manner gave him a philosophy professor's intense gaze. He stood with them at the security desk to view the images.

"You have exterior cameras. Let's see those too," the detective asked.

Henry found them. "There he is, exiting the limo."

Ana didn't see anything to help them. "The car in front of him blocks the plates."

"Unfortunate. Let's see the following day," Cazares urged.

This time the chauffeur walked into the camera's view, but the limo was parked down the block. "Do you think he's gotten more cautious?" Ana asked.

"Probably, although I can't be certain. You did have the name of one florist?"

Ana had brought the tag downstairs. "Do you suppose they have security cameras?"

"I'll call them and ask. Let's look at the other deliveries."

Henry scanned the camera footage, but commercial delivery trucks had brought the potted plants and chocolates. A man driving a van with kittens painted on the side had delivered the kittens. Ana murmured softly, "Gatitos Bonitos. Maybe the owner remembers who bought them."

They went upstairs to her apartment to make the calls. Ana opened the door carefully, but Fatima had shut the kittens in the bathroom as planned. She offered coffee, but Cazares refused politely.

He chose the floral wing chair and opened his notebook. "I never rush anyone. Often people know more than they realize." He called the florist, but there were no security cameras there. The friendly owner remembered the white roses and speaking to Ana, but could barely recall the chauffeur who'd made the purchase.

"Don't be discouraged," the detective offered when he ended the call. "The man who raised the kittens will have paid more attention." He found the number for Gatitos Bonitos and made notes as he interviewed the owner, a Mr. Güerra. He smiled as he ended the call.

"Mr. Güerra recalls the man vividly because he took his time deciding which kittens to choose. He was around six feet, had wavy dark hair with gray-blue eyes. Güerra thought he was in his late thirties, or early forties. He was dressed in a suit that looked expensive. Güerra operates his business from his home and has no security cameras. Does the description sound like anyone you know?"

"It would fit half a dozen advertising executives, but they couldn't keep a secret if they tried, let alone send me gifts anonymously. Does he remind you of anyone, Fatima?"

She stood in the kitchen doorway. "No one I recall. Where could he have bought the beautiful shoes?"

Ana opened her laptop and did a search for Lucien Lamoreaux. His website featured his beautiful high heels, and the store that handled them exclusively in Spain was there in Barcelona. There was no photo of him, however.

"If the shoes are sold only through a single store, the clerks will undoubtedly recall the man who made the purchase. May I take the shoes with me?" Cazares asked.

"Yes, do. May I go along?"

The detective closed his notebook and slipped it into his jacket pocket. "You've received flattering gifts, but it's possible the sender's motives aren't benign. I can't allow you to walk into a situation that could prove dangerous."

Fatima gasped. "Should Ana hire a bodyguard?"

"No, not yet. Let me see what I discover. You're well-known. He could simply have a crush on you and mean you no harm. I'll speak to you later in the day."

Ana felt worse after he'd left than she had before she'd called him. Unable to simply sit, she called a couple of the advertising firms she worked with regularly, but neither had done any commercial work for Lucien Lamoreaux. Paul Perez wasn't familiar with the name either.

"Shoes are an odd thing to send a woman," the agent said. "It has a Cinderella feel to it, but maybe he has a foot fetish and hopes to see you wearing the heels."

"Then he'd plan to watch me," Ana replied. "Thank you for that unwelcome thought. I'll talk to you next week when I come home from Mallorca."

"Yes, do. I'm sorry if I was short with you this morning, but you have such tremendous potential, and you mustn't waste a speck of it."

"Thank you." She ended the call and walked into the kitchen to speak to Fatima. "I should have talked to Mr. Güerra when Mr. Cazares had him on the phone. Maybe he'll take back the kittens."

"Let's leave them in the bathroom while you eat lunch. You can decide what to do with them later. I made your favorite salad, and the oranges are especially good. I'll get more at the market before I come in tomorrow."

Ana had forgotten to tell her she'd be out of town for several days. "It's on my calendar. Please check it to make certain you've made a note of everything, but that's the only new job that wasn't already listed."

"I'll do that right now."

Javier Cazares returned in the afternoon. "The clerks at the Lamoreaux shop hadn't seen these shoes. They exclaimed over them but thought they must be from the holiday collection that wouldn't reach the shop until fall. I picked up one of their brochures. Mr. Lamoreaux is on the front. Does he look familiar?"

Ana took the brochures. Lamoreaux was a dark-haired man with a sprinkling of gray and striking blue eyes. He stood in front of his Barcelona shop, and his dark suit fit his trim build perfectly. "I don't know him, but he does fit Mr. Güerra's description." Although the cat fancier hadn't mentioned how handsome Lamoreaux was.

"I thought so too, so I went to see Güerra. Lamoreaux is the man who chose the kittens for you, and he paid with cash."

Fatima came forward to look at the brochure. "Why didn't he just ask Ana to model his shoes?"

"This may not be about shoes," Cazares warned. "His real interest may be Ana herself."

"Fine." Ana sighed. "What do you suggest?"

"Don't wear the shoes," the detective advised. "I'll locate Mr. Lamoreaux, and we'll decide how to approach him then."

"I'll ask my agent to represent me," Ana replied. "If he's looking for a model, fine. If he wants something personal, Paul will set him straight."

"Do you frequently receive unwanted gifts?" Cazares asked.

"Yes, she does," Fatima answered.

"It isn't all that frequent," Ana argued. "Gifts usually go to my agent's office. I don't post my home address anywhere."

"But Lamoreaux found it," Cazares emphasized.

Ana sat back on the sofa. "I've never heard of him, so he must have begun designing shoes recently. Perhaps he believes his approach was a polite way to introduce himself."

"It helps to be positive," the detective agreed.

"But it isn't often wise," Fatima countered.

Ana feared Fatima was right.

Chapter Four

Wednesday afternoon, Ana flew to Mallorca with Galen Salazar. The designer was always in a rush, and his long, sandy hair continually blew into his face, while his dark drooping eyebrows made him appear perpetually morose even when he laughed. Ana knew the other two models. Valeria had flaming red hair and alabaster skin that gave her an ethereal glow, while Lourdes had a Gypsy's dark beauty. Along with the crew who'd work the shoot, there were seven of them altogether.

Galen had made arrangements to shoot in the Palau de l'Almudaina in Palma. The Moorish palace was the perfect backdrop for his fashions, but they had to begin early Thursday morning to be finished before the museum opened to tourists. After they'd checked into the Hotel Feliz, Leticia, who handled Galen's fashions, immediately set to work steaming them to perfection.

Valeria went for a nap to the room she'd share with Lourdes, while Lourdes was insulted she hadn't been given her own room and headed for the bar. "Will you keep an eye on her?" Galen asked.

Ana grabbed her carry-on bag. "Sorry, I'm dropping this in my room and going out for a walk. You're not paying for my time until tomorrow."

At five-eight, he was used to looking up at his models, but he shook his head sadly. "You always behave in a professional manner, but if my clothes didn't look so good on Lourdes, I'd never hire her again. I'll have to watch her myself. We'll all meet later for dinner."

"I'll see you then." Ana shared a room with Mimi, a makeup artist devoted to Galen who never caused anyone a particle of worry. Ana left her carry-on bag on the bed by the windows, pulled on her hat and dark glasses and went out to find a tourist shop with postcards so she could mail one to Alejandro and her mother and stepfather. She also looked forward to taking some photos of her own.

She walked down Avinguda D'Antoni Maura, found postcards,

and entered a café for tea and an ensaimada, a delicious local pastry spiral sprinkled with powdered sugar. She shuffled through the half-dozen cards she'd bought, looking for the perfect one for Alejandro. She'd made a mental note of his address when they'd entered his building on Sunday and wrote it on a photo card of the Moorish palace where they'd be shooting tomorrow. Her message was a simple one about the beauty of the island. It probably wouldn't reach him before she got home, but she'd send it anyway.

She couldn't confide any worries to her mother because the dear woman would simply remind her of how hard they'd worked to give her such a lucrative career. As Ana saw it, she'd been the one who'd done the work. She wrote only that she was on Mallorca for a fashion shoot. It was a blessing her mother was so happy with Andre, and Ana was thankful for it every day.

Still hungry, she bought an orange and peeled it slowly. When she noticed a couple staring at her, she nodded. The woman came to her table. "You look so much like Ana Santillan, you ought to be modeling too."

"Thank you. That's very flattering." She wondered how long it would take Alejandro to recognize her. Men noticed the sexy models on billboards even if they never saw a fashion magazine, but she didn't want to push her luck any further. It would be easier to call him tonight and tell him who she was while she didn't have to face him, but it would also up the risk he'd quit seeing her before they really got to know each other.

The waiter put her empty teacup on his tray. "You are too pretty to look so sad. I could show you around Palma and give you a very good time."

She picked up her bag. "Thank you, but I've other plans." She mailed the postcards and had started back to the hotel when their photographer, Jaime Campos, overtook her.

"I'm glad I found you so we can talk privately. Let's stop here."

Ana didn't want another cup of tea, but sat with him in the outdoor café. He ordered a beer and leaned back to enjoy it. "How many times have we worked together, Ana?"

Jaime had the haggard look of a photo-journalist, and she'd heard he'd worked in Iraq. He always wore baggy khaki shirts and pants and dusty boots as though he'd be ready if a war broke out that afternoon.

He was a fine fashion photographer, however, and she enjoyed working with him. "Half a dozen times, I suppose."

He nodded. "You're one of my favorites, and I'd like to work with you on some art photography for a gallery show."

Ana raised a brow. "Are you talking about nudes?"

"A woman's figure is a glorious subject, and with your long hair, you'd never look completely undressed."

She glanced away. It was such a beautiful afternoon, but she wasn't in a warm mood. "Jaime, you do excellent work, but I don't do nudes, ever."

"Has anyone else asked it of you?"

"Not since I let it be known that I'd not consider it. I do fashion, not so-called 'art photography'."

"But I plan a serious study of the female figure—everything elegant with artistic backgrounds. Nothing tacky like a cheap girly calendar."

Growing more emphatic, Ana rested her elbows on the table and leaned toward him. She kept her voice low. "I wish you good luck with the project, but I won't be part of it."

His lower lip bulged in disappointment. "I've always made you look as beautiful as you are, but if I let a shadow fall across your face each time you pose tomorrow, you might be cut from the final ad."

Ana grabbed hold of his sleeve and, nearly shaking with anger, twisted hard. "Are you threatening me? It's a very bad idea when I could shred your career with every designer I know. If your work isn't up to its usual high standard tomorrow, I'll tell Galen why not." She stood and tightened her hold on her bag. "Let's forget this conversation ever took place. I'll see you at dinner."

Jaime stared as she walked away, his mouth agape.

Ana knew she'd probably overreacted, but Jaime must have finally gotten her message. She walked back to the hotel and around to the courtyard. She sat down on the garden wall and called Alejandro while she was too mad to realize it wasn't a good idea. "Hi, it's Ana."

"Hi, Ana. How are things going on Mallorca?"

She smoothed her hair behind her ear. "Not all that well, but I hope they'll run more smoothly tomorrow."

"Sounds interesting. Do you want to add a few details?"

She bit her lip, then burst out with it. "Not about that, but Alejandro, my black hair is a wig. I'm blonde."

"You're kidding, aren't you?"

She sucked in a deep breath. "You don't like blondes?"

He laughed. "Blondes are fine, redheads, whatever. You could show up bald, and I'd still like you."

"That's comforting." Now that she'd blurted out the least important thing about herself, she grew cautious. "The crew is having dinner together tonight, and I need to get going."

"You don't sound happy."

"One of the models is probably passed out in the bar, and that's going to make tomorrow difficult."

"You could take her place, but that would make it hard to take the photos, wouldn't it?"

"It would. I'll call you when I get home."

"Call me tonight if you want to, or tomorrow, whenever you have a chance."

"Thanks." Ana ended the call and doubted he'd remain so agreeable for long. All she had to do was show up looking like herself, and the paparazzi would circle his building like sharks. She hated them, but she was used to their shouts for smiles. He'd not enjoy finding himself in the tabloids as her mystery lover. He'd just shake his head and wish her a good life.

Despite Ana's misgivings, dinner went rather well. Lourdes was only tipsy and thought every comment hilarious which made everyone laugh. Ana had taken a seat on the same side of the table as Jaime so she wouldn't have to look at him while they ate. Galen talked at length about what a beautiful background Palma made for his fashions. With the mountains of the Tramuntana and circled by the sea, he said he might bring them all back to Mallorca in the fall.

Valeria leaned close to Ana. "You're awfully quiet. Did you leave someone exciting at home?"

Ana was afraid saying so would jinx their affair and shrugged. "It's too soon to tell."

"You have the hope, then. I haven't dated anyone fun in months. Men want to be photographed with me, but that's the extent of their interest. I'm going to find some nice school teacher or attorney, a doctor maybe, someone with substance."

"Substance is good," Ana assured her. "We live in an imaginary world where the latest fashion is more highly regarded than anything of real significance. This should be a fun job, though."

"Yes, but location shoots are a challenge for me. Ten minutes outside and I'll resemble a lobster too closely. Galen promises he'll watch the time."

"I'm sure he will."

The dinner party ended early so they'd all be ready to work at six the following morning. As Ana left the table, Valeria touched her arm. "Come outside with me a moment. There's something I need to ask you."

Ana doubted she could give valuable advice on any topic, but she wasn't sleepy. "It's a lovely night. Let's go out to the courtyard."

Valeria led the way, and they strolled near the low wall. "Did Jaime ask you to do some art photography?"

Ana bet he'd told her she was one of his favorites too. "He did, but I'm not interested. What did you tell him?"

"I said I'd think about it. He insisted I could trust him to show off my figure to every advantage. I'm paid for not having much in the way of curves, so I'd be a poor subject, but he raved about my hair."

"You do have magnificent red hair, Valeria."

"I wouldn't go that far, but it gets me work. I have a bad feeling about Jaime's project, but I don't want him to be angry with me when we do the shoot tomorrow."

"He'll take the blame if we don't look good, so I wouldn't worry. Don't let him coerce you into posing nude. With digital photography, photos can go around the world in less time than it used to take to develop a single shot in a darkroom."

Valeria appeared to be really distressed. "That's what worries me. The tabloids would put us on the front page and make fun of us for being too slender to look at without high-fashion clothes."

Ana gave her a quick hug. "I'm thoroughly sick of the tabloids too. Tell Jaime after the shoot that you've decided not to do it. There are plenty of girls who will. Let them worry about the consequences."

"I knew you'd know what to do. You're always confident, and I admire you for it."

"Thank you, but I wouldn't go that far," Ana replied with a gentle laugh. "Have you ever heard of Lorenzo Lamoreaux?"

"The name's vaguely familiar. Does he do shoes?"

"Yes, he does. Someone sent me a pair. I'll contact him when I get home."

Valeria brushed her fingertips over her flying curls. "Let me know if he likes women with red hair."

"I will." They went inside to go to their rooms, but Ana was tempted to go right back out and call Alejandro. Really tempted, but rather than appear desperately needy, she let it go.

Mimi had a delicate touch with makeup and brought out each model's exquisite beauty without overdoing it. They were photographing print ads for Galen's holiday line, and the long, painted silks flowed easily on the morning breeze. The Palau de l'Amudaina had two tiers of beautiful arched arcades, and with that frame, even the most casual pose was extraordinarily lovely.

Ana followed Jaime's directions and struck graceful poses, but she loved the splendid setting. When the Moors ruled Spain, they'd built the same extraordinary structures they had refined in North Africa. Each was a monument to their precise mathematics and geometry. The plain exteriors hid interiors of lavish intricacy that still marveled tourists.

She doubted many of today's constructions would remain standing in seven hundred years. Unlike the glorious Moorish architecture, stark modern lines wouldn't be missed.

"Ana!" Galen called. "Give us more of a smile. You've stepped out of a lavish party to catch your breath, and someone's waiting for you."

Ana licked her lips and tipped her head slightly. She thought of Alejandro and found a seductive smile.

"Perfect! Now let's do the blue gowns," Galen called.

Lourdes yawned. "All this fresh air makes me sleepy, and I don't look good in blue."

Ana caught Galen's eye. "Do you want to put Lourdes in a brighter color and give Valeria and me the blue? The contrast might be more effective."

Galen rested his hands on his hips. "Are you directing the shoot now?"

"It was merely a suggestion," she replied sweetly. She was tired of keeping her ideas to herself. He designed the clothes but often didn't understand how to show them to the best advantage.

"Brighter colors do look better on Lourdes," Jaime added, without looking Ana's way.

"All right, fine," Galen agreed. "We haven't much time. Let's hurry through the next shots and then take a look at what we've got."

"Thanks," Lourdes whispered. "I look dreadful in pale blue."

"You're welcome," Ana replied. When they finished work for the morning, the group scattered, while she stayed to tour the palace's museum with its beautiful chapel of Santa Ana. Growing up, she'd missed a lot of school due to work, but wherever they'd gone, her mother had taken her to see the historic sights. She should have thanked her and used another of the postcards she'd bought to do so now.

She bought an ensaimada pastry, walked along the palm-tree-lined pathway to the Parc de la Mar and found a bench to rest. Naturally slim, she could have eaten a dozen of the delicious spirals, but she seldom ate sweets and one was enough. Once finished, she brushed the powdered sugar from her hands and pulled her book from her bag. She loved the water, and it was a beautiful place to read. As a child, she'd become adept at disappearing into herself. She could sparkle on cue and relax just as easily, but today she was sorry to be nearly invisible and alone.

She pulled out her phone and called Alejandro but her call went to his voice mail. "We're finished for the day, and I'm reading by the water." She'd ended the call before she realized she hadn't given her name, but she didn't call back. He'd know who she was, and if he didn't, then he had too many girlfriends, and she didn't care.

As she entered the Hotel Feliz, Galen waved to her from the bar. He was seated alone and drawing in his sketchbook. He closed it when she joined him. "This morning went well."

"It did." She ordered limeade, relaxed into a comfortable chair and crossed her legs.

"I still think we can do better tomorrow. I want to capture more of the romance of my designs."

Ana nodded. She was well-acquainted with designers' passionate love for their own work. "It should be another beautiful day for a shoot."

"I hope so. Jaime and I talked about having you girls run along the arched arcades, breathless, laughing. It will put more excitement in my gowns." He reached for her hand. "You inspire me, Ana. I want to work with you on my next collection."

Growing uneasy, Ana slipped her hand from his and grabbed her limeade. "I enjoy working with you too."

He lowered his voice. "I want you to be my muse, to be in my studio so I can design first for you, and you'll be the star of the collection."

Appalled by the idea, she struggled to find a sad smile. "That's so flattering, Galen, and I'll work with you when I can, but I don't work exclusively for any designer."

"Don't reject the idea out of hand. I intend to make it very profitable for you. Stay with me when the others fly home tomorrow afternoon and give me a chance to convince you."

The warm glow filling his glance made it clear he was suggesting something more personal than mere conversation. "Aren't your wife and children expecting you to be home tomorrow?"

He sat back in his chair. "I can tell them I've decided to stay an extra day if you will."

He didn't appear to feel guilty for offering to lie, which disgusted her all the more. "I have someone waiting for me to come home, so I can't stay. I don't date married men anyway, Galen, so let's concentrate on work rather than our personal lives."

He picked up his sketchbook. "Forgive me if I've insulted you. You'll still join us for dinner, won't you?"

"Yes, the food here is very good." She could have taken a flight home that afternoon, but she wouldn't cancel a day of work. She carried her limeade out to the courtyard and took a chair facing the sea.

Some designers were over-friendly, and she was used to the way they fussed with the fit of their fashions in a blatant excuse to fondle her. This was the first time a designer had propositioned her, though. She'd pretend it hadn't happened. She could do it convincingly too. Perhaps her acting skills really were good enough to play a small role in an Almodóvar film, although she couldn't see herself as a movie star.

She tried Alejandro again, and he answered. "How are you?" he asked.

"I'm fine, but it's been a strange couple of days."

"Are the models being temperamental?"

"No more than usual, but location shoots always pose challenges. How are you?"

"I've been better. Took the bike out this morning, and a truck cut me off at the corner."

Her heart dropped. "Were you hurt?"

"I've a few scrapes, but no broken bones. I reacted quickly enough to save my bike."

She imagined him a bloody mess. "Is that your idea of humor?"

"No, it's titanium, and they aren't cheap. When are you coming home?"

"Tomorrow night, but I won't come to see you if you should be resting."

His voice was low. "You could rest with me."

"Enticing thought." She needed to talk with him, and perhaps she could work up to it. "What if I bring dinner?"

"That would be good. I haven't had time to take cooking lessons yet."

"I'll see you tomorrow."

Friday morning went well, and, the shoot over, Ana joined the others in flying home. Fatima welcomed her with a hug, and Romeo and Juliet scooted by in a rush. "Could they have already grown?"

"I think so," Fatima replied. "I have to feed them separately, or Romeo will eat Juliet's food. You can't have one enormous cat and one little tiny one."

"They're still little and cute, so this is the time to find them a home. It sounds as though you've become attached to them. Wouldn't you and Bruno like to have them?"

The housekeeper's gaze narrowed. "I told you I'm not fond of cats, and I haven't changed my mind. Give me your laundry, and I'll run a load before I go."

Ana unpacked her bag and tossed her clothes in the hamper. "If you were taking dinner home to Bruno, what would you buy?"

"He'll eat anything, so I'd buy whatever I felt like eating, and he'd eat it too. Why do you ask?"

She wouldn't twist the truth with her longtime housekeeper. "I've met an architecture student I like, and he got scraped up in a bicycle accident."

Fatima had a sparkling laugh. "So you're taking dinner to a sick friend?"

"You could say that, and I've never done it. I'm not certain where to begin."

"Make it a picnic and take a big meaty sandwich for him, and a bag of vegetables for yourself. He'd probably rather have beer than wine."

"I suppose." She knew exactly where to buy a sandwich he'd like and would call ahead to have it ready when she stopped by. "Thank you for everything. Take Monday off if you'd like."

Fatima closed the lid on the washer and turned the dial. "I just came back from vacation, Ana."

"So what? I've been gone a couple of days, so the place is clean, and you've taken care of the cats."

"May I save the day for a time I really need it?"

"Of course. Put 'day off' on a Post-it and stick it on the edge of my calendar so we don't forget."

"I'll do it. Tell me one thing, Ana. I'm sure your student is a very nice young man, but is he sophisticated enough for you?"

Despite a slightly raised brow, Fatima was sneaking up on an obvious problem rather than asking if she'd lost her mind. "He has no idea who I am. I'm easing him into it. He's a grown man, not a kid anyway."

"I won't say another word." Fatima gathered up the laundry, and Ana didn't follow.

As Ana soaked in the tub, she fought not to panic over the evening. She was a natural blonde, and waist-length hair suited her well as a model, but a photographer would tie her hair back or wear it in a single braid. Deciding on the latter, she asked Fatima to braid her hair before she left for home.

"Let's leave a few loose strands around your face so you don't look like a peeled grape," Fatima suggested. She stood back to admire her work. "Looks good. You have a good time tonight."

"Thank you. I'm sure we will." At least she hoped so.

She liked wearing white shirts with slim blue jeans. She added only a couple of coats of mascara; her brows were dark enough on their own. A pale lip gloss made her look too sweet for her tastes, but she didn't want to shock Alejandro too badly.

Before leaving, she fed the kittens and corralled them in the guest bathroom. Gathering her courage, she drove her Porsche to El Gato to pick up their dinner and parked the car around the block from Alejandro's studio. Fearing she was imagining more problems than she actually had, she carried their dinner bag up the stairs.

Alejandro opened the door on her first knock. He stared at her, looked much too closely and then broke into a wide grin. "You're even prettier than you were." He reached for her waist and pulled her into a loving hug. "You disappear so often, I don't want to let you go."

"I'm here," she assured him. She patted his back, felt the muscles play under her fingertips and found his strength wonderfully reassuring. When he dropped his arms, she didn't back away. Barefoot, he wore a knit shirt and shorts rather than attempt to hide the bruises and scrapes running along his right side, but when he turned toward the table, he limped. She was certain he'd been hurt worse than he'd admit. "Do you fall off your bike often?"

"No, thank God." He'd cleared the end of his worktable and made brown paper placemats. He had laid out napkins and utensils and had pulled up two chairs. "I'd just like to look at you for a while. Do you mind if we wait to eat?"

"Not at all." She stowed the café bag in his nearly bare refrigerator and took out a bottle of water. "I like looking at you too. We ought to sit down, though. Do you want to use the futon?"

He took her hand and walked her to it. He lowered himself slowly, and she sat on his left side, stretched out her legs and crossed her ankles.

"It's nice to see you in something other than black."

She drank a sip of water and licked her lips. "Thank you. Tell me what you've been doing all week."

He reached for the water bottle and took a drink. "Classes, projects that have to be completed on time, nothing fun at all. I've been to Palma. I wish I could have been there with you."

"Me too." She couldn't believe he'd eyed her so closely and not thought she at least looked familiar. Looking forward to the night, she wouldn't admit anything he didn't see, however.

He set the bottle aside and laced his fingers in hers. "Tell me about the shoot. Did it go well?"

"All in all yes, but not entirely. It doesn't matter now, though."

"Are you sure?"

She closed her eyes and drew in a deep breath. "I work with different people every week, and I never know what to expect. I may think I know, but there are always surprises."

He squeezed her hand. "Not good ones?"

"No, never good ones."

He brought her hand to his lips. "Don't I qualify?"

The devilish glint in his light eyes made her laugh. "Yes, you're a delicious surprise." She leaned close to kiss him, and he lay back and pulled her down on his chest.

"If we don't get too rambunctious, I'll be fine," he promised.

"What if I get rambunctious and you just lie back and enjoy it?" She ran her fingertips down his arm in a teasing caress.

He moaned way back in his throat. "I've really missed you."

"I've missed you too." She slicked his hair out of his eyes, ran her hands down his belly and unzipped his shorts without breaking eye contact. "Condoms?"

"Pocket, but I don't want you to think…"

She silenced him with a lavish kiss that made him breathless. "Let's not think." She leaned back to pull his shorts down his legs and took care not to brush his skinned knee. He'd gone commando, and she raked her fingertips across his bare belly and watched him grow hard. "Take off your shirt."

He yanked it over his head and threw it aside. "You ought to remove something."

"Maybe after dinner." She pulled her hair out of the braid and leaned over to swish the gentle curls over his chest and hips.

He grabbed hold of her shoulders. "How can you talk about dinner?" he asked in a choked gasp.

"All right, I'll forget food for the moment, but we'll have to eat eventually." She played her fingers over his hairy chest. He looked like a real man, not a carefully waxed and manicured model. The next time she brushed her hair over him, she moved lower to straddle his left leg and slid her fingers around his rock-hard cock. "You've got a real mouthful here, but I'll give it a try."

"Ah." His voice ended in a grateful sigh, and he grabbed her hair to hold her close.

She teased him with soft licks, savoring the smooth head before sucking him in deep. Circling his shaft with gently twisting hands, she lured him nearer and nearer to the edge before sitting back. She pulled her hair free of his grasp, tickled his balls and pinched his nipples. "You liked what I did last time. Now you'll know what's coming."

When he could only manage a strangled moan, she bent down to swirl her tongue over the sensitive spot where his shaft met the head, and again took him deep. She held him so he couldn't thrust down her throat, rubbed the spot behind his balls, and pressed down with her thumb to delay his climax. He could only stand a few seconds of that erotic torture, and she slid his cock out of her mouth and pressed it to his stomach. She raised her thumb to give him another world-shattering climax and watched his cum spew across his belly. She wiped it up with a tissue from her pocket.

After rolling off the futon, she washed her hands in the kitchen sink and called over her shoulder. "I feel like eating, but you can take your time. I love the placemats."

Alejandro mumbled incoherently as he fought to regain his breath. He stared up at the ceiling. "You must have had a lot of practice with that technique, whatever it's called."

Indeed she had, and with a master. "I doubt it has a name, but I'm discreet and never name my lovers." Earlier, she'd slid the elastic band from her braid onto her wrist and used it now to make a low ponytail. She took the El Gato bag from the refrigerator. "If you want to eat, you have to wear clothes when you come to the table."

He propped himself on an elbow. "This is my studio, and I make the rules."

She found plates and carried his sandwich and beer to the table. She warmed her vegetable-filled pasta in the microwave. "You ought to please your guests, especially considering how easily I please you."

"You think I'm easy?"

The silly question made her laugh. "Of course, you're a man."

He eased himself up and pulled on his clothes. "I think I like the Goth girl better. Can you bring her back?"

That hurt, and she was angry with herself for not thinking he might have a favorite. She shrugged as though he'd been joking. "I'd still be the same person."

He came to the table, and when he found his favorite sandwich, he sat back. "We didn't exchange more than a half-dozen words that first Sunday, and you remembered what I like?"

"Goth Girl has a great memory. Thank her next time you see her." She took the chair beside him and had a bite of her dinner. The pasta held a comforting warmth, but her feelings were still hurt.

"No, wait. I'd rather you stayed one person, and you're so pretty with your blonde hair. How long did it take you to grow?"

It was a question she'd been asked a million times, and she didn't want to sound annoyed. She forced a smile. "I've had long hair since I was a child and trim the ends once in a while. Now tell me something. You must be at least six-three."

"I'm six-five when I stand up straight."

"Perfect."

He finished chewing a bite of his sandwich. "You wouldn't describe me as gangly and awkward?"

"No, not at all. You have an athlete's grace, and you're better looking than most of the male models I photograph."

He dipped his head as though embarrassed. "I'm not any good at standing still, so that career is out for me."

She played with a strand of pasta. "It's still nice to find a man who doesn't have to look up at me." She licked a bit of tomato off her lip. "It makes for a nice fit."

"I believe it. If I could climb the ladder up to my bedroom, we could try it."

She'd brought her water to the table and took a long drink. "There's no need to rush. I fed the kittens and don't have to hurry home."

"Good. We can spend the whole night together. I don't suppose anyone's died from too much sex."

"Sure they have. Men have heart attacks all the time. I've heard more often with a mistress or girlfriend than a wife."

"Have you ever been married?" he asked.

She finished a bite of grilled zucchini. "No, I haven't."

He frowned slightly and looked more serious. "What about your boyfriend who died? Would you have married him?"

Her breath caught in her throat, but it was unfair to both of them to think about Miguel when they were together. "Yes, but now you've depressed me thoroughly. Let's leave that subject closed and just eat."

He gave her shoulder a sympathetic squeeze. "I'm sorry. I always ask the wrong questions."

She curled her hand around his wrist. "I'd like to really know you, but I don't want to know about other women unless they were circus performers who had some unusual tricks we could try."

He jerked his hand away to grab his napkin. His mouth was full, and he couldn't laugh, so he shook his head and swallowed. "No, you're the wildest woman I've ever met, but I like it."

"Wild?" She regarded him with the enticing sultry glance she used so successfully in ads. "I'll take it as a compliment."

"It was." He glanced at her plate. "Don't you eat anything other than vegetables?"

She smiled. "I also eat fruit. You could call it the fruit-bat diet."

His gaze turned quizzical. "How could you recommend the restaurant's filet mignon?"

She toyed with another piece of grilled zucchini but didn't bring it to her mouth. "We don't discuss other people, remember?"

"So your dates, who shall remain nameless, said it was good?"

She set her half-eaten dinner aside. "Nothing matters, Alejandro, but here and now. Life is fleeting, and we should enjoy the moment and not worry about the past."

There were only a few crumbs left on his plate, and he turned his full attention on her. "You sound like a fortune cookie."

"True, but it's good advice. Now tell me something about Moorish art. The buildings on Palma are so beautiful, and it's difficult to believe they're seven hundred years old. Was construction that much better then?"

His brows dipped in disbelief. "You want to talk about architecture?"

"Why not? I'm curious, and you're an expert, aren't you?"

He nodded. "The Moors had superb craftsmen who built with local stone, and their measurements were so accurate that once built, their structures will stand indefinitely. If Spain were a country with frequent earthquakes, all we'd have now would be intriguing rubble, but the ground here is solid."

"There's no difference between one architect and another, though, is there?"

"No, they all combined the same elements. Now we can build whatever we want, or whatever we can convince someone to pay to build, but my little boxes won't last seven hundred years."

"They're meant as family homes, so they won't have to," she assured him.

He finished his beer and set the bottle aside. "Now I'm curious. Why do you go around in a Goth disguise?"

She smiled and hoped it would distract him until she could come up with an answer that made sense. "It's just fun. I work in advertising where we often make one thing look like another. On Sundays, it's fun to disappear into someone else, and it doesn't hurt anyone."

"I suppose not, but if there had been another table with a vacant chair at El Gato, I would have taken it and missed knowing you."

"A tragedy," she replied flippantly, but the possibility truly saddened her.

"For me, if not for you," he insisted.

She reached for his hand and gave him a quick squeeze. "Truthfully, for me too. One of the models who went to Palma is looking for a man with substance. She's not talking about money, but good character, someone really worth knowing. You're in that category, but I won't introduce you."

He looked at her askance and scoffed. "I don't believe I've ever impressed a girl with my character."

His skeptical expression told her much more than he'd meant to. "Maybe you've met the wrong women."

"You could say that." He caught her hand before she could pull away. "I want to take you out, go places, do things. We don't need to stay here."

"Out," she repeated softly. "I love holding hands in movies. Do you like that?"

"Of course. I still want to take you to the port."

"That's always fun. But we needn't go anywhere until you're better."

"I'll be fine by tomorrow night. Let's go to dinner again. Let me pick the place this time."

"Do you know someplace quiet, out of the way? Someplace tourists never see. I want to be able to talk the way we did last Sunday."

A slow smile slid across his lips. "Someplace romantic?"

"Yes," she insisted. "If you like places with crowds and loud music, go with your male friends."

"I don't like crowds and loud music, and most of my friends are married now. We haven't gone out looking for hookups with girls for a very long time." He coaxed her onto his lap. "I love having you here, but I'm not some kid you have to blow each time you come in."

She slid her fingers through the soft curls at his nape and widened her eyes in mock innocence. "You didn't like it?"

"A dead man would have liked it, but I don't want to stop there." He kissed the line of her jaw, sucked her earlobe to make her giggle and gave her a long, slow kiss. "I think there's some ice cream in the freezer."

She wrapped her arms around his neck. "Later."

"Will you tell me where you live so I can pick you up at your place?"

She rubbed her forehead against his. It was such a simple request and so natural a step she couldn't say no. She could substitute Miro prints for her framed magazine covers and welcome him in. "I'll give you my address when I leave. I'll meet you downstairs and invite you to come in and see the kittens after dinner."

"Fine." He ran his tongue over her lower lip. "I've been dying to see the kittens."

She laughed into his kiss. Everything about him felt good. She bet he had been gangly and awkward when he was a kid, but he'd definitely outgrown it. She ended the kiss to catch a breath. "I wanted to be ballerina. I actually had the talent, but by twelve, I was too tall. It was a huge disappointment."

"I know disappointment." He kissed her throat and unbuttoned the top button on her shirt and then the second. She had on lacy ecru lingerie, and he sat back as he unbuttoned the last buttons and eased her out of the shirt. "You have the most beautiful underwear."

"And not a single pair of black boxers," she teased. "I think we should go back to the futon before you fall over backwards and dump us both on the floor. I don't want to see you hurt any worse than you already are."

"Good plan." He eased her off his lap and stood. "Maybe if I went very slowly, we could go up on the loft."

She kicked off her flats. "Why don't you save your energy? We can climb up there the next time I'm here."

"You so sure I'll invite you back?" He pulled his shirt off over his head.

She peeled off her jeans and rolled them up to set aside. "You better, or I'll leave the kittens on your doorstep."

"You're threatening me with kittens?" He caught her hand and spun her around so he could unfasten her bra. He slid off her thong and stared at her heart-shaped pubic curls. "Do you change the shape with the seasons?"

She unbuttoned his shorts. "I rather like the heart, but I suppose

I could turn it into a little house just for you."

He laughed so hard he nearly tripped taking off his shorts. "I've never inspired that level of devotion in anyone."

"Don't gloat. You haven't inspired it yet."

"I'll regard it as a challenge," he growled against her throat as he eased her down on the futon. "You have the most beautiful skin." He kissed the inside of her elbows and sucked lightly at her breasts. Clean-shaven, he rubbed his cheek against her delicate nipples without leaving a scratch. He licked her belly button to make her giggle and then slid his fingers into her. He stretched out to kiss her inner thighs. "You smell so good. Do you put perfume behind your knees?"

"It works, doesn't it?" She slid her fingers through his hair.

"Everything works with you." He twisted two fingers inside her and licked her slit, teasing her open with the tip of his tongue. "Am I doing all right?"

Ana opened her eyes and smiled. "You're doing beautifully, but you can't stop until I tell you to."

"Is that one of your rules?" He stroked her with his thumb.

"One of them. You've created the most delicious ache." She placed her hand over his. "I like your mouth better."

He drew in a deep breath, and licked her until she writhed beneath him and thanked him with a soft sigh. He pulled on the condom he'd had ready and thrust into her slowly. "You've such a glorious heat, like bubbling honey."

Raising her arms above her head, she thanked him through a breathy sigh. He taunted her with deep thrusts and carried her into another shuddering release. When he buried his face in her hair, she wrapped him in her arms and held him tight as though she'd never let him go.

Chapter Five

Alejandro got up during the night and found a blanket to cover them, but Ana slept too deeply to stir. They remained in a blissful tangle until dawn, and she awoke still smiling. She eased herself out of his arms, dressed and, as promised, wrote her address and phone number on her placemat. Before leaving his studio, she took several photos of him hugging the twisted blanket as tightly as he'd held her. She left quietly and drove herself home. Fatima arrived soon after she'd left the shower.

"How was your date?" the housekeeper asked.

Ana's smile said it all. "We had a wonderful time. Thank you for suggesting I take him a sandwich. He was probably expecting some elegant French dish neither of us could pronounce, so something he recognized was a big plus."

"Men are simple creatures," Fatima advised. "Throw them a piece of red meat, and they'll be happy for hours."

"I'll remember that. I need to call Cazares and see if he's found Lamoreaux before he sends another pair of shoes."

"I could use some new shoes," Fatima remarked. "Maybe you could mention my size if you meet him."

"It never hurts to ask for samples." She called the detective from her room, and Javier Cazares supplied an update. "Lamoreaux divides his time between Barcelona and Paris. He'll be here next week, and I suggest you have your agent call him to make an appointment."

Ana took careful notes. "I've got it. Send me your bill."

"I will, and Miss Santillan, I have some other and perhaps disturbing news."

She shoved her still damp hair out of her eyes. "I'm afraid to ask what it is."

"I saw a colleague yesterday, and while he wouldn't disclose who'd hired him, he's being paid to provide information about you."

Alarmed, she sank down on the end of her bed. "What sort of information? My modeling jobs, or something personal?"

Cazares cleared his throat, but his voice remained hushed. "I believe a bit of both."

"That isn't good news. Could it be Lamoreaux?" she asked.

"It could be, but he wouldn't say. He isn't a friend of mine. We just happen to cross paths occasionally."

"Would you describe him as ethical?"

Cazares delayed a moment too long. "I don't recommend him."

"Oh fine. I don't lead a particularly exciting life, so he'll probably soon grow bored with the job. Can you describe him?"

"He's six feet tall and heavy set, bald, and he walks fast, as though he's on his way to an important meeting. If you see him, pretend not to notice and go on with whatever you were doing. You're not in danger, but be careful."

"Thank you, I will be." She glanced at her framed magazine covers and changed them for the Miro prints. It was a small precaution, but all she could handle right now.

That afternoon, her agent welcomed her with a cheerful smile. "Armand Levya wants you for a shoot on a cruise ship, the *Mediterranean Goddess*, this coming Monday morning. Bikinis, resort wear, that sort of thing. Meet him at the ad agency at seven, and you'll all go from there."

She made a note of the date on her cell phone. "Fine. Thank you." She handed him Lamoreaux's number in Paris and the brochure from his shop. "He sent me a magnificent pair of heels, so he must want me to model for him. Will you please call him while I'm here? I want to meet him before I agree to work for him."

Paul nodded thoughtfully and called the Paris number. He spoke French as well as Spanish, Catalan and English. Ana had learned French to work with haute couture designers, and English merely for fun. He put the call on speaker. "Monsieur Lamoreaux, this is Paul Perez, Ana Santillan's agent. She asked me to call and thank you for the beautiful pair of heels you sent to her."

When Ana heard Lamoreaux's soft-spoken reply, she whispered, "Find out why he sent me kittens."

Paul raised his brows. "Monsieur Lamoreaux, why are you sending Ana presents?"

Ana and Paul exchanged puzzled glances, but Lamoreaux admitted only that he'd wanted to make a good impression on a woman he greatly admired. Women loved flowers and kittens, so they were appropriate gifts, and he hoped he'd made her curious about him. He'd be in Barcelona the following week and wanted to discuss the advertising for his new line.

"Let's meet in my office on Tuesday at one." Paul gave him the address and directions. He ended the call and shook his head. "Let's face it, he adores your legs."

"Many of the designers are eccentric," Ana mused aloud. "Lamoreaux seems like the typical Frenchman. He'll dote on a woman, swiftly grow bored and look elsewhere for someone new."

"Many Spanish men suffer from the same failing, but if he doesn't impress us next week, you needn't work with him. Your skin has such a pretty glow. You must have had a very good time in Palma, or did you spend a day at a spa?"

Any color she had today would have come from Alejandro's lavish affection, and she blushed rather than give him credit. "We worked outdoors so it must be from the sea breeze and sunshine. Have you received the script from Ignacio Belmonte?"

"Not yet, but if it isn't here in the next couple of days, I'll call him."

"I'd rather you didn't, but go ahead. It shouldn't take more than an afternoon to film the part I read, so it isn't a big time commitment." They checked the work she had coming up and parted on a better note than they had the last time.

Ana surveyed her closet with the same exasperated sigh as she had last weekend. She wanted to look pretty, but not so pretty other people noticed. She decided upon a short green dress that matched her eyes. People recognized her from her long blonde hair, and she twisted it into a bun at her nape in the hope she wouldn't be noticed. She loved bracelets, loaded both wrists with silver and gold bangles, and finished with gold hoop earrings. She had dozens of pairs of heels and chose a tan wedged pair with ankle ties. All she'd need tonight was a small clutch and light sweater.

She went downstairs ten minutes before Alejandro was set to arrive, and Jacob was on duty. "How is your school going?" she asked him.

"Good. Thank you for asking, Miss Santillan."

She paused, uncertain whether she should ask him not to use her last name as she left for the evening, or when she came home. He'd think her daft, of course, and she didn't want to lure him into the gigantic secret she'd kept from Alejandro. She turned away from the desk and waited near the door. When Alejandro drove up in a black Mercedes SUV, she went outside to meet him.

He came around the car to open her door. "I have to haul stuff all the time. I hope you don't mind riding in this."

The car was spotless and the interior freshly vacuumed. "Why would I mind? Don't all architects drive trucks or SUVs?"

He got into the driver's seat and leaned over to kiss her. "They do, but this isn't the car for a romantic evening, and I apologize."

While he worried about his car, she just wanted another remarkably pleasant time. "I love SUVs. The view of the road is so much better with the high seats." It was so good she noticed the bald man in the dark sedan parked across the street. He hurriedly lowered a camera when she glanced his way, but she'd seen it.

"Why are you so quiet tonight?" he asked.

"I'm sorry. I should have prepared a list of conversation topics, but I was too busy today."

He laughed and reached over to pinch her knee. "What were you doing?"

"Just Saturday stuff, nothing interesting. What about you?"

"I felt good enough to ride my bike, but I took it out of town so I didn't have to worry about landing on a curb again."

"I've never learned to ride a bike. Do they make adult bikes with training wheels?"

"I've never seen one. Let's rent a tandem bike. I'll do all the work, and you can ride."

"I wouldn't want to plan a tour of Europe, but for an afternoon, it sounds fun. It really does." She'd done sportswear ads holding a bike, but growing up, she hadn't done much of the physical stuff other kids had. "I don't know how to play soccer either. Do you like it?"

"Sure, I played when I was a kid. I can teach you that too."

She'd never missed soccer but would love to have him teach her. He'd obviously earned his lean, athletic build, but he didn't sound as though he expected her to keep up with him. He took her to a quiet place where their table overlooked the port. "There are so many lights, it looks like noon," she exclaimed.

"The work goes on twenty-four hours a day. So there's plenty to see day or night. They have an excellent Parrillada de Mariscos here. Do you ever eat seafood?"

"Sometimes."

"Order whatever you like, Ana. I never talk about money, but I can afford to do whatever you like."

She'd rather not think about money, especially where he was concerned. She chose the Amanida, a salad with shellfish, and reached across the table for his hand. "Your company is enough excitement for tonight."

The woman at a nearby table kept glancing her way. People often asked for her autograph, and if this woman approached her, she'd have to deny who she was, or tell Alejandro the whole truth. Her appetite vanished with a soft thud.

The waiter approached, and she dipped her head to look out at the port until Alejandro had given their order and the man had turned away to bring their wine. "I've always wanted to go sailing on a clipper ship. There are a few left, aren't there?"

"Yes, there are. But it must be backbreaking work, rather than as romantic as movies make it appear. Almost nothing is real in movies anymore—but you must know that."

"I do." The woman who'd been observing her so closely was talking with her companion and had apparently decided Ana wasn't worth observing after all. Relieved, Ana talked easily about movies and music while they ate. They didn't like all the same things, but nothing they differed on mattered.

"I've waited a long time to meet you," he admitted. "I don't want to frighten you. If you only want to see me once a week, I'll have to manage."

He was such an open man and obviously unfamiliar with

romantic games. "It's good not to overdose on someone new," she offered. "But I'm sure we can work out something without having to block out days on a calendar. Is the crema catalana good here?"

He studied her expression a long moment. "We're going to be sensible, is that it? Fine. The crema catalana is superb. Do you want some?"

She played with a strand that had escaped her bun. "Yes, please. Fatima makes it for me sometimes."

He signaled the waiter and ordered two. "Will Fatima be there when I take you home?"

"She doesn't work on weekends, and she's never there at night, but I hope you'll meet her soon. She's a wonderful cook, and crema catalana is easy for her. I've tried to make it, but the custard is never rich enough, and I've yet to discover the secret to grilling the sugar topping perfectly."

He leaned back as the waiter brought their desserts. "There's a secret to everything."

His seductive glance made it plain he wasn't thinking of recipes, and she nodded. "Often multiple secrets, but it makes life exciting, don't you think?"

"Definitely."

Ana looked for the bald man as they left the restaurant, but didn't see him, and they weren't followed to her place. They parked on the street and held hands as they went through the main doors of her condo. Jacob was on the phone, speaking to a resident about a take-out delivery, and Ana waved and hurried Alejandro to the elevators. When they reached her floor, he took her key to unlock her door and opened it slowly.

"Where are the kittens?"

"I banish them to the guest bathroom when I go out. I'll get them if you'd really like to see them."

"Of course I want to see them. This is a beautiful place, but it doesn't look like you."

She grabbed a pillow from the sofa and threw it at him. "I've lived here for years, and it's exactly what I want. I work in stark modern sets all the time. This is as peaceful as it comes, pretty and comfortable, even if it isn't the latest in home design."

"You should decorate your home the way you please," he agreed. "I expected something more in the Goth tradition."

She pulled the pins from her hair and shook it loose. "Stone walls, wooden benches and flickering candles? That doesn't sound very homey." She let the kittens out, and they chased her back to the living room. "Juliet is the black one. So far, Romeo has shown more personality."

Alejandro loosened his tie, pulled it off and tucked it into his jacket pocket. "Do they sleep with you?"

She shook her head. "Sorry if it disappoints you, but no. Would you like coffee or tea, wine, a glass of water?"

He shook his head and came toward her. He caught her waist and tilted her head to kiss her with a gentle sweetness, and with her encouragement, he became increasingly insistent. "You always taste so good."

"So do you. Let me take your coat."

He shrugged out of it. "Have you ever been to a nudist colony?"

She laughed and stepped back. "No, and I'm not going. Do you like them?"

"I've never been either, but I spend so much time with you taking off and putting on my clothes, it might be fun to try one."

She unbuttoned his shirt. "I believe the idea is to enjoy the tranquility of nature, not to more easily ravish your partner."

"I've completely misunderstood the purpose, then." He took her shoulders to turn her around and unzipped her dress. She'd worn turquoise lingerie tonight. "You must have an endless supply of lingerie, and this is a cute dress. You have such beautiful legs, you ought to show them off with short dresses all the time." He knelt to untie her shoes and slipped them from her feet. Her toenails were painted a bright pink.

"Thank you. I have my own dance studio here, and dancing is the perfect exercise."

"May I see it?"

"It's the second bedroom. If anyone comes to visit, the living room sofa makes a bed."

He followed her down the hallway. When she opened the door, the first thing he saw was the mirrored wall. "Do you ever make love in here?"

She had, but shook her head. "I'm discreet, remember? No one will ever hear what you and I do." There was a straight-backed chair in the corner, and she pulled it out into the center of the room with the seat facing the mirror. She took hold of the back. "Does this give you any ideas?"

He walked up behind her and studied their reflections in the mirror. He unfastened her bra, let it drop to the chair and cupped her breasts. He rolled her nipples into tight buds. "You slip out of your clothes so easily. You ought to give me a head start."

She covered his hands with her own. Her skin was a creamy peach, while his was deeply tanned. "Just unzip your pants."

He kissed her shoulder. "No short cuts. I want to feel your bare skin against mine."

"You started this, but I didn't mean to rush you." Romeo dashed into the room and sped out while Juliet lay down by the door to watch. "We have an audience, although she's discreet too."

He let her go and circled the chair to sit down and remove his shoes. "Good, but I'm taking you first."

She kneaded his shoulders and leaned down to kiss his cheek. "There are hooks along the wall for your clothes." Her ballet slippers dangled from the first hook, and she had tutus in the closet. Not thinking they'd use the room, she'd stacked the framed magazine covers in the closet too. She'd have to keep him too busy to look.

Once undressed, he came to stand behind her and ran his hands over her shoulders and down her arms. "I'll bet you were a gorgeous child."

"All people saw was my hair." She dipped her head to let it spill over her breasts. "I was lucky, though, I liked being tall and didn't care that much for boys when they were too short to dance with me."

He kissed her nape with teasing nibbles. "I was born tall. We should have met sooner."

She leaned back to rub her shoulders against his hair-roughened chest. "Maybe we wouldn't have appreciated each other until now."

"I'm sure I'd have appreciated you."

She studied him in the mirror. He ran his hands over her hips and up between her legs to pull away the thong. Their reflections magnified the thrill of his slow caresses, and she leaned into him.

"Oh damn." He left her to get a condom from his pants pocket. "Hold this for me so I can touch you."

She placed a kiss in his palm before she took it. "Let's put on some music." She turned on a romantic piece she loved for dancing and swayed as she returned to him. "Do you like to dance?"

He shrugged. "I'm not very good at it."

"I'll teach you after I learn to ride a bike." She looped her arms around his neck and pulled his lower lip gently through her teeth. When she turned back to the chair, he leaned over her, wrapped his arms around her waist and slid his fingertips through the soft heart on her mound. Her moisture smoothed every stroke.

The mirror gave her a provocative view, and the luscious music swirled around them to create an exotic rendezvous. Craving his intimate touch, she relaxed against him and pretended they were floating in the sea. When he asked for the condom, she'd forgotten it lay in her hand.

He used it, bent his knees to ease into her, and, braced against the chair, she pushed back to take him deep. He swirled her hair around his wrist to lift her head and kissed her. He rocked her slowly, diving in and pulling back with a heartbeat's steady rhythm. She watched him in the mirror. With his ebony hair, he could have been another of her lovers, but she wouldn't let memory blur his image. He was always so gentle, as though he feared she'd break, and she loved his lazy loving. He coaxed her with a deep thrust only to withdraw and pleasure her with his hand. She hung on to the chair and closed her eyes to simply feel without the distracting view.

He made her so warm her whole body felt slippery. She was so close, teetering on the rim, and then tensed as with another thrust, he sent a searing orgasm jolting through her. She felt his body throb deep within hers and savored the thrill until only the chair kept her standing. When he picked her up and carried her into her bedroom, she was amazed he still had the strength to lift her.

The room was painted a pale lavender, decorated with lace and puffed pillows and a white rug as soft as a cloud. He set her down only long enough to pull back the wide bed's duvet and top sheet and eased her down beside him. "I want to hold you all night."

She snuggled against him. "I'll not set the alarm and make you go." Romeo clawed up the end of the bed and jumped around them in frantic circles. "Damn," she sighed. "I forgot the kittens."

"Give me a minute, and I'll feed them," he promised, but the kittens had already fallen asleep by the time he was awake enough to remember.

Alejandro stood by the window when Ana woke Sunday morning. She stretched lazily and blew him a kiss. He was already dressed, and she wouldn't beg him to come back to bed. "Good morning."

He sat down beside her and smoothed her hair out of her eyes. "I like waking up with you, but I have a project to finish before tomorrow. I'll try and see you at the beginning of the week. You finally gave me your number so I can call you."

He was so earnest she couldn't mistake his architecture assignment for an excuse to avoid her indefinitely. "Please do. Monday, I have a job that will probably take the whole day, but maybe we can have dinner together if you're not too tired."

He laughed and leaned down to kiss her. "Drawing blueprints isn't as exhausting as spending the night with you, but this is a good kind of exhaustion."

"I know." She stretched and hugged her pillow. She longed to tell him the truth, was finally anxious to do so and promised herself she'd do it Monday night. "There's something I need to talk to you about, but it can wait until the next time I see you."

"You don't have some deadly disease, do you?"

He looked horrified, and she sat up to hug him. "No, of course not. Please don't worry."

He returned her squeeze and stood. "I wish I didn't have to leave and we could go to El Gato this afternoon and on down to the port."

"Next Sunday," she replied. She covered a wide yawn and slipped back under the covers. "See you soon."

He kissed her cheek and left without disturbing the dozing kittens on the foot of the bed.

Sunday night, Alejandro picked up his cell phone on the first ring hoping it was Ana, and was disappointed to hear his father's voice. He couldn't ignore the call, or the man would persist in annoying him until he answered. It was better to get the conversation over now. "Hello. How is everyone?"

"We're all fine. I called to ask about you. Are you and Ana still dating?"

Alejandro drew in a deep breath. His father had a lengthy list of women he regarded as suitable mates for his eldest son, and Alejandro had never liked any of them. "Yes. I'm fine and so is Ana."

"Good. Is she also studying architecture?"

"No, she's a photographer."

"Really? I need you to come to the office tomorrow morning. There's something I have to show you. I'm sure you can work it into your schedule."

Instantly wary, Alejandro sat up straight. "What is it?"

"It's too involved to describe on the phone, but it will only take a few minutes of your time. You'll thank me, I'm sure."

Alejandro doubted it. "I'll be there." He ended the call and quickly wished he'd been too busy to go anywhere tomorrow except to see Ana.

The *Mediterranean Goddess* was a modern cruise ship booked months in advance for luxury cruises in Greek waters. In port for a week between voyages, it was the perfect location for a magazine spread on resort wear. The designer, a petite woman named Lee-Lee, knew the owner of the cruise line, and Orlando Ortiz met them as they came on board.

"Please let us know if there is anything you need," he announced graciously. "My staff is at your disposal. I recognize most of you from your photos, but it's a pleasure to meet you in person."

Ana returned his smile, but when his glance remained on her a moment too long, she grew uneasy. He was an attractive man, perhaps in his fifties, but she trusted her intuition, and the intensity of his gaze worried her. She was relieved when he didn't remain on deck to watch the shoot.

Ana always found working with Lee-Lee amusing. The designer insisted upon overseeing every detail of hair and makeup and emphasized her directions with whirling gestures that frequently made everyone duck. Teresa used her magic with makeup and hair to transform the models into flawless beauties and handsome hunks despite Lee-Lee's interference. When Armand was ready to shoot, they were all dressed in their first outfits.

Gian Carlo Maxim was one of men working that day. He gave Ana a begrudging nod, and just for spite, she responded with a dazzling smile. He was dressed in a ship's officer's white uniform, and she posed with him in a bright red bikini with red stiletto heels. With false eyelashes, her hair blown by Robert holding a portable fan, she stood at the rail and leaned against Gian Carlo, posed as every man's dream of a vacation lover.

She saw Orlando Ortiz approach out of the corner of her eye but didn't glance his way until Armand gave them a break.

"Miss Santillan," Ortiz called. "How pretty you are in red. Do you have a minute? I'd like you to meet my son."

When Alejandro stepped out from behind his father, she couldn't have been more surprised, but she was delighted to see him, even in her full Ana Santillan regalia with copper eye shadow and false eyelashes that were longer than a giraffe's. It was a secret she wanted to let go. Smiling widely, she took a step toward him, but he swept her with a disgusted glance, turned on his heel and stalked away. Orlando regarded her with a vicious smirk, clearly enormously pleased with the difficult scene he'd created. Instantly sure he'd been the one who'd hired a detective to follow her, she disliked him all the more. The models and crew on the deck had all fallen silent, but the noise of the port was only slightly louder than her wildly beating heart.

"What have you done?" she asked.

"Why nothing at all, Miss Santillan. I just wanted my son to meet you, but apparently you two are already acquainted."

Gian Carlo moved up behind her. "What's going on?"

Orlando Ortiz strutted away. Ana wouldn't chase him along the deck in a bikini, and she'd no idea where Alejandro might have gone. "I'm not sure, but I'll straighten it out when we're finished." Everyone gaped at her, including Lee-Lee, but this wasn't the time for a lengthy description of her love life. "What's next, Armand?"

"Do you need a minute?" the photographer asked.

"No, thank you. I'm fine." She just wanted the shoot over with quickly so she could see Alejandro and straighten out whatever hideous mess his father had created for them.

"Why did Orlando's son leave?" Lee-Lee asked. "We could use a beautiful young man with his dark brooding looks in the evening-wear scenes."

"I can be as brooding as you need," Gian Carlo quickly offered, and regarded the designer with a threatening glare.

Lee-Lee sighed. "I guess that will have to do. I want the other girls with Gian Carlo now. Wave as though you were telling someone good-bye on the dock."

Ana changed into her next outfit, and Teresa touched up her makeup, but Lee-Lee changed her mind about which girls she wanted in which clothes and Ana had to dress again. She stopped looking at the time, but it was late afternoon before they finished and rode back to the advertising agency's office. She went straight home from there to shower and dress. Fatima nearly danced around her, asking questions.

"Why are you in such a hurry? Just call the man and tell him you need more time. I'm sure he won't mind if you're a few minutes late for your date."

"We don't have a date, and I need to speak with him in person, Fatima."

"Oh, there's a problem? The weekend didn't go well?"

"The weekend went beautifully, or at least Saturday night did. I won't explain today's mess until I've solved it. Good-bye. I'll see you tomorrow."

Fatima picked up the kittens so they'd not be stepped on as Ana left, but she put them down quickly before they licked her fingers with their rough little tongues.

Ana's knock on Alejandro's door brought only a hollow echo. She pressed her ear against the wood, but there was no trace of life behind the door. She sat down at the top of the stairs and pulled her book from her bag, prepared to wait as long as it took for him to come home. When she heard his step on the stairs, she jammed her book in her bag and leaped up to face him.

He stopped when he reached the landing below her. He looked no happier than he'd been on board the *Mediterranean Goddess*. His deep voice held a low, growling threat. "You're not welcome here."

"Why not?" she countered.

He came on up the stairs and went around her to lean against his door. "How much did my father pay you to date me?"

Insulted clear to the bone, she clenched her fists. "I'd never met him before today, and I don't work as a paid escort. We met by chance. I didn't stalk you."

He folded his arms over his chest. "I'm not sure who you are, Ana, or who you'll be tomorrow. Your face is on billboards. You must have laughed at me the whole time we were together for not recognizing you."

"Never. It was wonderful." She took a step toward him, and he turned the key in his lock. "Could we please talk inside?"

He opened his door. "I told you you're not welcome here. Go home and forget we ever met."

"I will not. I didn't tell you I was a model because it was so nice to be treated like an ordinary girl rather than a celebrity. If you'd stayed with me yesterday, I would have told you. I said there was something I needed to tell you tonight. I may have omitted a few things, but I never lied to you, Alejandro. I love being with you."

He stared at her and shook his head sadly. "You look so damn sincere, but that's what you do for a living, isn't it?"

"No one is paying me now. When you walked away from me today, your father's face lit with a vicious triumph. Does he enjoy hurting you? Does he ruin every relationship you have? If he said he'd paid me, then he's a damn liar on top of being cruel."

"He just showed me a few of your ads and asked why I didn't know who you really were. You could have told me you were a model. It wouldn't have mattered to me."

"Why does it now?" she shot back at him. "Didn't your father have some tabloid photos to show you? I'm sick of being followed by paparazzi, and if I'd been recognized with you, you would have been on the front page of the tabloids too. Most men don't want that kind of notoriety. I wanted to date you without being followed and endlessly photographed."

He reached into his shirt pocket, pulled out a clipping and handed it to her. "Here you are with Miguel Aragon. Was he the man you would have married?"

Ana had the clipping at home. It had been taken a couple of years ago when Miguel was still healthy, and they went out often. He always smiled and waved for the paparazzi, while she hung back and dipped her head to avoid them. Just looking at Miguel's photo gave her heart a painful twist. She pulled in a deep breath and let it out slowly. "I loved him dearly, and he's gone. I want to be with you now. Is that impossible to believe?"

"How can you go from a famed matador to a complete unknown? No woman wants that."

"I do. Now can we please go into your studio and talk before all your neighbors open their doors to listen?"

He shook his head. "I want you to go home."

"Are you going to let your father win? How late does he stay at his office? I'd like to drop by and see him on the way home. Did he tell you he's had a detective following me?"

That stopped him. "You're kidding."

She shook her head. "How did he find out we were dating? Did you tell him?"

A look of tired regret swept his features. "I did, but I didn't know your full name, so I couldn't tell him."

"Speaking of names, why do you use Vasquez instead of Ortiz? Shouldn't you have told me the Ortiz shipping line belongs to your family? Or do you keep quiet about it so women won't date you solely for your family's money?"

"I prefer my mother's name. Do you imagine we're a pair because we're both liars?"

She kept her voice soft and conciliatory. "Neither of us is a liar, Alejandro. I understand perfectly why you'd keep your family name secret. I'd appreciate the same consideration from you."

He did not appear to be in a conciliatory mood. "Is that your Porsche parked out front?"

"It is. What's that got to do with anything?"

"Nothing, I suppose. I still want you to go home. If you don't leave, I will. I could be gone for days, and you'll get awfully sore sleeping out here on the stairs."

Clearly he meant it, and his hostile rejection hurt badly. She started down the steps, but turned back. "I'm not giving up. You're worth fighting for, and I'll go, but you'll know where to find me when you realize you're making the worst mistake of your life."

"I've already made it with you."

"Not even close," she shot back at him and ran down the stairs. She heard him slam his door before she'd reached the street. She hadn't shed a tear since Miguel had died, and she wasn't going to sob pathetically now, but she was furious with Orlando Ortiz. She'd not go to his office today, but there had to be another way to tell him what she thought of him in obscenely precise terms.

Chapter Six

Alejandro's studio looked empty without Ana. He threw his keys on the worktable and opened the refrigerator for a beer, but left the bottle on the counter unopened. He'd never seen the point of getting drunk over a woman when he'd be the one to suffer with a hangover. Hell, he'd never cared enough about any of the women he'd dated to turn the sorrow of a breakup in on himself, until now.

He'd felt more for Ana than he had for all the other girls combined, but nothing about the beautiful model had been real. She'd been as intangible as smoke, and she'd amused herself playing erotic games with him. If his father hadn't recognized her, she would probably have kept at it until he somehow stumbled over her fame. He'd never made such a gigantic fool of himself over a woman, and, disgusted for still wanting her, he did a computer search. Her website showed her work to every advantage. He lost himself in her again and couldn't turn away.

When Fatima came into work Tuesday morning, Ana was still in bed with an ice bag on her head. "I'd say good morning, but this does not look good," the housekeeper mused.

"No, it isn't." She gave Fatima a brief summary of her romance with Alejandro. "I can understand his being surprised I'm a model, but not to such an extent that he wouldn't want to see me again."

The housekeeper tied her apron strings. "Men are often slow to follow their hearts. Give him a few days, and you'll hear from him. Now, why don't I make you some crema catalana?"

"That's diabolical, Fatima. You know we shouldn't stifle our emotions with food."

She agreed with a slightly dipped head. "Of course not, but you do need to eat, and crema catalana is one of your favorites."

"That's true, and I have an appointment with the shoe designer this afternoon, so I should eat something." She remained in bed while Fatima got busy in the kitchen. She heard the buzzer from the security desk but let her housekeeper answer.

Fatima came into her bedroom. "There's a florist's deliveryman here with a bouquet of yellow roses. There's a card with them. Should they send him up?"

Elated to think Alejandro had come to his senses so soon, Ana left her bed and grabbed her satin robe. "Yes, please tell Henry I want the roses." She waited in her room until Fatima placed the bouquet on the coffee table, but when she opened the card, she was badly disappointed. "They're from Lucien Lamoreaux, the shoe man. He says he's looking forward to meeting me today."

"I'm so sorry they're not from Alejandro, but they're beautiful roses. We can still enjoy them."

Ana nodded and went back to bed.

Striving to lift her mood, Ana wore red to her agent's office. She arrived fifteen minutes early, but Lucien Lamoreaux had come earlier. "Miss Santillan, you're even more beautiful in person." He turned her hand to kiss the soft skin of her inner wrist. "What a delight it is to meet you. I'm sorry if my gifts didn't please you, so I've begun again with roses."

His tender kiss surprised her and shot a chill up her arm. It was as blatantly sexual as his glance. She recognized him from his brochure, although he was even better looking in person. His curls were tipped with gray, and a sly challenge lit his blue gaze, but she didn't appreciate being studied so intently. She'd worn her hair in a bun and pushed a stray curl into place.

"Today's yellow roses were a surprise, and thank you, but you needn't send more gifts."

His low voice was honey sweet. "Oh, but I want to. It's impossible to give a beautiful woman too many presents."

"Mr. Lamoreaux," she began again, "Mr. Perez will make certain I'm well paid for my work. You needn't do anything more."

Paul Perez guided Lucien into one of the comfortable chairs he used for informal conferencing. He took the one at his side rather than sit behind his desk, and Ana sat across from the men. "Tell us what you have in mind, Mr. Lamoreaux," Paul began, "and we'll move on to specifics and decide upon a fair payment for Miss Santillan's talents."

"There's no need for us to be so formal. Please call me Lucien." He winked at Ana. "You have the most extraordinary legs. All of you is sublime, of course, but for my shoes, I want to hire only your legs." He pulled some sketches from his briefcase. "This is what I have in mind. You could be seated in some ads, standing in others, but to emphasize the beauty of my footwear, I want to show only your legs."

"It's a shame my legs don't work on their own," Ana remarked softly. "You'll have to pay for all of me, no matter how little is photographed."

The Frenchman responded with a low chuckle. "I love a sense of humor in a woman. When can we begin?"

Ana wanted only the job, not to take a French lover, and her mind sped to Alejandro. She silently scolded herself for wondering about him, and hoped he missed her with an agonized pain worse than any lingering headache. Excruciating, torturous pain would be good. People saw her looks and imagined men fell in love with her with a single glance. The truth was, she had very little luck with romance, and the fiasco with Alejandro was another example of her sorry fate.

Paul brought the meeting to a close with the promise he'd have a contract for them to sign in a few days. Ana stood when Paul did, but Lucien appeared reluctant to have the meeting end.

"After we sign the contracts, we must all go to lunch to celebrate," he insisted. "I'm embarrassed by how much money I'm making with my shoes, and I intend to spend it on the people whose company I enjoy."

Ana managed a faint smile. "Lunch would be lovely, Mr. Lamoreaux—Lucien. I'll look forward to it."

He gave a mock bow. "What a thrill it is to meet you, Miss Santillan. Good day."

Ana and Paul remained silent until they heard the elevator doors slide closed. She dropped back into her chair. "He's a very charming man, and I won't have to sit through an hour of makeup if only my legs are posing."

"You do have lovely legs, Ana, and the money is just the same. He'll probably give you a lifetime supply of his shoes as a bonus. I received one other call late yesterday from Orlando Ortiz. He said he met you while you were working on the *Mediterranean Goddess* yesterday, and he'd like to book you for ads for his cruise line."

Ana had to bite her lip to keep from shrieking. "You're not serious."

Paul appeared puzzled. "Why, you didn't like him?"

"I've been dating his eldest son, and apparently he doesn't approve. Please tell him I won't go on board one of his ships until Alejandro and I are sailing on our honeymoon."

Paul's eyes grew huge. "Has the man proposed?"

"No, and he probably won't, but I'm not working for Ortiz. He's a mean-spirited bastard I'd rather forget."

"I assume his son is nothing like him?"

"Nothing at all." She picked up her bag and stood. "I'm sure you won't whisper anything I've said to the tabloids, but please don't tell anyone else I'm about to marry the heir to the Ortiz fortune, because I'm not."

The agent's expression lit with glee. "That's such a delicious secret, Ana. Couldn't I mention you know him?"

Fortunately, she knew he was teasing. "No, not a word. Please give Mr. Ortiz our standard refusal: my current schedule simply doesn't allow time to promote his cruise line. You needn't say I'm dreadfully sorry, though."

He walked her to the office door. "You lead such an exciting life, Ana. You should begin working on your memoirs."

Ana left without replying to his silly bit of unwanted advice.

A job kept her busy on Thursday, but the weekend appeared bleak. Saturday afternoon she put on her floppy hat and sunglasses for a long walk to burn off her restless energy. She stopped at a flower shop on Las Ramblas and had just picked up an iris and daffodil bouquet for her bedroom when she glanced up to see Libby Gunderson and Maggie Mondragon coming her way. She peeked over her sunglasses so they'd recognize her and said, "Hello."

"Ana!" Libby exclaimed. "Come have a drink with us."

Ana paid for the flowers and, eager for some company, joined them. They sat at a table at the closest café, and Ana ordered tea and a thin slice of lemon cake. "You're not carrying anything. How can you walk down Las Ramblas and not buy something fun?" she asked.

"I'll get some flowers before going home," Maggie replied. "We were talking about school and not paying attention to the vendors along the way."

"I'm coaching the women's sports at the same America high school where Maggie teaches Spanish," Libby explained. "Most of the kids are great, but others, are, well, a challenge."

"They believe they know everything?" Ana asked.

"Yes, exactly," Libby responded, "and they are sophisticated kids. Most of their parents are executives with American companies, and they've traveled and seen a lot of the world. That can make school seem a total bore, but they need to keep their grades up for admission to the best colleges. To make matters worse, parents put pressure on us if their students aren't applying themselves."

Ana sipped her tea. "I didn't spend much time in high school and didn't attend college, but aren't most teenagers obnoxious?"

"Maggie was never obnoxious," Libby exclaimed.

"I was the studious sort," Maggie added, "unlike my sisters."

The pair were half sisters and shared the same mother, but Miguel Aragon had been Maggie's father. Ana could see him in Maggie, but she'd known her for nearly a year and gotten used to the striking resemblance. Miguel had been an extraordinarily handsome man, and Maggie was a beautiful woman. It wasn't a thought Ana cared to dwell on. "It must be nice to have sisters. I'm an only child."

Maggie sat forward slightly. "It doesn't have to be a disadvantage."

Ana nodded. "True, but it would have been nice to have someone else around so my mother wouldn't have been so totally focused on me."

"Siblings are definitely an advantage there," Libby agreed. "I don't want to pry, but did you call Javier Cazares?"

"Yes. He's an excellent detective. It turned out to be a shoe designer who was sending me flowers, not an obsessed or dangerous fan. I still have the kittens, by the way, but I've gotten used to them."

Their conversation turned to the fashions Ana had recently

modeled, and she told them about the brief trip to Mallorca. "I love location shoots. I don't have time to travel otherwise."

Libby finished her drink. "We're going out to dinner tonight with Rafael and Santos. Would you like to come with us?"

"Seeing you this afternoon was fun, and thank you for the invitation, but Santos would choke if he had to sit through a dinner with me. Perhaps we'll see each other at another charity event."

Maggie and Libby watched Ana hurry away, swinging her flowers in time with her steps. "Does she seem sad to you?" Maggie asked.

"Why would she be sad? She has everything, doesn't she?"

"Everything except Santos," Maggie reminded her, "and maybe you shouldn't tell him we saw her."

"Good advice," Libby agreed.

Ana went to a French movie at a small theatre Saturday night and stayed in on Sunday. She hoped Alejandro would go to El Gato and sit on the patio all afternoon waiting for her, but she had too much pride to sit there alone hoping to see him. Instead, she danced in her home studio and even went so far as to don a tutu. Dancing always made her feel better, and so tired she slept all night without waking.

She'd just gotten dressed Monday morning, when Henry buzzed her condo. "Ms. Santillan, there are some detectives here to see you."

"Detectives? More than one?"

"Yes, two."

"I'll come right down." She turned to Fatima. "If they're looking for witnesses, I haven't seen a damn thing." She pulled her hair back in a ponytail and hurried on downstairs.

The men were waiting at the security desk. The taller was dark and heavy set, the shorter red-haired and wiry. Their expressions were impossible to read, instantly making her uneasy. "May I see your credentials, please?"

"Sergeant Robles," the taller man said, and both showed their badges. "This is my partner, Guillermo Mesa. We have a few questions for you. It won't take much of your time."

Ana would rather not invite them into her home. "We have a

conference room. Let's use it. I'm curious as to why you'd want to see me, but we needn't involve anyone else who lives here. Is the room free, Henry?"

"Yes, it is. Do you want coffee?"

The detectives shook their heads. "No, thank you, Henry." She led them down the hallway, past the elevators to the conference room. It was furnished with the requisite long table and ten comfortably padded chairs. A wall of windows lit the room. She waited for the men to enter and then propped open the door. She took the chair at the end of the table, and they pulled up chairs on either side. Uneasy, she folded her hands in her lap. "Well?"

Robles leaned toward her. "Do you have any idea why we're here, Miss Santillan?"

She looked between them, but there were no clues in their solemn expressions. "Absolutely none. I've not forgotten to pay any traffic fines, have I?"

Mesa's voice was high and sharp. "There's no humor in this situation."

"What situation?" she asked again. "I've no idea why you're here."

Mesa's pale blue eyes narrowed in an accusing stare. "Jaime Campos has been murdered. It's in today's papers."

Shocked, Ana sat up straight. "I haven't read the paper yet. Jaime Campos, the photographer?"

Robles nodded. "I believe you worked with him often."

Sickened by their news, she leaned away from them and sank deeper into her chair. "Sometimes, not often. We worked together with Galen Salazar on Mallorca week before last. He was a terrific fashion photographer with some war experience."

Mesa tapped his nails on the table. "You knew he was working on an exhibit of his art photography?"

With no reason to deny it, she answered truthfully. "He told me about it, but I wasn't interested. Do you think it had something to do with his death?"

"You've complimented his work. Why didn't the project interest you?" Mesa continued.

With a near constant frown, his sharp features gave him a ratlike appearance. She could almost see his nose twitch. She took a deep breath to dispel the image. "I model haute couture, gentlemen. I don't do nudes."

Robles opened a folder and laid an 8x10 photo in front of her. "How do you explain this?"

Ana picked it up and studied it closely. It was a frontal nude of a slender woman in a brazen pose with legs spread wide and hands on hips. "He's Photoshopped my head onto someone else's body. This isn't me."

Mesa glanced at his partner. "So you wouldn't have wanted to see it included in his exhibit?"

She wondered if they were being deliberately dense. "He may have played around with his photos, but he wouldn't have used something as obviously inauthentic as this."

"Why not? Would you have sued him?" Robles asked.

She handed the photo back to them. "He wouldn't have used it because it would have harmed his professional reputation immeasurably," she stressed. "This is something a paparazzo would fabricate and sell to the tabloids. I've no idea who might want Jaime dead, and if you've no other questions, I'd like to go."

"We have a few more," Mesa answered, his faint smile sliding into a smirk. "Where were you yesterday?"

"Here. I usually don't work on the weekends, and I enjoy relaxing at home."

"Did you have any guests?" Robles inquired.

"No." She certainly hadn't expected to need an alibi, or she would have invited someone in the condo building for dinner.

"Did you attend church?" Robles asked.

"No. Did you?"

Mesa shoved his chair back. "You'd be wise to watch your attitude, Miss Santillan. We may want to speak with you again, and you may want to have an attorney present."

Ana bolted to her feet. "Where was Jaime murdered? In his studio?"

"Yes, and his blood splattered many of his prized photos."

She'd not asked for details and shuddered. "I've never been to his studio, so you won't find my fingerprints. Don't you rely on clues?"

"The murderer would have wiped the place clean, Miss Santillan," Robles stated. "Here's my card. If you think of something we should know, call me."

Ana took the card and walked out the door ahead of them. She waited by the security desk while they passed through the front doors. "Did they sign in, Henry?"

"Yes, right here, Robles and Mesa. I'm sorry if they upset you, but if I'd said you weren't here, they would have kept coming back."

"You needn't lie for me. A photographer I worked with was murdered, and they're probably questioning everyone he knew. At least I hope they are."

Tuesday morning, the doctored photo of Ana appeared on the front page of the most popular tabloid in Barcelona. Her agent called to warn her before she left her building and walked straight into a swarm of paparazzi unprepared. "That's only my head, Paul, but I won't pose nude to prove it. Two police detectives showed it to me yesterday. One of them must have leaked it. I need an attorney to stop this before it gets any worse."

"How could it get worse?" Paul asked.

She had an easy answer for that. "They could arrest me for murder."

"Don't even think that, Ana. You don't have any work today; stay home and screen your calls. The agency has an attorney, Elena Covarrubias, and I'll ask her about suing the tabloid for harassment."

"How about defaming my image?"

"Perfect. I'll get her right on it."

Ana called Henry and asked him to find a copy of the tabloid. "It isn't my body, and I'm going to sue over it, so I'd like to have a copy."

"Right away, Miss Santillan."

Orlando Ortiz called Alejandro as soon as he heard about the photo. "I've sent you an email. Open it and tell me what you think."

Alejandro found the front-page photo and wouldn't give his father the satisfaction of sounding alarmed. "That isn't Ana's body."

"You know her that well? I'm impressed."

"Anyone could tell the proportions are wrong. She's all legs, and this photo shows a woman with an average height. Why would they publish something like this?"

"Read the article. She's a suspect in a murder."

He couldn't stand his father's gloating tone. "Nothing in the tabloids is true. You ought to know that."

"Perhaps not, but a man is dead. I'll talk to you later."

Alejandro sat down and read the accompanying article and then went out to buy a copy of a reputable newspaper. The bogus photo of Ana wasn't included, but her name was mentioned as one of the models who'd worked with Jaime Campos. There was no mention of her being a suspect, and relieved, he sat back and debated what to do. Doing nothing seemed completely wrong, however.

Henry buzzed Ana's condo. "There's a deliveryman here from El Gato Café. Did you order something?"

She looked at Fatima and rolled her eyes. "Please ask him his name."

There was a momentary pause. "He says he's Alejandro Vasquez, and you know him."

She did, and had liked him enormously, until he'd turned on her. Maybe he'd come to his senses. She turned to the helpful housekeeper. "Looks as though you were right. Alejandro's here." She made him wait a minute. "We're acquainted, Henry." She opened her door when he knocked. In a navy-blue windbreaker and a blue cap, he did look like a deliveryman. He handed her the bag.

"I know, I should have called, but I thought you'd probably tell me go to hell. I got past the half-dozen paparazzi out front without a second glance." He removed the cap and swiped his fingers through his hair. "You must be Fatima. How do you do?"

The housekeeper swept him with an appreciative glance. "You better be nice to Ana while you're here, or I'll toss you out myself."

He raised his hand. "I promise. I brought you some of the cakes you like."

Ana peeked into the bag. "A bribe?"

"It's part of the disguise. I needed to deliver something."

Fatima took the bag and went into the kitchen. "I'll make fresh coffee."

"Thank you," he said. The kittens came running by, and Romeo went right up his leg but his jeans protected him from sharp little claws. He caught the kitten and held him up. "He's grown."

"The real question is, have you?" Ana walked into the living room, and he put down the kitten and followed her.

"I knew that wasn't you in the paper, and you wouldn't have killed a photographer over a doctored photo. That's ridiculous. If you need a character reference, I'll be glad to give one."

She sat on the sofa and crossed her legs. "Wait a minute. You didn't think much of my character the last time we spoke."

He walked over to the window and looked out at the tree-lined street below. "I deserve that, but I thought you might need some help. There are corporate attorneys working for the Ortiz Lines, and they'd be able to recommend someone practicing criminal law, if you need one."

Fatima brought in two mugs of coffee, napkins and the sugary nut cakes on a fancy plate. "Would you like anything more?"

"Thank you, no." Ana reached for a cake. "The situation is simply bizarre, Alejandro. I had no reason to kill Jaime, and there's no evidence to even suggest I did, but the detectives who questioned me yesterday were creepy. I'd rather not see them again. They showed me the bogus photo, and today it's hit the tabloids. It can't be a coincidence."

He took the wing chair and reached for a mug of coffee. "Do you think you're being framed?"

"There are some models who'd like to earn as much as I do, but I don't think they'd resort to murder to boost their earnings. By the way, did your father tell you he called my agent to ask about my doing some promotion for your cruise ships?"

His eyes narrowed, and he swore under his breath. "Did you say yes?"

She brushed sugar from her hands and reached for a napkin. "Of course not. I don't want to be near him ever again."

He took a cake and chewed it slowly. "I should have thanked you Sunday morning for having a new toothbrush out for me in the bathroom. Are you always so considerate?"

She swallowed a sip from her mug. "You have an amazing gift for saying the wrong thing. I don't have a parade of men spending the night here. I have toiletries handy in case an occasional guest needs them. Don't feel bad. Women think of these things; men don't."

"I'll think of them now. Do you want to put on your Goth disguise and get out of here? The paparazzi wouldn't recognize you, and we wouldn't have to come back until late tonight."

He was looking at the rug rather than her. She found his shyness touching, but she needed to make a point. "I don't believe I heard an apology for the way you treated me last week."

He brushed his hair off his forehead. "Can't we just forget it?"

"Not without an apology."

He looked up. "All right. I'm sorry."

"Alejandro, you don't sound sincere."

His voice deepened. "Should I get down on my knees and beg your forgiveness?"

A fiery light shone in his silver eyes, and she knew when to stop. "Not this time, but if you make a habit of questioning my motives, I'll demand one in writing."

He stood and went to the door of the kitchen. "Is she usually this hard on men?"

Fatima leaned against the counter. "She's being very generous with you, and I wouldn't advise you to push it."

He turned back toward the living room, but Ana had disappeared. He hoped she'd gone to put on her black wig rather than lock herself in her bedroom. "Fatima, does this condo have a back entrance?"

"No, but in case of a fire there are stairs at both ends of the corridor. Are you expecting an emergency?"

"I think we already have one."

Chapter Seven

Ana took the time to put on the dramatic black eyeliner and changed into her baggy black clothes. Alejandro was sitting on the living room floor playing with the kittens when she returned ready to go. "They'd make good pets for you," she offered.

"Not when they have such a great home here." He rose with an easy stretch and stopped to stare. "Do you ever forget who you're pretending to be?"

"Sometimes, but I always know who I really am. I should warn you, the paparazzi can smell news from clear across town. If they discover you're Orland Ortiz's heir, they'll stick closer than the hair on your chest."

He laughed and shook his head. "I'm tougher than I look. I studied karate when I was a kid so I wouldn't get roughed up on the docks."

Fatima glanced out from the kitchen. "You may need it."

Ana reached for his hand before he could respond. "You need to go out as the deliveryman. Just brush by everyone as though you were positive they'd have no interest in you. If anyone speaks to you, ignore them. If they ask whose order you brought, shake your head. Don't give them any opening to talk to you, because they'll twist anything you say into an insulting weapon. I'll go out through the garage and meet you in back. I hope you have your SUV rather than your bike."

"I do." He picked up his cap and pulled it low. "It was nice to meet you, Fatima."

The housekeeper wished him good-bye and closed the door behind him. "He's almost too good-looking. Have you ever dated a homely man?"

Ana picked up Juliet and gave the inky-black kitten a loving squeeze. "Few people are truly homely, but unattractive men don't approach me. If Henry buzzes for anything else, please use your own judgment, but absolutely no more live pets."

"I understand, no puppies, no geckos, no fish, nor birds in fancy cages."

"No pet snakes either," Ana added. She handed Juliet to the housekeeper and slipped out the door. She went down the stairs rather than use the elevator and left the building by the workman's entrance in the garage. She found Alejandro waiting for her at the corner.

"I walked out looking as dull as a door and no one noticed me," he greeted her. "Won't the paparazzi give up soon and chase someone else?"

"It depends on whether there's someone more interesting to chase, but a murder involving high-fashion models makes compelling news. Let's continue to avoid them. Do you want to go down to the port?"

"It's a good place to be lost in the crowd. I'll give you a tour of the *Mediterranean Goddess* if you'd like."

"Will your father be on board?"

"No, his office building overlooks the port, but he's seldom on board one of the cruise liners. I worked as a steward in the summers while I attended university the first time. It was supposed to give me a feel for the business from the water up, but what I liked best was touring our ports of call. I came home with sketchbooks filled with drawings of classical buildings rather than a love for the cruise business. Naturally my father wasn't pleased with how I'd spent my free time. A college degree in business didn't inspire me either, so now I'm studying what I should have been studying all along."

Embarrassed by her own lack of formal education, Ana glanced at the passing scene. "I read a lot, and no one has ever called me stupid, but I've not spent much time in school. Unlike most careers, there's a time factor to modeling. An experienced architect would be sought after; an experienced model is often regarded as too familiar a face. God forbid there should be an early sign of a wrinkle."

"You're a long way from being wrinkled, and you don't need a college degree to prove you're intelligent. It's obvious from the sparkle in your eyes."

"Thank you." When they reached the port, he pulled his SUV into a slot marked for the Ortiz Line and took her hand. "Cruise ships are huge floating hotels, a thousand feet long, with room for nearly four-thousand passengers plus the crew to serve them. I love the sea, but I'd rather vacation on Tahiti and watch the waves roll in than cruise from port to port."

"I haven't been to Tahiti, but it sounds magical. Could we just walk and lose ourselves among the tourists for a while?"

"Sure. This is a good place to watch people."

They were near the end of Las Ramblas and often had to turn sideways to slip by other couples. Laughing, Ana looked over her shoulder and caught the bald man walking twenty feet behind them. She jerked on Alejandro's hand and pulled him into a shop selling Barcelona curios. "The man who's been following me is tracking us again today. He must have been following you, because he wouldn't have seen me leave the condo." She described him briefly. "Does he sound like someone your father employs?"

Alejandro glanced out the shop's door and saw the bald man at a nearby news kiosk. He gestured for Ana to come close. "Is he standing there?"

"Yes, that's him."

"Stay here." Alejandro walked down the sidewalk to greet him. "You've begun to annoy me. Follow someone else."

"I've no idea who you are and don't care where you're going. I'm buying a magazine for my wife."

"Fine, because I'm going to stand here and watch you walk away as quickly as you can."

"If I don't feel like moving?" Widening his stance, he took up more of the sidewalk.

Alejandro's voice was low and utterly convincing. "You'll swiftly regret it."

The owner of the kiosk came out to offer his opinion. "I don't need anyone disrupting my business. Both of you move along."

Alejandro tipped the kiosk owner and stayed put while the bald man paid for his magazine and walked away with a hurried step. The newsman straightened the stacks of tabloids. He pointed to the one with the pseudo Ana. "What do you think of this? Beautiful women are as deadly as cobras, but would a model kill a man over a bad photo?"

"No," Alejandro assured him. "Ana Santillan doesn't know a thing about the photographer's murder. The tabloids are smearing her name to sell papers."

"You know her?" the man asked skeptically.

Alejandro nodded and returned to the shop where Ana had bought a glass-domed paperweight containing shells from a Barcelona beach. "I don't have nearly enough souvenirs from Barcelona. What do you think?"

He picked it up and found it surprisingly heavy. "It will definitely hold papers on your desk."

"That's what I thought." She dropped it into her bag. "What did you say to the detective?"

"I growled at him, and he walked away. I'll have my father fire him. You have enough trouble without being followed by some idiot who's so easy to spot. Are you hungry?"

Ana suggested the place he'd taken her earlier. Alejandro took her hand and led the way. He knew the port better than any other part of the beautiful city, and they were there in minutes. The hostess smiled at him as they entered but looked surprised when she saw Ana in her Goth disguise. Alejandro pretended not to notice.

When they'd made themselves comfortable in a booth by the windows, Ana leaned close. "Did you see the way the hostess looked at you? She must think you're cheating on the blonde you were with the other night."

"She can think whatever she wants. If you own a red wig, we could confuse her even more the next time we're here."

"I do have a red wig." Ana looked for something new on the menu. "One of the detectives who came to see me had strange, fishy blue eyes, and even if I don't usually order fish, I won't order it today because of him."

"I wish you'd stop worrying about them. Campos must have photographed hundreds of models. Maybe his death had nothing to do with any of you. He could have been killed by someone he owed money."

She rubbed her toe up his calf and watched him jump. "I didn't mean to frighten you."

He grinned and shook his head. "Do it again."

"It has to be done when you're not expecting it." She ordered a raw vegetable salad and limeade and leaned back to study the view of the busy port in daylight. "I wonder how many people are murdered a day in Barcelona."

"I hope it's not many. Rather than look at the ship, let's find a movie after we eat, something funny."

The waiter returned with her limeade and his beer. She took a long drink. "I might have a part in an Almodóvar film. It's just a few lines, but I don't want you to be surprised if you see me on the screen."

"He's a remarkable director, but you don't sound excited. Why not?"

She described the audition with Gian Carlo. "Models usually aren't that good on the screen. Thank goodness it's such a small part I won't be mentioned in the reviews."

He studied her expression a long moment. "You don't smile often in your Goth outfit; you seem to sink into her. You should do fine with a scripted part."

The buttons on her black shirt were silver skulls. She polished one with her napkin. "I'm sorry, I'm sort of unfocused today. I often work long hours, and when I'm free, I like to go out to lunch and to movies, but I have a very bad feeling about that bogus photo. It just keeps whipping through my mind. I need to buy a notebook and write down where I am every minute of the day."

He reached across the table to take her hand. "I'd also be alarmed if detectives had come to my studio. It doesn't matter what they've been told to ask, or what ludicrous suspicions they might have. You didn't murder anyone."

"Innocence ought to be a strong defense," she replied. "But I feel the floor tipping under me, and I can't get my balance."

"Listen to me." His glance was as dark as she'd ever seen it. "You're not the only model who worked with Campos. All of you are probably on edge, and justifiably so, but while it might be a good idea not to be seen laughing as though we had no concerns, there's no reason to hide as though we're guilty."

His remark brought a smile. "I'm the one they've questioned, Alejandro, not you."

He leaned back as the waiter served their lunch, and waited for him to leave. "It could have been a model's boyfriend who didn't like Campos's photos."

She raised her fingertip to her lips. "Don't give the police any ideas they don't already have and implicate yourself."

He glanced over his shoulder at the others in the restaurant. No one seemed out of place. "We aren't being watched."

She shrugged. Just because they didn't see anyone, didn't mean someone wasn't there.

Alejandro took Ana to an American comedy that was so silly they laughed until tears rolled down their cheeks. She had to use the restroom to refresh her eyeliner and fluffed her black wig. She smiled as she rejoined him. "Thank you. That was so much fun, and I'd never have chosen it myself."

He hugged her close. "I don't laugh enough either. Let's buy your notebook for your timeline and use it to make a list of things we ought to do."

"Like ride a tandem bike?"

"Exactly."

They found a stationery store and bought a small notebook to fit in Ana's purse. Ready for a snack, they stopped at an outdoor café, and she doodled in the notebook's margins. "We should learn to cook."

"Both of us," he agreed.

Ana's cell phone chimed, and she checked the text message. "It's my agent." She frowned and dropped her phone into her purse. "My job for tomorrow has been cancelled. I've worked with the designer for years, but she gave Paul no reason why. Now I can add loss of work to the lawsuit. I'm afraid this is only the beginning."

"Won't there be other designers who'd want to hire you because of the controversy?"

"Probably, but they're not the ones I usually work with." Thoroughly depressed, she reached for his hand. "This has been a great day, but I need to go home. Just drop me off a block away, and I'll go in the front door. No one saw me leave, so if any of the paparazzi are still lurking, they won't notice me."

He stood and helped her to her feet. Even in the Goth outfit, she had her usual grace. "I'll help you any way I can."

She kissed his cheek. "I'll handle it." She sounded as tough as she looked. When he dropped her off, she strolled through the front door of her condo with a lazy swagger and drew curious glances from the three remaining paparazzi, but none raised his camera to photograph her.

Alejandro went straight back to the port. His father's office was in a high-rise building and had windows from floor to ceiling to provide a dazzling view of the harbor. "I've never understood your thinking. Why would you want me to stop seeing Ana Santillan and then try to hire her?"

Orlando leaned back in his chair and steepled his fingers over his chest. "It's always a pleasure to have you pay a surprise visit. Do sit down and stay awhile, but you needn't concern yourself with promotions for the cruise line."

"We're talking about Ana. I care about her, and you need to leave her alone. Stop having us followed. I spoke to your detective today. Did he tell you? The brute would stand out in any crowd, and it's easy to spot him."

Orlando sat up. "Other than her looks, what about the woman appeals to you? You weren't pleased to discover she's a model, and you're dating her again?"

It wasn't her modeling career that had appalled him, but his sickening suspicion she'd used him for her own fun. He'd gotten over it. "Yes, and I'll keep seeing her. Pay the detective for what little work he's done and let him go."

Orlando shrugged off the matter as unimportant. "He's served his purpose."

"In the future, if you want to know where I'm going or where I've been, call and ask."

"Fine. Were you with Ana last Saturday night?"

Alejandro could see right where his father was going, but he wouldn't lie. "Didn't your detective provide a report? I was home studying."

"Good. We can keep the Ortiz name out of the murder investigation, even if Ana Santillan is involved up to her beautiful neck."

Alejandro stared at his father. He'd never struck the man, but he'd never been so sorely provoked. "She won't be. On the remote chance she's called in for questioning, I'll go with her and pass out cruise brochures."

Orlando laughed. "Your loyalty is touching. She was just playing with you until she learned who you are. You needn't bother to wear cologne. Nothing smells better than wealth."

Alejandro left without describing how he'd always thought his father smelled.

Fatima was hanging up her apron when Ana arrived home. "How was your day?"

Ana leaned against the kitchen counter and folded her arms over her chest. "Alejandro did wonders at distracting me, but my job for tomorrow was cancelled, and I'm worried I'll lose other work."

"Eggs stay fresh longer than most scandals last, and this will blow over soon. Your veggies are ready to steam, and the salad is in the bowl. I'll see you tomorrow."

"Night." She noted the time she'd arrived home in her new notebook and took a quick shower rather than soak in a bubble bath. As she ate dinner, she began a list of reasons why Jaime Campos might have been murdered. All she succeeded in doing was frightening herself silly, and she called Alejandro.

"I never heard Jaime mention a wife or girlfriend or boyfriend, but aren't most people murdered by someone they know?"

"I've heard it, but a lot of provocations could push someone to murder. Are you trying to outthink the detectives?"

She'd barely tasted the vegetables on her plate and hadn't touched the salad. "It wouldn't be difficult, but I can't concentrate on anything else."

"You should have come home with me."

"Another time. Please help me think of reasons for Jaime's murder."

He was silent a long moment. "All right. He was a photographer. Could he have blackmailed someone, or photographed something he shouldn't have seen?"

"A drug deal?" She made a quick notation.

"That's possible, or a prominent man being with a woman who

wasn't his wife?"

She pushed her chair back from the table. "Millionaires who didn't want to be seen discussing business together?" she added.

"Government figures plotting," Alejandro offered. "There's also an entirely different angle with photography. You refused to pose for nudes, but could he have been producing porn, or bondage and S&M photos that attracted the wrong kind of people?"

"I see where you're going. Barcelona is a large commercial port, and it's possible to buy almost anything here, isn't it?"

"I've not looked, but yes, I suppose so. Call security and ask if the paparazzi are still out front."

"Give me a minute." She came back quickly. "They're gone, and I told the night guard to expect you."

"Is there anything you'd like me to bring?"

"Your company is all I need."

Alejandro parked at the side of the condo building. He scanned the street, but nothing struck him as being out of place. As he entered the building, he paused at the security desk.

"Good evening, sir," Juan greeted him.

"Miss Santillan is expecting me."

"Sign in, please."

Alejandro did. "Are you armed?"

Juan stepped back. "If I have to be, sir. We lock the entrance early and don't admit anyone we don't recognize, unless it's an expected guest. We all take this job seriously."

"Good. Thank you." Alejandro walked to the elevators and pressed the button. He was becoming as jumpy as Ana. When she opened her door wearing only a white satin robe, he framed her face with his hands and kissed her, licked her lips and spread tender kisses over her cheeks.

She kicked the door closed, took his hand and led him into her bedroom. "Let's talk about murder later."

He flung his sports coat toward the chair in the corner. She crawled up on the bed and leaned back to prop herself on her elbows. Her robe slid open to show a long, shapely leg. He grabbed her feet to pull her closer until her legs dangled over the end of the bed. He knelt between them. "Count this later when you want me on my knees."

He tickled her feet and made her laugh. "I have a very poor memory. You may have to do this often."

Kissing his way up her thighs, he grazed his knuckles along her slit in a teasing swipe. He leaned back to catch her foot and kissed her toes. "I've always wanted to do this."

"Are you talking about indiscriminate toe kissing, or am I something special?"

"It's only you. I'm no danger to barefooted sunbathers on the beach."

She pulled free of his light grasp and wiggled her toes. "Our whole bodies are sensitive, but my feet are too ticklish."

He danced his fingers up her thighs and kissed her knees. "I like all of you." He leaned down to lick her cleft. "You taste so good, sweet and salty like tears. Luscious."

His glossy black hair fell over his eyes in a boyish wave. "I like watching you. You have such a handsome smile," she nearly purred.

"Who wouldn't smile with you?"

"Or with you, Alejandro." She ran her foot up his shirt. "Take off your clothes."

"Later." He spread her legs wide, slipped his arms under her thighs and dipped his tongue into her. He'd known how to satisfy a woman, but being with Ana was a wild exotic trip rather than a hasty hookup. He slid crossed fingers into her core and twisted them in time with his tongue. He felt her first quiver of pleasure and sucked gently to bring her to a peak. He loved her grateful moan and savored every throb and grasp of her core. He didn't pull away until she lay too limp to desire more.

He pulled off his clothes and moved over her. "Is this too much now?"

She wrapped him in her arms and rolled her hips under him. "No. Come with me."

He loved going slow, plunging into her slippery heat until neither of them could stand another stroke. He'd been an idiot to stop seeing her for even a minute and vowed to make up for it tonight.

A wild pounding on the front door woke them at six thirty a.m. Alejandro sat up and threw the sheet aside. "The building must be on fire. I'll get it." He pulled on his jeans and pushed his hair out of his eyes as he opened the front door.

The detectives leaned in to look around him. "I'm Sergeant Robles, and this is my partner, Sergeant Mesa." They flashed their badges with a practiced swing. "We need to speak with Miss Santillan."

"At this hour?" Alejandro asked incredulously. "You could have called and made an appointment."

"We need to speak with Miss Santillan now," Robles emphasized gruffly.

Ana came up behind Alejandro, the belt on her robe tied tightly. She'd made no effort to smooth her hair and looked as though she'd just walked out of the jungle. "What is it, gentlemen?"

"We need to take you down to the station for a few more questions."

"I could meet you there," she offered.

"No, you need to come with us," Mesa stressed. He swept Alejandro with a hostile, dismissive glance. "Alone."

"Wait downstairs while I dress. I'll be ready in a few minutes."

"We'll wait right here."

Alejandro pointed out the padded bench under the window at the end of the hallway. "Wait there." He closed and locked the door before they could object. "Bastards."

"I love waking up with you." Ana caressed his back. His skin was warm and smooth. "I'll answer whatever questions they've raked up, and if I need to, bombard them with our suggestions of real possibilities in Jaime's murder."

"I'll follow you."

"Don't you have classes?"

"Not at this hour." He went into the guest bathroom where the kittens were stretching, meowing and looking for breakfast. He found the cat food in the refrigerator and fed them before getting into the shower. Needing more than a toothbrush, he was grateful for the basket on the counter with every grooming product he could possibly need. He was ready to go and had time to make coffee before Ana was dressed.

She appeared in a conservative gray skirt suit with a pale gray blouse and low heels. She'd wound her hair into a bun at her nape. "I don't wear glasses or I'd put them on. How do I look?"

"Like a loveable librarian. You'll be mistaken for an attorney down at the police station."

"Oh no, I need to call my agent and get the attorney there." She opened the door, and the detectives jumped to their feet. "Which police station is it?"

Mesa hurried toward her. "The main station. It isn't far."

"I know where it is," Alejandro offered. "It would easier if I drove her there so she'd have a way home."

"We'll bring her home," Robles replied.

Ana finished her call to Paul Perez, gave Alejandro a quick good-bye kiss and carried her travel mug as she left with the detectives. "An attorney should meet us there, but it may take her a while to arrive."

"We'll wait," Mesa assured her.

The backseat of their dark blue sedan was cleaner than she'd expected, and it had no grill to prevent passengers in the backseat from attacking the officers in front. She wondered what the pair had learned, if anything. When they reached Barcelona's main police station, she was surprised to see Valeria waiting on a bench near the door. Dressed in a black top and jeans, the model had pulled her hair back to form a huge red puff.

Valeria leaped to her feet to hug Ana. "Why do they want to see us?"

She looked near tears. Ana gave her a comforting squeeze. "I've no idea how their tiny minds work. I have an attorney coming. Do you?"

"No, I know absolutely nothing about Jaime's death and didn't want to pay for an attorney to sit beside me while I said so."

The detectives had gone to the front desk. Ana sat down beside Valeria. There were uniformed officers and people in plain clothes everywhere she looked. "This is a busy place. I'd no idea there was so much crime in Barcelona to warrant all this activity near dawn."

"I've no idea about anything," Valeria replied.

Alejandro saw them as soon as he came through the front doors and joined them on the bench. Ana introduced him, and he smiled. "I'm glad to meet you, Valeria, but wish it had been under better circumstances."

"So do I," Valeria responded. "This is the first time I've ever been inside a police station." She rubbed her arms. "It's not a place I'd like to visit again."

They waited nearly an hour before the attorney Paul Perez had called rushed through the door. Dressed in a black pants suit, with dark brown hair in a short stylish cut, her appearance was both striking and professional. She spoke in a hushed voice. "Miss Santillan, I'm Elena Covarrubias. From what I learned from Paul, the police are repeatedly questioning you without reason, which is harassment, and they've leaked a photo that has defamed your image and harmed your ability to earn a living. I'll handle whatever questions they have. All you need do is sit quietly and listen unless I encourage you to speak."

Ana was enormously relieved. "Thank you. Alejandro and I came up with some reasons Jaime Campos might have been slain, but none of them had anything to do with the models he knew."

Elena's proud posture stiffened. "Keep all speculation to yourself, Miss Santillan. Let the police do all the work in this case."

Alejandro winked at Ana, and she nodded. "I understand." She was puzzled when her name was called before Valeria's. "There must be some mistake. She was here first."

Sergeant Robles insisted there was no mistake. Ana and Elena followed him out of the room. Alejandro moved closer to Valeria. "I can understand their doing a thorough investigation, but they aren't looking in the right place."

Valeria responded with a shaky smile. "When we were on Mallorca, Ana said she'd met someone nice she wanted to see when she got home. I'm glad she wasn't disappointed."

She had such a wistful expression, Alejandro feared she had been disappointed all too often. "Thank you. We met by chance and just clicked. Do you know anything about Campos other than his work as a photographer?"

"I barely knew him. I've only been working professionally a year, and Ana's worked since childhood, so she knows more about everyone."

It jarred Alejandro to think Ana might know the murderer.

Elena Covarrubias and Ana sat on one side of the interview room's table and Robles took the other while Mesa paced behind him. Robles cleared his throat. "Why didn't you tell us you'd talked with Valeria Godina about Mr. Campos's art photography?"

Elena leaned in to whisper in Ana's ear, and Ana nodded. "You didn't ask if I'd discussed it with anyone."

"It didn't seem relevant?"

"No," Ana replied without prompting. She sat still to appear confident and unconcerned by the question, but she was more annoyed than frightened.

"We'd like to hear your version of the conversation."

Elena only raised a brow, and Ana took a moment to recall before she spoke. "She asked if Mr. Campos had mentioned his art photography, and I said yes. I told her I didn't do nudes and urged her not to let him coerce her into posing for him if she didn't want to."

Robles smiled. "So you spearheaded the models' opposition to Mr. Campos's project?"

"I spoke to Valeria, no one else. It was a casual conversation, not a diatribe against nude photography."

"Well, now, Miss Santillan—"

Elena brought her open hand down on the table with a loud smack. "You summoned Miss Santillan at dawn for this? We'd like to know how the bogus photograph of her reached the tabloids. It was in your possession on Monday and published Tuesday. Is your security here so incredibly lax? Or was it released in an attempt to focus blame on her while you scramble for viable suspects?"

Robles bristled at the attorney's questions and looked over his shoulder at his partner. "There was more than one copy, and we've no idea who released it."

"You're admitting this insulting photo of my client was widely circulated in your department?"

"Well, yes, but—"

"That is pathetic," Elena continued, her voice low and taut. "Publication of the phony photo has cost Miss Santillan work, and we plan to sue for damages for the harm you've done her career. Do you have any questions that actually pertain to the case?"

Mesa paused midstride and pressed against the table. "We are near an arrest, Miss Covarrubias, and are being thorough. You cannot sue us for doing our jobs."

"I most certainly can sue you for the way you're doing them." She dropped her card on the table. "Call me if you wish to speak to Miss Santillan in the future."

Ana restrained the impulse to cheer and silently rose as Elena left her chair. They walked out of the interview room at a stately pace, but Ana longed to run back to Alejandro. He stood when he saw them coming, and Valeria looked very lost and alone remaining on the bench.

"We're finished," Elena remarked. "We never discuss anything here." She handed Ana her card. "Come to my office. We've plenty of time before my usual office hours."

"This is close," Ana observed. "I'll take the Metro, and you can go on to your classes, Alejandro."

"I'm free until this afternoon," he said. Valeria was looking up at him, her enormous blue eyes shiny with unshed tears. "Did you call your agent? Someone ought to come to be with you."

The redhead shrugged. "The detectives asked me to stay until they'd spoken to Ana, so if you're done, I must be too." She stood and slung her fringed purse over her shoulder. "I hope I didn't get you in any trouble."

Elena lowered her voice. "We talk about nothing here." She handed Valeria her card. "Should you need legal advice, call me."

"Thank you." Valeria left the building first and ran right into a wall of paparazzi shouting for her to look their way.

Elena stepped in front of Ana and Alejandro. "It's important to look ethereal in photographs, not real life," she cautioned. "Let's lose this crowd in the Metro." She marched through the wide doorway with the bravado of a four-star general. Ana and Alejandro followed.

"Don't you look pretty today, Ana!" one man shouted, while his companions yelled only her name.

Valeria had already pushed her way free and disappeared. Ana gripped Alejandro's hand, ignored the paparazzi, and followed Elena zigzagging through the stream of people rushing toward the Liceu station. Without a clear shot for a photo, the paparazzi fell back. Elena pulled a transport card from her purse when they reached the bottom of the station stairs.

"I'll go back to my office on the Metro. What about you two?"

Ana checked with Alejandro. "I have a card. Do you?"

"I ride the Metro, just like everyone else. Let's go with Elena, and we can come back for my SUV later. If you'll let go of my hand, I'll pull my card from my wallet."

Embarrassed, Ana dropped his hand. "I'm sorry." People were moving around them to reach their trains, and she stayed close. They waited while one of the sleek silver Metro train cars emptied and pushed in with the other passengers ready to go. Ana grabbed a pole rather than sit with Elena, and Alejandro stood facing her.

"This is a great place to watch people." He had to nearly shout to be heard.

Ana nodded and leaned against the pole. At first she thought the man standing behind her had been jostled against her, and then realized he was rubbing against her butt. She jammed her elbow into his stomach so hard he cried out. Infuriated, she swung around to face him. He was a middle-aged man in a shiny suit. He had only a sparse fringe of hair circling his head above his ears, and even in his teens, she doubted he could have been handsome. He blushed deeply and looked as ashamed of himself, as he ought to be.

"What's the matter with you?" Ana cried. "Buy a blow-up doll if you need female company, but don't accost women on the Metro."

Alejandro moved to confront the man. "Are you bothering her? If you so much as touched her, I'm going to pull you off this car at the next stop and make you very sorry."

"No, no, I did nothing," the man swore, his lower lip trembling. "The train is crowded, that's all." He burrowed through the passengers behind him to put a safe distance between them.

"What was he doing?" Alejandro asked.

"You don't want to know," Ana assured him. "Elena's standing. We must get off here."

Elena's office was a couple of blocks from the station, and she talked as they walked along. "I meant what I said about suing the police. They've no reason to question you once, let alone twice, and if they dare to come near you again, I'll double the sum we'll ask."

Her office was on the second floor of a building packed with law firms. She had several partners and led them past the receptionist into her cluttered office. "The place is a mess, but I know where everything is. Sit. Do you want coffee?"

Ana had stowed her empty travel mug in her bag. "No, thank you."

Alejandro shook his head and pulled his chair closer to Elena's desk. "If you work with Ana's agent, do you have many criminal cases?"

"I do contracts mainly, but I know how to scare off the police. Now that nobody is listening, who do you think really killed Jaime Campos?"

Ana pulled her notebook from her bag and first noted the time they'd arrived. "I've no real clue. Maybe it was something personal, or he could have photographed something he shouldn't have, or have been blackmailing someone. We also wondered if he might have had a dark side, done porn photos and got involved with the wrong crowd."

Elena raised her hand. "Don't blame anything on the porn industry. It's a headless beast with a thousand waving arms. It's a good thought, however. The police must have searched his studio and computers for leads."

"What if he had a second studio?" Alejandro asked.

Ana's expression brightened. "Of course, he'd have had another studio to keep the porn crowd out of his regular business address. Where would that be likely to be? Down at the docks?"

Elena stood up and opened her door. "Begin writing a screenplay, but don't go knocking on doors looking for a porn studio. You'd never get out if you actually found one."

Alejandro stood and offered Ana his hand to rise. "Is there anything else we can do to discourage the police?"

"More than a lawsuit? No, not now. As for the tabloid that published the offensive photo, you don't want to waste your money suing them. It would just give them a reason to republish the photo."

115

"I've lost one job since it was published, and if I lose more, that's a good cause for a lawsuit, isn't it?"

"Let's concentrate on the police for now," Elena insisted. She walked them out to the office entrance. "Let's keep in touch."

Ana wasn't sure what that meant, and she took a firm grip on Alejandro's hand as they walked away. He sounded so sure of himself, while she feared being a suspect would end her career long before Jaime Campos's murder was solved.

Chapter Eight

Alejandro drove them to the docks where the *Mediterranean Goddess* was moored. "She sails at the end of the week, and her sister ship, the *Mediterranean Siren*, will come into port. Going on board ought to take your mind off the rest of the morning. There are several pools, so we could swim. My father reserves a cabin in case he decides to go on the cruise. There are swimsuits, whatever you need there."

The ship was painted a near-blinding white and sparkled in the morning sun. Ana raised her hand to shade her eyes and craned her neck to look up. "How many of these magnificent vessels does your family own?"

"There are a half-dozen of the cruise ships, more tanker ships, but I've lost count." He held her hand as they walked up the gangplank. The man guarding the gate at the top recognized him.

"Mr. Vasquez, welcome aboard."

Alejandro greeted him by name and pulled Ana close. "We won't be on board long."

"Stay and sail with us."

"Another time," Alejandro replied. He led Ana along beside him. "People board and take the elevators to their deck. Want to see the bridge?"

"I'd love to," she answered. "How do your passengers keep from getting lost?"

"Stewards offer directions, but I used to get lost all the time when I worked as a steward. Eventually I caught on. The bridge has the best view, and I'd come up here whenever I could at night."

While he wouldn't admit it, she saw the pride in his gaze. "Were the other stewards allowed such easy access to the bridge?"

He pulled her close for a hasty kiss. "No, but I was supposed to become familiar with everything, so I had special privileges. I wasn't cocky about it."

When they reached the bridge, a navigator smartly dressed in a white officer's uniform welcomed them. Alejandro introduced him to Ana, and the officer's smile grew wide.

"I saw you when you were here last week. I bought my wife a red bikini on the way home."

"I'm pleased our ad was so effective," Ana replied. She saw Alejandro wince, as though he'd rather forget the day. She hoped he regretted his own behavior rather than her posing in a bikini with Gian Carlo.

"Let me give you a quick tour," the navigator offered. "We have the same electronic navigational equipment as the largest naval vessels. We track our route, other ships nearby, follow weather forecasts and monitor all the technical systems on board."

The bridge was lined with computer screens and banks of controls. Ana wondered how anyone kept track of it all.

When Alejandro hugged her shoulders, she rubbed her cheek along his hand. "This is amazing. Thank you."

Alejandro found his father's suite without taking a single wrong turn. The glass doors to the balcony flooded the plush cabin with light. It was as beautifully decorated as a suite in a five-star hotel, and the bed was wide and inviting.

He followed her glance. "We don't have to swim if you'd rather not."

His thoughts were easily read in his relaxed smile, but her second experience with the detectives hadn't left her in a loving mood. "I love to swim. Where are the suits?"

He opened a narrow closet. "Here you are. There's no red bikini, but there are other choices." He grabbed a pair of baggy board shorts for himself.

Ana found a black one-piece suit and went into the bathroom to pull it on. "Are all the cabins this beautiful?" she asked through the partially open door.

"This is one of the deluxe cabins. Many Barcelona apartments aren't this large." When she came out carrying her folded clothes, he gave her a slow, appreciative glance. "That's almost better than the red bikini, but I don't know why."

She gave a saucy turn. "It leaves more to your imagination." She found a cap on the closet shelf and pushed her hair up into it.

It was a mild day, the pool heated and Ana swam laps with an easy stroke. She rolled over on her back, and Alejandro swam up beside her. The water felt like liquid silk against her skin, and she fluttered her hands to move closer to him. "I got up too early this morning to challenge you to a race. I'll add it to our list of things to do."

He whipped his wet hair out of his eyes, and water beaded on his eyelashes. He treaded water beside her. "Do you really think you could win?"

"I do. When I travel for jobs, I swim at the hotel if there's time. It's easier than bringing along my ballet slippers and searching for a parquet floor."

"I've never brought anyone else on board one of our cruise ships, but we'll come back and swim again. I think the *Mediterranean Siren* docks next week. Right now, I'm too hungry to race. We didn't have time for breakfast. Aren't you hungry?"

She dropped her legs to tread water. "When do you have a class? You shouldn't be late."

He gave her a watery kiss. "We have to eat, and I have an hour." He swam to the end of the pool, pulled himself out and used the pool phone to call the kitchen to request whatever they were serving the crew.

Ana regarded him with a slow smile. He didn't have an ounce of fat, and every muscle was firm and taut. He'd make a great menswear model. "Have you ever thought of modeling?" She swam to the steps and climbed out. She pulled off her cap and shook out her hair.

"I told you I can't stand still." He picked up a thick white towel and dried her off with gentle pats. "Although, if I could work with you, I might be able to manage it."

She'd brought her purse out on the deck and heard her phone. "Do you mind if I check this?"

He dried his hair with a couple of rough swipes of a fresh towel. "Go ahead."

"It's Gian Carlo. Whatever could he want?"

He pulled a deck chair close for her. "Answer and ask."

She slid into the chair and cocked her head to listen and then covered her cell phone. "He says he has something he has to tell me in person. Do you mind if he comes here, or should I have him meet me at home later?"

That was an easy choice. "Have him come here."

"He's only ten minutes away. We can shower and be dressed before he arrives. I'll go first."

She quickly ended the call, and he caught her fingers as she moved by. "Fine, because if we shower together, ten minutes won't be nearly enough time. Put showering together on the list." He wrapped the towel low on his hips and moved to the rail to wait for Gian Carlo. When he saw the red MG drive up, he recognized the blond man. He waved to the guard and went down to meet him.

"Have the police been after you too?" he asked the model.

"No, but that's not the problem." Gian Carlo wore khaki slacks, a black polo shirt and Italian sandals. As they entered the elevator, he eyed Alejandro's hairy chest. "Going with the natural look?"

Alejandro hadn't given it a thought. "I've got better things to do than shave my chest."

"Have it waxed. It lasts a lot longer." He strolled out on the poolside deck. Ana was waiting for them in her prim skirt and blouse. A steward placed a tray of sandwiches on the table beside her, along with beer and lemonade. "I didn't expect lunch. This is great." He reached for a sandwich and took a bite before he sat down beside Ana.

Alejandro thanked the steward and dismissed him. "We don't have much time. Tell us why you called." He took the chair on Ana's right.

Gian Carlo looked highly amused. "Us? You two didn't look like a couple last week." He reached for one of the excellent German beers.

Ana raised a brow, forcing Alejandro to answer. He didn't lie. "That was my mistake."

Gian Carlo leaned back, crossed his ankles and looked out over the pool. "We ought to let women rule the world. Men just screw up everything. I wish my dad owned a cruise ship. This is a great place for a party."

"Gian Carlo," Ana urged, "couldn't you have sent me a text?"

Chastened, he straightened up. "This is too important to trust to flying thumbs, and I wanted to talk to you before Jaime's memorial service."

Ana shot Alejandro a wary glance. "What memorial service?" she asked.

"Galen Salazar is having it at his home on Saturday afternoon. Didn't he invite you?"

Ana rested her cool glass of lemonade against her cheek. "Galen and I aren't on the best of terms."

Gian Carlo finished the last bite of his sandwich and wiped his hands on a napkin. "I thought he really liked you.What happened?"

"I'd like to hear it too," Alejandro added, curiosity lighting his gaze.

She told them. "He didn't seem terribly disappointed when I wasn't interested in working with him exclusively, or lengthening my stay on Mallorca, but maybe he thought it would be awkward to have me there with his wife."

Alejandro moved forward in his chair. "Does this happen often?"

"With designers, no. With ad execs, and photographers, sometimes. I always say no, and it hasn't hurt my career. Let's not digress. What was it you wanted to talk to me about before the memorial?"

Gian Carlo took a swig of beer. "You know Robert Mapplethorpe?"

"Of course," Ana answered, but she doubted Alejandro would have heard of him. "Mapplethorpe was an American photographer who did striking black-and-white photos, mainly of flowers and nudes. He died of AIDS in the late 1980s."

"I've heard of him," Alejandro replied. "Spain isn't at the end of the world."

Gian Carlo continued. "Jaime pointed out Mapplethorpe hasn't been around in more than twenty years, and he thought there would still be a big market for black-and-white photos of male nudes. He offered a percentage of the profits if I'd be one of the models. I've got the body for it, but it didn't feel right."

"Could you be more specific?" Alejandro requested.

"I asked if a gallery had an interest in a show of male nudes, or if he had a publisher ready to print the book. He told me not to worry because there was plenty of money behind the project, and he'd take care of everything. Anytime someone tells you not to worry, you know you're being screwed. I told him I'd think it over, but I wasn't going to do it. Sometimes even good money isn't worth earning."

"You're absolutely right," Ana readily agreed. "Could Jaime have planned to channel the photos into the porn market? Did he ever mention bondage or S&M?"

Gian Carlo frowned slightly. "A couple of years ago, he told me a woman asked him to take some bondage photos to jazz up her sex life with her husband. He said he'd dress me in leather and have me wear a mask. There wasn't any sex in it. It was just supposed to look like dominant and submissive poses. I told him I was too busy, but he probably found another man to do it."

Alejandro rose to his feet. "Did he say where he planned to take the photos?"

"No. His studio I suppose. Should the police question me, I don't want to tell them about either of the offers and give them the mistaken idea Jaime and I could have argued over them. I want to do all I can to avoid landing on their suspect list."

"Good luck," Ana offered. "Do you have an alibi for the day Jaime died?"

"I was with my sister and her family at my niece's third birthday party. But is time of death ever exact? I liked Jaime and want whoever killed him caught, but I don't want to land in the middle of it. You're good with a camera, Ana. Are you going after the jobs Jaime had lined up but can no longer do?"

Horrified by the idea, she paled noticeably and had to force herself to take a deep breath. "I hadn't even thought of it. If the police do question you, please don't mention I even own a camera. I don't want them to believe I had a motive for the murder."

"I won't tell them a thing, but they haven't called me and probably won't. From what I've heard, they're questioning the young women he photographed, not any of the men."

"At least they haven't leaked any bogus photos of you to the tabloids," Alejandro added. "Come on, I'll show you the way back to your car."

"I can find it. I have a clever rat's instinct for mazes," he announced with a grin.

"I'll watch to make certain you make it." Alejandro walked over to the rail, and Gian Carlo swiftly appeared by the gangplank below and waved. Alejandro untied his towel and picked up a sandwich. "He looked so damn good in an officer's uniform, but he's not very bright, is he?"

Gian Carlo's question about her taking over Jaime's photography jobs was so damn obvious, but she'd not seen it coming and wouldn't comment on his intelligence. "He's paid for how he looks, so let's leave it at that."

"All right. You haven't eaten anything. There must be something on the tray that appeals to you."

The sliced chicken sandwiches had crisp lettuce and thick slices of tomato. She picked up one and wrapped it in a napkin. "I've completely lost my appetite. I'll take this home. The cookies look good too." She filled another napkin with some.

"What about some grapes?"

He was teasing her, but she couldn't appreciate his humor. "This is fine. I'm really worried, Alejandro. When people are in trouble in the movies, they always get out of town. Maybe I ought to be on board the *Goddess* when she sails."

He rested his hands lightly on her shoulders and spoke in a soothing tone, "You're a model who takes photos in her spare time. You can't be the only one with a camera, and owning one shouldn't be considered suspicious."

"It shouldn't, but I doubt Robles and Mesa are reasonable enough to grasp the fact. I don't want to make you late. Better go and shower."

"I won't be a minute. Come to my place tonight. I'll provide the dinner this time and show you the loft."

Her mood was already so dark she didn't need to stay home and brood with the kittens. She managed a faint smile. "Thank you. I'll be there."

They'd left her condo early, and when Alejandro brought her home, she was relieved the paparazzi weren't camped nearby. Maybe they'd met their quotas for the day when they'd photographed her fleeing the police station. "Hi, Henry. I hope you're having a quiet day."

"Thank you. It's too quiet, but I always have a book handy, Miss Santillan."

She went on upstairs, greeted Fatima and the kittens, put the sandwich and cookies in the refrigerator and went on into her room and lay down across the bed. Sleep was underrated in her view, and she always found a nap helped no matter what the problem, but today she couldn't quiet her mind. She soon gave up the attempt to rest, put on a leotard and went into her studio to dance. Ballet required intention in every step and gesture, and she was grateful for the distraction as well as the exercise.

Once finished, she knotted the ties of a flowing dance skirt at her waist and entered the kitchen, looking for the sandwich she'd brought home. She saved the chicken for the kittens and ate the lettuce-and-tomato sandwich leaning against the counter while Fatima rearranged the cupboard holding the pots and pans. Romeo ran into the kitchen and right out.

"Are the kittens getting in your way, Fatima?"

"They see me coming and hide." The nested pans straightened to her ideal, she stood and brushed her hands. "You still look tired, Ana. Maybe you should tell Alejandro you need a night for yourself."

Ana opened the refrigerator and took out a bottle of stuffed olives. She ate three before responding. "This is a really good sandwich. We went on board the *Mediterranean Goddess* this morning. Have you ever been on a cruise?"

"In other words, I should mind my business. Bruno's taken me out in a fishing boat, which isn't comparable, but that's enough ocean for me. I made the lemon cookies you like so much. If there's nothing else for today, I'll go upstairs and look in on Mrs. Diaz. She needs a little company now and then."

"That's very kind of you. Take her some cookies and tell her I said hello." Fatima looked in on several of the elderly condo residents who lived alone. "I ought to have a tea in the afternoon and invite Mrs. Diaz and whoever else would like to come."

"When you have time," Fatima suggested and said good-bye.

Ana hadn't heard anything more from Paul Perez, but if she lost other jobs, she'd have plenty of time to entertain her neighbors.

Alejandro found a vegetarian restaurant and ordered their vegetable stew and several salads for their dinner. He drew new placemats and wished he had a real dinner table he could set more formally, but he bought a bouquet of mixed flowers and hoped that would do. In jeans with a dress shirt, he was comfortable and ready, but when Ana didn't arrive by the time he expected her, he feared she'd run into trouble.

A call to her cell went to voice mail. He tried again in ten minutes with the same result. Certain something had to be wrong, he drove to her building, and the night security guard came out from behind the counter to speak with him.

"The police came for Miss Santillan about an hour ago." He checked the sign-in sheet. "An hour and fifteen minutes ago. They were very rude."

"Did they arrest her?"

"No, but they insisted I not alert her before they went up to her condo, and they brought her down with them a few minutes later. She was dressed as though she planned to go out, but they didn't give her a chance to leave a message."

"Thank you." Alejandro strode out to his SUV and drove straight to the police station they'd visited that morning. He'd pay Ana's bail if she'd been arrested, but he feared she'd be stuck in a cold cell all night. She didn't deserve to be treated so badly. While he hadn't been waiting for a chance to rescue her, he was glad he had the wherewithal to do it.

Chapter Nine

Detective Robles and Mesa escorted Ana into the rear entrance of the police station rather than enter through the front doors as they had that morning. She doubted they had any desire to protect her from bad publicity, however. She wished they'd given her time to call Alejandro and hoped he'd know she wouldn't stand him up. After the morning they'd had there at the station, maybe he'd be relieved if she didn't show. Elena Covarrubias wouldn't appreciate being called out at night, which added another unfortunate layer to her situation.

A tall, slender, dark-haired man in a well-tailored gray suit met them in the back corridor. His deep voice echoed off the walls. "I'm Lieutenant Montoya. Please come with me."

"First, I need my phone to call my attorney," she answered, standing firm in her place.

Montoya nodded sympathetically. "Please forgive me, Miss Santillan. You're not under suspicion, and you won't need your attorney tonight."

The man was as smooth as glass, but like Robles and Mesa, he made her uneasy. "That's my decision, Lieutenant, and I want my phone."

Robles pulled it out of his pocket, and as her fingers brushed his sweaty palm, she wished for a pack of hand sanitizer wipes. She'd buy some tomorrow, if they let her out tonight.

Montoya dismissed the detectives and led her up the narrow rear stairs. He moved with a refined elegance and escorted her into a room with a cork wall covered in gory photographs. She shuddered and quickly looked away. "I didn't kill Jaime, and you can't frighten me into confessing."

He closed the door. "I'm so sorry, I should have warned you. I've seen so much blood over the years I've become inured to violence. Sit here so your back faces the photo wall." He pulled out a chair for her at the long table and waited until she was comfortably seated. "The murder scene showed such a vicious attack, we believe Jaime's assailant was male. In addition to Mr. Campos's fashion photography, we've discovered he also submitted work to several S&M magazines." He picked them up from the end of the table and took the chair across from hers.

The graphic glossy covers nauseated her. "I'd rather not look at those."

He shrugged sadly and opened a folder. "I'd rather not know such publications exist, but I've a crime to solve. We found Mr. Campos's original photos in his studio computer and printed these. I know they're distasteful, but would you please look at them and tell me if you recognize any of the men? The editors of the magazine can't name them."

It was the last thing she wanted to do. "First, I need to speak with my attorney." He nodded permission, and she called Elena but got her voice mail. She left a brief message, but doubted Elena would object to her looking through photos. "I had plans for the evening, and I need to send an apology."

Montoya reached for her phone. "Of course, but do not tell him where you are."

"If I'm supposed to be a secret informant, you shouldn't have brought me through the front door this morning."

He frowned with what appeared to be sincere regret. "Unfortunate, I know, but it was before we found these photos."

Although that didn't sound like an apology, she wouldn't push him for one. She licked her lips and tried to decide what to say when it wouldn't make any sense. Alejandro answered on the first ring. "I'm so sorry not to be there on time."

"It wasn't your fault," he replied. "I'm waiting on the bench where we sat this morning, and I'll take you home."

"Thank you." She ended the call. "He's here, so I've no secret to keep."

Montoya's eyes narrowed as he sat back. "Don't tell him why you've been brought in. He'll mention it to someone else, and it will swiftly become common knowledge. If the man who killed Jaime Campos is in these photos, we don't want him to know you've identified him."

She scanned the room. "Are you videoing this?"

"No, there are no cameras here, and I'm not recording our conversation either. Let's begin. Just look at the men."

The women were impossible to ignore, however. Some appeared terrified and others posed as the perfect submissive with a totally blank expression. Many had long blonde wigs tickling their bare breasts, but none resembled her. There was less variety among the men. They were bare-chested, clad in tight leather pants and gloves, and wore masks or hoods. She looked up at Montoya. "If you've seen one waxed chest, you've seen them all."

"I know this is trying, but look closer. They're not all the same man."

"I realize that." One of the masked men was blond, but his hair was long, unlike Gian Carlo, who always wore his fair hair in a stylish cut. She quickly scanned the photos. "Menswear models tend to be tall, broad-shouldered, slim, and designer suits fit them beautifully. Look at the muscles on these men. They're bulked-up like bodybuilders. You'd have a better chance of identifying them if you looked in the gyms that promote bodybuilding rather than healthy exercise."

She'd captured Montoya's full attention, and he leaned forward. "Excellent observation, Miss Santillan, but nothing about any of these men looks familiar?"

"Without being able to see their faces, no, not at all." She shuffled through the photos and sorted them into four piles. "There's the blond; this man looks to be the tallest; this one has really hairy forearms. I don't see tattoos on any of them, but there's a faint shadow on the fourth man's right arm that could be makeup covering a tattoo. I'll bet if you showed these photos to bodybuilders, you'd find someone who knows them."

Montoya stared at her a long moment, then shrugged unhappily and placed the photos in a single stack. He carefully neatened the corners. "I'll send Robles and Mesa out to do so tomorrow. You've been a great help to us, but again, don't tell your date the subject of our discussion. I may need to contact you again, but rather than send detectives, I'll call you myself." He rose from his chair with the sinuous grace of a cobra weaving above his basket.

She looked up at him and raised her hand. "Wait a minute. I need to leave another message for my attorney." This time she asked Elena to respond in the morning rather than tonight. She hesitated before

128

leaving the table. "The women in these photos aren't professional models. Have you been able to find any of them? Wouldn't they know the men's names?"

Montoya crossed the room and rested his hand on the doorknob. "Some are runaways who've scattered. Others are known, but drug-addicted prostitutes have few clear memories. That's why I wished to speak with you."

Not wanting any part in their investigation, she left her chair and gripped her bag tightly under her arm. "I'm sorry I couldn't be of more help. Galen Salazar is hosting the memorial for Jaime on Saturday. One of the men in the magazines might show up, and it would give you a chance to question him."

He nodded thoughtfully. "The murderer might attend. They love funerals where they can offer comfort to the family, even if they're not acquainted with the deceased. Sick individuals all. I'll plan to be there. Will you?"

His eyes were so dark a brown they appeared black and shone with a provocative gleam she recognized all too easily. "I can't say. Good luck with your investigation."

"Let me see you out." They moved along the office-lined corridor to the front desk. Alejandro rose from the bench, prompting the lieutenant to whisper, "Is he a model?"

"No, he isn't." She moved forward to take Alejandro's hand. She'd worn a caramel-hued top and a matching gored skirt that swirled around her ankles as she moved toward the doors. The gentle swish sounded to her like faint applause.

Alejandro glanced over his shoulder. "Who is he?"

"We don't talk in here, remember?"

He was parked close, and as soon as he'd started the SUV's engine, he turned toward her, looking concerned rather than simply curious. "No one will overhear us here. Who was he and what did he want?"

She fastened her seat belt. "He's Lieutenant Montoya, apparently Robles and Mesa's boss. He told me not to reveal what we discussed. He didn't order me to be silent or forbid me to speak, but it wouldn't matter if he had. I'm through holding back with you."

He pulled away from the curb and eased the SUV into the flow of traffic. "Thank you, but I hope you also consider me trustworthy."

"I do." She provided a brief description of the last hour. "Apparently I'm no longer a suspect, and I don't know anyone who's ever posed for S&M magazines. Maybe that's the last I'll hear of Montoya and his minions."

"I doubt it. Maybe he never thought you'd provide anything new and just wanted to meet you."

She took a deep breath and let it out slowly. "That's an angle I hadn't considered. Did you get a good look at him? He has a reptilian quality I don't find appealing, but he looked at me the way most men do."

"And how is that?"

"As though I'm something delicious, and they'd love to lick off the frosting."

"God, what an image. Let's stop at the market and buy some frosting."

She squeezed his arm. "Not tonight, please. Maybe the whole interview was a sham and Montoya thought I'd give something away when he handed me the S&M photos. Maybe none of the men had anything to do with Jaime's death. Elena told me to let the police solve the crime. I called her but had to leave a message."

"Let's go to the memorial Saturday."

It was a presumptuous suggestion and yet endearing. "Let's? As in you and me?"

He parked on the side street closest to his building and walked around the SUV to open her door. "Yes, as in you and me. I've been to the police station twice for you. That ought to count for something."

She ran her hand over his chest. "You've done a lot more than that. I hope whatever you'd planned for dinner isn't ruined."

He took her hand as they entered his building and held it for the slow elevator ride. "The vegetable stew can be reheated and the salads are in the refrigerator."

His loft was only a few steps from the elevator. She moved aside as he unlocked his door. "Is there anything for me to do?"

"You could slice the bread."

"I'll be happy to. I was afraid I'd end up spending the night in a damp cell. Let's forget about the murder."

"That's fine with me."

Other than to warm a meal Fatima had made for her, she seldom cooked, and standing beside him in the kitchen alcove was fun. She bumped her hip against his, but kept her eyes focused on the knife in her hand. "This is fun."

He laughed and hugged her. "With the right person, everything is fun."

"You're speaking from experience?"

He'd poured the stew into the only pot he owned and stirred it gently with a wooden spoon. "Yes, because I know how awkward everything feels with the wrong woman."

"Or the wrong man." He felt like the right man, but his father had blown them apart once, and she couldn't help but feel something bad would happen again. The gory photos Montoya had told her to ignore flashed in her mind. Terrible things happened to people every day. She'd just been very lucky to avoid them.

"You've gotten awfully quiet. Is something wrong?" he asked.

"I'm simply quietly enjoying the moment. That smells so good."

He gave her a taste on the spoon. "Does it need more salt?"

"It's delicious now." She licked her lips, and vowed silently to be happy the whole evening. With Alejandro's very pleasant company, it wouldn't be a challenge. She buttered a slice of the freshly baked bread, gave him a bite and took one.

He set soup bowls on the counter. "Let's put the bowls on the table, and then I'll fill them. I've never worked as a waiter, and I'd probably spill most of the stew on the way to the table if I filled them first."

"Sounds good. I've never had any job other than modeling. Other than being a steward, have you done anything else?"

He brought the salads to the table so they could serve themselves. "Something useful, you mean? No, I've never done any other work. We'll have to avoid becoming stranded on a deserted island, or we might starve before we figure out how to catch a fish and roast it over a fire."

"I'll add gaining survival skills to our list." She loved the vegetable stew and said so often. "This is the perfect dinner. I hope it's enough for you." She heaped a second serving of spinach salad on her salad plate.

He sat back and smiled. "This is fine, but I wish I had a fireplace. A fire would make the dinner perfect."

"I do have a fireplace, but I seldom light a fire unless it's the dead of winter, and it isn't cold enough to snow here."

He broke off a bite of bread, scattered crispy crumbs from the crust and brushed them into his napkin. "Do you know how to ski?"

"Ski? I've posed in ski clothes in Switzerland, but I've never actually skied. Have you?"

"I learned as a child. My father thought I ought to 'experience' winter and learn to ski and skate. I prefer riding a bike."

"I've posed with bikes." She had to laugh. "There are photos of me looking as though I play tennis, or ice skate, so many things, but a big cardboard doll would be equally adept at sports." She blotted her mouth with her napkin. "I've been modeling for twenty years, Alejandro. Standing around looking as though I'm having an absolutely wonderful time, or in haute couture where I must appear to be above it all, but that's not really living, is it?"

He reached for her hand. "Think of the opportunity you've had to travel and see the world."

Time and again, she'd told herself the same thing, but it still didn't seem as though she'd lived a life that mattered. "Yes, I've the photos to prove it."

He regarded her with an encouraging smile. "And you supported yourself and your mother."

A spoonful of the vegetable stew filled her with a peaceful warmth, and, unwilling to complain any further, she nodded to concede the point. "True. I have an enviable life and should enjoy living it."

"That's a good piece of advice for me too. Would you like more stew?"

"Yes, I would." She sat back as he refilled her bowl. "I wish I'd met you at a different time."

He refilled his own bowl and returned the pot to the stove. "When I owned a home with a fireplace?"

"No, you're fine the way you are. It's just that I'm so unsettled. I refused to mention Jaime's murder, but..."

"I'd rather forget it too. Are these pale cubes in the stew eggplant?"

She understood he was also sick of the subject of murder. "They are. I love eggplant. They're a luscious color, aubergine, and they can be prepared in so many ways. When I learn to cook, I'll bake them and broil them or whatever it is one is supposed to do with an eggplant." She wiped away a tear with her napkin.

"I'm sorry. I shouldn't have cut you off. My father often tells me I should be more appreciative of the life the Ortiz wealth affords me. I'm not, and you shouldn't be satisfied with your life either, if you want more. Maybe you should change careers now and go after the jobs Jaime can't do."

Appalled, she laid her spoon on her plate and sat back. "That's ghoulish."

"True. It's also an opportunity you didn't expect, but maybe it shouldn't be overlooked."

She picked up a piece of bread and slathered it with butter. "Is that the way you think, or your father?"

"Some of his ideas have probably rubbed off on me without my consent. Just think about it."

"I'd have to start with babies and weddings, Alejandro. I couldn't just step into haute couture fashion. Designers consider me a model, maybe a bright one, but they wouldn't take a chance on my doing any fashion spreads for them."

"Why not? Couldn't you show them samples of your work? Valeria would pose for you. I bet Gian Carlo would too. I look good enough in a suit to pass for a model in a few photos."

He was challenging her to work for her future, to seize it, rather than simply dream it. She wouldn't admit to cowardice, but the prospect terrified her. "You're making my head hurt." She reached for another piece of bread.

"I'm sorry, but if you're tired of being a model and want to switch to photography, you'll have to do something to move toward it. Unless you want to wait for the first dreaded wrinkle to doom your career."

He made her laugh in spite of herself. She gave his shoulder a playful punch. He was the youngest man she'd ever dated, and he'd fallen for her when he'd thought she was a taciturn Goth girl. That still amazed her. "I've some candid photos of you. They're on my camera. Would you like to see them?"

He looked startled. "You're kidding."

133

"No. Let's finish dinner, and I'll show you." She immediately doubted the wisdom of mentioning them and finished eating in silence. They cleared the table and piled the dishes in the sink. "We should do the dishes now," she suggested. "All it takes is a little soap and water."

"We can wait until after dessert. I want to see the photos. Let's put them on the computer."

She brought her camera and sat down in front of his Mac, but hesitated. "The afternoon we met, you fell asleep almost immediately. It was such a great pose of a student, and I took photos before you woke."

He looked over her shoulder and remembered meeting her, but not how tired he'd been. When she loaded the photos, he was as impressed as he'd been with her photos of his tiny model houses. "Those are good. It's strong as a composition, with my body curved over the round table, and the straight lines of El Gato Café behind me. All the angles are good. You ought to put these in your portfolio. Do you have one?"

"Only for modeling."

"Start one of your photography. Put everything on a disk and hand them out every time you model."

Ana loaded the photo of him stretched out on the futon and held her breath. The sexy photo showed off his lean body to perfection. "What do you think?" When he didn't respond, she turned to look up at him. "I'll never show it to anyone. It was just for me because you looked so handsome."

He pulled up a chair from the worktable and sat beside her. "My face doesn't show, so no one would know it was me if you did sell it to the tabloids."

Jarred to the bone, she had to swallow hard to speak. "What made you think of them?"

"They print every embarrassing photo they can get their hands on, don't they? But I'm not embarrassed. This is another great shot. Jaime pointed out Mapplethorpe has been dead a long time. Maybe you ought to give some thought to showing men, mostly undressed, for your own show."

"I'm not going to compete with a dead man," she objected with a grimace.

He smoothed a curl behind her ear. "Are you referring to

Mapplethorpe or Jaime Campos?"

She would love to do a hundred candid shots of Alejandro, but solely for herself. "Both. Now what's for dessert?"

"You're trying to distract me, but I get your message. I bought some lemon tarts. Do you want coffee or tea?"

"Tea, please." She left her chair, put her camera in her bag and followed him to the kitchen alcove. She raked her lower lip through her teeth. Although she wanted to be honest with him, it was a risk she really didn't want to take. "I have sold photos to the tabloids, Alejandro, but they were of well-known people, and there was nothing scandalous about them."

He filled the teakettle with water, put it on the stove and leaned back against the counter. "Would you care to name them?"

She looked down at her ballet flats. "No, I'd rather not, but you needn't fear I'll sell any photos of you."

"You look so damn apologetic, it must not have turned out well."

After a poignant shrug, she answered honestly. "You could say that, but it's all over and done."

He pulled her into his arms. "You're the most remarkable creature. Do you have an endless number of things to confess?"

She might have deserved that but wouldn't admit it, ever. "I wouldn't call them confessions."

"Fine. Unlimited fascinating facets. How's that?"

His warm embrace soothed her temper. "I'm trying to tell the truth. You shouldn't make fun of me."

He reached over to turn off the kettle. "Dessert can wait. I love the way your skirt flows around your ankles when you walk." He took her hand and pulled her out into the main room. He raised his arm and twirled her a couple of times. "I have to take dance lessons."

She moved close and rested her hand on his chest. "You're changing the subject."

"Yes, I am. I promised to show you the loft, but I don't want you to trip on your skirt when you climb the ladder."

"How considerate of you. Suppose I did. Do you know any first-aid techniques?"

"Apply pressure to slow the flow of blood from a wound."

"That's a good one." She unfastened the hooks at her waist, stepped out of her skirt and laid it over the back of her chair. She slipped off her gold ballet flats. "There probably isn't much room to undress up there, is there?"

"Not really." He unbuttoned his shirt.

She pulled off her top. Her lingerie was bright red. She crossed to the ladder and started up. "Is there a trick to this?"

"I should go first and pull you over the top."

"Too late." She climbed to the top of the ladder, a little more than seven feet from the floor, and gazed into the loft. There was room for a big bed and a closet at the end. She could have used something to hold on to but got over the end of the ladder not too ungracefully and stepped into the loft. The studio had such a high ceiling, she could walk around the bed without bumping her head. "This is like a tree house."

He followed her wearing only his black briefs. "I should put tree houses in all my little cities. How could I have forgotten them?"

Wanting to think only of him, she lay back on the bed. "Make a note of it later."

He crawled over the side of the bed to catch her. "You'll remind me if I forget?"

She giggled against his chest. "I may have no memory of the night."

"Is that a challenge?"

She answered with a deep, luscious kiss to block all thought save those of him. His sleek body fit so well against hers. She slid her hand over his chest, tugged at the hair hiding his nipples and then found them with her tongue. He uttered a welcoming moan, and encouraged, she licked the leathery buds. He smelled like soap, but something exotic with a sandalwood base. She eased over him to nibble an earlobe.

"You smell awfully good. You always have, but tonight, your scent is something darker, more mysterious."

"I'm not giving away my secrets." He pulled her down into his arms. "I'm going to find a huge oak tree where I can build a tree house and make love to you there all night."

"Not in a public park, please."

He smothered his deep laugh in her soft curls. "No, somewhere deep in a forest where no one will hear us laugh and wonder what we're doing cradled in the branches."

She wound her hair in a coil to sweep it out of his way. "Mallorca has La Serra de Tramuntana."

"It does, but a tree house on the coast might be chilly at night."

She slid her hand down his flat belly. "I don't suppose we could light a fire to keep warm."

"Definitely not." He pulled her close. "I'll find somewhere not so far away. For now, we can imagine whatever we choose."

Nuzzling against him, she nearly purred, "I don't need to imagine anything better than being here with you." She licked his shoulder. "Now I wish we'd bought the frosting. I'd put just a tiny bit here." She touched the base of his throat. "A dab here. All the spots you wouldn't expect and make you delicious all over."

"We could probably make frosting. What does it take? Sugar, butter, what else?"

She ran her fingertips up his inner thigh to make him shiver. "It must need some flavoring. Do you have a bottle of vanilla?"

"No, but I'll buy a gallon tomorrow. Could we use a liqueur?"

She kissed the inside of his elbow, and he wove his fingers in her hair. "Probably, but I'm not in the mood to cook. Are you?"

"You are enough," he whispered.

The lights he'd left on down below veiled the loft in pale shadows, but his sexy grin still showed, and his silvery eyes glowed with a teasing light. He was enough, more than enough for her. She unfastened her bra and tossed it away before crawling over him. She loved kissing him, and he wrapped his arms around her waist and rolled over to hold her. He nuzzled her throat, and she rubbed against him.

He covered her breasts with kisses and sucked gently at her nipples. Feeling adored, she pressed close and combed her fingers through his hair. Making love was a game that never grew old, and she welcomed his every lick and caress. She held her breath as he tongued his way to her navel and raised her arms above her head to stretch and lengthen the path. His tender kisses tickled her inner thighs, and his warm breath promised so much more.

He slid her thong down her legs, dropped it to the floor and kissed her instep and ankles. He trailed tender kisses to the tops of her thighs, spread her open with his fingertips and didn't make her wait for the delicious thrill. He smoothed his tongue over her, circled her clit with the tip and lapped gently.

"You're so good at that," she murmured.

He slid a finger into her and then two. "This makes it better, doesn't it?"

She gave an appreciative squirm. "Hmm, it does."

He made her feel warm all over, and heat pooled low in her belly. He licked her, paused to blow across her damp slit, and then sucked until she reached for him. "Come here. I want you this way."

He pressed the heel of his hand against her mound. "Don't you want me to finish?"

"Inside me this time."

There were condoms in the nightstand, and he quickly donned one. "I can't even think when I'm tasting you."

She bucked as he slid into her, surprising him, catching him, drawing him in deep. She flexed her muscles to pump him, and he withdrew to plunge into her again, and again. Already close, she clutched his shoulders and felt every inch of him sliding in, filling her, stretching her to fit, and arched her back in a demanding surrender. Her breath caught in her throat, and the joy he always gave rushed through her in trembling waves. He chased his own climax with a final surge, and she clung to him, never wanting to let him go. When he could stir, he moved beside her, pressed her head against his chest and wished her beautiful dreams.

In a playful mood before dawn, she spread teasing kisses up his spine to wake him. "Do you like this? You have such a handsome back, and backs are so often neglected." She ruffled his hair and kissed his shoulders.

"You're right. You're the only one who's ever kissed my shoulder blades. Keep going."

She moved down to place wet, sloppy kisses in the dimples on his butt before refocusing her attentions on his spine. "What about your ribs? Does this feel good?" She whisked the ends of her hair across his skin to accent her kisses.

"Everything you do feels better than good," he murmured softly.

Moving astride his hips, she rubbed his shoulders. "Sorry, I can't resist you."

Completely relaxed, he cradled his cheek on crossed arms. "I like that in a woman."

She leaned down to kiss his cheek. "I'm spoiling you."

He rolled over to catch her in his arms. "Yes, you are, and now it's my turn."

"Just for variety, why don't you start on my front and work around to my back."

He gave her a long, slow kiss and touched her breast. "If I start here, I'll never get to your back."

"What a shame. Another time, then." She wound her arms around his neck and welcomed every bit of loving he could give.

Fatima was vacuuming the living room when Ana came home. She went into the kitchen for a piece of fruit and found Romeo sitting on the kitchen counter. She flicked water on him from the sink, and he jumped down as though he'd been scalded. "I have a lunch date, so you needn't make me anything."

Fatima shut off the sweeper. "I beg your pardon?"

"I'm having lunch today with Paul and the shoe man. He called me early this morning, so it's not on the calendar. I'll add it." She did and bit into an apple. When she entered the living room, Fatima eyed her with an expression she knew all too well.

"I'm not getting out of bed with one man to get into bed with another," she exclaimed.

"I didn't say a word."

"You had that look, though," Ana insisted. "I've never had multiple lovers. You know that."

The housekeeper gave an innocent shrug. "I'm just taking care of the house today, that's all I'm doing. You're free to live your life as you choose."

Apprehensive, Ana took a step toward her. "Is there some reason you don't approve of Alejandro?"

Fatima kicked the vacuum cord out of her way. "He's good-looking and rich. What more could you want?"

"There's lots more, but maybe he'll decide I'm not the girl for him. So far, we're doing fine, and I'm not going to worry about what tomorrow might bring. I'll do my best to get you some free shoes from Lamoreaux. Will that make you happy?"

"Free shoes would be nice. I wouldn't refuse them, but you don't want to give him the wrong impression."

"Believe me, I won't give him any ideas." She threw the apple core in the kitchen trashcan and went into her bedroom to shower and dress. She loved wearing Alejandro's scent and hated to wash it away, but she wanted nothing on her mind other than business that afternoon.

Ana met Paul at his office, and they drove to the five-star restaurant Lamoreaux had selected. The shoe designer gave the contract Paul had prepared only a careless glance before signing. He ordered an expensive bottle of wine for them to share, but Ana took only a sip. Lucien made conversation easily but directed all his comments to her. Such unbridled admiration made her uncomfortable.

"Tell us about yourself," she encouraged. "Do you have a wife and children?"

For the first time that afternoon, he looked away. "I'm a widower. My two sons are grown—a doctor and an attorney."

She had meant to remind him of his wife if he had one, not depress him. "I'm so sorry for your loss. You must be very proud of your sons."

"Of course, but I would have loved to have daughters as well."

His sly glance promised he was open to remarrying and having a second family, but she wouldn't encourage his interest. Something about him set her on edge, and she was relieved when Paul steered the conversation toward business.

"Our single Lamoreaux store here in Barcelona is doing exceptionally well, and I hope to expand to other locations soon. A photographer with the French advertising firm that usually does our ads will be coming to Barcelona for the shoot."

"I always enjoy working with someone new," Ana offered. It would also be an opportunity to learn from another photographer. Alejandro was right, though. She really did need to assemble a portfolio of her photographs for tangible proof she intended to change careers.

"The women in Paris walk everywhere," Lucien observed, "and continually need new shoes. It's a commodity that's always popular. The women in Barcelona also appear to enjoy walking."

"It's excellent exercise," Ana added. She could have mentioned how much her housekeeper admired the black heels he'd sent her, but the words stuck in her throat. The salad she'd ordered was very good, but she had little appetite and merely rearranged the chilled vegetables on her plate.

"You're not hungry?" Lamoreaux asked. He refilled her wineglass. "Let's order something else for you."

"No, this is fine." She scooped up another forkful. "I love the way they've sliced the carrots and beets."

"It's a colorful salad," he agreed. "But something's wrong. Don't you want to work for me?"

Ana flashed her most charming smile. "I love your shoes, and I'm looking forward to doing the ads. Forgive me if my mind wandered."

Lucien nodded. "I've seen the tabloids. I'm sure you're not involved in Jaime Campos's murder, but it must weigh heavily on you. Let's order something for dessert with piles of whipped cream. It should make you feel better."

Whipped cream would work as well as frosting, and this time, her smile was genuine. She thought of Alejandro with every bite and not once of gorgeous French shoes.

Chapter Ten

Alejandro took her to dinner at a new place located atop one of Barcelona's tallest buildings. Seated beside a floor-to-ceiling window, they had a beautiful view of the city from a near-dizzying height. "This is as close as I could get to a tree house for tonight."

Ana reached across the table for his hand. "The lights are so pretty, but I'm afraid to look down. I'd like a tree house I could jump out of easily without needing a parachute."

"I won't give you any reason to jump," he promised.

He had such a sexy smile, and she knew he meant it. She urged him to talk about his classes while they ate. He had one particularly amusing instructor, and his fellow students ranged from extremely serious to comical. "You'll be finished soon, won't you?"

"In a couple of weeks. I've interviews set up, but few firms are hiring."

Last night, he'd been free with his advice, but she wanted only to offer encouragement. "That doesn't mean they won't hire you."

He refilled her wineglass. "No, it doesn't. I shouldn't have given you career advice while I'm out of work."

She appreciated his apology without gloating. "Your ideas made sense. Has your father given up on your working for him?"

"As long as I'm breathing, he won't. Do you want to stay for dessert? Or we could go to my place and play with frosting. I bought both vanilla and chocolate."

"That sounds so exciting, but I'd like to see the dessert menu before I choose," she replied with forced innocence.

"Of course. They might have a crema catalana we wouldn't want to miss."

They did have one and their waiter described it as the best in all of Catalonia, but she blotted her mouth on her napkin and shook her head. "Let's wait until the next time we're here to try it."

Alejandro requested their check, and the waiter bowed slightly but didn't step away. "Pardon me, but several people have asked if you're Ana Santillan, and I didn't wish to disturb you."

Lost in Alejandro's company, she'd not worried about being recognized. Relieved to be herself, she smiled and nodded. "Yes, I am. Will you please wait until after we've gone to answer anyone who's curious?"

"I will."

Alejandro paid with cash and tipped the man well. He held Ana's hand as they rode the elevator down to the parking level. "Do people usually recognize you when you go out?"

Uncertain what his real question might be, she hesitated to answer. If he was again criticizing himself for not recognizing her when they met, she didn't want to make the matter worse. "Sometimes, like tonight, someone might think I look familiar and wonder who I am. If possible, I try to be gracious rather than standoffish."

"That's undoubtedly wise, but if there's somewhere you'd rather not go, please say so."

There was an edge to his voice, but she wouldn't call him on it when the fact she might draw a stranger's notice was still so new to him. It was easier to be quiet and think about frosting.

"Vanilla or chocolate?" Alejandro asked.

She leaned against the counter beside him. "Let's begin with vanilla, but it will have to be a tiny bit or we'll quickly get sick of the taste and each other."

"That's unlikely." He opened the can, swiped a little on his finger and slid it across her lips. When he kissed her, she couldn't stop laughing. "What's so funny?"

She licked her lips to catch the last sweet taste. "This was my idea, I know, but maybe it wasn't a very good one."

"I say it was." He washed his hands and unbuttoned his shirt. He reached for her arm, pushed up her sleeve, and put a little frosting on her inner elbow. He licked it off. "Is that better?"

"Hmm, yes. Take off your shirt, and I'll try it on you." He hung the white shirt on a cupboard knob and offered his arm. She reached for

143

his hand, turned it and placed a drop of frosting on the veins showing on his inner wrist. She sucked it off and looked up. "Well?"

He let out an appreciative sigh. "I didn't expect it to feel so good. Do it again."

She obliged, but the frosting was so sweet, she used only a dot. He wrapped his hand around hers as she kissed his wrist, and she looked up at him. "Maybe it's just the kisses, not the frosting that's making it feel so good."

The frosting forgotten, he pulled her close and kissed her. She tasted unusually sweet, but he still wanted more. "We'll have to be careful where we put it. Let's use a little more frosting just to make certain we don't need it."

She'd worn a short blue-green dress and turned for him to unzip it. They moved to the worktable. He held her hand while she stepped out of it and flung it toward the closest chair. She peeled off her black lace bra, dropped it on the table and put a dollop of frosting on a nipple. "Let's start here." He eased her into the chair and knelt between her legs to be at the right height. He sucked away the frosting, licked her other breast and tugged the rosy nipple gently between his teeth.

Leaning into him, she raked her fingers through his hair. They made magic together so easily, and she'd never have enough of him. "Hand me the frosting," she whispered. He reached for the can on the table. She put a smidgen on his earlobe, sucked it off and licked the tender hollow behind it. "Your ears are as handsome as the rest of you." She licked his other ear without bothering with frosting.

"Thank you." He put frosting in her navel and tongued it away to make her laugh. "Maybe we should always go this slowly." He pushed her knees farther apart and nuzzled his cheek against the smooth skin of her inner thigh.

"Take off my heels."

He pulled them off and set them aside. "I've never understood how a man can have a foot fetish when there are so many more delectable parts of a woman's body."

Now barefoot, she rubbed her toes along his erection. "Why are you still dressed?"

He gave her a quick kiss, stood and unbuckled his belt. He kicked off his loafers, took a condom from the pocket and discarded his slacks. He wore a pair of leopard-print briefs. "You have such pretty lingerie, and I didn't want you to grow bored with me."

"Impossible—but the leopard print suits you." She rose slowly and raked her fingernails lightly across his belly. He had great abs, and she caressed the hard muscles and outlining dips before sliding her hand lower to cup his familiar weight. "I appreciate the effort too." She reached for the can of frosting and put a dab on the hollow of his shoulder. She had given him only a couple of licks when he caught her waist, sat down and pulled her astride his lap.

She dipped her finger into the frosting and, with a seductive smile, licked it off. "Are you already tired of this game?"

"No, but I'm calling a time-out."

She eased his rock-hard cock from the slit in his briefs and rolled it between her hands. "Were you thinking of a quick break, or something longer?"

"About this long." He covered her hand with his, took a deep breath and rolled on the condom. He pulled her thong aside and guided himself into her.

She rose up on her tiptoes to take him deep and twisted on her way down to his lap. She rocked, but he held her waist to hold her still. His silver eyes had a smoldering glint, and she was always eager to play. She clenched her inner muscles to demand more.

"That isn't fair."

"Of course it is," she argued with another fluttering squeeze demanding he thrust.

He raised a hand to the back of her head and silenced her with a fevered kiss. She clung to his shoulders, rocking so he'd have to dive deep, and when he slid his hand between them to thumb her clit, she pulled him into a searing climax that melded their very souls. Locked in his arms, shivers of pleasure surged to her toes and the delicious sensation faded so slowly she floated in his embrace, completely and utterly sated.

In a lazy mood, she slid her fingers through the soft curls brushing his nape. He hadn't used the word love, and she wouldn't speak it first, but this was how it felt to be loved until she couldn't ask for more.

Friday, Alejandro had class work he couldn't avoid, and Ana didn't see him again until Saturday afternoon when he picked her up for Jaime's memorial service. He wore a whiskey-brown suit and striped tie, and she'd chosen a dark green wrap dress with a hemline brushing her knees. "We look appropriately sedate, don't we?" she greeted him.

"We do. I'm not fond of memorials, but I want to go to this one. There will be people weeping, but no one will confess to killing Jaime the way they'd do in the movies. Still, I'd like to see how everyone behaves."

"I'm curious too. Lieutenant Montoya will be there. Let's do whatever we can to avoid him."

"Gladly."

Gian Carlo had given them Galen Salazar's address, and Ana had left a message for the designer to let him know they'd be coming. When they arrived, Galen's wife, Lena, met them at the door. She wore a black sheath with a lace collar and had pulled her dark brown hair into such a tight bun she'd raised her eyebrows into a permanently surprised arch.

Ana gave her name and Alejandro's. Lena swept her with a critical glance and waved them on into the house without any effort to make them feel welcome. He whispered in Ana's ear, "Was she close to Jaime?"

"I've no idea who is close to whom anymore." There was a memorial book where guests signed their names, and they had to begin a new page to add theirs. There were folding chairs on the patio. They took two in the last row. Valeria waved from a seat at the front, and Ana pointed out other people she knew. Lourdes found a seat in the front. Ana was tempted to point her out to Alejandro and mention the Mallorca trip, but thought she better keep still. The seats were nearly filled when Gain Carlo dropped into the seat beside hers.

"I hope they get this over with quickly," he leaned close to whisper.

Alejandro reached for Ana's hand and laced his fingers in hers. She squeezed his hand and thought his effort to claim her was sweet rather than obnoxiously possessive. She watched Lieutenant Montoya move around the side of the patio. In a dark gray suit, he faded into the shadows near the wall. He appeared to be closely observing everyone who'd come. He nodded when their glances met, but she quickly looked away.

A man sat down next to Gian Carlo who looked like a bodybuilder, and his chair groaned under his weight. Montoya must have noticed him. She hadn't seen a blond man other than Gian Carlo, but thought she'd have a better chance to sight suspects when people were standing and talking later. No one had regarded her with an accusing stare, and she wondered who'd also been questioned by the police.

Galen's sister, a beautiful young woman with long, dark curls, began the memorial singing a hymn with a haunting melody. She had a soaring soprano, and when Alejandro's cell phone buzzed in his pocket, he looked horrified. He checked the number and, with a nod to Ana, carried the phone inside.

Another woman? Gian Carlo mouthed.

"Idiot," Ana whispered back at him. It was none of her business who'd called him, but she began to worry when he didn't quickly return. Friends were now going to the front to share their memories of Jaime. She wished she'd made a list of the jobs they'd done together to cite one. He'd always been easy to work with and professional, if she didn't count his recent request for nude shots.

Alejandro came in quietly and retook his seat. "My father has had a stroke, and my stepmother is hysterical. Will you take Ana home, Gian Carlo?"

"I'll be glad to."

Ana grabbed Alejandro's sleeve. "I want to go with you."

"Believe me, you don't want to meet Carlotta under these circumstances, and it might take several hours for the hospital to have the test results. My father argued about going there, so he can't be that ill. I'll call you when I can."

She let him go without argument, but she was apparently more worried about his father than he was. Maybe his stepmother was an alarmist, and he didn't expect anything the woman said to be accurate, but some people didn't recover from a stroke. If Alejandro had to give up his dream of becoming an architect to oversee the Ortiz family's shipping interests, she doubted anyone would be able to console him. Tears filled her eyes. She pulled a tissue from her purse to wipe them away.

"I didn't realize you were so close to Jaime," Gian Carlo

murmured.

"We were dear friends," she responded. When there was an opening for her to go up and speak, she praised Jaime's talents as a photographer with sincere enthusiasm. Inspired by her remarks, Gian Carlo told about a shoot he recalled and how much Jaime's respect for the models had meant to him.

"That was lovely," Ana told him when he returned to his seat.

"I meant it," he insisted.

A photographer who'd known Jaime from his war days told a frightening story of how they'd gotten cut off from the troops in Iraq and had to crawl back to camp after dark, certain they'd be mistaken for insurgents. All had ended well that night, but he missed Jaime's friendship deeply.

Galen's sister closed the memorial with another song. While Ana told her how much she enjoyed her voice, Lieutenant Montoya appeared at her shoulder. "Mr. Campos had a lot of friends," he remarked.

"Don't you?" Ana asked before she could catch herself.

"Perhaps, but I won't be able to count them at my memorial service. Is there anyone here who seems out of place?"

Ana refrained from mentioning him, but nodded toward two well-built men who might possibly be bodybuilders. "There are people here I don't recognize, but those two might have been the S&M models."

"I noticed them and plan to question them when they leave rather than disrupt the memorial. By the way, Robles and Mesa toured local gyms but failed to learn anything significant. As for today, I thought your remarks were especially touching."

"Thank you. They were sincere." She saw Gian Carlo on the opposite side of the patio, apparently staying out of the lieutenant's reach, and hurriedly covered a yawn.

"A late night?" Montoya asked.

"Yes, and a very enjoyable one. Will you excuse me?" She turned away before he could object and circled the crowd to reach the refreshment table. There were plates of cookies, small cakes, and candies along with wine and lemonade. She took a cup of lemonade and sipped it while she scanned the group. Valeria and Lourdes were talking with a male model Ana worked with occasionally. Apparently the three were close friends. With a lean build, he didn't look suspicious, and in the soft-spoken crowd, no one appeared to be hiding murderous intentions. She made her way to Gian Carlo, who now stood alone.

"I'm ready to leave whenever you are," she confided.

"Now would be fine with me. Let's tell Galen and his wife good-bye."

Galen winced as they approached him, but Ana focused on his wife. "This was such a nice memorial for Jaime. Thank you so much for hosting it."

Lena looped her arm through her husband's before she nodded to acknowledge the compliment. "Let's hope we won't have another such sad occasion anytime soon."

Gian Carlo agreed and took Ana's hand as they left the patio by the side gate. He opened the door of his MG for her and looked back at the house. "Why do you suppose Galen married her?"

She waited for him to get into the driver's seat. "Maybe her father had the money to finance his first collection, or they fell madly in love when neither had a dime."

He turned the key in the ignition and revved the engine. "Whatever the reason, we can say we were here. Is there anywhere you'd like to stop on the way home?"

A long walk would have been so nice with Alejandro, but she'd had enough of Gian Carlo's company. "Thank you, but I've things to do at home. Don't you?"

"Sure, but I do my best to avoid them. What's your next job?"

There was no news on the Almodóvar film, but she wouldn't have mentioned it if there were. "I'm working with a French shoe designer, Lamoreaux. He wants only my legs, however."

Turning left, he looked toward her. "You do have great legs. Oh hell."

He'd taken the turn too fast, and Ana grabbed for the dashboard to brace herself. He wrestled with the wheel. The tires screamed for purchase, and the sports car skidded out of control. She saw a bright flash of blue sky.

Orlando Ortiz had been rushed to the hospital closest to his home, and, certain a moment of garbled speech wasn't serious, he was an extremely poor patient. He submitted to a CT scan under duress, but no blockage or bleeding was found in his brain. "I told you there was no reason for alarm."

His doctor disagreed. "You probably had a TIA, or transient ischemic attack. The symptoms your wife observed were real, but quickly passed. She was correct to insist you come to the hospital, however. I've warned you to quit smoking. Alcohol and a high-fat diet are also contributing factors in strokes. You need to make some changes in your habits soon. When was the last time you went on a vacation? Do you ever sail on one of your cruise liners?"

Thoroughly annoyed, Orlando shook his head. "I've no time to waste on vacations."

"Clearly you're a Type A personality. They believe they thrive on stress, but the opposite is true. They often die of massive strokes long before their time. You have young boys to consider. What about your eldest son? Is he any help to you?"

Orlando barely contained a rude snort. "He intends to be an architect and build homes for the poor. He's not interested in the business."

"That's unfortunate. I want to speak with your wife before you go, but you must regard today's episode as the warning it is and make your health a priority."

Orlando nodded, and checked his watch, eager to go.

Alejandro found his stepmother in the emergency waiting room. She was a petite woman with henna-tinted hair and several years too young to be his mother. They were polite to each other but had never really bonded. He sat down beside her. "How is he?"

Carlotta grabbed his hand. "He always knows everything, but when I couldn't understand him, I told him slurred speech is a bad sign, and I refused to wait for him to get worse. His doctor met us here and is seeing him now."

She'd always been devoted to his father. Alejandro gave her hand a comforting squeeze. "You were wise to make him come. I know it couldn't have been easy."

"Nothing is easy with such an obstinate man, but you know him."

That was the first critical word he'd ever heard her speak about his father. He nodded rather than add his own lengthy list of complaints. He recognized the doctor approaching them and stood with her.

"I have good news." The physician explained his findings and the warnings he'd given Orlando.

Alejandro understood his description of a TIA, but Carlotta had multiple concerns. "I make sure my husband eats healthy food at home, but he goes out with his friends and orders thick steaks. He doesn't smoke around our boys, but he smokes in his office. I've no idea how much he drinks. It must be too much."

The doctor laid his hand on her shoulder. "He's the one who has to see the value of changing his habits. Compliment him when he does and ignore his poor choices. You can't control his behavior and shouldn't try. There's no reason to keep him here. He'll be ready to go home in a minute."

As the physician walked away, Carlotta looked up at Alejandro. "He's going to argue he didn't need to come here, but he really did."

"He should be grateful you're looking after him so well."

She shrugged. "He's grateful for some things but not others. Thank you for coming so quickly."

"Call whenever you need me." Alejandro stayed until his father was ready to leave, but Orlando looked more annoyed than pleased to see him.

"I'm fine," Orlando insisted. "You didn't need to leave your studies to come here. I don't want you to get behind and not graduate with your class since it's so important to you."

Carlotta rolled her eyes, and Alejandro understood why. His father intended to control everything and everyone he could, or die trying. They'd come in an ambulance, and he drove them home but quickly told them good-bye. Before Alejandro pulled his SUV out into traffic, he called to see if Ana had gotten home. Gian Carlo answered her phone. He was crying so hard Alejandro couldn't understand him. "Take a deep breath and tell me what's wrong."

Gian Carlo gave an audible gulp as he swallowed hard. "There's been an accident. We're at L'Esperanza." His voice broke. "Ana's hurt, and you need to hurry."

Alejandro cursed under his breath. He'd thought he could trust Gian Carlo to see Ana home safely, but if she'd been hurt, he'd blame himself. "Calm down. How badly is she hurt?"

"Badly! And it's my fault."

Alejandro broke the connection and sped to L'Esperanza. The hospital treated accident victims, and Ana would receive excellent emergency care, but he damned himself the whole way for foolishly leaving her behind when she'd wanted to come with him.

He walked into the second emergency room for the day and found Gian Carlo huddled in the corner, hugging Ana's purse. There wasn't a mark on him. He sat down beside him. "Are you trying to tell me Ana is dead?"

"No," Gian Carlo exclaimed, his blue eyes growing huge. "She's alive. I rode with her in the ambulance. She hit her head and has a broken leg. Other things could be wrong, I don't know. The doctor hasn't come out to talk to me yet."

Alejandro shoved himself back in his chair and folded his arms over his chest. "If you have Ana's phone, did you call her mother?"

"I didn't even think of it, and I don't want to terrify her. Maybe things aren't as bad as they looked."

Alejandro felt sick. "It sounds as though they might be worse. Tell me how it happened with every detail."

Gain Carlo shook his head as though he could clear away the bloody mental images. "We were talking about work. I took a corner too fast, lost control and hit a light pole. People came running to help. An ambulance was there in minutes. Ana was unconscious. She didn't feel anything."

Alejandro could easily imagine the red MG wrapped around a light pole and Ana lying crushed in the wreckage. It sickened him clear through. There had to be something he could do to help her. "If Ana's unconscious, and her mother is in France, I'm going to say I'm her next of kin. Don't dispute me on it. I'll make whatever decisions need to be made until she can make them on her own."

Gian Carlo looked around to make sure no one was seated close enough to overhear and still whispered, "You're not her husband."

Alejandro gave him a vicious glance and silenced that argument. "The hospital won't know it, will they? We kept our marriage a secret so it wasn't in the tabloids. Ana will be able to speak for herself when she comes to, but if anything has to be decided before she does, I'll do it. Now give me her purse. You look ridiculous sitting here hugging it like a doll."

Gian Carlo wiped his nose on his sleeve. "It was down by her feet, so her phone and camera weren't smashed."

Alejandro reached for the bag, but the side was wet where Ana's blood had soaked through. Sickened, he set it on the floor by his feet. "If we lose Ana, I'll kill you."

"Don't bother, I'll kill myself. She was so beautiful. She didn't deserve this. I should have been the one hurt. I've never been in an accident. Never. I wasn't drinking either. I was cold sober, just stupid and driving too fast."

Alejandro didn't argue with him. They drank coffee from a vending machine and regretted it. They'd been waiting nearly two hours when a pretty young woman in a white coat came their way. They rose and stepped toward her.

She directed her first question to Gian Carlo. "I'm Dr. Pallares. Are you Miss Santillan's brother?"

"No, just a good friend. This is her husband."

Alejandro gave his name with his usual pride, but Dr. Pallares frowned slightly. "I hadn't heard Ana Santillan had married, of course, I don't follow popular culture as closely as some people do."

Alejandro lowered his voice. "It was a quiet ceremony, and we hadn't announced it to the public as yet. How is she?"

"Come with me, I'll show you her X-rays."

Alejandro brought Ana's bag. Gian Carlo tagged along behind them. They were led to an empty treatment room where the physician put the X-rays on display. "Her lower right leg was broken in three places. An orthopedist will insert a rod through the center of the tibia to hold the bones in alignment. It will take several weeks to heal, but with time for rehabilitation, she should still be able to strut a runway gracefully. I do need your signature, Mr. Vasquez." She had a clipboard with the proper forms, and he scanned them hurriedly before signing.

"Thank you. Ana suffered a concussion, and she'll recover with rest. A plastic surgeon will repair the cut in her head. It sliced through her cheek, but again, with time to heal, she'll be as beautiful as ever."

"May I see her?" Alejandro asked.

"She's being prepped for surgery, so you'll have to wait until she's in the recovery room. You'd be more comfortable at home. I'll give you a call when she's out of surgery."

Alejandro shook his head. "My wife wouldn't leave me. I'll stay."

"If you insist." Dr. Pallares directed him to the waiting room on the surgery floor.

"I can't leave either," Gian Carlo explained and followed him. The small waiting room had more comfortable furnishings than the one in the emergency department, but neither man could relax.

Alejandro paced while Gian Carlo sat and shifted his position every other minute. "Do you suppose the cafeteria makes milkshakes?" he asked.

Sick with dread, Alejandro shook his head. "How can you think about food?"

"Milkshakes aren't food, are they?"

"Yes, they are, but what does it matter? Go look for whatever you want."

"Do you want me to bring you one? Milk has soothing qualities. It's why people drink warm milk when they can't sleep."

Alejandro doubted he'd ever sleep again. "I'd only throw it against the wall." He remembered licking frosting off Ana's delectable body and had to sit down and rest his head in his hands. He ought to call her agent and Fatima, but he couldn't find the necessary will. The same worry spun in his brain—if he hadn't left Ana at Galen's, she wouldn't have been hurt. No matter how guilty Gian Carlo felt, Alejandro would always feel a thousand times worse. He'd known Ana only a month, but calling her his wife had been so easy. Their sudden marriage would only last until she woke. She'd probably be too sore to laugh, but she'd want to, and he'd have to pretend she hadn't broken his heart.

Gian Carlo drank his milkshake in the cafeteria and fell asleep in his chair soon after rejoining Alejandro. Unable to sit still, Alejandro paced the long corridor with his hands clasped behind his back and his eyes focused on the shiny linoleum tile. He avoided glancing toward the clock in the waiting room each time he passed. He thought it cruel to post the time where frantic family members and friends had to wait hours for news of their loved ones and a second stretched forever.

He'd never considered medicine as a career, but he wished he knew more. He doubted a ballerina could easily regain her former strength and agility after suffering a badly broken leg. It would probably take months to recover, maybe more than a year. Dr. Pallares was either overly optimistic or admired Ana too highly to admit they couldn't magically heal her injuries.

He found a wrapped mint in his jacket pocket and ate it. A patient was wheeled out of an OR at the end of the corridor, bound for the recovery room, but it wasn't Ana. Bored walking the silent corridor, he sat down opposite Gian Carlo in the waiting room and stretched out his legs.

The model opened his eyes. "Any news?"

Alejandro shook his head.

Gian Carlo shoved himself out of his chair. "Want some hot chocolate? I'm going to get some."

"Just bring me a bottle of water."

"I'll bring two."

Gian Carlo reminded him of an overgrown puppy, desperate to please. He closed his eyes and woke with a start when Gian Carlo rushed in and turned on the television set suspended on the wall.

"The accident is on the news. I saw it downstairs." The next story was up, and he cursed. "I didn't get up here on time. They had photos from the scene."

Alejandro opened a bottle of water and took a long drink. "You don't want me to see those."

"I'm just warning you what to expect. The paparazzi have to be gathered outside, hoping for a chance to get in."

"The hospital must have security."

"Of course they do." Gian Carlo turned off the television and sipped his cup of hot chocolate. "How long do you think Ana will have to stay here?"

"Not long. I'll move her to a private hospital as soon as she can be released."

"Do you ever have to worry about money?"

Alejandro failed to respond. He knew absolutely nothing about private hospitals, but he wanted somewhere Ana wouldn't be pestered by paparazzi and tabloid journalists eager for a story. He'd have to find a place celebrities chose for the security. Someplace with lovely rooms and a peaceful view. He was uncertain what to do until he realized he could provide everything she'd need on a cruise ship. It was the perfect answer. She couldn't work, so she'd have no reason not to go on a cruise. On board one of their ships, he'd make her recovery as pleasant as he possibly could.

When the orthopedist entered the waiting room, he looked as tired as Alejandro felt. The physician sat on the arm of an upholstered chair. "Everything went well, but it was a bad break. The plastic surgeon has worked on Ana's cuts. She's being taken to recovery and won't be awake until tomorrow morning. Go on home and come back for visiting hours."

"Even if I have to look through a window, I need to see her tonight," Alejandro insisted.

"I'll wait here," Gian Carlo offered.

The weary orthopedist rose slowly. "I'll give you one minute, that's all."

Alejandro did have to stand at the window at the end of the room, but Ana was in the closest bed. She'd have been unrecognizable to others, but even with her head bandaged, he knew her. A nurse stood on the other side of the bed adjusting an IV drip and smiled when she saw him.

He sagged against the wall. "I'll go."

The doctor grasped his shoulder. "Patients' families faint so often I've become good at catching them. Go back to the waiting room and rest before you drive home."

Alejandro nodded, but what he really wanted to do was return to the lounge and strangle Gian Carlo. Perhaps anticipating such a threat, the model had disappeared. Ana's bag sat on the table beside the model's chair. Taking the orthopedist's advice, Alejandro sank into his chair and leaned back. When he felt better, he'd go home, but he ached clear through that all he could take with him for comfort was Ana's bloody bag.

Chapter Eleven

Alejandro returned to L'Esperanza the next morning looking as haggard as when he'd left. He'd showered, shaved and put on clean clothes, but it hadn't improved his dark mood. He entered from the parking garage to avoid any paparazzi lurking at the front entrance. If the TV news had photos of the accident, they had to be in the tabloids, but he refused to look when seeing Ana so badly injured was pure torture. He carried the bouquet of yellow roses he'd bought on the way and went to the main desk to ask for Ana's room number.

The receptionist smiled apologetically. "I'm sorry, but only family members are allowed to see her. I'll have the roses sent to her room."

"I'm her husband," he argued persuasively. "Dr. Pallares will tell you who I am."

Appearing convinced by his earnest manner, the receptionist checked her computer screen. She wrote Ana's room number on a slip of paper and passed it to him.

He glanced at the paper and slipped it into his pocket as he entered the elevator. The door to Ana's room was ajar, and a nurse was with her. "May I come in?"

"Please do. I'm Maja, Ana's nurse today. Please put your vase of pretty roses on the windowsill with the other flowers."

He saw Santos Aragon's name on a gorgeous mix of pink roses and carnations. Ana had mentioned Miguel, but never his son, Santos. Alejandro wondered just how well acquainted the two were, but it was another worry he didn't need. Paul Perez had sent a leafy philodendron. Rather than search the other bouquets for cards with men's names, he turned away.

"Use the call button if you need me," Maja offered on her way out.

"Thank you." Alejandro stood beside the bed, uncertain what to do. Ana needed rest to get well, but he longed to tease her awake with gentle kisses. When her lashes fluttered and she opened her eyes, he reached for her hand. "I'm so sorry I left you yesterday."

She blinked, rubbed her eyes and stopped when she felt the bandage covering her right cheek. "You're all blurry, but that's my fault rather than yours. What happened? Did the ancient elevator in your building crash with us inside?"

"You don't remember the accident?" She looked so fragile and pale, and spoke slowly as though she were underwater. He'd thought he couldn't be more disappointed in himself for leaving her, but the torment became even more painfully deep.

"Obviously not," she breathed out through a yawn.

Maja entered, carrying a bouquet of daisies. "I'm glad to see you're awake. These are from Valeria." She fit the vase into the last open space on the windowsill. "I'll bring you some broth to make you feel better."

"I doubt it." Ana raised her hand to touch the bandages encircling her head. "Why am I wrapped up like a mummy?"

Alejandro pulled the visitor's chair over to the bed. He described the accident as briefly as he possibly could and glossed over her injuries without admitting he'd been scared to death he'd lose her.

"What happened to Gian Carlo?" she asked.

"Other than emotional distress, nothing. He was here with me last night. It's probably better you don't recall anything after Jaime's memorial."

She licked her lips and frowned. "Give me a minute."

He pulled her hand to his lips. "I have all day."

"Won't they make you leave soon? Can you make out the time on the clock over the door?"

He followed her glance. "It's midmorning, but they won't ask me to keep my visit short. I told them I was your next of kin."

"Like a brother?"

"No. I told them I'm your husband."

Astonished, she raised her left hand. "Where's my ring? I don't remember marrying you, but you must have given me a ring."

Before he could explain, Maja returned with the bowl of soup on a tray. She placed it on the rolling table at the end of the bed, pressed the bed control button to raise Ana's head, and rolled the table close to her. She handed her a spoon. "Try and swallow it all."

Ana's hand shook, and she dropped the spoon. "Maybe I should just drink it."

Alejandro picked up the bowl. "I'll help you."

"I wish all my patients had such thoughtful husbands. It makes my job so much easier. I'll check on you again soon."

Ana rested her hands on his and took a couple of sips of the broth. "This doesn't have any taste. Try it and you'll see."

He did. "It's warm and liquid. You must need liquids."

She swallowed a little more. "That's enough. Now let me think what I do remember."

He put the bowl back on the tray and rolled the table out of her way. "You know me."

"Alejandro something. Was I going to use your name?"

He'd not thought she'd actually believe they were married, but he couldn't see any harm in the convenient lie for the time being. "No, of course not. Everyone knows you as Ana Santillan."

"I can't remember a wedding. Did my mother come?"

"No. We planned to have another wedding in Rouen. We haven't told her yet. I haven't called her about your accident either, and I should." He pulled her phone from his pocket. "The accident has been on the news. You're well-known in France, and I wouldn't want her to hear about it before we call."

"What should I say?" She plucked the top sheet.

Clearly she'd been shaken up by the accident, but he hadn't expected her to be so apprehensive about making a phone call.

"Tell her you're fine and then mention the accident. You broke your leg and won't be dancing for a while, but she doesn't need to come and take care of you. Promise to visit her soon." He scanned the names in her phone, found her mother's and handed her the phone.

She held it in shaky hands. "I'm fine, broken leg and I'll see her soon."

"That's it." He held his breath, but the conversation with her mother went more smoothly than he'd dared hope. "Tell her you'll call her again soon."

She nodded, but first asked about her stepfather. "I can't wait to taste his new recipes. Love you." She handed him her phone. "Will you

159

keep it for me?"

"I will. The *Mediterranean Siren* is in port this week, and as soon as you're released, you'll be more comfortable there than at home. We need to call Fatima." He again scrolled through the names on her phone. "Do you want me to talk to her?"

"Fatima will be worried, won't she?" She covered another yawn. "I'll call her. What should I say?"

He'd never seen her unable to handle her side of a conversation, but with her vision blurry and her memory hazy, he couldn't fault her. "Tell her you're fine and ask about the kittens."

"Kittens?" She closed her eyes and frowned. "Are they black or white?"

"One of each. Romeo and Juliet."

"I remember them now. Maybe all I need is a little push. Call her and give me the phone."

He did and walked over to smell the flowers perfuming the room. Ana had to reassure Fatima several times, but eventually convinced her she was doing well. She promised to call her every day.

He came back to the bed to take the phone. "Can you smell the flowers? Santos Aragon sent pink roses and carnations. Do you know him well?"

A bright blush filled her cheeks. "Santos? That's a long story, and I'd fall asleep before I finished."

"So you do remember him?" He hated himself for asking about Santos when the story was clearly more than he wished to hear.

She licked her lips. "I remember you. Is there some water?" He held the cup, and she drank from the straw. "Thank you. Don't you have to be somewhere?"

He set the cup on the nightstand and took her hand. "I've finished most of what I had to do for the university."

"You should go finish the rest," she mumbled sleepily. "Did you say you brought me flowers?"

"Yellow roses." He pulled one from the vase and gave it to her. "Can you smell it?"

"I love yellow roses." She brushed it against her cheek. "I'd like to go to sleep. You needn't sit and watch. Come back later, if you like."

Being casually dismissed hurt, but he did have things that had to be done. First of all, he'd buy her a wedding ring.

It was after two when he returned with fresh strawberries and peaches she could eat without needing a bowl or spoon. "I washed them. Try a strawberry and tell me how it tastes."

She rolled a strawberry from the container between her fingers and bit off the pointed tip. She licked juice from her lips. "This is delicious. Thank you for bringing them. Maybe I'll feel like eating more later."

He put the fruit on the rolling table at the end of her bed. "I'll bring anything you'd like."

"You're so sweet, but I just don't feel like eating. I'll be better tomorrow."

Alejandro feared it might take much longer for her to feel like herself. He pulled the plain gold band from his pocket and slid it on her finger. He'd guessed at her size, and luckily, it fit perfectly. "We hadn't told anyone we'd gotten married, so you weren't wearing your ring."

She twisted it on her finger. "How could I have forgotten getting married? Did we take photos?"

She had him there. "No, we intended to have a proper wedding later. Can you remember going to the memorial for Jaime?"

She closed her eyes. "Maja said this is Sunday, and I try to count back, but my thoughts won't go in a straight line."

"Please don't worry." He kissed her forehead but hid how frightened he'd been, and still was.

Lieutenant Montoya rapped lightly on the door and looked in. "Good, you're both here."

Ana looked up at Alejandro with a fearful gaze. "It's Lieutenant Montoya, Ana," he responded. He held her hand to cover the ring. "I hope you've no more questions."

Montoya gave an apologetic nod. "It's an inopportune time, I know, but things must be covered. Can you tell me something about the accident? Were you being followed? Did Mr. Maxim turn to escape a pursuit?"

Tears filled Ana's eyes. "I don't know what happened. You'll have to ask Gian Carlo."

"I'm so sorry to upset you, but we've been unable to locate him," Montoya replied. "His MG is totaled, and he must provide an accident report, but he left the scene of the accident in the ambulance with you and has disappeared."

"He hasn't disappeared," Alejandro countered. "He was here at the hospital until Ana got out of surgery. He didn't mention being chased. He would have told me had it happened."

Montoya took out his notebook and pen. "When did you last see him?"

"I was trying not to look at the clock, but it was late last night. I thought he'd gone home."

"He didn't return home last night."

"Girlfriend," Ana whispered.

Alejandro squeezed her hand. "He'd wrecked his MG, so he must have called someone to give him a ride home. Maybe he stayed at her home rather than his own."

"Ah yes, it's a possibility. He should surface soon. I need for you to look at some photos from the memorial service. You left rather early, and there were a couple of men who arrived later. It's possible you know them."

"Why didn't you ask them their names?" Alejandro inquired.

Montoya's smile slid into a predatory smirk. "I did, of course, but that doesn't mean the ones they supplied or wrote in the memorial book were accurate." He pulled a manila envelope from his coat pocket and shook out the candid photos taken at the memorial. "Do either of these men look familiar?"

Alejandro slid Ana's hand under the covers to hide her ring before he reached for them. "Ana suffered a concussion and her vision isn't clear yet, so she'll need a few days before she can identify anyone from a photo. They don't look familiar to me, though." He returned the photos to Montoya. "Maybe someone else at the memorial knows them."

"Perhaps." The lieutenant did not look pleased. "How are you, Miss Santillan? I was so sorry to learn you'd been hurt on your way home from the memorial."

"How do I look?" she asked.

Alejandro tried not to laugh, but that was the Ana he knew. "As you can see, she's doing very well for the injuries she sustained. She needs to rest, though, so please don't stay long."

Apparently losing interest, Montoya moved toward the door. "I've stayed long enough, Mr. Vasquez. Good afternoon to you both."

Ana closed her eyes. Alejandro thought she'd fallen sleep, but after Montoya closed the door, she looked up at him. "I don't like him, do I?"

"No, not at all. He's working on Jaime Campos's murder. Do you remember Jaime?"

"Please hand me another strawberry. Thank you." She ate it in small bites. "Someone killed him. What a waste. He was an excellent photographer. What could have happened to Gian Carlo? Does he blame himself for the accident?"

"It was his fault, and he readily admitted it, so I doubt he'd hide." He turned as Dr. Pallares came to the door.

"Good afternoon," she said. "I'm happy to see you're awake, Ana. May I speak with you privately, Mr. Vasquez?"

"Are you in trouble?" Ana whispered.

"I hope not." He stepped out into the hall and followed Dr. Pallares to a secluded spot in the hallway around the corner. "What's wrong? I thought Ana was doing as well as could be expected."

The physician stuck her hands into her coat pockets. "She is. We ran several tests when she came in yesterday, and one will show if a woman is pregnant even before she knows it herself."

Afraid he knew what was coming, he braced his hand against the wall. "Are you saying she's pregnant?"

"Yes, but she'd not have missed a period yet. After being so badly injured in the accident, she could miscarry. I think it would be a kindness if we didn't mention the possibility of a baby just yet. Were you two hoping to have children?"

Dumbfounded, he didn't know how to respond. Ana had said she would have married Miguel Aragon had he lived, but they'd never talked about marriage or children as a general subject of conversation. He had no idea what she'd want. Hell, they weren't married in the first place, and he'd gotten himself in much too deep. "Don't most couples want to have children?"

"Some do and some don't. You're both young, and I thought you might want to postpone becoming parents."

He straightened up. "Let's concentrate on getting Ana well, and then we'll talk about having babies."

"Whatever you wish, but I wanted you to know the truth. I don't usually keep things from my patients. Ana is bruised from head to toe, and with the pain meds, she might not make a decision she'd be comfortable with later. I doubted you'd want that to happen."

"No, of course not. Thank you for telling me first." He waited in the hallway while she went in to see Ana. He continued to feel sick that she'd been hurt so badly, but she'd shown him a glimpse of her usual feisty sparkle. A broken leg would impact her career, although she could pose for ads seated, if the scar on her cheek healed to a faint scar. She'd balked when he'd urged her to pursue photography, so apparently she wasn't ready to retire from modeling. Or she hadn't been prior to the accident.

Where a baby fit into her life, he didn't know. She could hire a nanny, but somehow, he thought she'd want to raise a child herself. *If* she wanted to raise a child. Sometimes condoms failed, so he thought he was the likely father. He'd assumed she took the pill like most young women he'd dated, apparently not. He swallowed hard. He'd claimed to be her husband, but there was a huge difference between that ruse and being slammed in the gut with fatherhood.

Chapter Twelve

After Dr. Pallares left, Alejandro looked in on Ana, but her eyes were closed, and he wouldn't disturb her. He called Fatima before leaving the hospital. She'd gone to Ana's condo to feed the kittens and wanted him to come and tell her everything Ana hadn't disclosed.

The kittens rushed to him as he came through the door. He scooped them up and scratched behind their ears before setting them down. "They're getting big. Did Ana really think she'd find a good home for them?"

"At first, I believe so. But I don't want to talk about Romeo and Juliet. Would you like some coffee?"

"Yes, please." He'd grown up with servants, but Fatima was far more than a housekeeper to Ana, and she might know important things he didn't. She was dressed in a navy blue dress, probably the one she'd worn to church. They took chairs at the dining table rather than move into the living room, and she brought a plate of lemon cookies along with the coffee mugs.

"These are Ana's favorites."

"Give me a bag, and I'll take some to her."

The housekeeper studied him closely. "You look as though you haven't slept. Now tell me the truth. How is Ana?"

She was right—he hadn't slept more than an hour or two last night, if that. The coffee was the best he'd tasted since his last visit there. He reached for a cookie. "I don't think she likes being fussed over."

"No, not at all. Now stop stalling."

He smiled at her gentle scolding. "She can't remember the accident." He gave her a brief summary of Ana's injuries and didn't make them sound less serious than they were. "It's going to be a long while before she can walk a runway. Makeup artists will be able to cover the scar on her cheek, but by the time she's well, she could have lost interest in modeling."

Fatima pulled a tissue from her pocket and wiped the tears from her eyes. "This is just so awful and unfair. She's such a good person, she really is." Romeo jumped up on a chair and onto the table. She brushed him off. "The kittens are incorrigible."

"Of course they are; they're cats. I won't tell you not to worry, but Ana is receiving the best of care. When she's able to leave the hospital, I plan to take her on a cruise. She'll be much happier on board one of our ships than in a rehab facility, or here watching her favorite movie videos over and over."

Fatima offered a faint smile. "You really care for her, don't you?"

It was easy to admit. "Yes, I do, but we haven't been seeing each other long. Is there someone else she's also been dating who'd like to know how she's doing?"

Fatima's posture stiffened. She drew in a long breath and exhaled slowly. "Ana sees just one man at a time, Mr. Vasquez. She doesn't juggle her time between lovers."

He reached for her hand, but she pulled away. "I didn't mean to insult you, or Ana. She's a beautiful woman, and I thought she might have other men who cared for her."

She looked away. "She's not been seeing anyone since Miguel Aragon died last summer. She adored him. I met him once when he came by to pick her up, and he had, well, I suppose magnetism is the word. He was such a handsome man, and when he spoke to you, he made you feel as though you were the only person in the universe. Santos has his looks, but I doubt he can work the same magic with women."

Uncertain whether to be proud or appalled he had to be the father of Ana's child, he shifted in his chair. He knew he ought to confide in Fatima and admit to a sham marriage, and the real stunner, that Ana was pregnant, but since yesterday afternoon, things were moving too fast, and he couldn't find the words. "Would you please pack a suitcase for Ana for the cruise? She'd be able to wear long skirts and tops. I don't think she'd want her short dresses. I'll ask her when she's ready to leave the hospital to be sure, but you probably know what she'll need."

"I'll have everything ready. A cruise will be a good thing for her. Being on the sea will keep her from worrying too much about missing work."

"I hope so." He thanked her for the coffee and cookies and took some for Ana.

Ana was certain she ought to remember getting married, and she twisted the new gold ring on her finger. She liked Alejandro so much, and thought she might have married him and agreed to keep it a secret for a while. Perhaps they'd not wanted to announce the marriage while a murder investigation swirled around her. Wishing there was something more than a billowing fog in her brain, she struggled to recall details of her childhood and go from there. There had been pretty clothes, bright lights and cameras, but there had been so many years of the same routine, she couldn't separate one from the other. Her mother had kept a diary. She was sorry she hadn't had one of her own.

When Alejandro returned in early evening carrying a takeout bowl of vegetable stew, she was as elated as she could be with every part of her body aching. "Thank you, that smells so good. Clearly there are benefits to marrying you."

"Thank you. Few women can be seduced with vegetables, but I'm doing my best."

She couldn't see his face clearly, but thought he must be smiling. She slurped the stew from the container rather than fumble with the spoon. "Was I no challenge at all for you?"

"You were a challenge in every respect. A major point might have been that I'm taller than you."

"Are you calling me shallow?"

He pulled the visitor chair to her bedside. "Not at all. Can you remember when we met at El Gato?"

She closed her eyes to focus. "Wasn't I in my Goth Girl outfit?"

"Yes, and I didn't discover who you really were for, well, a while."

Before she'd eaten half the stew, she couldn't swallow another drop. "Do you want to finish this? It's really good, but I'm full."

"I brought some of Fatima's lemon cookies. Would you like one?"

She reached out her hand. "You went to see her? Is she frantic over this?"

He gave her the smallest of the cookies and used the spoon he'd brought to finish the stew. "She's worried, quite naturally, and I tried to reassure her. More importantly, I'm growing more fond of vegetables every day."

"I'm glad to hear it." She drew her lower lip through her teeth. "Alejandro, can we be serious for a minute?"

"You're in a hospital bed. How could we be more serious?"

She frowned and winced when her cheek hurt. "I'm in real trouble here. Modeling can be unpredictable, and I've money set aside to live on, but I'm not going to be able to work for a long time. With a broken leg, I can't even do Lamoreaux's shoe ads. I don't think I'll feel up to having sex any time soon either. If no one knows we're married, do you want to have it annulled?"

He got up to toss the empty container into the wastebasket in the corner. "There's more to a marriage than sex, Ana."

"I agree, but I don't want you to be disappointed, and you must be."

"What if I'd broken my leg cycling? Would you end the marriage?"

She ran her hands over the blanket. "No, that would be cruel, and silly when it doesn't take long for a broken bone to heal."

He came back to his chair and pulled her hand to his lips. He rubbed his thumb over her gold wedding band. "Let's just take each day as it comes rather than worry about what we'll do next week or next year. You needn't worry about money when I've got more than enough."

She squeezed his hand. "There's a big calendar in my home office where I keep track of jobs. I hate to think how long the days will be blank, as if I don't exist."

"Stop it. There's more to your life than work. We'll fill up the calendar with whatever you'd like to do."

"With whatever I *can* do," she amended. "I'm sorry not to be thinking more clearly. Will you come back tomorrow?"

He leaned over to kiss her. "Yes, I'll be here in the morning."

"Good. Leave the cookies. I'm sorry you'll have to sleep alone," she mumbled through a yawn.

"Me too. I keep forgetting to thank you for the postcard you sent from Mallorca. It came when I thought I'd never see you again, but I couldn't bear to throw it away."

"Should have told you something."

"It did. See you tomorrow." He kissed her once more before leaving.

By the time Alejandro arrived home, he was too weary to climb the stairs and took the moaning elevator. He made a quick call to his father before he fell asleep where he stood. "I wanted to check on you."

"I'm surprised you have the time. Ana Santillan's accident is in all the tabloids. Will she be as hideously scarred as they say?"

He sank onto the futon. "I'll tell you again, nothing in those papers is true. She'll be as beautiful as ever."

"With the damage her friend's MG sustained, I'm surprised she survived."

"I don't want to see the photos, but she'll be well soon. I'd like to take her on a cruise so she won't be stuck in a hospital bed. Did you hold your cabin on the *Siren*?"

A long moment passed before his father responded. "I did, but will Ana be well enough to sail?"

"She will. Would you give me a discount rate on the cabin?"

Orlando responded with a low chuckle. "How can I charge you when you want your pretty girlfriend to recuperate in comfort? Are you sure you'll like playing nurse?"

"There are medical personnel on board," Alejandro reminded him.

"I know who's on board. I pay their salaries," Orlando countered, his voice flavored with sarcasm. "Go ahead and use the cabin. All I'll ask is that you give me a report on the cruise."

"Thank you, but we're sure to be treated well."

"Look around at how everyone else is treated. We want our passengers to come back again and again. You know what I mean. Put on a steward's uniform and work undercover if you must."

"Yes, sir. I'll do what I can. Now, how are you?"

"I'm fine. Carlotta strives to be the perfect wife, and yesterday, she

169

went too far. The next time she calls, tell her you're sure a hospital visit isn't necessary."

His cautious stepmother might be right, and there could be dire consequences if his father's treatment was delayed. "I won't promise anything until she has a reason to call."

"She won't have a reason to call. That's the whole point. Now have a good time on your cruise and then cut Ana loose. You don't need to be saddled with an invalid."

"Neither does Carlotta. Good-bye." He was so angry he nearly threw the phone across the room. Ana would soon recover from her injuries, so she couldn't be described as an invalid. He lay back on the futon and rested his arm over his eyes. What if she had been so badly injured she couldn't walk again? He thought too much of her to abandon her even then. After all, he'd married her, hadn't he? With a baby coming, he'd have to arrange a legal marriage to have a say in the child's upbringing. He was positive he'd be a much better father to their child than his father had been to him. He promised himself he would.

When Alejandro arrived at L'Esperanza Monday morning, a new physician stood beside Ana's bed. "I'll wait outside."

"Please come in," Ana urged. "You'll tell me the truth even if Dr. Hibiscus won't." She held one of the bright red flowers in her hand.

The surgeon turned and nodded a welcome. He was of medium height with curly gray hair and a bright sparkle in his brown eyes. "Good morning. It's Dr. Higareda. I have hibiscus bushes covered with flowers and brought your wife one. I'm just changing her dressing, and while I'm known for my absolutely exquisite work, she won't believe me."

Alejandro came to the foot of her bed. He'd brought a bag of cakes from El Gato to tease her into eating breakfast. "Is your vision better today?"

"Sadly no. The whole world's still shimmering out of focus."

Dr. Higareda removed the bandage looped over her head and uncovered her cheek. He'd shaved a strip of her scalp before stitching the beginning of the cut, but the bald spot could be easily hidden by her long hair. The fine line of stitches extending across the apple of her cheek made Alejandro sick. Had the cut been an inch higher, she might have lost her eye. He took a firm grip on the foot rail to remain steady. "It looks good to me, Ana."

"Thank you," Dr. Higareda said. "I'll apply a light bandage, and you'll be fine for today."

"We'd like to leave on a cruise Friday. Will Ana be able to go?"

"Yes. I'll remove your stitches before you sail, my dear. My wife and I went on a cruise on an Ortiz ship a couple of years ago. It was the best vacation we've ever taken. We should go again."

Alejandro expected Ana to reveal he was part of the Ortiz family, but she didn't give it away. He'd picked up some unsolicited praise for the cruise line to report to his father, if he ever spoke to him again.

Later, they were eating the little nut cakes when Ana's cell phone chimed. Alejandro pulled it from his pocket. "It's Fatima. Do you feel well enough to talk with her again?" When Ana reached for her phone, he held back. "Don't mention we're married. It's our secret, remember?"

"No, I don't remember," she reminded him, but she found a cheerful voice for Fatima. "The food here isn't nearly as good as yours, but Alejandro is sneaking in my favorites. How are Romeo and Juliet?"

New flower deliveries had been placed on a table against the wall, and the room smelled like a lush greenhouse. He leaned over his yellow roses on the windowsill to watch the traffic in the street below. The day moved on with a restless rhythm and an occasional strident horn blast, but with no regard for last weekend's casualties.

The doctors and nurses referred to him as Ana's husband. He'd grown used to it, but apparently they were discreet and hadn't called a tabloid. He hoped their marriage would remain a secret awhile longer. Once they got to sea, they'd have the calm and quiet they'd need to make plans for themselves and for a family. He laughed to himself at the thought the tabloids might have been alerted, but couldn't find any proof he and Ana had wed and weren't publishing the story. He didn't expect anything in the way of ethics from the tabloid press, but for once, they were proving useful. As for his own ethics, he was only doing what was best for Ana. He assured himself it couldn't be wrong.

Ana ended the call and left her phone in her lap. "I told her to spend her time with the widows in the building who need company. I'd hoped to invite them all for an afternoon tea, but it will have to wait until after the cruise. I hope I'll feel better by Friday. I'd hate to spend our time at sea in bed."

He pulled up the visitor's chair. "I thought you already felt better. Are you in a lot of pain?"

She still had an IV drip and nodded toward it. "They're keeping me on painkillers, but it's difficult to move without something hurting. At least I'm not dead. Now what do you suppose has happened to Gian Carlo?"

"You have his number on your phone. Why not call him?"

"You'll have to find his number for me." He did, and Gian Carlo answered on the first ring. "Hi, where have you been, Gian Carlo? Haven't you had time to come visit me?" she asked.

"Ana! Oh God, I'm so sorry. If you're well enough to talk, please forgive me."

"It was an accident. Montoya is looking for you. You need to file an accident report."

"He scares me. My insurance company is handling the accident, and I'm staying with Lourdes until someone's been arrested for killing Jaime."

Ana smiled at Alejandro. "You might have a long stay."

"I hope not. Now tell me how you are."

She covered her phone. "How am I?"

"Tell him you're in pitiful shape and going on a cruise to forget the accident ever happened."

She repeated the message. "I'll talk to you when I come home." She ended the call. "I should call Paul too." She waited for him to find the number. "Hi, Paul. I'm doing well. Thank you for the plant. I'm going on a cruise with Alejandro and will be gone next week and don't want you to worry about me."

She again covered the phone. "He asked if we're going on a honeymoon. Does he know we got married?"

Alejandro shook his head. "He couldn't know."

"It's just a cruise, Paul. Have you spoken with Lamoreaux? Right now, I've only one good leg to use for a shoe ad, so he should hire someone else." Ana said good-bye and handed Alejandro the phone. "As always, Paul is focused on my career. As long as I have a head and can smile, he advises me to work. Apparently Lamoreaux is so enchanted with me, he still wants me to do his shoe ad even if I have only one foot. Can you find a wheelchair and get me out of here for a while?"

He stood and swung the chair aside. "Do you really feel up to it?"

"I don't know. We'll see."

He found Maja at the nurse's station. "Is it too soon for Ana to use a wheelchair?"

"We could give it a try." Maja found a chair and rolled it into Ana's room. She moved the rolling IV stand out of their way. "Ready for a little adventure?"

"I just want out of this bed." Ana tried to sit up and fell back. "Give me a minute."

"I'll wait," the nurse replied. "Take a couple of deep breaths, and we'll move you to the chair."

With her leg in the cast, Ana could barely shift position, but with Maja's help, she eased herself onto the side of the bed, and Alejandro scooped her up and into the wheelchair.

She sat back and scrunched her eyes closed. "I'm sorry, but I'm too dizzy to do this."

"Wait a minute," Maja urged. "Let the room stop spinning around you."

Ana frowned and shook her head. "I need to go back to bed."

"I'll help you," Alejandro offered, and with a gentle grasp, he placed her on the bed. "You'll feel better tomorrow."

She settled against her pillows. "We'll see. Just go home. You needn't come back again today."

"Gian Carlo recommends milkshakes. I'll go down to the cafeteria and get you one. What would you like, chocolate or vanilla?"

She reached out to catch his hand and gave him a fond squeeze. "Some things you can't fix, Alejandro, and you needn't try. Please just go on home."

He looked to the nurse, but she just shrugged and rolled out the wheelchair. "All right, I'll go, but have Maja call me if you need anything."

"Go live your life. I'll be fine."

"My life's right here." He leaned down to kiss her and drank up her spicy taste. He took care not to overwhelm her with affection and left the bag of little cakes in her lap. Too concerned for her to be wary, he left the building for the parking garage and walked right into a ring of paparazzi.

"Mr. Ortiz! Is it true you've married Ana Santillan?"

Another shouted, "Is she dying?"

"No, she's not," he answered, and immediately regretted it when the half dozen camera-toting men lunged closer. He pushed his way through them and made his way to his SUV, but he was disgusted with himself for believing he could call her his wife and not have it reach the tabloid hounds. Ana believed she was his wife, so the so-called news in a tabloid wouldn't hurt her. Then he remembered his father. "Oh hell."

Ana wasn't sure if it was the lingering effect of the concussion or Alejandro's delicious kisses, but she felt warm all over. He smelled so good, and his tender kisses were most welcome, not affection she'd rather avoid. Everything about the man drew her close. The way he'd caress her hand or touch her hair—it was all comfortingly familiar, as though they'd been together for years rather than a few weeks. She thought it was a few weeks, but nothing was certain right now.

Tuesday morning, Libby had everything ready for her first-period class when Joe Taylor, who taught boys' physical education at the American high school, entered the gym. Tall and slim with bright red hair, he was always in motion. He waved a tabloid. "Do you believe this? Ana Santillan is dying, and she's married the heir to the Ortiz shipping fortune. I've been in love with her since I was sixteen. I don't know which is worse, that she's near death or that she's married someone else."

"May I see it, please?" Libby took the paper and quickly scanned the brief article. "Santos sent her flowers, but I didn't think the accident left her that badly injured. Maggie and I talked with her a couple of weeks ago, and she didn't even mention Alejandro."

Joe's eyes grew huge. "You know her? Can you get me an introduction, if she survives?"

"She will," Libby assured him, but she wouldn't promise he'd meet her when she doubted Ana would enjoy meeting him.

At lunchtime, she shared a table with Maggie. Joe came to sit with them, still carrying the tabloid. "Have you seen this? Libby says you both know Ana."

Maggie hurriedly read the article. "We know her. Alejandro looks a little like Santos, don't you think, Libby?"

Libby studied the photo between bites of salad. "How can you tell? He looks as though he's telling the paparazzi to go to hell, but he's still a handsome man."

"He's got the looks and the money, but I doubt he can play basketball worth a damn," Joe interjected.

"Do you still have her number?" Maggie asked. "Maybe you ought to call and ask how she's feeling."

"You have her number?" Joe moved his chair closer to Libby. "Do you mind if I listen in?"

"Yes, I do," Libby replied. She carried her phone out to patio opening off the teachers' lounge. When Ana answered, she greeted her warmly. "It's Libby. I'm so glad you're well enough to answer the phone."

"Despite what the tabloids print, a broken leg isn't fatal."

Libby turned to send Maggie a thumbs-up. "That's a relief. Maggie and I would love to come visit you."

"Please don't. Let's plan to get together when I'm better."

Libby leaned against the doorway. "We'll look forward to it. Is anything the tabloids report true? Have you married Alejandro Ortiz y Vasquez?"

"Yes, and he's a devoted husband who insists I end our call to rest. I'll talk to you soon."

Libby returned to her table. "She did break her leg and got married, although I'm not sure which came first."

"Well, she's not going to die," Joe remarked. "People do get divorces, so there's still a chance for me if you'll help me meet her."

"You mustn't impose on your friends," Maggie advised. "It's a very bad habit."

"Well, I had to try." He bit into his sandwich and let the matter drop.

Ana kept hold of her phone. "Libby's engaged to Santos Aragon. She's a sweet girl."

Alejandro knew he'd sound like a jealous ass, but he couldn't keep his mouth shut. "You told me you knew Santos, but the story was too long to tell. We've got the whole day."

She smoothed her hair out of her eyes. "Isn't there a disaster somewhere—wild fires or floods, a war or famine to discuss?"

"Does Santos belong in such a dismal category?"

"It depends on who you are. All I'll say is that we were close when his father was ill. Please let it go at that."

He tried but failed. "It's difficult to believe a matador could offer much in the way of sympathetic comfort."

She sat up but quickly collapsed into her pillows. "I'm still dizzy. Maybe I'll be able to use a wheelchair tomorrow. I'd hate to be carried on board the *Siren* on a stretcher." Her phone chimed, and she handed it to him. "Who is it?"

"Speak of the devil, it's Santos Aragon. Should I leave the room?"

"No, stay. I thought he wasn't speaking to me, so this ought to be good. "Santos, Libby just called to say hello."

His voice was hushed, as though he didn't wish to be overheard. "I wanted to make certain you weren't near death."

"That's very kind of you. Thank you for the beautiful roses. It was thoughtful of you to send them."

"I'm sorry you were hurt. I hope you know I mean that."

"Thank you, Santos. Stay well." She ended the call and kept the phone. "He has his father's deep voice, but now I know who's calling."

His heart sank. "When Miguel was alive, you couldn't tell them apart?"

"I hate to disappoint you, but we were never a ménage a trois. If you have any other questions, ask Santos."

He got up and paced by the bed. "I doubt he'd enjoy the

conversation any more than I would. Maybe I should meet him, just to say I'd shaken hands with a matador. I need to check on the details for the cruise. You must have a passport."

"I do. It's in my office desk. Fatima knows where it is."

"I'll get it Thursday when I pick up your clothes. Do you want me to bring you anything?"

"Some chocolate, please, but don't go out of your way."

He kissed her brow. "I'll find something good."

Even his lightest touch brought a teasing tingle that made Ana wish for more, even if she weren't well enough to do more than kiss him back. She struggled to fluff her pillow and was sorry she'd not asked him to bring one from home. He'd been so accommodating, and she didn't want to take advantage. Still, she wished she'd thought about a softer pillow sooner. She simply wasn't cut out for bed rest. After he had gone and Maja brought her some juice, she was grateful for her company.

"Where's Prince Charming?" the nurse asked.

"He's running errands. He must have lots to do if he's not going to stay with me. All the people here are wonderful, but I'll be so glad to leave."

Maja moved the visitor chair back to the wall. "That's our mission. We want everyone to feel good about going home."

While Alejandro waited for the elevator, a man wearing a white doctor's coat and holding a clipboard came through the stairwell door at the end of the hall. He was about six feet tall with shaggy blond hair and a burly build. While Alejandro possessed no psychic traits, he had a very bad feeling. The man wore no identification badge attached to his pocket. Alejandro took a backwards step into his way. "Maybe you can answer a question for me, Doctor."

The man brushed by him. "Sorry, not today."

Alejandro watched him walk on down the hallway toward Ana's room and alerted the nurses at the desk. "Call security."

"Wait a minute!" he called and loped down the corridor to overtake him, but just as the man reached Ana's room, Maja came out carrying an empty tray. The man caught the nurse's arm, flung her into Alejandro, and the tray clattered to the floor. Sidestepping the spinning tray, Alejandro caught Maja before she fell, and the white-coated man darted through the exit doorway at that end of the corridor.

Maja grabbed hold of Alejandro's arms to regain her balance. "Who was that?" she cried.

"Someone who shouldn't have been here." He looked into Ana's room. "Are you all right?"

"Of course. You left only a minute ago. What's going on out there?"

Two uniformed security guards came sprinting from the elevator, and Alejandro pointed them toward the exit door. "He's a big blond guy in a doctor's coat."

Alejandro picked up the tray and handed it to Maja. "Did he hurt you?"

She straightened her uniform. "He just rattled my teeth, that's all. He'll be on the security cameras. They'll catch him."

"I hope so." He went into Ana's room and gave her a quick account of the scuffle in the hall. "I'm calling Montoya. Maybe the guy is an ambitious paparazzo, but he could have been someone more dangerous."

"A big blond guy you said? Ask Montoya to bring the S&M photos from Campos's studio. There was a blond with a mask, but maybe you can recognize him from his build."

"I will, and as soon as we've talked to Montoya, I'm taking you out of here," he said, his tone emphatic.

A wide yawn took her both hands to cover. "It would be so nice to go home, if they'll let me."

"Not home. We'll board the *Siren* a few days early."

She cocked her head slightly. "Can we do that?"

He laughed and kissed her. "It's an Ortiz ship, Ana. I can do whatever I like."

"I suppose that's good." She caught his hand as he drew back.

"You don't look convinced."

She licked her lips. "Some believe it's important for people to earn things for themselves in order to really appreciate them."

He squeezed her fingers before releasing her hand and leaned against the foot rail as he pulled Montoya's card from his wallet. "Even if you don't count how difficult it is to be Orlando Ortiz's son, I deserve credit for earning two college degrees on my own."

"Of course you do."

It was a quick call, and Montoya promised to be there within ten minutes. Alejandro shoved his phone back into his pocket. "Do I strike you as being ungrateful?"

"No, not at all. You're generous and kind."

"Thank you. I'd hate for you to suddenly decide you've married the wrong man."

She finished her juice and set the glass on the night table. "Not yet. Did you make a wonderfully romantic proposal?"

He paced beside her bed. He'd already strayed so far from the truth he might as well embellish it. "It was extraordinary, poetic and so passionate you threw yourself into my arms."

"I'm trying to picture it but just draw a blank. It must be worth repeating. Please propose to me again so I'll remember it this time."

With a befuddled gaze, she was so innocently appealing he wished he had actually proposed. "It was spontaneous. I could never recapture the moment."

"You could give it your best effort."

"I don't want to disappoint you. Let me work on it."

"Please do. The *Siren's* captain could marry us, couldn't he? Then I'd have a wedding ceremony to remember."

He swallowed hard, but with a man posing as a doctor to get into her room, this was an odd time to plan a wedding. "Captains can marry people at sea, but let's talk about it after we're safely on board."

Her voice was feather soft. "Have you decided you don't want to be married to me?"

"Impossible," he assured her. He was grateful her beautiful green eyes still couldn't see clearly, because his perplexed expression would have instantly given away the whole preposterous fantasy. Marrying her on board the *Siren* would simplify everything. He was grateful she'd thought of it before he had to convince her an ocean wedding would be wonderfully romantic and suit them perfectly.

Chapter Thirteen

Montoya spoke with the director of the hospital security force before entering Ana's room. "The hospital security cameras caught it all. The man came through the kitchen carrying what appeared to be a food delivery. It proved to be a carton containing a white coat and clipboard. He went up the service stairs, pulled on the white coat, grabbed the clipboard and came out on this floor. He dropped the clipboard running back down the stairs, and we're checking it for prints. He eluded the guards and walked out the front entrance with the white coat tucked under his arm. The whole time he kept his chin tucked to his chest, so we have no clear images of his face, but he could very well be the blond in Mr. Campos's S&M scenes."

Alejandro studied the photos Montoya had shown Ana at the police station. "From the width of the shoulders, he could have been the man here. Didn't Jaime have any photos of him without a mask?"

"He may have, but they weren't in his files when we went through them. You said the man spoke to you. Did he have an accent, or an unusual way of speaking?"

"He was brusque, as though he were needed elsewhere. It was his size that caught my attention. He simply looked out of place, but the fact he had no ID badge gave him away."

"What do you suppose he planned to do if he'd gotten into my room?" Ana asked.

Montoya shrugged and straightened his tie. "He may have only wanted to make certain you aren't half-dead as the tabloids reported. Or, he could have planned to take a photo to prove it. He ran when you confronted him, Mr. Vasquez, but if he'd meant to do Miss Santillan any serious harm, he would have struck you hard enough to knock you out and incapacitated the nurse."

"You've no proof of what his intentions actually were," Alejandro replied. "If a man without an ID can get so close to Ana, it's clear she isn't safe here."

"With a well-known patient, it's an unusual situation," Montoya began, "but I believe hospital security can handle any other intruders."

"Really?" Alejandro challenged. "If no one is observing the security cameras until after an event occurs, they aren't a force I'll trust. We'll move to the *Mediterranean Siren*. She's in port, and on Friday, we'll leave on a two-week cruise."

The detective regarded Alejandro with a dark stare. "I don't believe it's necessary for Miss Santillan to leave the country."

"I don't care what you believe. If the elevator had come any faster, I'd have been gone when the man reached this floor. He could have easily knocked the nurse senseless and done whatever he intended to do. I won't risk it happening again."

"Alejandro is right," Ana added softly. "It's bad enough to be confined to a bed. To have to be on guard for dangerous intruders is too much. If Dr. Pallares won't release me, I'll leave on my own. I can ride in the backseat of your SUV, Alejandro. You needn't hire an ambulance for me."

Montoya sent a disapproving glance between them. "Do as you wish. I'll contact you if I have any news. I do hope your recovery will progress smoothly, Miss Santillan."

"Thank you."

Alejandro closed the door behind the detective and leaned against it. "He may be hiding more than he's willing to reveal. He's looking for *who* killed Jaime, but I'm also interested in the *why*. One of Jaime's last projects had to have been the art photography he mentioned to you. He'd have gotten greater publicity if you'd been involved."

"Don't make this about me," Ana answered crossly. "If he'd told me there had been threats to his life, I'd have done it. He pitched an art series, and Valeria said he'd asked her to be part of it too. Lourdes was also there on Mallorca. He might have spoken to her as well."

"Do you have her number?"

"No, but I could call Gian Carlo and see if he's still at her place." Her phone was beside her bed, and she handed it to him. "Will you find him, please?"

He did, but spoke to Gian Carlo first and described the man who'd tried to get into Ana's room. "Do you know anyone he might have been? He would have known Jaime Campos."

"I saw Jaime on shoots. I didn't hang out with him. I've no idea who his friends were, although whoever murdered him couldn't have been much of a friend. How is Ana?"

Alejandro handed Ana her phone, went out into the hall and fought to control his rioting imagination. At best, a paparazzo had gotten into the hospital hoping for a quick photo of Ana. It would have been worth quite a bit to the tabloids and kept readers buying papers to follow the story. At worst, the intruder had been sent for another reason entirely, but what?

Maja came up to him. "Would you like some candy? A good chocolate bar is the best medicine for the scare we've had today."

He felt too sick to want candy. "Ana would like whatever you have." He followed her down to the nurses' station, where she pulled open a drawer filled with a variety of chocolate bars. He chose a couple. "Let me pay for these."

"Absolutely not," Maja insisted. "Although we do take donations to replenish our supply and be prepared for emergencies."

He pulled out his wallet and gave her a couple of bills. "I just hope there aren't any more involving us."

Ana was still on the phone when he returned to her room. He went to the window and waited for her to tell Lourdes good-bye. There were no armed men standing in the street, but he still felt uneasy and the candy began to look a whole lot better to him.

Ana ended the call. "Campos did ask Lourdes to be part of his nude series. She agreed, and in addition to being paid for posing, she wanted a percentage of the sales of the book. They were discussing money when he was killed. I asked if she knew any big, muscular blonds, and she doesn't. Maybe they'll identify him from his fingerprints on the clipboard."

"I hope so." He gave her a choice of chocolate bar and opened the wrapper for her before opening the other for himself. "I want you to tell Fatima what clothes you'd like her to pack. She thought she knew, but you might want something she'd not thought of."

"Give me a minute to savor this. I love almonds wrapped in chocolate. Did you know that?"

"We hadn't gotten to candy preferences, so I'm glad I picked one you like."

"You're the dream husband, Alejandro. I hope you don't tire of my

182

saying it."

"Never," he assured her between bites, increasingly grateful she couldn't recall they weren't really man and wife. If they got married at sea, she'd believe it was for the second time, and he'd not have to tell her otherwise. A good marriage, however, ought to be based on truth, and he'd not uttered a word of it.

With doctors to see and luggage to pick up, it was nearly sunset by the time they were ready to leave the hospital. Alejandro had brought a deep blue wrap dress Fatima had been sure Ana could wear and her Goth wig. She brushed it forward to cover her bandaged cheek and donned her sunglasses. An orderly pushed her wheelchair out to the parking garage where Alejandro waited. They hadn't attracted any notice before driving away, but she couldn't relax until she smelled the sea as they neared the docks.

"That was too easy," she murmured.

"Some things have to go our way," he assured her. "I called to let the ship's staff know we're coming. They'll meet us with a wheelchair, and once we're on board, security won't be a problem."

"I hope not." She clutched the roomy handbag Fatima had sent along after her favorite had been ruined in the crash. It contained her camera, passport, wallet, notebook for listing her whereabouts and her makeup. "What do they call the medical unit on a ship?"

"The sick bay."

"Right, I knew it wasn't the brig. That's the jail, isn't it?"

"Yes. We have physicians on board all our ships—nurses, pharmacists, hair stylists, anything you could possibly need."

"Good. Do you suppose there will be a walker I could use? I'm well-coordinated, and I'd rather hop around using a walker than have to depend on a wheelchair."

"Can you see clearly?"

She slumped back in her seat. "No, but I'm getting better."

"Then let's wait until you can see where you're going before you strike out on your own."

"Are you always this sensible?"

"I hope so. One of us has to be."

"What makes you think I'm not? I've been taking care of myself since I was in my teens, and I don't do foolish things." Unless she counted marrying a man she barely knew, and time would tell how foolish *that* had been.

He parked where they could board with their luggage and reached over to squeeze her hand. "I didn't say you made foolish choices. I just don't want you to worry you'll have to keep doing everything on your own. Let me handle whatever I can."

She bit her lip. "I hadn't planned to even think about marriage before I reached thirty, so I'll need a while to get used to the idea of having a husband. I don't want to fight over things."

"Like what?"

"I don't know. I've never been married, but some couples fight all the time, and I don't want that."

"Neither do I. Here's a steward with the wheelchair." He left the car to open the back, and a second steward handled their luggage.

Their cabin was a duplicate of the one she'd seen on board the *Goddess*, even to the bathing suits in the closet. She'd been eager to leave the hospital, but the move left her completely drained. She'd been too shaky to attempt using crutches and hadn't left the hospital with a pair. She loved to walk and dance, and being confined to a wheelchair was torture. It couldn't be easy for him either. "This cruise isn't going to be much fun for you."

"Describe fun."

"I have the energy of a teabag left too long in the pot. How am I going to be able to do anything with you?"

He laughed. "I can visualize having fun with a teabag."

"I'm imagining the sly gleam in your eye even if I can't see it clearly. What time is dinner?"

"We'll eat at the captain's table once the voyage begins, but now we can eat as soon as the kitchen prepares whatever you'd like. Are you hungry?"

"Not really, but I can eat, if not much else."

"We'll concentrate on what you can do then. The library has audio books. Do you ever listen to those?"

"I love them for trips." She took a deep breath, but felt so uncomfortable in her own skin it brought no relief. She rubbed her arms. "Maybe it's post-traumatic stress, but I don't feel right."

Clearly concerned, he knelt beside her. "I'll see if the physician is already on board."

"No, don't bother him, or her. I'm not used to feeling so helpless. For now, we can't do anything about it."

He kissed her cheek, stood and pulled open the small refrigerator hidden in a cabinet. "Maybe it's low blood sugar. Would you like some orange juice?"

"Yes, thank you. I could pretend I'm a princess who's used to being waited on, rather than a runway model who's unable to stand. Is there a limit to the number of requests per day?"

He handed her a glass of juice. "I'll let you know when you're close."

She looked up at him and wanted to believe he was a little bit clearer. "Then what?"

"We'll start over."

The teasing promise in his voice made her giggle, and she nearly sprayed juice through her nose. "Hotel refrigerators usually have mixed nuts. Are there any here?"

"A big jar." He poured some into a napkin and carefully laid it into her hand. "I need to move my car into the long-term garage. Will you be all right while I'm gone?"

"Look, I'm sitting up without being dizzy, and that's real progress."

"Maybe I should move you to the bed."

"No, I'm fine. Just turn me around so I can look out at the port. It's such a colorful, relaxing blur."

He moved her close to the balcony but left the sliding door closed. "This is why I wanted to bring you here, where you'll never tire of the view."

"Not as long as you're in it."

He squeezed her shoulder. "So now you're a flirtatious teabag?"

"A flirtatious Goth teabag," she corrected. "Hurry back."

"You won't even notice I'm gone."

Alejandro moved his SUV and spent several minutes debating

185

whether or not to stop by his father's office. He hadn't forgiven him for telling him to dump Ana, but he'd relied on the man's generosity for a cruise on the *Mediterranean Siren*. They had nothing in common other than the family name he refused to use, but he felt he ought to take the time to see him. He found his father pacing his office with a drink in his hand.

"My God, Alejandro, you've come by so often lately you'll soon be mistaken for one of my staff." He raised his glass. "May I offer you a drink?"

"No, thank you. I just came by to tell you Ana was able to leave the hospital and we've boarded the *Siren* a couple of days early."

Orlando leaned back against his desk. "Fine. I hope you noticed I didn't call when the tabloids reported you'd married her. You insist they print nothing but lies, and it struck me as a particularly preposterous one. At least I hope it is."

Alejandro hadn't planned to stay long enough to sit down. He remained standing and told the truth. "We aren't married, at least not yet."

Orlando took a step toward him. "Keep it that way."

From long experience, Alejandro recognized the threat in his father's voice, but now grown, it no longer fazed him. "I'll see you when we get back."

"Does your mother know you'll be visiting Greece?"

He paused at the door. "I'll call her."

"Do, and send her my best."

From what Alejandro remembered of his parents as a couple, his mother had had incredible forbearance where his father was concerned, and she certainly hadn't seen his best, if he even had one. "I will. Good-bye."

He offered Ana an apology as he came through their cabin door. "I'm sorry to be gone so long. I stopped by my father's office, and while our conversations are never long, I didn't want to keep you waiting."

She raised her hand to his cheek as he leaned down to kiss her. "I don't require such doting care, Alejandro. I don't mind sitting alone with my thoughts. We're not sailing until Friday, and weren't you going on some job interviews?"

He sat on the end of the bed to be beside her. "I postponed them because I couldn't pretend I cared about getting a job now. You can argue I should care, but I don't. So let's not fight about it."

"I didn't expect something like this to come up so soon, but I'll make you a deal. I won't offer career advice, if you'll refrain from giving me any."

"How about casual suggestions?"

"What if we differ on what constitutes 'casual'?"

He laughed and shrugged off his jacket. "Should we draw up rules on how to disagree, since neither of us wants to fight?"

"Perhaps agree to only discuss disagreements on Tuesdays?"

"Why Tuesdays?"

"Nothing much happens on Tuesdays, and it would give us something to look forward to."

His voice held a low teasing growl. "I don't need anything but you to brighten the week." He got up to answer a knock at the door and found the ship's captain.

The officer's spotless white uniform made his bright blue eyes all the more vivid. Sun-bleached streaks lightened his brown hair, and his tan had clearly come from time spent on deck rather than lying prone in a tanning bed. He appeared to be in his early forties. He extended his hand.

"I'm Gabriel Reyes, and I want to welcome you on board, Mr. Vasquez."

"It's Alejandro." He returned the captain's firm grip and glanced toward Ana who was looking over her shoulder. He should have introduced her as his bride, but hesitated as he searched for the proper words for the fanciful lie.

"My husband appears to have forgotten my name. I'm Ana."

The captain frowned slightly. "We didn't speak the day you were here shooting a clothing ad, but aren't you usually blonde?"

"Usually. It's so nice to meet you. Commanding this ship has to be a great responsibility, and we won't be in the way. Will we, Alejandro?"

"No, of course, not," he agreed.

The captain clasped his hands behind his back. "We provide all our passengers with exemplary service, but if there's anything special you require, Mrs. Vasquez, don't hesitate to let me know. We don't begin the formal dinners until we sail. I hope you won't mind dining here in your cabin until then."

From the moment Ana had spoken, Captain Reyes had addressed his comments to her, and Alejandro swiftly grew annoyed. "We're fine here, and I won't keep you from your duties."

Reyes nodded. "Perhaps I'll see you on deck tomorrow."

Ana replied before Alejandro could. "I'll look forward to it."

Alejandro nodded a quick good-bye and closed the door. "He was flirting with you."

"Oh my God, this is Tuesday, isn't it? But I'm in no mood for a fight. I couldn't see him well enough to tell, and your family owns the ship, so he has to be accommodating. Men like to flirt with me, Alejandro, and while I don't flirt back, I can't be rude or my professional reputation will suffer. People have to describe me to their friends as one of the nicest women they've ever met. We probably should have had this discussion earlier, but when I didn't want to be recognized, there wasn't a problem. Maybe I should stay in hiding as a Goth girl for the cruise."

He opened the refrigerator and took out the bottle of nuts. He poured himself a handful, began with the pecans and ate them slowly. "You're right. Any man who marries a beautiful woman should expect men to flirt with her. I just don't want Captain Reyes fawning over you."

"Come here and kiss me."

He brushed off his hands and complied. "How far are you willing to go to distract me?"

"How much distraction do you need?"

"An enormous amount apparently."

"Since I can barely pucker my lips, I'll have to owe you." She raised her hands to cover a wide yawn. "I'm sorry. I think the pain pills make me sleepy. Cruises are supposed to be relaxing, but..."

He kissed her again, slowly, tenderly, and straightened up. "I'm going down to the kitchen to see what they're serving tonight. It won't be one of the spectacular meals they'll have when we sail. I could get us something else while we're still in port."

"Soup is all I'll need, and a soft drink. Pain meds and alcohol don't mix."

"What about some warm bread and butter?"

"Hmm...that does sound good. Maybe some ice cream?"

He gave her another kiss and went straight to the bridge rather than the kitchen. From there, he was directed to Captain Reyes's cabin. The door was open. "Captain, do you have a moment?"

Reyes left his desk and welcomed him in. "I read about your wife's accident. Does she have health concerns you didn't wish to discuss in front of her?"

"Rest is all she requires, and she'd prefer whatever privacy you can afford her rather than your solicitous attention."

The captain folded his arms across his chest. "We provide everyone on board with solicitous attention, Mr. Vasquez. As I'm sure you're well aware, it's what makes the Ortiz Line so popular."

Alejandro gritted his teeth. "Attention can be overly tiring, and Ana needs rest."

A slow smile teased the corner of the captain's mouth as he nodded. "As you wish."

Alejandro doubted he had accomplished anything other than to make himself look ridiculous, and he headed for the kitchen without further delay. Although he'd not sailed on the *Siren* in years, he recognized the chef and was relieved their meals wouldn't be a concern.

A steward brought their dinner on a rolling table, and Ana thought the potato soup was especially good. She buttered a piece of the warm bread. "This is perfect. Thank you for bringing me here."

"You're welcome." Alejandro had a chicken dish with a buttery crust. "You have to try this." He scooped up a taste on a spoon, but she raised her hand.

"I'm a vegetarian, remember?"

Embarrassed, he laid his fork on his plate. "I'm sorry."

"I've lost whole days, so you needn't apologize for missing a few details when there's so much to learn about each other. I hope you won't mind my asking about money. You've told me it isn't a concern, but do you have a trust fund or some other way to receive money from the Ortiz Line?"

He took another bite of chicken before answering. "When my parents divorced, my mother received an enormous settlement and put most of the money in an account for me, so I'd be independent when I reached twenty-one. 'Escape' my father's control, is the way she put it. She made wise investments, and the money keeps growing. It's not an inexhaustible fund, but more than enough for us to live comfortably. You should keep your money in your present accounts. It's yours."

"So I can escape being under your control?"

He reached across the table for her hand. "I'm not ever going to try to control you, Ana. What would be the fun in that?"

"I agree, but some people are into it." She finished her soup and looked up. "I'm sorry, the word control sent my mind straight to S&M and then on to Mapplethorpe's nudes. Do you remember Gian Carlo telling us Jaime had asked him to pose for the nude project, but couldn't supply the name of a gallery interested or a publisher for a book? He said something about having the money to do it, but Gian Carlo didn't want any part of such a vague deal. If Jaime had a silent partner with enough money for him to complete the project, publish and promote it, shouldn't he be a suspect? People are often murdered over money."

He focused on his plate. "Montoya must be looking into Jaime's finances. There would have been a contract, wouldn't there?"

"I suppose. It was just an idea that crossed my mind. It doesn't mean it's true."

"You told me you didn't mind being alone with your own thoughts, but I hope you're not dwelling on the murder. Please forget Jaime Campos and concentrate on getting well."

She leaned back in her chair. "I'm working on it, but my leg won't heal any faster regardless of my thoughts. Could we go out on the balcony when we're finished?"

"Of course." He left the table to slide open the door and rolled her out into the night. The air was still comfortably warm. He pulled a chair up beside her and held her hand.

"Speaking of thoughts, you still owe me a proposal."

He sucked in a breath. "I'm sorry. The day got away from me."

"It needn't be perfect, Alejandro. I've already said yes."

He brought her fingers to his lips. "You did."

The port was ablaze with light for the night shifts, and he could see clearly. He wanted to keep Ana and wished it hadn't become so damn complicated. Dr. Pallares's request they keep her pregnancy secret for a while had made sense at the time, but he was hiding too much to feel comfortable about it now.

"I wish we could dance. They do have dancing on board the *Siren*, don't they?" she asked.

"It's part of the romance and fantasy of the voyage. We want this to be the best vacation our passengers have ever had, so they'll come back as often as they possibly can."

"I earn my living projecting a fantasy, but let's make a pact not to spin fantasies around each other."

Already guilty, he leaned close to spread a light trail of kisses along her jaw. "You're wearing the same Goth wig you wore when we met, so I'd say some fantasies can be a good thing."

"True, but..."

He ran his fingertips down her arm. "I don't want you to get cold. Let's go in."

She caught his hand. "I am tired. Stay up and watch movies— whatever you want to do. You won't wake me when you come to bed."

"First, we have to get you there. There are women among the staff, and some will already be on board. I should have arranged to have a maid for you earlier."

"Alejandro, please, I don't need a lady's maid. Just roll me into the bathroom and I'll take care of myself. I can grab hold of the sink or wall for balance." She pulled off her black wig and shook out her hair.

"No, there's too great a chance you'll fall and hurt yourself worse than you already are. If you don't want me to call someone, I'll help you myself."

"Absolutely not. I feel better than I did when we left the hospital, and I don't want to star in my own reality show."

He raised his hand. "I won't look. I promise."

"You're very sweet, but no, bathrooms are off limits. If you must, go find some willing female to play maid."

"Sit right here and don't move while I'm gone."

"Like a rock."

He didn't trust her as he went to the cabin phone. They were the only passengers on board, but a concierge answered and promised to send a maid immediately. Alejandro thanked him.

"Apparently the captain has staff ready for us."

"Your father pays his salary, and he wouldn't want any complaints coming from you."

"Are you saying our service is less than sincere?"

"I'll pass on that. Would you please find my nightgown? My toiletries are in the small flowered bag in my suitcase."

"I'll get it." Fatima had folded her clothes in an organized fashion, and he pulled out a pale aqua satin nightgown. It held a faint hint of floral perfume. She'd posed in perfume ads, but he didn't recall her ever wearing any. He carried her things to her. "Do you have a favorite perfume?"

"Not really. I rinse off everything when I finish work and don't bother with it when I'm not."

He answered the knock at the door. A petite maid in a black uniform and white apron greeted him. "Please come in. My wife would be happy for your help, wouldn't you, dear?"

"Most certainly. Let's go into the bathroom and close the door. What's your name?"

The maid rolled Ana's chair into the large powder-blue tiled room and shut the door behind them.

"I'm Marie, and I'm so happy to meet you. I've seen you in so many ads, but I didn't believe anyone could really be as perfect as you."

"I'm a little less than perfect for the moment, Marie, but without makeup and a hair stylist, I'm not that different from anyone else."

"Oh, but you are! Look at your hair." She picked up the trailing curls, held them up like wings and let them float down over the back of the wheelchair. "How long did it take you to grow it so long?"

Ana gazed at the mirror, but saw only swimming colors. "I've had long hair forever, Marie. Now help me out of this dress and into my nightgown, please."

"Yes, ma'am."

Alejandro paced their cabin and searched for what else he might have forgotten she'd need. He'd never had dates who needed special care, but a wife required far more tender concern. She wouldn't be his wife until Captain Reyes married them at sea, and as she had pointed out, the captain couldn't refuse his requests, so it was as good as done.

When Ana rolled out of the bathroom dressed in the pretty gown, his glance was immediately drawn to the deep purple bruise crossing her shoulder where her seat belt had held her during the crash. Her hospital gown and wrap dress had covered it, and seeing it now, he fought not to grimace, but his smile wavered.

"I know. I'm several shades of purple where I shouldn't be. The bruises will fade long before my leg heals, so I won't be that hard to look at for long."

He tipped Marie and showed her out. "You'll never be hard to look at, Ana. Don't even think that."

"Right now, I don't want to think at all. Will you help me into bed?"

He picked her up from the wheelchair and carried her to the bed. He'd already turned down the covers and eased her between the sheets. "Would you like some music as you fall asleep?"

"Please, that would be nice."

He tuned in a classical station on the radio set into the wall and turned it low.

He couldn't sit through a movie and went up on deck to walk off the energy he could barely contain. Once they left port on Friday, he'd have to weave in and out through the passengers strolling the deck. It was a popular pastime on a cruise, and while no one would recognize him, he'd not considered how quickly Ana would be sighted by fans. She'd be sweet and sign autographs, but he didn't want to share her with anyone. He supposed he'd have to get used to it. He laughed as he thought of being called Mr. Santillan, but so what? Ana would be his wife.

Chapter Fourteen

Ana had fallen asleep in the center of the king-size bed, leaving plenty of room for him on either side. He wondered if couples argued over who took which side of the bed. Some must. He settled into the side on her left so he'd not bump her broken leg. He slid his arm around her shoulders to cushion her head against his shoulder. She murmured his name sleepily. He kissed her forehead, and she looked up at him.

"This is nice."

"It is." Her lips were soft and inviting, and one good-night kiss melted into a dozen. He reluctantly reminded himself she was too bruised to want more and drew back. "We never talked about having a family."

"Little girls and boys who look like us?"

He combed her hair away from her face. "I'm going to be very suspicious if they don't."

She laughed. "Are you warning me to take lovers who look like you?"

"I don't want you taking any lovers, no matter how they look."

She snuggled against him. "I wouldn't have married you if I hadn't thought I'd be faithful. Don't you intend to be?"

"Yes, but don't change the subject. We're talking about children."

She drew her lower lip through her teeth. "I'd like a few. We'd make very pretty and tall babies."

"Being tall is good, but they'd also be smart."

"I should have added smart. What about you? Do you have a certain number in mind?"

"No, but a few sounds good."

"What else didn't we discuss?"

He pulled her closer. "We won't know until it comes up."

"Hmm…"

Her breathing slowed as she fell back asleep, but a long while passed before his conscience let him close his eyes.

When he woke Wednesday morning, he was alone in the bed and the wheelchair sat outside the bathroom. He threw back the covers and quickly crossed to the door. "Ana, is Marie in there with you?"

She slid open the door a crack and peered out. "Good morning. My vision's better, and I don't need her. If you'll help me put on my mascara, I'll be ready for the day."

Her breath smelled of peppermint toothpaste, and she looked so sweetly innocent he swallowed the string of curses hovering on his lips. "At least let me help you back into the wheelchair."

"I got out and I can get myself back in."

"If your vision has improved, can you see my face well enough to tell how little I think of that idea?"

"No, but I can imagine it." She relaxed against the jamb and let him slide open the door. She took his hand to sit down, and waited while he used the bathroom. When he came out, she was right where he had left her.

They spent the morning by the pool. Alejandro swam laps, and Ana relaxed on a chaise longue in her own pretty blue one-piece bathing suit. She recognized the captain's voice when he greeted her. His white uniform was nearly blinding, but today she could see his blue eyes. "Good morning, Captain. I'm enjoying doing absolutely nothing, but I suppose you're always busy."

"Always." He sat down on the end of the chaise beside hers. "Your husband is a fine swimmer."

"Yes, he is, but let's hope he doesn't have to rescue us if the ship sinks."

Reyes's laughter caught Alejandro's notice, and he swam to the end of the pool.

"What's so funny?"

"Your wife made a joke about the *Siren* sinking, which it won't. The Ortiz Line has never lost a ship, and the *Siren* won't be the first."

"I suppose it was in poor taste," Ana remarked.

"It's all right in port," Alejandro replied. "Just don't do it when the ship's crowded with passengers who could be frightened."

The captain stood. "Good advice. I hope you enjoy the rest of your day."

"Thank you." Ana waited until she was certain the man had gone. "He wasn't flirting," she whispered.

Alejandro hauled himself out of the pool and grabbed a towel. "Of course he was, but other than for dinner, we won't see much of him once the cruise begins."

She pursed her lips. "He may not want to flirt after Dr. Hibiscus removes my stitches."

"Higareda, wasn't it? You'll be a walking advertisement, so he would have done his finest work on you. You're allowed to worry, but don't obsess over it."

"Do you actually expect to govern my thoughts?" She smiled, and there was no threat in her voice. "We should stay out of each other's thoughts, Alejandro. Let's agree to that."

"We only argue on Tuesdays and stay out of each other's thoughts. It sounds reasonable for the time being."

"I suppose I could let you in on one thought."

He brushed his hair dry with the towel. "Fine. What is it?"

"There are multiple ways to have sex that won't leave me more bruised than I already am."

"Fascinating. Let's go to our cabin and try them all." He scooped her up and placed her in her wheelchair.

She laid her hands in her lap. "I hope you're always this agreeable to my suggestions."

"Why wouldn't I be?"

"Some men grow deaf to their wife's voices, or so I've heard."

"Where would you have heard that?"

She looked up at him. "A clever woman never reveals her sources."

He pushed her to the elevator and pressed the button. "Are many of your model friends married?"

"None of them are. What are you trying, a process of elimination?"

"Am I that transparent?" He rolled her into the elevator.

"You're very pleasingly solid." She could almost make out the numbers on the elevator panel. She remembered him very clearly.

The bed in their cabin had been neatly made and the curtains opened to let in the sun. Alejandro helped Ana from the chair and pulled her close. "You have an energy that makes holding you feel incredibly good."

"Tingling chemistry? You have it too." She raised her arms to encircle his neck and rubbed against his hairy chest. "Everything about you feels better than good. I could stand and hold on to the balcony rail, but we should probably wait until after dark."

"Unfortunately, the ship's lights would prohibit it, but I like the idea." He glanced around the room. The bathroom mirror showed through the partially open door, and he nodded toward it. "You could hold on to the sink."

"Yes, I like watching you. Help me out of my suit."

He took a step back but kept hold of her with one hand. "I got you into it, and I'll be happy to peel it off."

Her voice was low and suggestive. "Go slow rather than yank it off."

"Peel you like a banana?"

She licked her lips and rose up to kiss him. "I'd rather think of myself as a peach."

"You'd be delicious as a peach or plum or mango. Let's go into the bathroom first, just to be safe."

She held on to his side and hopped through the doorway. "See? I can get around now that I'm no longer dizzy. A ballet dancer has incredibly good balance." She watched him in the mirror as he lowered the narrow bathing suit straps to uncover her pale pink nipples. Even if his features weren't distinct, she appreciated his smile, but the bandage on her cheek bothered her. "If I'm not pretty enough to model any longer, you'll tell me, won't you?"

He paused with her suit at her waist. "The scar will barely show, Ana. Wait until Friday, and you'll see."

If she could see clearly, she didn't add. She placed her hands over his, and he met her glance in the mirror, or at least she thought he did. "I'd been in El Gato a dozen times before I met you."

"So had I. The stars must have aligned, or fate filled the other tables so I'd have to share yours."

She rubbed her bottom across his erection. "What if I hadn't come back?"

He brushed his hand over her breasts and plucked her nipples. "You would have come back."

"I wanted to, but I didn't allow my imagination to go this far. This is all a luscious surprise."

"For us both." He dipped his head to kiss her bruised shoulder.

She grabbed hold of the sink. His touch always made her feel cherished, and she leaned into his kisses. His hands were callused, and his rough palms tickled as he lowered her suit. He helped her hop out of it and tossed it over the shower door. "I told you I didn't need a maid."

"I may be a rather clumsy maid, but you definitely need me."

"You're my lover, Alejandro, not a maid."

He wrapped her in his arms and hugged her tight. "I'm also your husband. How well can you see us in the mirror?"

"Well enough. You're tan and I'm pale, and we blend into each other very nicely, harmoniously."

"We should have photos made in this pose," he teased.

"With a mirror behind us too, the image would repeat like an echo." She closed her eyes and tilted her head against his shoulder. "Just for us though, no one else." He slid his hand between her legs and rubbed her gently. "That feels so good, but I can't touch you while I'm hanging on to the sink."

"We'll take turns," he promised. He loosened his hold on her to shake off his trunks. He had condoms in his shaving kit sitting on the counter, donned one and eased into her.

Caught between him and the sink, she could barely move, but the sensations he created with slow, gentle lunges took her to the brink of release before he paused to ease them both down to an anxious calm.

It was such delicious torture. She wiggled against him and clenched her inner muscles to pull him deep.

"Slow is better," he breathed against her ear. He crossed his hands over her chest and fondled her breasts tenderly. His thumbs brushed her nipples in time with his surging hips.

She curved her spine to roll her back against his chest, slanted her shoulders to brush against him and closed her eyes to savor the joy they created so easily. It had to be more than mere chemistry and a deeper, stronger link. "Ah, that's it, stay right there," she nearly purred. He rocked back on his heels, and a final thrust sent her tumbling into perfect bliss. She locked her arms over his to ride his orgasm and doubled her own. Heat flooded her limbs to her fingers and toes, and it took a long while for her jagged breathing to slow.

Alejandro carried her to the bed and kept her in a warm embrace until their stomachs began to growl, and laughing, they remembered they had to eat.

On Friday, Ana had an early morning appointment with Dr. Higareda. His office was located in a medical building adjacent to the hospital, and after parking, Alejandro unfolded the wheelchair and helped her into it. "I don't think you'll need this much longer."

"I hope not." Her vision was nearly perfect, but rather than tell him, she waited so she could gauge his true reaction to her scar. She also loved watching him apply her mascara. He moved slowly, as though he were restoring a treasured piece of art rather than helping her with makeup. She shouldn't have worried, however, because when the physician removed her stitches, Alejandro's expression was one of mild surprise rather than anguished alarm.

Dr. Higareda was ecstatic. "The scar is so faint, it will soon disappear. I'll refrain from asking you for an endorsement of my work, but I'm sorely tempted." He gave her a hand mirror. "I'm sure you'll be pleased."

She had to gather the courage to look, but the thin pink line on her cheek struck her as a glaring flaw. She worked in a world where perfection mattered, and when her skin fully healed, she could cover the scar with makeup, but she'd still know it was there. Thinking she was lucky it wasn't worse, she forced a smile. "Thank you. I'll talk to you about using my photo when we come back from Greece. Unless it has to be taken right now."

"For my files only today," the physician assured her. He took photos at several angles. "You're sure to have a wonderful time on your cruise. The pastries on the Ortiz Line are the best I've ever eaten. All the food is good, but the pastries are lighter than an angel's caress. The pestiños bathed in honey syrup are beyond compare."

"I can't wait to taste them," Ana assured him. She had his card and promised to call when they came home. They returned to the ship before the passengers had begun to board, but there was far greater activity along the dock as the final supplies were loaded.

She wouldn't complain in front of Alejandro, but being scarred hurt more than she'd ever reveal. "It was so nice having the ship all to ourselves," she said. "I brought my red wig as well as the Goth girl. Maybe I should wear a disguise."

"You could alternate. People would think I'd brought two women on the cruise."

"The wheelchair would give it away. I hope I'll be enough for you no matter what color my hair."

He pushed her chair out on their cabin balcony so they could watch the activity below. "Of course you're enough. We already agreed we'd be faithful, and you're far more likely to attract admirers."

"They're drawn to the illusion, not the real me. Do you suppose the chef has already baked the pestiños Dr. Higareda loves?"

"Yes. Would you like to send him some?"

"Could we?"

He kissed her soundly. "I'll see to it right now. Do you want to send anything to anyone else?"

She licked her lips to savor his kiss. "No. Just bring a few for me, will you?"

"Of course. We ought to sample them. I'll be right back."

She blew him a kiss as he left. She raised her hand to her cheek and quickly pulled it away. She'd not expected to remain in modeling many more years, and if the accident ended her career, she'd not waste a minute crying over it. It was just the way life worked. As for acting, special effects created all sorts of magical creatures, and her scar wouldn't be a challenge to cover. Still, the accident had changed her life so suddenly, it was difficult to cope as easily as she pretended for Alejandro. She wanted the truth from him, but as a woman, she ought to be allowed a few secrets.

Alejandro was such a good man, he probably wouldn't even see her scar. She was so lucky to have met him. They'd been together constantly since she'd checked out of the hospital, and she wasn't in the least bit tired of his company. Things would be different when they came home and resumed their usual lives, but for now, they got along so beautifully, she wouldn't ruin it complaining about her looks.

There were eight places at the captain's table. The chair on Gabriel Reyes's right had been removed to accommodate her wheelchair, and Alejandro had the seat beside hers. She'd had Fatima pack gowns appropriate for the evenings and wore the silvery white dress she'd traded with Libby Gunderson at the charity benefit. The captain was in his uniform, and the men wore dinner jackets. Alejandro's fit him beautifully.

Joseph and Maricela Lopez were seated beside him. Newlyweds in their sixties, they could barely keep their hands off each other. Ana thought it was sweet, but Alejandro looked more distressed than amused. She reached under the table to squeeze his knee, and he caught her hand.

A married pair of dentists, Olga and Memo Talleda, had blinding smiles, and Linda Suarez was at the Captain's left. A sultry brunette wearing a low cut red gown, she introduced herself as a psychologist who worked with bright children to ensure they received the finest in education.

"I'm happy to have all of you at my table," Gabriel Reyes said. "The Ortiz Line serves quality meals to everyone on board, but I believe the food is even more delicious at my table, perhaps due to the entertaining company. Have you all settled into your cabins?"

Ana smiled as the others shared more about themselves, but when Gabriel glanced her way, her mind went blank. He'd given her name earlier, and she could not recall the last time she'd had to say anything more about herself. She'd been the first to visit the *Siren's* hair salon, caught her hair loosely in a clip at her nape, and left gently curled strands free to cover her cheek, but no one would expect a model to be in a wheelchair. Horribly embarrassed she couldn't think of anything intelligent to say, she looked up at Alejandro.

201

"My wife is too modest to admit to being one of Europe's most popular haute couture models, but we've come on the cruise to relax rather than promote her career."

Linda Suarez peered at Ana more closely. "I'm sorry, I must not have been listening when the captain introduced you and your husband. Otherwise, I don't know how I missed recognizing you. Are you also a model, Mr. Vasquez?"

"I'm an architect."

"How wonderful," Linda continued. "Two diverse careers will create a nice balance."

"We hope so," Alejandro replied.

The dentists flashed their sparkling smiles. "This is a second honeymoon for us," Olga remarked. "How long have you and Alejandro been married, Ana?"

Alejandro again answered for her. "We were married last week."

"Then this is also your honeymoon," Joseph Lopez exclaimed and hugged his giggling bride.

Maricela Lopez leaned in to speak to Ana. "You must have had a fabulous wedding. Who designed your gown?"

Ana whispered to her husband, "What did I wear?"

Alejandro brought her hand to his lips. "Ana suffered a concussion in an accident last weekend and has a slight memory loss. We plan to be married again soon so she'll remember the ceremony."

Linda Suarez studied them more closely. "You were there. What did she wear?"

"It was a civil ceremony, and she wore a gray suit."

Ana frowned unhappily. "You're not serious."

"I didn't pick it out, you did," Alejandro countered. "You were beautiful as always, so what does it matter what you wore?"

"It's such an odd choice," Ana mused aloud. "Captain, could you marry us again so I'll have something to remember while we plan a formal wedding?"

"I'll be happy to conduct a ceremony. Would Sunday afternoon be a convenient time for you?"

"Could we all come?" Olga Talleda asked.

"Yes, let's make a party of it," Ana replied. "The chef makes the most wonderful pastries. Could he bake us a cake on such short notice?"

Alejandro squeezed her shoulders. "We won't need a multitiered cake for those of us at our table, but I'll ask him to bake something very special for us."

"You know the chef?" Linda Suarez inquired.

Alejandro had given away too much, and Ana quickly covered for him. "He takes special requests, doesn't he, Captain?"

"For you, Ana, I'm sure he will."

Now that she could see the captain clearly, she had to agree with her husband that the intimacy of his glance went well past friendliness. That he'd flirt with her with Alejandro seated beside her was jarring, but she'd not flirt back. Ever. Memo, the dentist, appeared to be focused on her too. She had beautiful teeth, but doubted her smile had caught his interest.

When they returned to their cabin after dinner, she hopped out of the wheelchair on her own, but nearly fell into one of the cabin's comfortably padded armchairs. "You were right about the captain. He is flirting with me. Must we dine at his table every night?"

"It's an honor to be seated with him." Alejandro pulled off his tie and wound it around his hand. "I expected everyone to recognize you, and when they didn't, maybe I should have kept quiet about who you are."

"Someone on board would soon recognize me, if they haven't already. It's your identity you want to hide."

"Do you think I should have welcomed everyone on board? 'Hello, my family owns the *Mediterranean Siren*. Please come to me if there's anything you need.'" He removed his white jacket and hung it in the closet. "They'd be after me for extra rolls of toilet paper before we left the dock."

Ana laughed before she realized he was serious. "I'm sorry. If the cruise is going to be too difficult for you, we shouldn't have come."

"You needed somewhere to rest and heal, and the man who tried to get into your room at L'Esperanza can't bother us here."

"Whoever was backing Jaime Campos could afford this cruise—

but we weren't going to talk about murder."

"No, we weren't, and I checked for new passengers. The *Siren* was fully booked more than a month ago. Maybe he was just a burly paparazzo, not anyone wishing you any real harm."

"Let's hope so. A photo of me looking all bedraggled in a hospital bed would be worth quite a bit. The paparazzi don't believe celebrities deserve any right to privacy. Let's forget about them. It's such a beautiful night. Do we have to do anything other than watch the moonlight glisten on the water?"

He cocked a brow. "There's a great many things we could do. There are bars with live music, a lavish musical show, as well as a small theater where talented casts perform popular plays. There are first-run movies, and an ice cream parlor where we could sample all the flavors—or I could handle tonight's entertainment."

Ana couldn't hide a wide yawn. "You sound like the most fun. Could we begin working our way through the rest of the list tomorrow?"

"Of course, but please tell me when you're tired." He helped her stand and hop into the bathroom. She had just pulled the door closed when she opened it again.

"What about the crew? Was anyone hired in the last week?"

He swore under his breath. "I'm sorry, I should have thought of the crew. I'll ask the captain as soon as you're safely in bed."

"I hope I won't be all that safe," she replied in a husky whisper, promising a great deal more than pleasant slumber.

"Probably not, but I want you to have a memorable voyage."

"It already is." She leaned out to kiss him before closing the door.

Alejandro found Captain Reyes on the bridge and stood for a long while just enjoying the incredible view. "This is my favorite place on the ship."

"Mine too. Is there something I can do for you, Mr. Vasquez?"

He hated to ask him for anything. "A photographer Ana worked with was murdered. The police questioned her, and someone may believe she knows more than she actually does. A man tried to enter her hospital room, and he could have followed her here. He was a big, muscular man. Have you hired any men for the crew in the last week?"

Gabriel scanned the multiple computer displays. "There are new members to the crew every time we sail, but no one was hired that recently. I don't recall any muscular men either. The chef hired a woman who looks as though she could handle herself in a fight, but the gender's wrong." He pointed to the computers tracking the weather. "We'll be crossing through a storm by tomorrow night. It will keep people off the decks and out of the pools, but we'll keep everyone entertained."

"I'm sure you will. One other thing—I want to register our wedding ceremony on Sunday as a legal marriage."

The captain turned his back to the other men on the bridge and lowered his voice. "Aren't you and Ana already married?"

"We may get married a dozen times, but because Ana can't recall the first time, I want to register this one too. Bill me for whatever you usually charge for a wedding."

"You own the ship, Mr. Vasquez, so you'd simply be paying yourself. I'll waive the fee. There will be flowers in the chapel and champagne on ice. If you speak to the chef about the cake, he'll have it ready."

"I'll do it tomorrow." He hadn't realized a wedding on board could be planned so easily, and that accomplished, he walked on deck until he was sure Ana had had time for a brief nap.

When he came through the door, she sat up and pushed her hair out of her eyes. "What did the captain say?"

"I would have come back sooner had I known you were so worried. No one has joined the crew who resembles the man I saw, so you can relax."

"Not unless you come here and relax with me." She slid back under the covers.

He shrugged off his clothes and joined her in the wide, comfortable bed. "Is it too warm in here for you? The temperature is easy to adjust."

She snuggled against him. "It isn't nearly warm enough, but your heat will do."

He hugged her closer. "I'm sorry I ever have to let you go. I've been happier with you than I've ever been. That's what I said when I asked you to marry me."

She brushed a fingertip across his lips. "You didn't promise to make me equally happy?"

"Yes, there was more to it. I wish I could remember it all."

"So do I." She kissed him with sweet, tender nibbles and his passionate response took her breath away. She loved kissing him, holding him, feeling the hairy roughness of his body against the smoothness of her own. He turned her to her side to spoon her. "I'm so pleasantly numb from the pain meds, you won't hurt me," she murmured.

"Let's not take the chance." He nuzzled her neck, drew her hand to his lips and sucked on her fingertips. "All of you tastes so good."

"You too. Maybe we're simply a successful accident of chemistry."

He nibbled her earlobe. "I'm very good at chemistry."

She giggled and pushed her bottom against his erection. "Show me."

"We have all night. Let's not hurry." He circled his palms over her silk-covered nipples. "You have gorgeous breasts."

Other men had also said so, but the softness to his voice made him sound doubly sincere. "Thank you. I like all of you, but your light eyes are especially handsome."

"Not strange or weird?"

She curved her back to rub against his chest. "There's nothing strange about you." She pulled his hand to her mouth to taste his fingers. "You taste like toothpaste."

He silenced his laugh in her hair. "You're more of a vanilla flavor."

She brushed her hand along the easy curve of hip and felt his muscles tense. They fit together no matter what their pose, and he knew where to touch her, and when to pull away to leave her eager for more. His breath quickened, and she understood he'd teased himself along with her. She pushed against him as he entered her and clenched her muscles to lure him deep. The next time he pressed her clit, an orgasm caught her with a blinding flash. She rocked against his hips to push him over the edge and felt his body shudder as he came.

Thoroughly loved, she savored the afterglow and laced her fingers in his. "Let's always be this close."

He squeezed her fingers. "Always."

Alejandro had closed the accordion partition to separate their bedroom from the sitting room, but the delicious aroma from the breakfast cart woke her. She moved off the bed and hopped around it to catch hold of the partition's recessed handle. He shoved it open just as she did, and she toppled into his arms. She laughed and grabbed hold of his shoulders.

"I meant to serve you breakfast in bed, but since you're up..."

"No one's ever served me breakfast in bed. I'll go right back so you can carry on with your original plan."

He scooped her into his arms. "I don't want you to fall on the way."

He was dressed in jeans and a dress shirt, already clean-shaven and looked as though he'd been awake for hours. She didn't even try to finger comb her tangled hair, and because his loving had wrinkled her silk gown, she didn't apologize for looking rumpled when it was all his doing.

He pushed back the partition, rolled the breakfast cart up to the bed and placed the silver tray in her lap. "I thought the french toast with blueberries sounded good, but there are muffins, eggs, grapefruit, tea. Is there anything else you'd like?"

"You're like a genie, Alejandro."

"Thank you. Rub me anytime," he teased.

She licked her lips. "You're supposed to rub the lamp, not the genie, but I'll look forward to it. Sit down with me. Have you already eaten?"

He circled the bed to sit down beside her and waited for her to start on the french toast before he tasted the scrambled eggs. "I had to make certain the breakfast was up to the Ortiz standard, so I've already sampled it all."

The thick french toast was dusted with powdered sugar, and the maple syrup was warm. "This is so good, but I never eat this much for breakfast. You'll have to help me finish."

He poured her a cup of tea. "You could stand to gain a few pounds."

"True, but not all in one sitting." A firm knock at the door jarred them both. "Did you order something more?" she asked.

"No, I'll get it." He rolled off the bed and eased the partition closed before going to the door.

A steward addressed him with a slight nod. "Good morning, Mr. Vasquez. Captain Reyes says there's a message for you, and he asks that you come to the bridge."

"Can't it wait?"

"No, sir. He told me it's urgent."

"I'll be right back," he called to Ana and left with the steward.

Ana was curious but not alarmed and swished another bite of french toast in the puddle of syrup pooling on her plate. It was almost too sweet, but she chewed each bite slowly to savor every single morsel. When Alejandro returned and pushed open the partition, his dark expression told her something was very wrong. "What's happened that they had to call you?"

"My father's suffered a massive stroke. My stepmother couldn't wake him this morning, and he was rushed to the hospital. His doctor doesn't expect him to survive the day. A helicopter is coming for me. I hate to leave you again, but you'll be more comfortable here. I'll make travel arrangements for you just as soon as I can. Although you needn't be caught in the mess if my father dies."

Shocked that he'd dismiss her so easily, she struggled to remain calm. "Mess? Is that how you'd regard it?"

"My father runs a huge corporation. If he dies, the stock value will drop and..."

She rested her fork on her plate. "That's your only concern, the stock value?"

"We weren't close for a good reason, Ana. I won't pretend to be devastated if we lose him. Start planning for our wedding. You must have a favorite designer who'd love to make your dress."

She drew in a deep breath, but his sudden change in subject was difficult to grasp. "I'll think about it." She didn't utter another word as he packed up a few things and left her with only a maple-syrup-flavored kiss.

Chapter Fifteen

The ship's library was larger than she'd expected and had an old-world charm with oak bookcases and comfortable leather armchairs and hassocks where she could prop her legs. She took a book from the mystery section, eased herself into a chair, then let Maria move the wheelchair out of the way and go. A young man in a dark suit soon joined her.

"I'm Edwardo Mendoza, the librarian. Please let me know if there's anything you need."

She raised her book. "Is this any good?"

He frowned as though he hated to offer an opinion. "It's not a book you'd keep forever, but for a quick shipboard read, it's good enough."

She handed it to him. "I need something more involving, riveting, if you have one." She raised her skirt hem to show off her cast. "The most active thing I can do is read, so I need something really, really good."

He pursed his lips. "Have you read R.J. Ellory's *A Quiet Belief in Angels*?"

"No, is it good?"

"It's one of my favorites. It's beautifully written, and you won't guess who did it until the very end." He brought her a copy. "Let me know when you'd like something to eat or drink."

"After the breakfast I had, I won't have to eat for days, but a cup of tea would be wonderful."

"Give me a moment."

He disappeared behind the desk and soon returned with hot water in a white teapot decorated with the Ortiz Line insignia and a wooden box filled with a wide variety of teas. He poured hot water into a pretty china cup, set it on the table beside her and waited for her to select a tea. "Ah yes, the orange spice is particularly good."

"Thank you. I'm not used to being waited on so attentively. Please don't let me distract you from whatever you usually do."

He closed the box. "I keep the library neat, order new books, and offer suggestions to anyone requesting them. I have plenty of time to read, so in my view, this is the best job on the ship."

He left her to read, and from the first page she was hooked. She didn't look up until Maria returned and suggested she might enjoy going to the tearoom for tea. "Is it afternoon already?" She glanced at her watch and discovered it was already past three. She'd brought her cell phone with her but hadn't heard from Alejandro. She supposed there was nothing to say, or he would have called long before now. Her world had changed so quickly, and if he lost his father, his would too. She'd continue being a loving wife, although that didn't seem like it would be nearly enough. "All right, tea sounds lovely. I'll see you tomorrow, Mr. Mendoza."

"Take your book. You'll want to read more tonight," he suggested.

"Do you need my cabin number?"

He walked ahead of them to open the door. "I know who you are, Miss Santillan."

She thanked him but felt very foolish. Many people recognized her, while a great many didn't, but his smile had been friendly rather than condescending.

The tearoom was beautifully decorated to look as though it had been plucked from a small town in the English countryside. The furnishings were delicate, all in white and blue, and the air was scented with cinnamon and cloves. Maria rolled her to a small round marble-topped table and said she'd wait for her outside. Ana had just picked up the menu when Linda Suarez appeared.

"Are you all alone?" the psychologist asked. "Where's that gorgeous husband of yours?"

"He was called away." He hadn't warned her not to mention his father's health crisis to avoid a stock market catastrophe, but she knew better than to provide any such intimate news. Linda would have no idea who Alejandro's father was, but she still wouldn't confide in her. "Would you like to join me?"

"Yes, thank you." Linda's navy blue slacks and seductively loose navy blue sweater complemented her curvy figure. She sat and rested her arms on the table. "Do you mean 'called away' like off the ship?"

"Yes. I'm ordering the little sandwiches. Do you want to order something sweet, and we can share?"

Linda glanced at the narrow menu card. "I'd like the fruit tarts."

Their waitress's dark curls were topped with a ruffled cap. "Let me bring you a pot of the lemon zest tea. It will brighten your afternoon."

"Thank you. I ran around the deck this morning and worked out in the gym, so a few fruit tarts won't hurt me. How do you manage to stay so slim?"

After questions about her hair, fans always wanted to know how she maintained her weight. "I'm nearly six feet tall, so I burn more calories than most women, and I prefer vegetarian fare."

"I've heard vegetables are the key, but can't give up bacon. Is your husband going to rejoin you soon?"

"He may." Ana sat back as the waitress appeared with their order and poured their tea. Linda was too inquisitive for her tastes, and she was sorry she'd have to see her later at dinner. The tea had a definite zing, which she surely needed. She took a bite of a tiny watercress sandwich. "These are good."

"Everything on board the ship is good," Linda replied. "I expected the captain to be somewhat older. Not that I'm complaining."

A woman and her little girl approached their table. "My daughter insists you're Ana Santillan, but I wasn't sure."

Ana smiled at them. "Yes, I am." She pulled the small notebook from her purse and tore out a page. "I'll write you an autograph. What's your name?"

"Julie." Her eyes grew wide as she watched Ana write. "You're so pretty. You ought to have dolls like Barbie."

"Thank you so much. You're very pretty too." She waited for the pair to return to their table before taking another bite.

"Does that happen often?" Linda asked.

"Yes, but I don't mind."

Linda edged one of her fruit tarts onto Ana's plate. "Was it difficult to get used to?"

Phoebe Conn

"I've modeled most of my life, so it's what I know." She took a couple of bites of the fruit tart, and it was so good she finished it. "I didn't realize how tired I was when I came in. Will you excuse me, Linda? I need to go back to my room." She rolled her chair to the foyer where Maria met her. Even without looking back, she could feel Linda watching her. When she reached their cabin, she checked her cell phone, but Alejandro hadn't called. Maybe his father was clinging to life after all.

Gabriel Reyes came to her cabin to escort her to dinner. She'd put on the long black sheath and shawl she'd almost worn for a Goth girl dinner with Alejandro. Tonight, the somber outfit suited her mood perfectly.

"Thank you, but you needn't come for me yourself, Captain."

"Humor me, Mrs. Vasquez. We have an especially fine dinner planned for tonight, and I wanted to make certain you'd be there."

"Are you always this enthusiastic?"

"I'm happy to be of service to you, but general enthusiasm is part of my job. We'll be passing through a storm later and my presence tonight will reassure everyone they're in no danger."

"Is it the truth?"

"Yes, it is. The *Mediterranean Siren* is a beautifully engineered and constructed ship, all the Ortiz ships are. I'm sorry our dinner company isn't more exciting."

They were the last to be seated at his table. Linda Suarez looked between them and frowned, but Ana had no romantic interest in the captain, and obviously, Linda did. Ana smiled and greeted everyone. The table linens last night had been a near eye-blistering white. Tonight, they were the heavenly blue of the Ortiz Line logo and the centerpieces were filled with bouquets of fragrant white carnations with accents of blue.

"How pretty everything is," Ana exclaimed.

The dentists nodded and smiled. The Lopezes agreed and hugged each other. "Where is your husband?" Joseph Lopez asked.

"He was called away," Ana replied. "I spent most of the day in the library reading. What did everyone else do?" She was relieved when the

212

others recounted their day. They were served a delicious sherried onion soup with saffron topped with sliced almonds and parsley, and she concentrated on swallowing with silent sips.

Memo Talleda looked up from his bowl. "How could your husband have been called away? Isn't he still on board?"

The captain answered before Ana could. "We arranged for a helicopter. Now tell me if the lamb isn't the best you'd ever tasted."

Linda thought the roasted lamb with red onion salsa looked incredibly good and took note as Ana was served menestra, a dish of spring vegetables. "Is the vegetarian food good?"

"Scrumptious," Ana replied, but by the time everyone finished the sorbete de limon for dessert, she was thoroughly tired of her dinner companions.

The captain rolled her chair away from the table, but when the others had left, he turned her wheelchair around and pulled up to the closest chair. "Give me a minute please, Mrs. Vasquez. Your husband told me he wanted the wedding we'd planned for tomorrow to be a legal ceremony he could register, because you couldn't recall your first wedding."

"Without a groom, there won't be any need for one tomorrow."

"I realize that." He looked away briefly. "I don't want to make trouble for you or Alejandro. Please believe me. He said you'd been married in a civil ceremony. Do you know when and where?"

"Some courthouse in Barcelona, I suppose. It had to have been last week, Thursday or Friday, but I'm not sure of the date. Why do you ask?"

"After couples marry, there's a legal requirement to register the wedding at the Civil Registry. It was just curiosity that made me go online to search for the details of your wedding so you'd know them, but I couldn't find any record of a marriage between you and Alejandro Ortiz y Vasquez."

His expression was dead serious, lacking any hint of his usual charm. "Maybe there's a backlog, and our wedding hasn't been posted yet," she suggested.

"This week's are already posted and those from last week are readily available. Yours simply isn't among them."

After the speed with which Alejandro had left her that morning, discussing their marriage held no appeal, and she laced her fingers in her lap. "What are you suggesting, that we aren't married?"

"I'm not suggesting anything. I'm just remarking on the fact there's no record of your wedding. Alejandro may have told you you'd married him, but do you have another source, or any evidence that you actually did?"

His shocking question forced her to wonder. Last Sunday, she'd woken from surgery with the world a blur and found she had a husband. Wasn't it true? The possibility it had been a convenient lie, or a cruel hoax, sent her heart tumbling. "I'd like to go to my cabin, please."

He rose to his feet. "I didn't mean to upset you."

"Of course you did. Don't tell yourself otherwise. I'll ask my husband for the details. You needn't bother to search elsewhere. His word will be enough for me."

"He's a very lucky man."

Ana told him good night as she rolled through her door, and he behaved as a gentleman and left her to her own thoughts. She sat in the middle of the cabin, staring out at the night, too confused to move to a chair or the bed. She could only dimly recall last Sunday but thought Alejandro had said something about telling the hospital he was a relative—not a brother, but her husband. Was that how it had started? He'd said it, and she'd been loopy with drugs and believed it?

When her cell phone chimed, she feared she'd be too upset to make sense, but she sucked in a deep breath and said hello. "How is your father?"

"There's been no change from this morning. He's alive, but just barely. I miss you. What did you do all day?"

His voice had a low echo, as though he were standing in a hospital hallway. "It doesn't matter. I have a question for you. When you told the hospital you were my husband, it wasn't true, was it? We're not really married. Why did you let me continue to believe we were?"

He sighed softly. "This is the conversation I'd meant for us to have."

She gripped her phone tightly. "But you didn't. You even said I'd worn my gray suit to the wedding. I should have known you were lying then. What were you after, Alejandro?"

He spoke after a long pause. "I wanted it to be true. You're the one who asked to have a wedding at sea, so you were happy with me."

She was furious with herself for seizing on his conveniently fabricated farce as though they were meant to be together. It was the stupidest thing she'd ever done. Rain splashed against the balcony doors as the predicted storm reached them. The weather couldn't have been more perfect. "I was happy, which makes your lies hurt all the more. I'm going to forget we ever met. If you sell a word of this to the tabloids, I'll sue you for every ship the Ortiz Line owns." She ended the call before he could apologize and vow to do whatever it took to win her love.

He called her right back, but it went to her voice mail. "I don't blame you for being angry with me. I'm disgusted with myself for not speaking up before you discovered the truth. Let's not fight over the phone. I'll come back as soon as I can. I love you. Good night." He hated being stuck in the hospital again where he could do nothing to help his father or reach Ana. There was also the baby to consider. She'd have to call him when she realized she was pregnant, and he'd have to pretend he didn't know. It would be another convenient lie, but it was all he could do. If she called.

The bouquet of yellow roses arrived with the breakfast cart. Ana was up and dressed, but she hadn't ordered anything. "This all looks wonderfully good, but are you sure it's for me?"

The steward assured her it was. "Mr. Vasquez left orders for the week."

"How considerate of him." Ana tipped him and waited until he'd gone to open the card on the roses. Alejandro had written he missed her. She wondered if he'd left bouquet orders with notes for the whole cruise. If he hadn't, she was sure he'd called them in that morning. There was a vegetable omelet that smelled too good to ignore, and she sat down and placed the plate in her lap.

There were women who believed all men were incredibly stupid but trainable. She'd never been of that opinion, but thought she was even more stupid than Alejandro. He'd scooped her up so easily, and she'd been a willing party to her own kidnapping. That was the real story. She'd never been so gullible with any other man. If anything, she was too cynical for most men's tastes. The omelet was gone before she'd decided what to do, and the crumb cakes didn't help either. She poured a cup of tea and looked out at the gray day.

Rather than sit in her cabin brooding, she returned to the library.

The rainy day brought more people in looking for something to read, but she didn't glance up from her book. The hero suffered so much pain and loss, she readily identified with him.

Eduardo came over to her when they were alone. "You look so sad. Maybe I suggested the wrong book."

"No, this is fine. It's just that my life has taken a strange turn, and I'm not sure what to do. Please don't worry about me. I'll pull myself together."

"Perhaps some tea and muffins?"

"Tea only, please."

He returned swiftly with her cup. "There are good movies playing in our theaters. You might like one of the comedies, and there are many films available to watch in your cabin."

She wasn't in the mood for a comedy, and with anything serious, she'd only sit in the dark and cry. As for entertainment in her cabin, it was too full of Alejandro to be bearable. His clothes were still in the closet and held his scent. "Thank you for your concern, but I'll just finish my book and maybe begin another."

The captain came to escort her to dinner, but she hadn't changed out of the long skirt and knit top she'd worn all day. "I should have called and saved you a trip, but I'd rather eat here in my cabin than join the others."

"They are a regrettably uninteresting group, aren't they?" he replied. "I can send another officer to take my place if you'll join me for dinner in my private dining room."

He'd ruined her life with a little detective work, and she didn't trust his motives. "That wouldn't be a good idea."

"Do you think Alejandro would object?"

"I'm the one who objects, Captain. Our first stop is Corfu. Will I be able to fly home from there?"

"You want to leave the cruise early?"

He looked so aghast at the thought, she almost laughed. "Yes. The *Siren* was supposed to be a fun place to rest, and without Alejandro, I can't bear it."

"You choose, dinner with me or the others, and then I'll help you make your travel arrangements."

He was a very good-looking man, certainly personable, but one-on-one was more than she could manage in her present mood. "The others. Let me get the shawl I wore last night, and I'll go." She'd begun using her wheelchair as a walker in the cabin and quickly hopped to the closet, came back to him and sat down in it.

"I admire any woman who can get ready that quickly." He rolled her out the door and closed it behind them.

"I spend most of my working life changing clothes, so I don't play around with my own clothing when I'm not. Besides, I don't care how I look tonight."

"You're beautiful as always." He paused a long moment. "I'm sorry. I wish I'd never looked for your wedding data."

She knotted the ends of the shawl to keep it loosely draped around her shoulders. "I should have searched for it myself, so you needn't apologize. Please don't say anything to the others at your table. I don't need anyone laughing at me."

He stopped and knelt beside her. "I won't say a word, but no one would laugh at you. Alejandro's the one who's at fault."

"Keep it to yourself," she emphasized. "The tabloids would make fun of me forever if they learned how easily I'd been tricked."

He stood. "You'd been in an accident. It's no wonder you weren't thinking clearly."

"True, but I am now."

They reached the table last again, and the group was talking about the storm and how safe they'd felt on board the *Siren*. Ana didn't feel safe. Her dinner tasted as delicious as the other meals, but she felt full after a few bites. The wheat rolls were good slathered in butter, and she finished one.

Linda peered across the table at Ana's plate. "Aren't you feeling well? You've barely touched your dinner."

The captain passed Linda a bowl of olives. "These are especially good. We pick them up in Corfu on each cruise. I'm fond of Spanish olives, of course, but these are wonderful too. Are you all fond of Greek food?"

Ana was relieved he'd spared her from Linda's unwelcome observation on her appetite. She turned the gold band on her finger and blinked away tears. Alejandro had also been so thoughtful and kind. Clearly she'd placed far too much faith in him, and it carried a terribly painful price.

Alejandro flew into Corfu in the afternoon of the day the *Siren* docked. He'd left messages on Ana's voice mail so she'd know he was coming, but none of her things remained in their cabin. He called on the ship's phone to locate the captain and met him on deck.

He was afraid he already knew the answer. "Where's my wife?"

"Miss Santillan flew home to Barcelona this morning. Had I known you were coming, I would have done what I could to delay her."

"She knew I'd meet her here. It's not your responsibility to keep track of her."

The captain nodded slightly. "Still, I would have done my best. I'm sorry you two were unable to enjoy the cruise you'd planned."

Alejandro lowered his voice. "I'm not one of your vacationing passengers, and you needn't pretend with me. I'll take my things with me this time. If you have a chance to book the cabin for the return voyage to Barcelona, do so."

"I will. There's one thing you ought to know. Ana didn't take off her ring, so it must mean something to her."

Alejandro doubted it. He searched their cabin for a note, but Ana hadn't bothered to write one. The flowers he'd sent were still fresh. He was angry enough to eat them, but he couldn't blame Ana for avoiding him. She'd complained people only saw the illusion she created without ever really knowing her. He'd created his own wonderful mirage, but maybe he'd made the same mistake as everyone else, and dreamed of a future that couldn't exist. He wanted their baby. It frightened him to think maybe she wouldn't.

Chapter Sixteen

Ana left the *Mediterranean Siren* on a pair of crutches from the sick bay, and once home in Barcelona, Henry carried her luggage from the elevator to her door. "Thank you. It's so good to be home."

"It's always good to see you, Miss Santillan."

She'd called Fatima from El Prat airport, and her housekeeper opened the door for them. The kittens came bounding up, nearly grown now. "Thank you for taking care of Romeo and Juliet and my condo. I'm flying to France this afternoon, so will you help me unpack and pack again? Henry, please take my luggage to my bedroom. Thank you."

Fatima waited until the guard had gone downstairs to his post to speak. "Wait just a minute," she cautioned. "Let me take a look at you. I'm glad to see you can get around on your own, but you certainly aren't at your best. I'll fix you a cup of peppermint tea, and you'll have time for a bowl of my vegetable soup, won't you? I've a new batch in the freezer."

"Yes, of course. I've missed you and your delicious soups." She sat down at the dining table and dropped her crutches to the floor. There was a stack of mail waiting for her, and she laid the bills aside to pay before she left.

Fatima thawed the block of soup in the microwave and transferred it to a pot to heat thoroughly. She brought Ana the cup of tea. "I didn't expect to see you home so soon. Didn't you like Greece?"

Ana's hands shook as she raised the cup to her lips. "I didn't see much of Corfu before I left. I might as well tell you the whole wretched story." She'd played it over and over in her mind as she'd flown home, and supplied the facts without embroidering the pathetic tale. When she finished, Fatima stared at her wide-eyed.

"He seemed so concerned about you when he came here, but he said nothing about marrying you. I'm shocked he'd take advantage of you. What could he have been thinking?"

"That he'd get away with it. I'll never speak to him again. I'm horribly embarrassed to have been so naïve. I watch the people I meet on jobs so carefully, but he fooled me completely. Please don't even whisper what happened to your family, or anyone else."

"You know I'm discreet, but if you'd planned to marry Alejandro last Sunday, he must have been, how shall I say it, adequate as a husband."

Ana took another sip of tea and nearly choked. "Believe me, he's more than adequate, but he lied every time he opened his mouth, and I believed him. I've called my mother. I don't know how long I'll stay with her, but if Alejandro comes here looking for me, please tell him I've gone to Brazil for a bathing-suit shoot and won't be home before Christmas."

Fatima got up to stir the soup. "He won't believe it. I should probably say August. That sounds better."

"Fine, August is good. Then when he comes around in August, you can tell him I've gone to Africa to photograph cheetahs."

Fatima set her place and brought the bowl of soup to the table. "Maybe you should talk to him yourself."

"What could I possibly say? He had to be laughing at me the whole time." Fatima made wonderful vegetable soup with every fresh vegetable available at the market. "This is so good. Thank you for being here."

Fatima sat with her at the table. "I work here, remember? I've visited the widows and done some mending for them. We even had an afternoon tea party with little sandwiches it took me all morning to make. I hope you'll come home soon so we'll have our usual routine."

Ana doubted her life would ever be the same. She leaned back in her chair. "I'll probably stay only a week or two at my mother's. Lamoreaux wants me to do his shoe ads even if I have only one good foot. Then there's the movie. I can't take off so long everyone forgets I exist."

"You needn't worry. You're as lovely as always, if a bit thin. You'll probably have more work than you can do when the cast is removed."

"Let's hope. Do the widows play cards? Maybe you could organize some sort of a tournament."

"Excellent suggestion. While you finish your soup, I'll see to the laundry."

"Thank you. I want to take many of the same things." She couldn't get into a pair of pants, so long skirts would have to do. Her mother had a beautiful garden, and her stepfather grew herbs and vegetables for his café. Maybe she could stand out in the yard, play scarecrow and make herself useful.

On his way home from the airport, Alejandro stopped at Ana's condo. Henry informed him she'd left for the airport a couple of hours prior. "Did she say where she was going?" He signed his name in the visitor's book to prove he'd been there, if she cared to look.

"She's visiting her mother, who's a very charming woman, although she hasn't visited in a while."

Alejandro lounged against the counter. "I'm looking forward to meeting her. She lives in Rouen, doesn't she?"

"Yes, Miss Santillan has brought us pastries from her stepfather's café, and they are beyond delicious. The French have many faults, but they must be born knowing how to cook."

"And design haute couture," Alejandro added. He kept Henry talking a few minutes more so he wouldn't appear as desperate as he was to find Ana. He ached for her, and he'd do whatever he could to make things right.

He'd noted Fatima's number the first time Ana had asked him to call her and phoned her the next morning. "Please don't hang up on me."

"I told you I'd deal with you if you hurt Ana, so don't you dare ask me to help you make up with her. She's finished. Done. Through. Do you understand?"

"Yes, but I'd still like to come talk with you."

"Why? It wouldn't do you any good."

"I want to adopt the kittens."

"You what?"

"You heard me. Ana doesn't really want them, and I do. I'll come get them this morning if you're at her condo."

Fatima answered after a long pause. "I'll let you have them on the condition you'll return them if she wants them."

"I'll put it in writing."

He'd spent more time at the hospital with his father than at home since he'd left the cruise, but the cats would have each other and as long as he fed them, they'd be fine on their own. He drove over to Ana's condo and signed in. "How are you this morning, Henry?"

"Fine, thank you, Mr. Vasquez. You know Miss Santillan isn't home."

"I do, but I came by to pick up the cats. They need more attention than Ana can give them."

"Are you sure that's what she wants?"

"Yes, I am. Fatima knows I'm coming."

Henry reached for the phone at the desk. "I'll give her a quick call to let her know you're here."

Alejandro held his breath, but Fatima hadn't changed her mind and invited him to come up. She let him in at his first knock. He was relieved she wasn't holding a knife.

"I've worried Romeo and Juliet are here alone too much of the time, or I'd not be giving them to you. There's a piece of paper on the dining table. Go ahead and sign for them."

"I'll be happy to." He pulled a pen from his pocket, and after addressing the note to his darling Ana, he promised to take excellent care of the kittens and return them if she so desired. "There. Pin it up in her office so she'll be sure to see it."

"Don't worry, she will. The real challenge will be to corral Romeo and Juliet and put them into their carrier."

"I'd love a cup of coffee. If I sit here for a while, they should come to me, and it will make everything easier."

Fatima rested her hands on her ample hips. "All I'll give you is a glass of water."

He took the chair at the head of the table. "That would be nice too."

She plunked the glass down in front of him. "We both know the cats are an excuse to see Ana again, but you shouldn't be sure it will happen."

"Even if she hates me now, I still have hope."

A perplexed frown crossed her brow. "You don't understand." She sat down beside him. "She's more angry with herself than with you. She's cautious about letting men into her life, and she's furious to have made such a gigantic mistake with you. She blames herself for being gullible. I shouldn't have told you, but I want you to see just how much damage you've done."

He stared at his water. Even if he told Fatima about the baby, she'd see it as an excuse to trick Ana into marriage. Plenty of women had done that to men, but it didn't justify his actions. "You're right. I should have told Ana the truth. I didn't have a choice about coming home early, but I should have taken her with me rather than leave her alone on the *Siren*."

"And what, continued your lies? That's not the right answer, Mr. Vasquez."

"Maybe not, but it would have given me time to straighten out things before she discovered the truth on her own."

"Well, it didn't happen."

Romeo brushed against his leg, and he picked him up to cuddle. "One down. Where's the carrier?"

"I put it in the guest bathroom. If you'll carry him in there, he won't see us sneaking up on him with it."

"Good plan."

"Well, of course," she scoffed. "*I* think things through."

He scratched under Romeo's chin. "Good advice, but I doubt cats plan anything at all." The kitten stared up him as he carried him into the bathroom, and Alejandro pushed him into the carrier and closed the door. Romeo pushed his nose against the wire grid in the door and meowed to get out.

"When we get home. Now where's your sister?"

"She's the hard one to catch," Fatima opined.

Just like her mistress, Alejandro thought.

Cats captured and all their gear stacked out in the hallway, Fatima leaned against the open door. "I was supposed to tell you Ana has gone to Brazil for a bathing-suit shoot."

He smiled in spite of himself. "Fatima, you know that isn't true."

She shrugged. "I work here and pass on whatever messages I'm given."

"I've always wanted to see Brazil."

"I wouldn't leave too soon."

That was all the help she was likely to offer, and he thanked her for it.

Ana ate a delectable croissant her stepfather had baked that morning and licked the butter from her fingers. "This is the absolute best croissant ever baked, Claude."

"Better than the chocolate-filled?" he asked.

"For breakfast yes. The chocolate are luscious for dessert."

They were seated on the terrace of the charming stone cottage he shared with her mother. "I'm so happy you could come for a visit. Your mother has worried herself sick since your accident. She was certain you weren't telling us all you should."

Reclining on a chaise longue, she gestured toward her cast. "It's only a broken leg and a scar everyone tells me barely shows. I wanted to come visit you."

Claude studied her closely. "There's something in your eyes, a sorrow you're not revealing."

"I hate being unable to work, that's all," she lied smoothly.

Claude was in his sixties with thick gray hair he wore smoothed back. He described himself as merely plump, and he had such a charming personality no one ever remarked on his weight. "There is a musician who plays at the café on Sunday afternoons. You might find his company entertaining."

From the day he'd married her mother, he'd been seeking the perfect Frenchman for her. She smiled at his latest effort. "I'm sure he's a nice man, but I'll be gone soon."

"You're too pretty to be alone. Your mother is so happy with me. You must give a nice man the chance to please you."

Restless, she shifted her position but still couldn't get comfortable. "Claude, enough, please."

"Forgive me, but I must try. Now it's time for me to go to the café."

He stood and leaned down to kiss her cheek. "Your mother is thrilled you're here."

Ana had outgrown a need for a mother to manage her career in her late teens, and while they still shared a love of fashion, they hadn't remained close after Carol had remarried and moved to France. Carol was tall and slim despite Claude's butter-laced cooking, and had swiftly taken on a Frenchwoman's elegance. Ana smiled as her mother joined her on the terrace.

"What would you like to do today?" Carol asked. "We've toured the cathedral, and it would be difficult to do again with your crutches. I've been meaning to buy some new lingerie. Why don't you come with me, and we'll have lunch at Claude's café."

Ana wanted to do absolutely nothing, but her mother would keep proposing activities until she gave in. "My lingerie is a bit ragged, so let's go."

"Your lingerie is never ragged, my sweet, but a woman always needs something new."

Ana had been to the shop with her mother on an earlier trip, and again posed for a photo with the owner, a Madame Cotillard, who often posted ads featuring her from *French Vogue*. The shop held a delicious lavender fragrance from the sachets hidden among the satins and lace.

"I'm so glad to see you looking well," Madame Cotillard exclaimed. "When I read about your accident, I feared the worst and said many prayers for you."

"Thank you. Clearly they were effective." She sat in the pink damask chair men used when accompanying their wives and girlfriends there. It was discreetly placed at the rear of the shop so they'd not be seen through the window. Alejandro would have loved the place and insisted she buy lingerie in every color of the rainbow. She shut her eyes tightly to force away his image, but he stubbornly lingered in her thoughts. When her mother had made her purchases, she bought the blackest lace bras and panties Madame Cotillard carried and folded the pink bag into her purse.

Claude's café overlooked the Seine and was popular with tourists and locals alike. Ana liked the tables out front but today asked for something inside.

"Of course, you do not wish to be troubled by admirers," the chef replied. "I have the perfect cozy table for you and my bride."

Ana had always thought his devotion to her mother was sweet, and clearly her mother thrived with his loving attention. She had to remind herself she was only twenty-four and had plenty of time for true love to find her too. For today, she'd satisfy the longing with a dozen escargot, dripping with garlic and butter.

Alejandro stood with Carlotta beside his father's bed. She had wept continually since her husband had entered the hospital, and he marveled at how anyone could hold so many tears. The doctors had yet to recommend they take his father off life support, but he knew it had to be coming. He'd prepared himself for it, but Carlotta would never agree. They had the resources to maintain his father in a coma forever, but that wouldn't be what Orlando would have wanted. He'd been far too ambitious and active a man to welcome a vegetative state for even a day, let alone the years he might live on the edge of twilight.

"I need to check in at the office," Alejandro told her.

"I'm sorry everything has fallen on you when you wanted another life," Carlotta whispered between sobs.

Amazed by her unexpected sympathy, he hugged her shoulders and left rather than agree. He'd worked for his father before returning to the university and knew exactly what was expected of him. His father had a responsible staff, but they were in a daze along with his stepmother, and no one had stepped forward to oversee things. He'd train someone himself if he had to, but he wasn't going to devote the rest of his life to the Ortiz Line. Although his father had tried to trap him, he'd broken free, and he'd do so again at his first opportunity.

When he returned home that evening, the cats were asleep in the middle of his model village. They hadn't swatted the little cubes onto the floor, just curled themselves around them. They lifted their heads and focused their yellow eyes on him. "I hope your day was better than mine." He hung his coat on the peg by the door and went to them. Romeo pushed against his hand while Juliet sat up and watched. He dropped Romeo to the floor, and Juliet jumped down by herself.

"I thought you two liked your bed." Before he left in the morning, he'd pack up the little houses to keep them safe, and maybe put their bed on the table. He'd be spoiling them, but why not? He filled their bowls and went into the kitchen to see if he had anything he could possibly eat for dinner. Sorry he hadn't bought something on the way home, he ate a cheese sandwich, leaning against the counter.

No matter how he added up the days, Ana had to realize she was pregnant soon. He needed to work on how he wanted to respond, but the words wouldn't come any easier than his so-called proposal.

Ana was chopping chili peppers when she made the mistake of touching her eye. "Oh damn," she cried.

"Did you get pepper in your eye?" Carol grabbed a clean dishtowel and wet it. "Just press this to your eye and let the tears wash away the sting. I'll get the eye drops."

Ana was seated at the kitchen table, and while she didn't need another reason to cry, she struggled not to be overwhelmed by tears after the burning sting finally abated. "I haven't cooked anything for myself in so long, I'd forgotten to be careful. I won't forget again."

Her mother smoothed back her hair. "You should visit us more often. This is the real world, not the make-believe paradise I raised you in."

"I know the difference, Mother. Now what can I do for the salad that won't involve peppers?"

"First scrub your hands to get rid of all the juice and cut the tomatoes." When they sat down to eat, Carol paused after taking a few bites. "There's the nicest young man working at the bookstore near Claude's café. We should have stopped there the other day."

"I'm sure he's a sweetheart, but I don't belong with a man from the ordinary world. He'd soon tire of the attention I receive, and it wouldn't last long."

"He's a poet, so he might be more understanding."

Ana speared a bite of cucumber with a fierce jab. "A poet? That's even worse. They're such sensitive souls and need to comfort themselves. They have little time or emotional strength to sympathize with anyone else."

Carol swallowed a sip of tea and added more lemon. "No one from the ordinary world, nor poets? Who does that leave? Only the men you meet on jobs?"

"I'm not looking, so please let it go." The plea worked until Claude came home carrying a tabloid with Alejandro and her on the front page.

Claude handed it to her. "One of the waiters saw this and showed it to me. If you went on a cruise with your husband, where is he? Why haven't you mentioned him? Did you think we didn't care? God help us, did he fall overboard and drown?"

Ana sighed unhappily and quickly scanned the story. They'd been photographed on the deck of the *Siren*. Alejandro had knelt beside her wheelchair, and they were laughing at some shared joke. Anyone could have taken it, but the comments on how little she ate had to have come from someone seated at their table. Linda Suarez was the likely source, and she hated the fact the psychologist had pretended a friendly interest simply to gather material to sell to a tabloid.

She looked up at her mother and stepfather. They were all the family she had and deserved the truth. "Why don't we make tea, and I'll tell you all about Alejandro Vasquez."

Carol put on the teakettle, and Claude produced a box of pastries from his café. "I need more than a tepid cup of tea." He opened a bottle of his favorite chardonnay and poured himself a glass. "Please begin," he urged.

They stared at her as though expecting a damning confession, but she hadn't done anything wrong. Fatima had met Alejandro and knew most of their story, so Ana hadn't had to provide more than a few details of the end of their romance. She couldn't use the same verbal shorthand with her mother and stepfather. "I should start at the beginning."

Claude refilled his glass. Carol poured Ana a cup of tea and fetched a stemmed glass to join her husband with wine. The box of pastries sat unnoticed on the table.

Ana fortified herself with sips of sugar-laced tea and began her story in a calm, detached manner, without prejudicing them against Alejandro until she disclosed his lie about their marriage. "It doesn't matter what the tabloids say. We aren't married."

Carol reached across the table for her daughter's hand. "I'm astonished. A man who'd lie about something so important would lie to you again and again. You're better off without him."

"Wait just a minute," Claude cautioned. "He's from one of the wealthiest families in Spain, so clearly he can afford you. He's handsome, so he'd be an attractive partner. He wanted to marry you, which is honorable, even if he went about it poorly. I think you should give him another chance."

"Another chance at what?" Carol responded. "To create another preposterous fabrication? No, you did the right thing to leave him, sweetheart."

"If she did the right thing," Claude countered, "she wouldn't look so miserable. You must listen to your heart, regardless of what your mother says. Men make more mistakes than women, and you should be generous with your forgiveness."

Carol got up to wash out her wineglass. "I think I'm going to be ill."

Ana had felt ill for a long while and understood completely. Alejandro kept leaving her phone messages, and she was disgusted with herself for listening to each one more than once. He had such a marvelous voice. She wished she could trust what he said. "Can we agree not to talk about him?"

"Of course," her mother replied.

Claude looked between them and shrugged. "If you insist, but if you're heartbroken without him, you already know what to do."

"It would be like walking into a burning building," her mother chided.

"We just agreed to drop the subject," Claude replied. "I need to go back to the café for the dinner hour. I'll see you both later. I may stop at the cathedral to pray for wisdom on the way home."

Once he was gone, Carol returned to the table. "I knew there was something wrong. Why didn't you tell us about Alejandro when you first arrived?"

"I'd rather you didn't think me a fool." She opened the pastry box and removed a cherry tart. "These are always so good."

Carol leaned back in her chair. "At least you're eating. That's good. Do whatever you truly want to do about Alejandro, and we'll back you either way."

"Thank you. I've been here a week and should think about going home."

"Stay forever if you like. You're safe here." Carol reached for the pastry box. "Oh good, he brought two cherry tarts."

Ana didn't think of her personal calendar until she returned home and found it in her lingerie drawer. When she realized her period was three weeks late, she quickly recounted. Unfortunately, it didn't matter how many times she checked the days. She was still late. She'd been in a serious accident, had anesthesia, taken pain meds, and maybe the combination had upset her body's rhythm. But with the way her life had been going lately, she doubted such a convenient explanation would prove true. Condoms weren't 100 percent effective, and things had progressed so quickly with Alejandro, she hadn't even had time to think about going back on the pill. Clearly it had been another gigantic mistake on her part.

Fatima wasn't there on a Sunday afternoon to go out for a pregnancy test, and while some pharmacies delivered, she'd have to use an assumed name and ask Juan at the security desk to watch for it. She could send for a whole list of health supplies—Band-Aids, cotton balls, antibiotic ointment, her favorite hand cream and bubble bath. That would fill up the bag, but the pregnancy test would be all that mattered, and whoever filled the order would know it.

She wondered if Alejandro would be glad to hear the news. With her leg in a cast, she couldn't dance away her choking fear, but she'd wanted a clear break, not an everlasting tie to him. He'd left a message for her when he'd picked up the cats. *After* he had them. He'd not asked beforehand. If he had asked, she'd probably have let them go rather than return his call. His calls since had all included an update on Romeo and Juliet's welfare. He certainly knew how to hang on when she wanted to let go. She lay down on her bed and stared up at the ceiling for more than an hour, but no escape for her newfound dilemma appeared. No matter how much she didn't want to do so, she'd have to get up and call Alejandro. Her voice shook as she said hello.

"My God, Ana, have you finally returned one of my calls?"

"I'm home, and I need you to do a favor for me."

"Do you want the kittens back? They've made themselves at home with me, and I don't think it's a good idea to disrupt their lives again so soon."

"Shut up and listen. I need you to buy a pregnancy test and bring it to my condo." She ended the call before he could give her a smart reply, and he didn't call back. Maybe he'd been so shocked he would stay home and pretend she hadn't finally called him after all.

Piles of papers and files were stacked on his father's desk, and he'd only worked halfway through them. He got up and stretched. Unlike Ana, he'd had time to adjust to her pregnancy, but that didn't mean he'd found the best way to respond. He'd played out a dozen dialogues in his mind, and each always ended with her furious with him. If he admitted he'd known since she left the hospital, she'd damn him for keeping the secret. If he played dumb, he'd be lying to her. There was no way to win, but he'd have to face Ana all the same. He wouldn't keep her waiting and grabbed his coat to run her errand.

Along with the pregnancy test, he bought pink roses and a box of chocolate-covered almonds. His mouth was so dry when he knocked on her door, he was afraid he wouldn't be able to speak.

Ana hopped to the door and welcomed Alejandro with an impatient nod. "Thank you, but you needn't have brought flowers and candy."

He carried everything into the kitchen, found a glass and took a drink before she could toss him out. "I thought if we had something to celebrate, we'd need candy and flowers."

"Possibly. In your many messages, you didn't mention you were growing a beard."

"You listened? I thought every word zoomed straight into the ether. I need to look mature and solidly responsible to run the Ortiz Line. Does it work?"

His beard grew low on his cheeks and accented his features

handsomely. That he was even better looking twisted her insides. "I'm not the one to ask. The vases are under the sink. If you'll put the roses in one, I'll go and take the test."

He handed her the box. "Do you want to talk about options first? That way there won't be any pressure afterward."

She leaned against the counter. "I'd rather not speculate."

He opened the box of candy. "Have a chocolate almond or two first. Maja told me chocolate works wonders."

She took them and hopped away. He was equally on edge and ate a couple. He trimmed the stems of the roses the way his mother had, placed them in an elegant crystal vase and carried them into the living room. If he were going to tell the truth, and damn the consequences, he'd have to do it before she told him what the test showed. He didn't want to hover outside her bathroom door, but thought he could sit in the chair in her bedroom corner without upsetting her too badly.

When she came out of the bathroom wiping tears from her cheeks, he spoke softly so she'd notice him without being frightened. "I already know what the test shows. Dr. Pallares ran tests when you entered the hospital, and one showed you were pregnant."

Astonished, she eased down on the foot of the bed. "Why didn't she tell me?"

"She thought we should wait until you felt better."

"We? Oh, I'd almost forgotten, you were pretending to be my husband. So you've known all this time and didn't tell me?" She closed her eyes for a moment and sniffed away the last of her tears. "What's your excuse? You've had plenty of time to dream up something really creative."

No excuse would justify his silence. "I don't have one."

She glared at him. "I'll give you one. If we married on board the *Siren*, then you'd have a claim to the child before I even knew I'd have one. Perfect. You don't need a beard, although it's attractive, as everything about you is, but you'd remain darkly sinister without it."

He didn't move. "I wanted you and the baby and still do."

She looked away. "Will you please go? My life keeps lurching out of control, and I need time to think."

"My life isn't going as well I'd hoped either, but we'll make great parents." He stood and leaned down to place a light kiss on her hair.

"What do you want for dinner? You ought to eat, and you don't look in the mood to cook."

"Must I summon security to make you leave?"

"No, of course not. Besides, offering to fix dinner isn't a threat. Do you want to have a gallon of the vegetable stew you like delivered?"

"Another attempt to seduce me with vegetables?"

"I'll use whatever I have to." He laughed in spite of himself. "I know a place that makes the best pisto manchego and artichoke rice cakes. If you don't feel up to going out, they deliver."

"Are we living in the same universe?" she countered. "When we met, I was a successful model. Now with a scar, a broken leg and pregnant, I'm barely photographable. I'll probably have to work as a hand model. I've also been married and unmarried with amazing haste, to say nothing of being on the fringe of a murder investigation. My life has fallen into dismal chaos, and you want to go out to dinner?"

He nodded. "It would be a good distraction."

"You're driving me to distraction right here."

"I'll consider that a vote for the manchego. I'll let you know when the food arrives." He walked out of her bedroom before she could insist he had to leave. She was talking to him, so things weren't going too badly.

A savory aroma filled the condo. He hated to wake her, but she was sitting up in bed, reading or pretending to. "Do you want to eat in here or in the dining room?"

She marked her place and closed the book. "The dining room." She grabbed the headboard to rise and get her balance and hopped along behind him. There were two places set at the table. "I'd rather not have your company."

"Ignore me if you like. The food is so good I won't be offended." He pulled out her chair and pushed it in for her. Along with the rich mixed vegetable dish and artichoke rice cakes, he'd ordered green salads and ice cream he'd put in the freezer. When she stared at her plate without lifting her fork, he grew concerned. "Can you remember the last time you ate?"

She appeared confused for a moment. "Last night. My stepfather made something wonderful with eggs, mushrooms and asparagus. I've forgotten what he called it."

He handed her a fork. "Take a bite. This tastes as delicious as it smells." He watched her slowly chew her first bite and was relieved when she took another. "I've been researching restaurants with vegetarian choices. This one makes the blue cheese dressing fresh for each salad."

When she continued to eat on her own, he broke apart a rice cake and put half on her plate. The cheese filling oozed out invitingly. "Other than meeting you, my life is also bordering chaos. My father loved the Ortiz Line; it filled him so completely he never needed anything or anyone else. But I see it as a malevolent force, and whenever I break free, it grabs me again, the way a cat tortures a mouse."

She glanced toward him. "How is your father?"

"The same. My stepmother believes one of us should always be with him, but I do need to sleep a few hours a day. I'm not asking for sympathy, nor do I want to toss complaints back and forth in an effort to decide who has the most pathetic life." He got up. "May I bring you more?"

"This is enough, thank you."

He'd placed a generous order and scooped up another helping. When he brought his plate back to the table, he continued as though he'd never left. "When I first told you I was your husband, why did you believe me?"

She ate a bite of rice cake before answering. "I was too laced up with drugs to think clearly, and you were convincing. You always sound so sincere. Is it a struggle?"

"Not at all. I am sincere. You easily convinced me you were a photographer, remember? But there's no point in fighting over what each of us made up for the other. We're going to be parents and ought to be civil."

She pushed her plate away. "You've had several weeks to consider parenthood. I was already numb, and it's too much for me to absorb easily. Will you excuse me? I'd like to go to bed early."

"There's chocolate ice cream for dessert. Wouldn't you like some?"

"You are a devil."

He finished his manchego and salad. "If you're not going to finish your salad, do you mind if I do?"

"Help yourself."

"Thank you. This is too good to go to waste. Will Fatima be here in the morning?"

"Yes. Why do you ask?"

"She'll be able to give you some support. I'll bet she loves babies."

She reached for his arm. "I'm not telling anyone yet. I need to work as often as I can, with what's left of me to photograph. When the pregnancy can no longer be kept hidden, I'll announce it, but not a moment before."

"I'll get the ice cream." He returned with two bowls. "Try it. In case you haven't thought that far, I've also been married and unmarried with unseemly haste. I feel worse than numb, if there's a level below it, and I've no one to blame but myself. I'll clean up the kitchen so Fatima doesn't have to do it in the morning."

"I can do it."

He shook his head. "On one leg? No, I can wash our plates and bowls without breaking them."

She stirred her ice cream into a smooth blend. "I need you to keep quiet too, Alejandro. Let me be the one to announce the baby."

"I'm tempted to ask for something in return, but I'll restrain myself tonight."

"And tomorrow?"

He leaned over to kiss her. "Ask me again tomorrow."

Chapter Seventeen

Ana tore the pregnancy test box into little tiny bits and put them and the damning test wand in a paper bag she wadded up and shoved into her purse to throw in the trash somewhere far from home. It took her a long time to get to sleep, but she was up, dressed and seated at the dining room table and reading the newspaper when Fatima arrived Monday morning.

"How was France?"

"Restful, which is what I needed. Would you make me a poached egg for breakfast? I haven't had one in a long time."

The housekeeper's eyes widened. "It's been a year at least, but if you'd like one, it will only take a few minutes. How is your mother?"

"She's well, and she and Claude are fun to be with. I should visit more often. They have a lovely home. Claude has to be one of the best chefs in France. Remind me to put a note to visit on my calendar."

"Will do."

Ana was grateful Fatima didn't ask about Alejandro, and she wouldn't speak his name. While she waited for breakfast, she called her agent. "I'm back. When can we schedule the shoot with Lamoreaux?"

"He'd want to do it today, but he needn't believe you're short of work, so I'll call him and say you'll be available on Wednesday."

"That's fine, thank you."

"Do you want to come to the office today so we can talk about the rest of the month?"

She thought what he really wanted was to see if she looked as battered as she felt. "I'll be there in an hour or so."

The poached egg was even better than she'd remembered and the buttery toast perfect. "I should ask for these more often, Fatima."

"It probably doesn't compare to the food in France."

"It doesn't have to. If I ate Claude's food every day, I'd balloon to two hundred pounds."

"It would look good on you. Shall I bake some of the cookies you like?"

"Would you please? We need to plan another tea party. Would tomorrow afternoon be too soon?"

"Not if I go to the market right now and buy everything we'll need."

"We could wait until later in the week."

"The ladies would be thrilled whenever you have it, but let's do it tomorrow before you begin working again."

"Fine. I'll call them all when I come back from Paul's." Hosting a tea was a ridiculous thing to do, but it would occupy her thoughts for an afternoon, something she desperately needed.

Paul welcomed her into his office. As usual, he was well dressed in a muted whiskey plaid suit and maroon tie. "How much longer do you have to wear the cast?"

"Another three weeks or maybe more. I get around all right, but I miss dancing."

"You look beautiful as always, and the scar scarcely shows. With your hair tumbled around your shoulders, it will be easy to cover. Lamoreaux was delighted you could work for him this week. He wants to do the shoot in his apartment, but it will be with a makeup artist, a wardrobe person, and the photographer who does his French ads. Ask someone to go with you if you'd rather not go alone."

Alejandro immediately came to mind, and she barely silenced a hysterical shriek. "I'll be fine on my own."

"The contract is already signed for your usual rate. If the shoot goes into a second day, you'll receive double."

"Then what's my incentive to get the shoot done quickly?"

"He's the one we want to hurry, Ana. If you're just holding a shoe, even an incredibly beautiful shoe, you'll not want to spend more than single day on it."

"Probably not. Is there anything else lined up?"

Paul shuffled the papers on his desk. "Not today, but once the word gets out that you're working again, we'll get plenty of calls. The tabloids have kept you on the front pages, and while obnoxious, all publicity is good. What's happened with you and Alejandro Vasquez? Just so I'll know and be able to tell people to mind their own business when they ask."

His gaze kept straying to her cheek. She couldn't blame him. "Please tell anyone who has the audacity to ask that I won't discuss him."

"Oh, I see. Fine. The film news isn't good. Apparently Almodóvar is reworking the script. It could be a complete rewrite that will delay the filming for months, or merely a tweak or two. I'm staying on top of it."

"Good. I should have thanked you for the philodendron. It's doing well in my condo."

"That's what I'd hoped. Flowers are lovely but soon wilt, while green plants survive a little benign neglect." He helped her stand and gave her Lamoreaux's address before he opened the office door. "Let me know if the shoot isn't going well, and I'll come right over. Lamoreaux is infatuated with you, but you'll be there to work, not hold his hand."

"I'll make certain he understands."

Paul laughed. "Yes, I know you will with a single glance. That's why you're so popular, Ana. You can convey whole paragraphs with a slight tilt of your chin."

She hoped she hadn't lost the ability. There was no point in worrying when all Lamoreaux needed was a shoe model. She pushed the incriminating evidence left from the pregnancy test into the waste bin in the ladies' room on the floor above Paul's, relieved to be done with it. She wouldn't pretend she wasn't pregnant, but she had so much to deal with now.

On board the *Siren*, Alejandro had asked her thoughts on having children. They'd been in a playful mood, but she'd been at a terrible disadvantage when he'd known the truth and she hadn't. She refused to replay the same tiresome argument when they should be planning for a family. She ought to buy a pair of booties, or a little sweater, some snuggly soft something to make the baby real. That's what she needed to do, make the dear little child real and love him dearly. Clearly, Alejandro already did.

In the afternoon, she helped Fatima make little nut bread

sandwiches with cream cheese for tomorrow's tea. The ladies had all been so excited by her call, she was sorry she hadn't entertained them all sooner. By the time Fatima left for the day, they had everything ready. There was the pisto manchego to reheat for dinner, but she wasn't hungry after nibbling nut bread all afternoon.

If Alejandro wanted something for keeping still about her pregnancy, then he'd better hurry up about it. Maybe he was so pressured by work for the Ortiz Line he'd forgotten all about her. She might slip his mind for several days, a week maybe, or two. She didn't have much of a hope, though. When her phone chimed half an hour later, she knew who it would be.

"I'm sorry not to have called earlier. Let's go out to dinner tonight. I've found a place with incredibly good vegetarian food that's so dark no one will recognize us and paparazzi don't even know it exists."

"Is dinner your price for keeping quiet?"

"No, but we need a neutral location to discuss it."

"Alejandro..."

"I'll pick you up at eight."

"Fine. I'd like to get it over with. Good-bye." It took her a long while to decide what to wear, and she finally chose her Goth look. With heavy eye makeup, her wig, a short black sheath, the jacket she'd worn to their first dinner, and one flat-heeled boot, she was dressed the part of a strong girl who could take care of herself. Alejandro would have to be equally prepared, or she'd make him part of the dinner menu.

Alejandro helped her into his SUV and paused with his hands on the keys. "That's a startling transformation. You look tough. Is that your goal?"

She fastened her seat belt. "You said once you liked the Goth girl best, so I thought I'd bring her out again."

"Was I teasing?"

"No, I don't believe so, but I'm in a Goth mood tonight."

He pulled the SUV away from the curb. "I wish you'd waited for me in Corfu. It would have been a beautiful place to work out our differences."

His deep voice echoed around her, soft and smoothly seductive.

"We don't have differences that can be easily resolved, Alejandro, no matter what the setting. You took advantage of me, and I caught you. We were careful but somehow created a baby. The problems keep compounding, and I don't even want to think about what tomorrow might bring."

"So you're about to have a baby with a man you'd rather not know?"

"Thanks for putting it so succinctly."

"You forgot to mention the accident that's left you suffering from post-traumatic stress. That has to be a factor."

"Thank you again. When we reach the restaurant, you ought to make notes for future reference."

He was quiet the rest of the way. "Here we are. The reviews are all good. Have you been here?"

She looked out at the sign above the door showing a buxom farm girl carrying a heaping basket of vegetables. "No, but it looks promising."

The restaurant was as dimly lit as Alejandro had promised, and the warm, crusty bread had the most appetizing aroma. She buttered a thick slice while reading the menu. "The scrambled eggs with asparagus sounds good."

"It does, but I'm going with the mushroom zucchini pasta. We'll want to begin with soup."

"I'm not really that hungry."

He picked up the nearly empty breadbasket. "Some of this was supposed to be for me, but I'll order more."

She laid her knife on her bread plate. "I'm sorry..."

"Don't be. You're supposed to be hungry."

"Please don't remind me."

He added gazpacho to their order, and the waiter brought them a second basket of bread. He took a slice. "This is good. They probably churn the butter here."

He had polished manners and was an exemplary companion in most respects. None of it mattered now. "Alejandro, what would you have done, if you'd been the one in the accident, and I'd told you we were married, when we weren't?" His eyes narrowed, and she knew exactly what had crossed his mind. "You'd believe I'd posed as your wife for your money, wouldn't you? You were furious when you discovered I've hidden my identity, and you'd never forgive me for lying about a marriage."

The restaurant was busy but quiet, and he responded with a lazy whisper, "But you wouldn't have said you were my wife to stay with me, would you?"

"Your father would have beaten me to the hospital, and I wouldn't have had the opportunity. But I would have been there for you."

"Thank you, but let's hope neither of us is in another accident."

That wasn't the way she'd hoped the conversation would go. She'd wanted him to understand why she couldn't forgive him, but he'd slipped right out of the question. There was no reason to press the issue now.

The gazpacho was filled with crisp green pepper chunks, and she paused to savor the mix of flavors. "This tastes as though it were made in the last ten minutes."

"It probably was. When I was a kid, asparagus was the only vegetable I liked, and I'd eat it with my fingers when my mother wasn't looking. Finally you're smiling. Did you do that too?"

"Of course, and green beans." She concentrated on her chilled soup rather than her handsome companion, but she could feel him watching her. "What?"

"You're a very beautiful Goth girl."

"Thank you. The scar gives me a steampunk edge."

"The scar isn't noticeable, Ana."

Their entrées were served before she could argue. Her savory dish was sprinkled with paprika for color and tasted as delicious as it looked. Living in the moment had many advantages, but each time she glanced up, he was still admiring her, although his food was disappearing more rapidly than hers.

"You might as well tell me what it is you want in exchange for your silence. Isn't it the reason we came here tonight?"

"We're here because I wanted to see you, and the subject is too important to discuss on the phone."

She laid her fork on her plate and knotted her hands in her lap. "You have a sly twinkle in your eye, so it can't be good."

"Ana, really. I wouldn't suggest anything mean. All I want is to

241

come with you on your doctor visits so I'll know everything is going well."

She pressed her nails into the backs of her hands to remain calm and was only partly successful. "I won't be treated like your broodmare."

He shoved away his empty plate. "Then marry me so you won't mistrust my motives."

"I've no idea what your motives are, but I still mistrust them." He'd never said he loved her, and it suddenly struck her as a damning omission. It was clear he wanted her and the baby as though they were treasures he could order from a high-end catalog. He was definitely his father's son, even if he failed to recognize and acknowledge it.

"What did you do with your wedding ring?" he asked.

"Isn't that off the subject? I put it in my jewelry box. I might need it for a shoot someday if I'm reduced to being a hand model in a detergent ad."

A teasing smile tugged at the corner of his mouth. "That's not why you saved it."

"It isn't?" She picked up her fork for a bite of asparagus.

"No, you kept it because it means something to you. Even if you were my wife for only a week, it was the best week of my life."

She'd loved it too and had to swallow hard to force back tears. She spoke in an anguished whisper. "That's why your underhanded trick hurt me so badly, and you can't undo it."

"Why not? Let's go back to the first dinner we had together. You were in your Goth disguise, and we were getting to know each other. I already had your purple bra draped over the lamp beside my bed, but you disappeared in a cab rather than let me take you home."

She remembered that night well. "Even if I didn't take you there, I didn't lie about my condo."

"No, but it struck me as odd you'd sleep with me if you didn't want me to know where you lived."

Rather than defend herself with a lame excuse, she picked up an olive and ate it slowly while she struggled for something believable. "I'm not sorry I slept with you that afternoon. Goth Girl is far more daring than I am."

"I like you both. Let's go back to your condo and finish the ice cream."

Only a smear of scrambled eggs was left on her plate, the breadbasket was empty, and yet nothing had been settled. "If you'll agree to just talk."

"Of course. All night if I have to."

The damn twinkle was back in his eyes, and she didn't trust herself now.

He seated her at the dining table, made coffee and served the ice cream. "Let's get back to the appointments with your doctor. Could you consider me a concerned friend rather than a despicable, conniving bastard who wanted to spy on you?"

She twirled her spoon in her ice cream. "I've never thought of you as despicable."

"Thank you, that's a point in my favor. I'll go in the backdoor and meet you at the doctor's office so we couldn't be photographed together on the street. Would that help?"

She sat back in her chair, took a deep breath and exhaled slowly. "We're avoiding the most obvious solution—we don't have to have a baby we didn't plan."

He'd finished his ice cream and set the bowl aside. "I would never have suggested it, but since you have, I'll tell you again that I want him or her. What's your real worry, that having a child will ruin your spectacular figure, or the bother of a baby will keep you from working as much as you'd like?"

Deeply insulted by his softly voiced accusations, her expression turned fierce. "I'm really fond of these dishes, or I'd hurl my bowl at you. I've not once thought about my figure or modeling. My only concern is having you as the father."

"But I'm not despicable at least. My father set such a poor example, I know what a good father ought to be. If I'm responsible enough to run a shipping line, you can count on me to handle whatever responsibilities you want to send my way. There's no question about my ability to pay for whatever our child needs."

"Your multitude of assets isn't the issue, Alejandro. We were so close, and none of it was real. I don't want to be fooled like that ever again. It hurt much too badly."

His voice turned soothing. "What if my attorney handled the child support, and a nanny came to pick up our child and returned him or her to you so you never had to see me?"

She regarded him with a skeptical glance. "You'd agree to that?"

"I suggested it, so yes, but it isn't what I want for us, Ana. You've only known about the baby for a day. Please take more time to consider what you really want to do."

When she looked at him, sweet memories betrayed her, and she could scarcely think at all. "My mother wanted more children, but my father died young, and she didn't meet Claude until she was in her forties and thought it too late to begin another family. It would be easier for us both not to have a child. This might be my only chance though, and my mother would love to have a grandbaby."

"My mother would too. I meant to call her when we were in Greece, then had nothing to say." He reached for her hand. "If we're going to have a child together, we ought to get married. We could agree to separate later. It would make everything so much easier, not only for us, but for our baby too."

She pulled her hand free. "Now we're back to why you wanted to marry me on board the *Siren*."

"I thought you were a wonderful wife, all I've ever wanted in a woman. I'd never really expected to meet anyone like you, and suddenly, there you were."

Until she'd discovered his lies, she'd have said he was all she wanted in a man. She wouldn't let her mind stray in that sorry direction ever again. "We haven't known each other for two months yet. Let's not rush things."

He stood to scoop her into his arms and shifted her to his lap. "We've already rushed things, so there's no reason to slow down. We could marry in France, or have your parents come here. My mother is so involved with her second husband she might not be able to attend, but I'd like to ask her. Her husband does huge modern paintings based on Greek myths. At least that's what he says, but they look like big splashes of color to me."

She stiffened her posture rather than lean into his embrace, although his warmth nearly melted her bones. "Maybe he's catching the emotion of the myth."

"That's exactly what he says. People see different things when they look at his work. He might use shades of blue to depict a tragedy, while viewers see a peaceful, restful scene. Look, Ana, we're talking to each other without either of us wanting to scream. That's progress."

"For you perhaps."

He raised her fingertips to his lips. "Only for me? I want you to be happy so we can laugh together the way we used to."

She made the mistake of looking into his smoky gaze, and he took it as an invitation. His kiss tasted of chocolate, and his lazy affection made her crave more. Ignoring the stern warnings of her conscience, she wrapped her arms around his neck. Her life in free fall, she clung to him, all the while knowing she shouldn't.

He broke away to catch his breath. "We need to declare a truce."

"This tastes like one." She shut out everything except how good it felt to be with him again. He kissed her as though he adored her, and she believed it just for tonight. When he carried her into her bedroom and placed her on the bed, she leaned back on her elbows while he yanked off her single boot. She hadn't had a drop of wine, but desire alone made her woozy. When he pulled her sheath over her head, he looked startled by her new jet-black lingerie.

"I may wear nothing but black from now on. Don't you like it?"

He ran a fingertip along the lacy edge of her bra. "I expected something more colorful, rather than a sexy widow's bra and thong."

"Please don't use the word *widow*," she begged. "Let's not tempt fate." She straightened up to unbutton his shirt.

He caught her hands. "That's another reason for us to marry. If a crane toppled and flattened me on the docks, you'd be a very rich widow."

"Don't joke," she begged. "Let's imagine we'll live well into our nineties."

"Together?" He shook off his shirt and sat beside her to remove his shoes. "Imagine it, at least."

"Let's stay in the here and now." When his sleek body looked so good, she couldn't focus on problems. He joined her on the bed with a single stretch. He kept his neck shaved so his beard looked handsome rather than scruffy, but when he raked his cheek up her thigh, it tickled. "Is it impolite for a woman to laugh at the man in her bed?"

she asked.

He kissed her knee. "It all depends on why she's laughing." He placed a sloppy wet kiss in her navel to make her giggle.

She ran her fingers through his hair. She longed to stay with him, but her mind raced, searching for the next rude shock. A truce was wonderful, and she pressed her whole body against his to enjoy it, but she felt as though she were making love to a ticking bomb. She gulped in a breath of air.

"What's wrong? No, don't tell me," he urged. "I don't want to hear anything other than grateful moans."

He tossed away her thong and used his mouth to pleasure her, and her worries drifted away on breathy sighs. He tilted her bottom so he could go deeper, and she clutched his inky hair to press him close. He teased her, made her hover on the edge of release and float down still wanting more. When he at last pushed her into a throbbing orgasm, she moaned his name and lay limp in his arms.

"You're the one who's in danger of being widowed," she murmured when she could finally speak.

His warm breath brushed her shoulder. "Not if you don't marry me."

"They might have to carry me into the church on a stretcher."

"A white satin stretcher with trailing ribbons," he added. He hugged her close and nibbled her earlobe.

She glowed in the lingering bliss. Sex might not be everything in a marriage, but when it was this good, did anything else matter? Undecided, she ran her hand down his flat belly to encircle his rock-hard cock. She'd not removed her wig and stared up at him with a sultry Goth-Girl gaze. "I'm so slippery wet, you won't hurt me if you bury yourself deep."

"Tell me if I do." He shifted over her, and she bent her left knee to welcome him. He caressed her slit with an easy thrust, dipped into her and withdrew. His calculated moves became a passionate dance, and when he had to give in, he carried her along with him into a shuddering ecstasy that left them both too sated to move apart.

"I've missed you," he whispered against her cheek.

"Hmm." She knew he'd want more, and so would she, but for now, she wished she could purr as loudly as Romeo.

Chapter Eighteen

The tantalizing aroma of freshly brewed coffee woke Ana Tuesday morning. Alejandro's scent lingered in her bed, and she rolled herself in the sheets to soak him up. When he didn't bring her a mug, she rose. She'd removed the wig before dawn, and her hair streamed about her head in wild disarray, perfectly suiting her mood. She donned her white satin robe and hopped into the kitchen. When she found Fatima rather than Alejandro, she forced a smile to hide her disappointment. "Good morning."

Fatima nodded toward the dining room table. "Your visitor left a note. I won't offer an opinion on the company you keep, but I'm sorely tempted."

Ana turned and found a beautiful drawing of the cats curled around each other. Alejandro had used paper from her printer, written they'd all missed her and signed with a fancy A that could have come from the cover of a Gothic novel. She hopped by her housekeeper into her office and added it to a folder to be filed later.

She wouldn't justify how she'd spent her night to Fatima or anyone else and promptly changed the subject. "I haven't decided what to wear this afternoon. Do you have a suggestion?" she asked.

Fatima poured a mug of coffee and carried it to the dining table for her. "You don't really do ruffles and frills, but you have a floral dress that would do."

"You're right. That is pretty." She took her chair at the dining room table and glanced through the paper. She suspected the editors of printing the same sad stories every day and just moving them around so readers would mistakenly believe the reports were current. She enjoyed working the crossword puzzles; those were always new.

"Are you in the mood for another poached egg?" Fatima asked.

"No, thank you, fresh fruit will do."

Fatima removed berries and melon from the refrigerator. "I've been thinking of baking some little creampuffs for this afternoon. It won't take me long to make a custard filling. Dusted with powdered sugar, they'd go nicely with what's left of the nut bread sandwiches."

"What's left?" She hadn't told Alejandro about the tea, and it tickled her to think he'd taken a handful on his way out. "I must have eaten more than I thought."

"Apparently so, but it can swiftly be replaced." She brought a serving of fruit to the table in a crystal bowl.

"Thank you, Fatima. I don't thank you often enough." She opened the paper to the crossword puzzle and ate her fruit slowly as she worked it.

Alejandro shoved away from the desk and stood to watch the activity along the docks. The view had fascinated him as a child when it had all been a game with a thousand moving parts. What he felt now was the burden to keep everything moving where it should. The *Mediterranean Queen* was in port that week, and he couldn't look at her without wishing the voyage he'd planned on the *Siren* had gone his way. He rubbed his neck, stretched, and had to admit he really needed to get more sleep than he'd had last night. He hoped Ana didn't have plans for the day so she could stay in bed, but he wished he could have remained with her until Fatima had yanked the covers off the bed and insisted they get up.

The tea was more fun than Ana had thought possible. Fatima put on a black dress and white apron to serve, and the ladies had dressed in their finest for the party. Ana had little in common with the four widows she'd invited other than a home address, but they told such entertaining stories she was sorry she hadn't gotten to know them sooner. Vivien had married a childhood sweetheart. Ingrid had eloped with her father's business partner. Judith and Helen had married men their families had encouraged them to wed, but only Judith had been happy.

Helen had had a difficult life. "I'd have left my husband long before he died, but I couldn't disappoint our children or force them to take sides."

"Life goes by so swiftly," Vivien observed. "I'm sorry you didn't have a loving marriage."

Helen shrugged. "I'm grateful he left me well provided for, and I may be luckier the second time."

"You'd marry again? Aren't you afraid you might do worse?" Ingrid asked.

Ana enjoyed a creampuff as the ladies laughed about the possibility of happy second marriages at their age. By the time they were all ready to leave, they'd talked away the afternoon, and Vivien promised to give the next tea soon.

"They were all really fun," Ana told Fatima. "I don't think people change much with age, do you?"

"Not from what I'd seen. Sweet people stay sweet, and the nasty ones just keep on getting nastier. Do you want me to fix dinner before I go?"

"Thank you, but I ate one creampuff too many, and I'll wait until later." She stretched out on the sofa and read through the latest edition of *French Vogue*. She'd hoped to hear from Alejandro, but when it grew late and he hadn't called, she warmed the leftover pisto manchego. It was even better than it had been Sunday night.

The call Alejandro had dreaded came late in the afternoon. His father had suffered a heart attack and died. Carlotta had been with him at the end and had left for home to tell their sons. Alejandro thanked the doctor for all he'd done, and remained at his desk to write a brief announcement for the staff. He gathered the department heads in the conference room and told them himself. Several sobbed into their handkerchiefs, but he felt nothing and remained dry-eyed.

"While not unexpected, this is still a blow," he said. "My father was not a religious man, and he often told me rather than a traditional funeral, he wanted to be cremated and have his ashes scattered at sea. It's appropriate for a man who gave his life to the Ortiz Line. I'll let you know when arrangements have been made. Take off as much time as you need."

There were questions, and he gave the best answers he could, but what was really needed was the assurance he would continue to head the firm.

"Yes, I will," he promised, his voice firm, but it wasn't an honor he welcomed or would continue indefinitely.

It was late when Alejandro came to Ana's door, but the seriousness of his expression made it plain he hadn't stopped by for sex. "Come in and tell me what's wrong."

"My father died this afternoon. I wanted you to know before it's on the news, but I won't stay."

She caught his arm and pulled him through the door. "I'm so sorry. You'll stay long enough to eat a creampuff, won't you?"

A skeptical frown crossed his brow. "A creampuff?"

"There were some left from the tea I gave this afternoon, but all the nut bread is gone. Let's have coffee and sit quietly together if you'd rather not talk."

"I'd rather not talk, but I'm sorry if I ate the nut bread you'd planned for a party."

She leaned close to give him a gentle kiss on the cheek. "You're welcome to whatever is here. From now on I'll put notes on anything I want to save." She hopped into the kitchen, and he followed.

"Go sit down, and I'll make the coffee," he urged.

"Fine." It amazed her how easily he glided into her life, and it was more than mere excellent chemistry. Whatever the intangible was, it exerted a constant pull even when she'd been furious with him. She returned to the sofa where she'd been reading. They'd called a truce last night, and she wouldn't mention a need to extend it when he'd come with such tragic news. He brought the whole plate of creampuffs into the living room, and thinking he might finish them all, she took the first one.

"How is your stepmother?"

He placed her coffee on the end table beside her. "She's taking it better than expected. She was with my father and swears she felt his spirit drift away. He would have hated being an invalid. It's a blessing he's gone. I don't feel anything, not sorrow, or relief, nothing at all. I called my mother when my father first entered the hospital, so his death didn't come as a shock. She said she'd pray for his soul." He took a creampuff. "How was the tea?"

She searched his face for a shadow of emotion, but he looked as cool as he sounded. This was a man who never mentioned love, so maybe today's lack of reaction was nothing unusual for him. Maybe he simply welcomed a distraction. "It was a lovely afternoon. I didn't grow up going to tea parties, and my mother never hosted one, but it was fun. I invited the widows in the building I've only seen occasionally and wanted to know. It's one of my efforts to sample the real world. Does that sound strange to you, or simply silly?"

"Neither. We get wedged into our lives, and it's good to step out on our own whenever we can. I don't suppose you told them about the baby?"

He was closely studying his creampuff. He never looked at her when there was something he really wanted to know. In gambling, such a giveaway was referred to as a *tell*. She stopped analyzing him to respond. "It's too soon, Alejandro, and they aren't dear friends. None would call the tabloids, but they'd tell someone, who'd tell someone, and soon everyone would know."

He swallowed a bite of creampuff. "How would that be bad?"

"Let's not go there." She licked a drop of custard filling from her finger.

"I should go."

"Have another creampuff and finish your coffee first."

He loosened his tie and kicked off his loafers. "I didn't mean to stay, but clearly you don't want me to go."

She laughed. "I don't?"

"No, or you'd not have offered a creampuff in the first place."

"Are you doubting my motives?" She still mistrusted his but couldn't help herself.

"Ask me later."

His father had died, and while he refused to admit it, it had to affect him. Maybe it had seeped so deep he couldn't feel it yet, but it would hit him someday. Every death was a loss, and Orlando Ortiz had cut a wide swath through Alejandro's life. Maybe Alejandro hadn't come for sex, but clearly he'd wanted a friend, and she didn't mind at all.

"Fatima could work as a pastry chef," he said.

"She could, but please don't encourage her. I love having her work

251

for me and would rather not have to train someone new in the way I want things done."

He nodded. "I understand. My father set out early to train me. He began taking me to the office when I was five or six. He talked to me as though I were an apprentice he expected to learn quickly. He cautioned me not to praise people for doing the job they were paid to do. He expected excellence and paid good salaries, so he didn't waste his breath on praise. One of his employees had to do something extraordinary to win an accolade. 'Keep them hungry,' he advised. I didn't know the word manipulation then, but I knew what he did was wrong and people deserved to be recognized for their work beyond a paycheck."

Now that he'd spoken about his father, she encouraged him to continue. "So his business lessons didn't take?"

He sipped his coffee and kept the warm mug clasped in his hands. "I learned his rules for success and could repeat them verbatim, but I didn't believe them. Now I have the choice of following his strict silent way of doing business or turning the Ortiz Line on its head. It's a tempting thought, but I won't do anything to harm the people depending on us for work. In the not too distant future, however, I hope to turn the whole operation over to someone who'd be much better qualified than I."

"Where do his younger sons fit in?"

"One of them may develop a passion for business when he's grown, and I'll drop the whole mess in his lap. But they're still kids and can't run anything yet. I'm sorry, I didn't mean to burden you with this."

"I don't feel burdened at all," she responded and had to cover a yawn. "I have an early shoot and should get to bed, but there's no rush if there's anything more you'd like to say."

"I've already said too much. I'll have just one more creampuff and go. I didn't come by for a sympathy—"

"Don't you dare say that word," she cautioned sternly. "That's never been what happens between us."

He flashed a killer grin. "You're finally admitting it's more than great sex?"

She'd meant to be strict, but he melted her resolve so easily, so continually, she doubted she'd ever be able to say no to him. She'd

252

never let him know, though. "You're pushing your luck, Mr. Vasquez. Last night's truce won't last forever."

"Why not?" He got up and carried the plate into the kitchen, wrapped the last two creampuffs and put them in the refrigerator. When he returned to the living room, he gave her a hand to rise. "We agreed to fight only on Tuesdays, but I can't handle discord tonight. Why don't you keep a list, and we'll argue about it the next time Tuesday comes around."

"There's nothing new," she replied with a shrug. She rested her hands on his chest to kiss him good-night, and he blurred the first kiss into so many more she lost count. He needed her tonight even if he couldn't admit it. "Stay," she breathed softly against his lips.

"What about your early job? Don't you have to look well rested?" He smoothed her hair back to kiss her ear.

It tickled, and she brushed him away. "It's a shoe ad. My one foot that can work will look great regardless." He slipped his arm around her waist to support her as she hopped into her bedroom. "I hope the kittens don't get too hungry before you come home."

"You caught me. I fed them before I came here," he confessed.

He pulled her so close she couldn't mistake how badly he wanted her. She slid her hand between them to rub him and felt him grow harder. "The ability to plan ahead is a significant plus in an executive, and you have other talents as well."

"I didn't sleep my way to the top," he murmured between kisses.

"No, but you surely could have."

They'd been together often, but he showered her with a fierce passion tonight. She welcomed his lavish kisses and deep thrusts and clung to his broad shoulders. She rolled her hips to rock against him and cried out as she came. He hovered above her, and she clasped her core to stoke him into bliss and lay pleasantly limp beneath his comforting weight. When he moved, she held him tight. "I like holding you."

"You don't feel crushed?"

"No, only warm and safe."

He kissed her tenderly, nibbled her ears and licked her breasts until his beard tickled. He rolled over to pull her up on top and wound his arms around her to keep her close. "Tomorrow will come too soon, but I'm not tired."

She kissed his cheek and wiggled against him. "Neither am I. What shall we do, count sheep?"

He smoothed his hand over her bottom. "I can't remember the numbers above one when you're so close."

"I can get closer," she promised, and he welcomed her delicious kisses and created another night neither would ever forget.

Rafael Mondragon listened to the news on the drive to medical school each morning, and he was shocked to learn of Orlando Ortiz's death. Maggie would already be at the American high school preparing for her classes. He called her as soon as he parked. "My mother may wait a year before marrying another millionaire, but I doubt it'll be much longer."

"Will she expect us to attend the funeral?"

"She might, but I'm not going."

"I don't blame you. How old was he?"

"Sixty-two, which doesn't sound all that old to me anymore. Love you."

"Love you more."

Maggie didn't see her sister, Libby, until lunch and drew her out onto the patio where they could eat at a table by themselves. "Orlando Ortiz died. While Rafael refuses to speak to his mother, I have the awful feeling she'll contact him to demand his support."

Libby opened her salad container and dribbled on the dressing. "Carlotta can demand whatever she wants, but your husband won't give in. You have to know that."

"Of course I do, but he doesn't need the aggravation and neither do I."

"Send flowers to the funeral and let it go. Ana Santillan married Orlando's son. I wonder if she'll keep modeling or simply run their social life. The family is probably involved in several charities, so she'd have plenty to do. We should call her and offer our sympathies."

"You're more curious than sympathetic," Maggie chided.

Libby's blue eyes shone with mischief. "True, but what harm could it do to stay in touch?"

Maggie gestured in the air. "Connect the dots. Carlotta is Ana's mother-in-law, or stepmother-in-law, and that's coming much too close to trouble."

"I suppose," Libby agreed, but she still wondered aloud. "We spoke to Ana after the accident, so we could call and ask how she is."

"Give it up, Libby."

Libby dropped the subject, but just because Maggie wouldn't call Ana didn't mean she couldn't do it on her own.

Lamoreaux sent his limousine for Ana. This was the first time she'd gotten a good look at his chauffeur. She'd recalled a larger man from the security videos, but this fellow was short and as lean as a jockey. "Have you been working for Mr. Lamoreaux long?" she asked.

"Awhile," he answered and remained focused on his driving.

She understood he was paid to drive rather than to keep her company, but something about him struck her as off. She made no further attempts at conversation and gazed out at the city as they drove through Old Town to Lamoreaux's apartment. It was located on the third floor of a beautifully restored building and had a spectacular view of the colorfully landscaped Parc de la Ciutadella. Ana loved coming to the park, and being so close lifted her spirits more than the prospect of modeling for the shoe designer could. He welcomed her into his home with a glass of champagne, but she took only a pretend sip and set it aside.

"I never drink when I'm working," she told him, unwilling to reveal her pregnancy. "What a beautiful place this is."

Lucien gazed up at the high ceiling circled with decorative gold molding. "I love nineteenth-century architecture. This building has been fully remodeled and well-maintained. What do you think of the color scheme?"

The entry and living room's soft greens and gold lured her in. "It's lovely."

The photographer had set up lights in the middle of the living

255

room and came forward to meet her. "Miss Santillan, this is a great pleasure. I'm Pierre Duvernay. I wonder if we could do some shots with you standing partially hidden by a door. It would be a way to show you wearing one shoe." He pointed to a rack of long and short gowns, all black. "We have clothes for you."

"Is there someone doing hair and makeup?" she asked.

"Yes," Pierre assured her. "My wife, Nanette, is setting up her cosmetics in the master bedroom."

"I'll show you the way," Lucien offered. "I hope you'll not be on crutches too much longer."

"So do I." Ana feared he'd lurk while Nanette worked, but he left her at the bedroom door. Decorated in dark blue and tan, the spacious room faced the park, but what immediately caught her eye were three stunning Robert Mapplethorpe floral photos. Her stomach dropped, but she licked her lips and made her way to the chair Nanette had placed in front of a full-length mirror.

"Whether I wear my hair up or down, you can use curls to cover my scar," Ana suggested. "What are your thoughts?"

"The scar won't even be noticeable under your makeup, and your long hair is so pretty, let's try several hairstyles. I'm very quick, so you won't spend the whole morning seated here."

"Fine," Ana agreed with forced calm. The striking photographs were visible in the mirror. She couldn't shake the uncomfortable feeling they told more about Lamoreaux than a decorator's whim. Her agent knew where she was, but suddenly he wasn't enough.

She pulled her cell phone from her purse. "I need to make a quick call before we begin. Will you excuse me?"

"Yes, of course."

When Nanette stepped out of the room, she called Alejandro. "I don't want to bother you, but I'm working this morning at Lucien Lamoreaux's apartment overlooking Parc de la Ciutadella." She supplied the address. "Will you please make a note of it? I'll talk to you when I'm finished."

"Is something wrong? Should I call the police?"

"Not yet, but I want you to know where I am should anyone be looking for me."

"Ana, are you just being mysterious, or are you in real trouble?"

"Too soon to say. I'll talk with you later."

Nanette returned, carrying a long black jersey gown. "This has a side slit and would be good to show off your leg and Lucien's shoes."

Ana entered the master bath, which was a masterpiece of cream-and-gold marble, to change from her long skirt and top. The gown had a high neck and long sleeves and looked perfect to her.

Nanette proved to have a delicate hand with a cosmetics brush. She added layers to Ana's mascara, a shocking red lipstick, and fluffed Ana's curls over her left shoulder.

"You look so elegant," the makeup artist exclaimed. "Let's begin with this look."

Lucien raised his hands in admiration as Ana returned to the living room. "You're even more striking than I dreamed. The doors are so beautifully carved and painted, it will be easy to hide your cast in the photos. Take your pick of the shoes I'm showing in the fall."

Shoeboxes were stacked to the side, each open to show a left shoe. Ana picked a black heel with a high lace vamp that hugged her ankle. "Let me go to the door before I put this on or I might not get there safely." She moved to her place, propped her crutches against the wall behind the door, took hold of it and removed her flat. Before she could wiggle her toe into the party shoe, Lucien knelt at her feet.

"Let me help you," he exclaimed. "Just like Cinderella. I always design my shoes with a princess in mind, and you'd make a lovely princess."

She held her breath as he slid his hand over her ankle, but he quickly fit the shoe on her foot and stood. "Thank you. Do you want me to look as though I'm peeking from behind the door, or coming around it?"

Pierre stood back to judge. "She ought to peek, don't you think, Lucien? Let's make it saucy so all we'll get is a hint of her figure and your magnificent shoe."

Lucien moved back to be out of the way, but his glance remained on Ana. "We have so many ideas for poses, but I don't want to tire you, so we might not finish today."

Ana smiled as though it were no concern. The man's shoes were gorgeous, but if he were a fan of Mapplethorpe's, he could easily have backed Jaime's nude project. Knowing how badly that had ended gave her chills. Suspicions weren't clues, however, so a second day might be worth it to provide information Montoya could actually use.

Lucien checked his gold Rolex often, and at one brought the shoot to a close. "Your agent said you'd be available for two days. I want to dress you in bright colors tomorrow. I'm thinking red, or maybe greens and blues. Let's talk it over while we have lunch."

The dining table was set with white damask and crystal, and a chef waited at the head of the table. "I always bring Etienne with me when I come to Spain. I love Spanish food, but there's nothing like familiar flavors from home."

Pierre and Nanette disappeared together; the table was set for two. Lucien helped Ana into her chair and set her crutches aside. Etienne returned to the kitchen, and his white-coated assistant brought a soup tureen to the table and filled their bowls with a mushroom soup with a bouillon base.

"This is one of my favorites," Lucien said. "Will you have wine now that you've finished working?"

"Thank you, but I prefer not to drink during the day." She smiled as though she were sincerely sorry to miss whatever expensive vintage he'd chosen.

"Then I must invite you to come for dinner soon. You're not wearing a ring, so should I assume the rumor you've married Alejandro Vasquez is untrue?"

He was an attractive man, and his teasing smile made him look harmless, but Ana remained on guard. "Our situation is complicated. Do you go out for walks in the park? The Museum of Modern Art is close."

"I've been there. It's an interesting collection, but I prefer the French museums. You must have been to France in your travels."

"Yes, many times." She kept silent about her mother and stepfather, and the conversation remained focused on art. While she didn't prompt him, he spoke of Mapplethorpe on his own.

"I collect modern photography. Perhaps you recognized the Mapplethorpe photos in my bedroom."

With his accent, he made the word *bedroom* sound like an invitation. "I did. He was a master of black-and-white and died much too soon. I'm interested in photography myself, and may someday turn it into a career."

"Really, it would be a shame for you not to be in front of the camera."

They were served a thick slice of roast lamb with small parsley potatoes and green beans. She sat back and stared at her plate. "I'm so sorry, I should have mentioned I'm a vegetarian when you first asked me to stay."

"I had no idea." Lucien looked up at Etienne's assistant. "Please remove Miss Santillan's plate and replace it with something she'd enjoy."

"I'm so sorry. I should have spoken up earlier." She certainly would have had she not been so distracted by her companion. At dinner parties, she could leave the meat on her plate and no one would notice, but with only two of them, Lucien would ask why she'd not eaten her lamb.

Lucien touched her hand. "Please, don't be embarrassed. Too often I assume others enjoy what I do, and I appreciate a reminder to be more considerate."

A new plate swiftly appeared with sliced fruit substituted for the lamb. She ate a green bean and exclaimed at the flavor. She hadn't worn a watch because they were too often misplaced during shoots, but Lucien took such small bites she feared it would be late afternoon before she could leave for home. Etienne served heavenly berry pastries for dessert, but she needed heaps of whipped cream to swallow each bite.

When she at last said good-bye to Lucien, she pretended an interest in his limo, and memorized the license plate before he helped her slide in. She called Alejandro and spoke as though she didn't care if the chauffeur overheard. "I'm finished working for the day and on my way home. See you soon." She ended the call before Alejandro could question her, and he surprised her by being there when she reached her condo. He nodded to dismiss the chauffeur and opened the door of Ana's building to escort her in.

"You needn't have come, but now that you're here, I need your opinion." She went to the security desk and asked to see the security tapes she'd studied when she'd wanted to know who'd sent her presents. Henry recalled the dates and put them on the screen.

Ana held Alejandro's arm. "Lamoreaux sent me several presents, including Romeo and Juliet. You can't see the chauffeur's face in any of the shots, but he doesn't look anything like the man who just brought me home, does he?"

Alejandro leaned against the counter to study the images. "No, this is a taller man, broader in the shoulder and more muscular. He's tucking his chin to hide his face. He could have been the man who came to the hospital."

"You think so? It makes me wonder what prompted Lamoreaux to hire a new chauffeur. Thank you, Henry. Let's go upstairs and decide what to do."

As the elevator doors closed, Alejandro pulled her into a lingering kiss. "Were you trying to scare me to death this morning?"

"No, that's not my idea of fun." Ana waited until Fatima had made coffee before she explained how uncomfortable she'd become working with Lucien Lamoreaux. "There was nothing unusual about today's shoot, but he's a wealthy man who could have backed Jaime Campos's nudes, although that doesn't mean he had anything to do with the murder, does it?"

Fatima brought a plate of hazelnut meringue cookies to the dining table and surveyed Alejandro with a coldly disapproving glance before returning to the kitchen.

"What did you tell her?" he whispered.

"The truth, but that's a story for another day. Do you think there's a reason to call Montoya, or should I wait to see what I can discover tomorrow?"

"I don't know which would be worse, calling Montoya or for you to risk going back." He reached for her hand. "That Lamoreaux has Mapplethorpe photos might merely be a coincidence, but that he's hired a new chauffeur could be significant. Montoya could get information on the former chauffeur that might lead somewhere. We ought to tell him."

"I'd hate to go to the police station." She picked up one of the light meringues and took a bite of the heavenly fluff. "These are so good, Fatima. Thank you."

"You're welcome," the housekeeper called from the kitchen.

After worrying about Ana all day, Alejandro had no appetite for sweets. "Let's make him come here. I still have his number."

"Let me talk to him." She gave the detective a call to inquire about the case, and when he had nothing new to report, she told him she might have discovered something. He came directly to her home.

Dressed in dark gray, he looked as smugly proper as ever and paced while Ana described her newfound suspicions about Lucien Lamoreaux. She handed him the limo's license plate number, and he nodded thoughtfully. "We weren't able to get clear prints from the clipboard the man dropped at the hospital, but it's possible he thought we could and left town. Thank you for the limousine license. I know just how to use it. Tomorrow an officer will go to Lamoreaux's apartment to inquire about unpaid traffic tickets. They'll have your address and a time when you were receiving gifts, so a ticket could be plausible. Lamoreaux will undoubtedly claim to know nothing about any traffic tickets, and the officer will inquire about his chauffeur." He stopped and turned toward her and Alejandro.

"Go back and work with him again tomorrow so he won't connect you with an investigation of his chauffeur."

"I don't think that's wise," Alejandro argued. "Maybe Lamoreaux is deep into the porn industry. He could be far more dangerous than a women's shoe designer."

"You could come with me," Ana suggested. "Lucien asked about you today, so he wouldn't be surprised if you were with me."

Alejandro glanced between them. "What do you want me to do, search the place while you're working?"

"No, absolutely not," Montoya replied. "Just be there so Ana will feel safe while our investigation continues."

"Ana shouldn't be used as bait."

"Of course not," Montoya exclaimed. "You brought me this information, and I'm pursuing it. Ana won't be in any danger."

Alejandro looked at her and shook his head. "I have a very bad feeling about this."

Things got out of hand for them so often, Ana knew exactly how he felt. "Please give us tonight to think about it, Lieutenant. I'll let you know what we decide in the morning."

"I trust you to make the right decision. We need to solve Mr. Campos's case before anyone else is harmed."

Alejandro showed the detective to the door and then strolled into the kitchen to talk with Fatima. "I deserve whatever name you might call me, but Ana and I have declared a truce. For her sake, I'd appreciate it if you'd pretend cool indifference rather than open hostility whenever I'm here."

"It will be a struggle," Fatima answered tersely.

Certain that was all he could get from her, he rejoined Ana in the living room. He removed her shoe and rubbed her foot. "Despite your suspicions about Lamoreaux, how did the shoot go?"

She wiggled her toes. "That feels wonderful. I looked at it as a day of work, which I need. It went well in that respect. The French photographer was very good, and had I been anywhere else, I'd have been happy with the job."

"I'm going with you tomorrow, but for now, I need to get back to work. I'll call you later about dinner."

"I'd like to stay in."

He leaned down to kiss her. "I'll bring dinner."

When he left, Fatima came to the doorway and shook her head. "I know," Ana confided. "If I've caught him in a lie, he'll work doubly hard to keep me from catching him in the next one."

"Or the following dozen," Fatima emphasized.

Ana bit into another cookie. "I like the hazelnut flavor."

"I don't care what flavor Alejandro is—just be careful not to take too large a bite."

Knowing she already had, Ana felt her cheeks fill with a bright blush.

Chapter Nineteen

Alejandro disliked Lucien Lamoreaux the instant he set eyes on him. Ana had called the Frenchman that morning to let him know she wouldn't need his chauffeur, but the designer's eyes widened as they came through the door.

"It's Mr. Vasquez, isn't it? How wonderful that you could come with Ana. The most provocative poses come to mind. Would you mind joining her in a few shots?"

"It's Alejandro, and that depends on how provocative you care to get," he replied with as charming a smile as he could fake. "Ana told me she wouldn't mind if I came along if I promised to stay out of the way."

Lucien offered his hand and looked Alejandro up and down. "The suit's handsome on you. Maybe we could have you dancing, and we'll focus on Ana's shoe. There's a new rack of clothing for you, my dear. Choose whatever you like, and Nanette will help you."

The photographer came forward. "Pierre Duvernay. Ana is the most photogenic model I've ever worked with, and you look as though you might be equally good in front of a camera."

"As long as I'm here," Alejandro responded with a careless shrug. "Just tell me where to stand."

Lucien opened a shoebox and removed a gold lace shoe. "Shall we do Cinderella? Your arm would hide Ana's cast."

"Fine, as long as I don't have to wear tights."

Lucien and Pierre laughed, and the designer assured him he wouldn't need a wardrobe change. Alejandro was grateful for the relaxed mood, but he found it difficult to stand close to Lucien. Miguel Aragon had been significantly older than Ana, and not having grown up with a father, she might be drawn to older men. Lucien's blue eyes and graying hair were a handsome combination, and Frenchmen were known for their charm. He silently cursed himself for being jealous, but if Ana weren't so suspicious of Lucien, the designer might pose some real competition. The baby held Ana to him, but he shouldn't have to rely on a child to keep her faithful.

When Ana appeared in a red ruffled gown, Pierre placed her in a gold occasional chair upholstered in silver brocade. "Turn toward me and, Mr. Vasquez, Alejandro, if you'll kneel and hold the shoe. It's the shoe we want to feature."

Ana pulled the ruffled hem of her gown over her cast. "Wait a minute. Alejandro needs a touch of makeup so his skin won't shine."

"You're right," Pierre replied. "Nanette, give him a light dusting."

Alejandro followed the makeup artist into Lucien's bedroom and immediately noticed the Mapplethorpe photos. He sat down as directed but flinched at the first brush of powder. He raised his hands to his nose. "Sorry, I have to sneeze."

Nanette stepped back until he'd finished. "Your dark, dangerous look sells cologne and whiskey. You should let my husband do your portfolio."

"Thank you, but this is the only day I'll model."

"What a shame. There, you look fine now."

Alejandro followed her into the living room. "I love the Mapplethorpe prints. He knew how to make a calla lily look erotic, and he did amazing nudes."

"Indeed he did," Lucien replied. "Now let's try again. How does he look to you, Ana?"

She smiled at Alejandro. "Very fine, as always. How much of us will be in the ad? Just the shoe, or both of us?"

"Both of you look too good not to use. Give me your best smile, and Alejandro, you have a fine profile and should concentrate on her foot and ignore the camera."

Alejandro gazed up at Ana. "You should have warned me I might have to pose."

She raised a finger to her lips. "Hush."

He slid the shoe on her foot more than a dozen times before Pierre and Lucien were satisfied. "Now stand together as though you were dancing. Do you want another shoe, Lucien?"

"No, let's use the gold again and switch for the next pose."

Alejandro held Ana tightly so she wouldn't fall, but they'd never danced together, and now he wished they had. "We need some music," he whispered in her ear.

"Hum to yourself, but if you make me laugh, we'll be here all day."

"I'll be serious," he promised, but it wasn't easy, and the tunes he hummed in his mind were all silly jingles for products he never used.

Although he appeared in only half the photos they took that morning, he was relieved when he finally had time to sit and observe. As promised, he kept quiet and was impressed by how easily Ana summoned a gorgeous smile on cue. It reminded him of the day he'd discovered her true identity. He'd thought every minute they'd spent together had been a cruel hoax, and if Jaime hadn't been murdered, he might not have seen her again. With his father's influence, the damning pieces had fit together perfectly, but Ana had blown them apart with the truth.

They were preparing to stop for lunch when a blue-uniformed policeman arrived at the door. Alejandro winked at Ana, and she responded with a slight nod.

The conversation at the front door could be easily overheard. "I'd no idea my chauffeur had any parking tickets. I'll take care of them today," Lucien said.

"It's really the chauffeur's responsibility," the policeman insisted. "May I speak with him?"

"I'm sorry, but he's left my employ."

The policeman scribbled in his notebook. "I should make a note of his name."

"René Charles," Lucien replied. "If you'll give me the tickets, I'll see they're paid."

The policeman handed them to the designer, thanked him and left. Lucien shuffled the three tickets and placed them on the entry table before rejoining the others. "It looks as though René parked in the wrong zone when he stopped at your condo. It isn't like him not to tell me, but I doubt I'll ever see him again."

"I hope they won't cost you much money," Ana exclaimed.

Lucien laughed at her dismay. "Please don't worry. My sales are so good here in Barcelona, a few parking tickets are of no concern, although I'm surprised someone would come to my door to make inquiries. Perhaps the Spanish are always so thorough. Now I hope you're hungry. I asked Etienne to make a vegetable dish he promises will be superb. Are you also a vegetarian, Alejandro?"

"No, but I've found everything Ana chooses is quite good, and I may become one someday. Right now, I bicycle to keep in shape, and I can't do it on a carrot salad."

"Will you excuse me?" Ana asked. "I need to change into my own clothes before we eat."

Lucien nodded. "Of course, take your time."

When the three reached the dining table, Lucien motioned for Ana to again take the seat on his right and put Alejandro on his left. As soon as they were served, Lucien concentrated on Ana. "I'm developing a perfume, a delightfully fresh and yet intoxicating blend of scents, and I'd love to feature you in the ads. You could do them now, and you wouldn't have to stand. We'll surround you in roses, orchids, all manner of colorful blooms, and all you'll have to do is hold the elegant bottle and smile."

"I don't work exclusively for anyone," Ann replied.

"You'll be free to work with whomever you choose," Lucien assured her. "I merely want you for the launch of the fragrance. We're aiming for the fall to market during the holidays."

"Aren't there enough perfumes on sale now?" Alejandro asked, and he caught a bright spark of anger cross Lucien's gaze. "Of course, I know nothing about ladies' perfumes."

"Apparently nothing about women at all," Lucien countered. "Women never tire of shopping. When they become tired of a favorite scent, they want something new, something captivating. Ana's face and figure are perfect for my new perfume."

"So there's always a market for perfume and shoes?" Alejandro surmised.

Lucien regarded him with a condescending smile. "Always. I love women and never tire of designing for them. Ana doesn't drink while she works, but I should have offered you wine."

"Thank you, but not today." Alejandro asked a question about shoe manufacturing, and Lucien supplied such intricate details, they had finished lunch before he concluded.

"I can see you're tired, my dear. I believe we have enough to work with today. I'll speak to your agent about scheduling the perfume ads.

We have the bottle now, a beauty of spun glass, and we could use it even while it's empty."

"Advertising always makes the product look better than it is," Alejandro offered.

"I disagree," Lucien countered. "I can't guarantee happiness or success in love, but my name is synonymous with excellence. I hope you'll forgive me, Ana, but I couldn't resist getting a small present to thank you for the last two days."

Alejandro squeezed her hand as they entered the living room. "Presents aren't necessary, Lucien," she told him.

"Gifts are a wonderful surprise, not a tiresome obligation." He opened a small chest and removed a white box with a big silver bow. "I hope you don't mind, Alejandro. Ana appears to be confused about her marital status, so I don't feel as though I'm giving presents to another man's wife." He handed Ana the pretty box.

Caught off guard, Alejandro nodded rather than argue they were married when they weren't. "Ana makes her own decisions."

"Thank you, Lucien." Ana untied the bow and opened the box to find a white gold bangle circled with pave diamonds. It was gorgeous, but she immediately replaced the lid. "I can't take this."

"Why not?" Lucien asked. "I've seen you wear bangles, and the dusting of diamonds doesn't make it a costly piece. Try it on and see how you like it."

Ana slid the beautiful bracelet onto her wrist. "This is lovely, but it's too much, Lucien."

"Nonsense," the designer argued. "I want you to keep it and give me an occasional thought. That's all I ask."

Ana hesitated, and then left the bracelet on her wrist and dropped the jewelry box into her bag. "Thank you so much. I've enjoyed working with you, and the perfume ads should be fun. Let's go home, Alejandro."

Alejandro wouldn't have forbidden her to take the exquisite bracelet, but he was annoyed that she'd kept it. "Yes, let's go while there's still time for me to get in a ride."

Lucien accompanied them to the door. "Are you a serious cyclist, Mr. Vasquez?"

"Not serious enough to train for the Tour de France, but it's good exercise for staying fit."

Lucien swept him with an appraising glance. "Clearly it is." He brought Ana's hand to his lips and turned it to kiss her wrist. "Goodbye, dear. I'll speak with you soon."

Alejandro held his breath as they walked down the hall, and waited until they'd entered the elevator to speak. "Did you have to keep the bracelet?" he asked.

She turned it on her wrist. "It's just a bracelet, Alejandro, and I want him to believe I'm looking forward to working with him again. We can't make him suspicious about our motives."

"Oh, of course not," he replied in a hoarse whisper. "Refusing a gift might make him believe we don't trust him."

"You already know I don't trust him. You needn't be jealous."

"I'm not jealous," he insisted through clenched teeth.

She gave him an ear-tickling kiss. "You certainly sound like it. Be sure to rinse off the powder before you go out for a ride."

He yanked a handkerchief from his pocket and rubbed it off with angry swipes.

Barcelona had few bike lanes, but Alejandro still liked cruising the city. Early mornings were the best time, but that afternoon, he needed to get out and ride to clear his head. He chose the streets leading to the docks and zigzagged in and out until a black Mercedes sedan came out of a side street and began following too close. To get out of the driver's way, he rode up on the sidewalk and grabbed a light pole for balance. As the car sped by, he made a note of the license number. Remaining uneasy, he kept a close watch on the traffic behind him, and when the sedan again appeared, he made a quick turn into a narrow alley.

He hadn't gotten a good look at the driver's face, but he had an impression of a big man. Whoever he was, Alejandro wouldn't take a chance on seeing him again. He cut from alley to alley and raced for the Ortiz Line building. He left his bicycle and helmet at the security desk and went up to his office in his shorts and sweaty shirt.

Carlotta was poring over the papers on his desk. Her black suit fit her lush curves to voluptuous perfection and reminded him of a suspect in a murder mystery. "Are you looking for something in particular?" he asked.

She swept him with a disbelieving glance. "You can't possibly expect to do business dressed like that."

He had only meant to find a quiet place to make a phone call. "I took the day off. Please don't move the papers on my desk, or I won't be able to begin where I left off."

"*Your* desk?" she cried. "My beloved Orlando's body isn't even cold."

"He died two days ago and couldn't still be warm. That isn't the point though, is it? I'll be happy to help you with whatever you need, but you can't walk in and out the way you did when my father was alive."

"You can't shut me out," she hissed. "The firm belongs to me and my boys as well as you."

Alejandro had read the will and being the principal heir, he wasn't fazed by her anger. "We'll see. We could meet with the attorneys tomorrow morning to read the will if you're free."

"Of course, I'm free. My husband is dead. We can make plans for the funeral then. His associates are asking for details, and they need to be decided."

"You know my father didn't want a funeral. His directions are clear in his will."

She clenched her fists. "He will have one of the finest funerals ever seen in all of Spain."

Alejandro sent her a darkly disapproving glance, and she stamped out on teetering stilettos. He vaguely recalled the television coverage of Miguel Aragon's funeral. Thousands of fans had surrounded the cathedral, but his father hadn't been a popular matador, and the church wouldn't be crowded if they held a funeral, which he was determined they would not.

He leaned against the desk and called Montoya. "Lucien believed your traffic-ticket story, but a black Mercedes followed me this afternoon, and the driver could have been the chauffeur he said no longer works for him. Fortunately, I was faster on my bike than he was in his car, but I have the license plate number for you."

Montoya wrote it down. "I have the officer's notes. There are a great many Frenchmen named René Charles, and several live here in Barcelona. Was the Mercedes merely following you, or did you perceive it as a threat?"

"The driver came too close the first time, and the second time I saw the car, I didn't give him a chance to do it again."

"I'll take that as a yes. Shall we keep this from Miss Santillan?"

Alejandro pulled in a deep breath and exhaled slowly. "I don't keep anything from her."

"Really? How brave of you. I'll call when we know who owns the sedan."

"Thank you." Alejandro looked over his desk. Carlotta hadn't made too big a mess. She had to have been searching for bank records, and he didn't leave those out for anyone who might wish to look. He locked the office, went downstairs to fetch his bike, and rode home in a weaving circular path. While he saw many black sedans, none was the one he'd spotted earlier.

Alejandro brought vegetable empanadas, a green salad and ice cream to Ana's that night. He looked relaxed in a shirt and jeans, but his ride had left him more jumpy than when they'd left Lamoreaux's. She was dressed in a long, pale blue skirt and top, and with her hair flowing free, she resembled a serene angel. He combed his fingers through her curls to pull her close for a hungry kiss.

"Someone followed me while I was riding this afternoon. I reported it to Montoya, and he'll let us know who owns the car."

She grabbed hold of his biceps. "You're sure they were following you?"

"Positive. I only got a glimpse of the driver, but it wasn't the chauffeur who's currently working for Lucien." He helped her to the table, and she slid into her chair.

Their places were already set, and she played with her napkin. "Could it have been one of your stockholders?"

"The price of the stock did fall after my father's death announced, but today it's bouncing back to its former level, so no one could be that incensed. There's my father's widow, who will never make things easy for me. We're not reading the will until tomorrow morning, so I should have been safe from her today." He went into the kitchen to toss the salad.

"Didn't your father leave her well provided for?"

"Yes, he did, and there are trust funds for the boys, but the majority of the family stock was left to me. She may assume there will be an equal distribution for her and her sons, but that's not what my father wanted. Now let's talk about something else."

"Thank you for again bringing dinner. This looks delicious. Everything you bring does. I wish I could cook something for us, but..."

"Learning to cook is on our list, remember?"

She brushed a crumb from her lips. "Yes, I do. We haven't added anything."

Alejandro had brought beer for himself, and he'd given her a glass of water. He swallowed a long drink before speaking. "We thought we were staying together when we began the list. Lamoreaux said you were confused about your marital status. What did you tell him?"

She plucked a black olive from her salad. "Only that it's complicated, and I changed the subject. I don't discuss my personal life on jobs. That's not included in my fee."

He ripped an empanada in half. "I understand, but we do need to make plans, Ana. My father's family lives in the penthouse of the Ortiz Line building. There are apartments for guests to use. I could move into one so I'd be close to the office, but I intend to keep my studio. You love your home, and I should bring the kittens back. Meeting for dinner every night is nice and sleeping over is great, but don't you think we ought to try actually living together?"

She regarded him with a wistful smile. "I suppose we could, and I do miss the kittens."

"Could you try for a little more enthusiasm?"

She reached for his hand. "We have such a great time together, but when I'm as round as I'm tall, your bed in your loft will look awfully good to you."

He laughed in spite of himself. "You can't get that big, and you're having my baby, so I wouldn't complain. Is that your real fear? That I won't find you attractive the minute you begin to show?" He had a call and checked his phone. "It's Montoya. Let's see what he's found."

"It's a rental car," the lieutenant reported. "And I'll bet you can guess the name on the rental agreement."

"René Charles?"

"Correct. He gave an address that doesn't exist and returned the car this afternoon after having had it only half the day. Paid in cash."

"Wonderful, so he may come after me next time in a red convertible. I won't be doing any riding for a while."

Montoya hesitated a moment. "You may want to reconsider."

"Now I'm going to be the bait?" Alejandro asked.

"It's a thought."

"Good-bye, I need to finish my dinner." He slid his phone into his pocket. "Where were we?"

"What does it matter? Does Montoya want you to ride around the city until René Charles comes after you again?"

He shrugged. "That doesn't mean I'll do it."

She pushed her plate toward him. "I'm not hungry."

He pushed it back. "You should eat all these nutritious vegetables to have a healthy baby. Do you want to work on names?"

"Names?" She put her head in her hands to smother her laughter. "You're like some crazy amusement park ride tonight, one of those with buckets of people whirling in circles and barely missing each other."

"Is that bad?"

It took her a moment to become serious. "You've lost your father and become CEO of the Ortiz Line, which is a huge responsibility, and you'll have to postpone becoming an architect. Your stepmother may order a hit on you, and someone's following you, apparently with bad intentions, when you ride your bike. You've got problems coming at you from all directions, and you want to work on baby names?"

He looked puzzled. "Does it strike you as an inappropriate time?"

"Inappropriate, inopportune, and flat-out crazy." She picked up her empanada and took a bite.

His eyes widened. "Now you're questioning my sanity?"

"No, you're so normal it's frightening. You're as steady as the Rock of Gibraltar, and all I can do is hang on while the world disintegrates around me."

"Eat so you'll have the strength."

She took another bite. "This is awfully good. The vegetables are crisp, and the crust is flaky." She took several more nibbles. "I can't get used to the idea of having a baby." She looked into the living room. "My home would be small for the two of us, and it's much too small for three with all the things babies need."

"A crib, a stroller, what else?"

There were only crumbs left on his plate, and she was full with half an empanada. She placed the remaining half on his plate. "We had a big lunch, and I'm full."

"Thank you. I forgot a highchair. What else does a baby need?"

"Toys."

"We'll buy a toy chest. I'll take the little guy to work with me if he'll be in your way here."

"Fatima will take care of him, or her. It's not that, Alejandro. I'm simply overwhelmed with the thought of caring for someone else."

"Ice cream will make you feel better. Calcium is soothing."

"It won't make me feel any worse. There should be more of the meringue cookies. I'll make coffee."

He finished the empanada and got up. "I'll handle it."

She sat back and attempted to fold her napkin into a rabbit, but gave up. "You'll make a wonderful husband."

"Thank you," he called from the kitchen. "You'll make a wonderful wife. I brought butter pecan tonight. I hope you like it." He returned with generous servings for both of them.

"I love it." She hummed as she swallowed a spoonful.

"Back to making plans..."

She waved her spoon. "I don't want to plan anything more than finishing this delicious ice cream. I thought you'd brought me too much. It's so good, though, I may have a second bowl. There's nothing that has to be decided tonight, is there?"

"Just the kittens' residence."

"Fine. Bring them with you the next time you're here."

He regarded her as closely as he would an exotic museum exhibit. "You make it sound as though I might not be invited back."

She brushed a curl away from her face. "Did I? I'm sorry. I'm just tired, and maybe nothing is coming out right."

That was a lie if he'd ever heard one, but he wouldn't call her on it. "I understand. Maybe I should go back to my studio tonight. I'll clean up the kitchen first." She didn't argue with him, and he left her seated on the sofa with a book. She looked more lost than tired to him, but clearly she didn't crave his company as badly as he longed for hers.

When Alejandro got up the next morning, it hurt to stretch, and he hadn't slept nearly as well alone as he did after spending hours making love to Ana. The overcast morning contributed to his dark mood, and the hot water and steam from the shower just made him wet. He rubbed his hair dry as he surveyed his closet. He had bespoke suits, monogrammed shirts and designer ties, so he looked the part of CEO of the Ortiz Line whenever he had to, and it was required for the reading of the will.

As he dressed, he replayed his last conversation with Ana, but no matter how he shuffled the exchange, she'd simply brushed off his suggestion they live together with a halfhearted concern they might feel crowded with a baby. Their baby wouldn't be born for months, so it was a lame excuse and made him wonder if she cared for him at all. He thought she had to like him a little. Clearly she liked the sex as much as he did. Maybe he hadn't given her enough time to get over his lie about their marriage. If that held her back, he hoped time would take care of the problem long before they became parents.

Carlotta was the last to enter the boardroom, and she'd brought her sons, Rodrigo and Francisco. They were ten and seven respectively, and while handsomely dressed, looked as though they'd prefer to be in school. They had neatly trimmed black hair and their father's gray eyes. Alejandro had been aware of their existence but had never played the role of big brother. He supposed he really ought to own up to it now.

There were also half a dozen members of the Ortiz Corporation's board present, men who'd admired Orlando and expected Alejandro to follow his lead. The corporate attorney, Jacob Tabladillo, had also handled Orlando's personal affairs, and he had the will ready to read.

He was a thin man with intense black eyes who looked as though no aspect of any maritime law had ever escaped his notice.

"I'm reading this will with great sorrow," Jacob began. "If you have any questions, Mrs. Ortiz, I'll be happy to explain in greater detail."

Carlotta was dressed in a black long-sleeve dress and wore no jewelry other than her wedding ring. "Thank you. I'll listen closely."

The attorney made eye contact with all those seated around the table. "Orlando had a gift for seeing the future, and he planned thoroughly for every eventuality. He left explicit directions there is to be no funeral or memorial service. He requested cremation and wanted his ashes scattered at sea."

Appearing shocked, Carlotta leaned forward. "Didn't he realize the boys and I would need to say good-bye?"

Jacob squared his shoulders. "Mrs. Ortiz, you and your sons will certainly be able to ride in the boat and distribute Orlando's ashes. Flowers are often thrown into the sea at such times, and you can bid your husband good-bye then."

"It's not right," she maintained, her eyes filling with tears.

"Pray for his soul whenever you attend mass, but there is to be no funeral of any kind," Jacob stressed. "Your late husband left a generous trust fund for you and his sons." He passed her the appropriate papers for her review. "As for his share of the stock in the Ortiz Lines, it is to be divided between you three and Alejandro, his eldest son, with seventy-five percent going to Alejandro and twenty-five percent to be shared by you, Rodrigo and Francisco."

"Twenty-five percent?" Carlotta nearly shrieked. "That's not fair. There are three of us, and he's only one person."

Alejandro spoke softly. "The trust fund will provide more than you'll ever need, Carlotta, so in every respect, the stock division is fair."

"I believe I need my own attorney," she countered. "Do I have to listen to anything more?"

"There's just one additional item. Orlando had known you'd had two children before you met him. He regretted the loss of your daughter, but admired Rafael Mondragon's courage and believed he'd inherited it from you."

Carlotta's complexion drained of all color. "How long had he known?"

Jacob concentrated on the will rather than the increasingly distraught widow. "For as long as he knew you, I believe. He was a man who kept a great deal to himself, for whatever his reason, and he allowed you to keep your secrets as well."

Carlotta rose and, taking her sons by the hand, fled the room as quickly as she could herd the boys through the door.

"You should have spoken to her in private," Alejandro admonished. "There was no need to embarrass her in front of us."

Jacob nodded. "I agree, but it was what Orlando desired, and I'm following his wishes to the letter as I always have."

Alejandro glanced around the table. The board members were as astonished as he. That his father had kept quiet about having a matador for a stepson amazed them all.

"I'm sorry Orlando didn't discuss his will with his wife while he was alive to defend his choices," Jacob stressed. "If any of you have made the same mistake, you ought to correct it immediately. Now let me continue."

There were charitable donations his father had wished made, and Alejandro nodded as each was named. There were letters for each of the board members and one for him that outlined his hopes for the Ortiz Line, but no word of love or praise. Alejandro slipped his into his pocket and promptly forgot it.

Lucien Lamoreaux called Ana midmorning. "I'm fascinated by the prospect of your becoming a photographer. I have a project in mind that should intrigue you. Will you meet me for lunch at one?"

Ana sat back in her chair. She'd been working the crossword puzzle at the dining table. She hadn't bothered to dress yet, but that scarcely mattered. She had a good idea what Lucien's project was. Because there appeared to be no other way to obtain evidence linking him to Jaime's death, she had to say yes but needed to appear reluctant. "I haven't done any professional work as yet," she stressed. "You might need someone with more experience."

"You have a wealth of experience in front of a camera, and that's what's needed. Let's meet at Can Culleretes in Old Town. Do you know it?"

"Yes, of course. It's the city's oldest restaurant and has wonderful food."

"This will be only a preliminary conversation, so there's no reason to include your agent as yet. Shall I send my chauffeur for you?"

"No, I'll meet you there." Alejandro would be busy with his father's will, so she couldn't call him, and she hated to bother Montoya over a lunch date that might fail to prove enlightening. "I'm meeting Lucien Lamoreaux at Can Culleretes for lunch, Fatima, so you needn't prepare anything for me."

"Any hope of samples?"

"I'll try." She couldn't very well accuse a man of murder and ask for shoe samples in the same breath, but she wouldn't let him guess she even suspected him.

Ana had been at Can Culleretes often and felt comfortable there, although she would have much preferred a different companion. As soon as they were seated at their table, she gave Lucien one of her prettiest smiles. "I'm so flattered you'd consider me as a photographer. Does the project involve your beautiful shoes?"

He laughed and shook his head. "No. You know I collect Robert Mapplethorpe's work, and he's my inspiration. Let's order first, shall we? I've heard their calamares a la romana is good. Do they have a salad you'd like? If not, perhaps we could give the chef a special order."

Ana surveyed the menu. "They have a wonderful fruit salad with delicious rosemary rolls, so I'll be fine." She requested iced tea rather than wine and offered no explanation for her choice. "Photography has changed completely from the time Mapplethorpe worked. Digital cameras make everything easier, although I'm sure the purists must miss their darkrooms."

"I'm sure they do. Traditionalists slow the progress of every art, but creativity can't be contained."

"I agree. You have three of Mapplethorpe's floral photos in your apartment. You sent me so many beautiful roses, were you thinking of doing something new with flowers?"

He had selected a fine white wine and waited while the waiter poured a sip into his glass. He tasted it and nodded, and the waiter filled his glass. "No, I prefer his studies of the human body. He had a way of highlighting the curve of a back or shoulder and made his models look as elegant as the finest Greek sculpture."

"He did," she agreed. "I never pose in the nude, so I'm not sure I'd be the right photographer for you."

"The models can cover themselves with a robe until you're sure of the shot. I'd like to give the impression of nudity without actually showing it. If a woman held a thin scarf over her breasts, there would be only a hint of her nipples. Do you understand what I mean? I want to produce tasteful photos, not create nude shots for cheap magazines."

Ana nodded thoughtfully. "Do you have a publisher interested?"

"I don't plan to produce a book, but instead a limited edition of stunning photographs that will appeal to men with, shall we say, discriminating tastes."

Ana's salad was served along with his meal, and she concentrated on the fresh melon. She was tempted to ask him if he'd approached Jaime Campos with the project, but although they were surrounded by people laughing and talking in the popular restaurant, she thought it would be too dangerous a question to ask. She smiled and nodded as though she were interested in producing the artful photography he described, but her heart beat much too fast, and she had to keep wiping her sweaty palms on her napkin.

Alejandro returned the kittens in their carrier with all their paraphernalia. "Did Ana tell you the kittens were coming back?"

Fatima held the door wide open for him. "She failed to mention it, but here they are, so it must be all right. Did they give you too much trouble?"

"No, but I'm not going to have much time to spend in my studio, and they need a real home. Isn't Ana here?"

"No, she's gone to lunch with Lamoreaux."

Astonished Ana would go near the man alone, he searched Fatima's expression for more. "Did she say where they were going?"

"She did, but you ought not to stalk her. If she wants to see you, she'll be here when you call."

He silently debated her advice only briefly. "Lamoreaux may know who killed Jaime Campos, and I don't believe she's safe with him."

"*Dios mio*, you're not serious."

"Dead serious. Now where is she?"

The kittens were chasing each other around the living room, and she watched them while she caught her breath. "They're at the Can Culleretes."

"I know it." He grabbed her shoulders and kissed her forehead on his way out.

Chapter Twenty

Alejandro joined Ana and Lucien at their table. He kissed her cheek and took a chair. "I wanted to make certain you had a ride home. Hello, Mr. Lamoreaux. I hope the photos Pierre took of us are what you needed." He slid his hand under the table to squeeze Ana's knee.

Lucien appeared only mildly disconcerted. "Indeed they did. Would you care to join us for lunch?"

"No, I'll wait for dessert. They have an incredible crema catalana here, don't they?"

"Yes, it's superb," Ana replied. "Lucien believes I'd be the right photographer for a series of figure studies he's envisioned, but I'm not sure I'm ready for such a big step."

Alejandro responded with a wide grin. "Of course, you're ready. Do you still have the photos of me on your camera?"

"I do. I always carry my camera so I don't miss an opportunity to get something unique." She hurried through the photos she'd taken on board the *Mediterranean Siren* and found the two of Alejandro. "I love this one of him curled over the table."

Lucien nodded as he studied it. "This is a remarkable composition. Do you have more?"

"The one of me in bed is good. Go ahead and show him," Alejandro urged.

Lucien's face lit with a bright smile. "Yes, we could use this one. This is exactly what I want. You'd be handsome in any pose, Alejandro, but this candid photo is far more appealing than a posed nude would be."

"You see." Alejandro leaned over to hug Ana. "This would be a great opportunity to not only gain experience but to launch your new career. You should do it."

She chewed her lip. "Your confidence is so flattering, Alejandro, but let me consider it, will you, Lucien?"

"Of course, and let's meet again to discuss details when you decide to say yes." He smiled as though she'd already agreed.

"I wish I had your confidence in my talent," she remarked.

"Confidence is vital to any pursuit," Lucien replied. "Wouldn't you agree, Alejandro?"

"Indeed, I do."

Alejandro finished his dessert first and watched as Ana licked her spoon. "I love desserts, so it's a good thing I'm going to ride again this afternoon. It also takes my mind off the constant stress of running the Ortiz Line."

"It must be a great burden," Lucien offered. When they were ready to go, he offered his hand. "Thank you for your enthusiasm for my idea, Alejandro. I'm sure we'll see each other again soon."

As soon as they were seated in his SUV, Alejandro kissed Ana hard. "You played that so well, Lucien will never guess why you're so reluctant to work with him."

She looked at him askance. "You overdid it with the encouragement, or do you actually believe I'd care more about my career than catching a murderer?"

"You're not going to do it, so I made it look as though I were on Lucien's side. It was an act on both our parts."

"Really? Didn't you refuse to be bait for Montoya—and now you're eager to go out and ride?"

"I did, but I've reconsidered. Working with Lucien really would build your photography career. Unfortunately, it's far too dangerous to even consider. I want him caught before you've taken a single photo for him."

"What about you? It's too dangerous for you to ride hoping René Charles will pursue you again. What if he shot at you rather than attempt to crowd you off the road?"

Already on guard, he studied his rearview mirror. "It has to be difficult to shoot a cyclist."

"Undoubtedly, unless he's a good shot."

He glanced toward her. "He used a knife on Jaime."

"So what? Maybe he has a wealth of lethal weapons. He could

blow poison darts at you."

He reached over to give her hand a loving squeeze. "Have you always had such a lively imagination?"

She looked out at the people on the street. "I'm an only child and learned early to amuse myself."

He laughed but reined it in when she scowled at him. "If you don't count Carlotta's boys, I'm also an only child, or I was brought up as one. Maybe that's why I took to drawing and didn't need anyone else."

"Fascinating to hear, but what are you going to tell Montoya?"

"That I let Lamoreaux know I plan to go out for a ride, and if René Charles shows up again, they can catch him."

"How is Montoya going to protect you? Will he take to a bicycle himself?"

Alejandro shrugged. "He looks fit. He might own one."

"You told me I'd be well provided for if a crane toppled and crushed you. Do you already have the baby in your will?"

"Would it surprise you to learn I do?"

"Yes, I'd be shocked."

"I updated my will this morning after our attorney finished reading my father's. It's signed and witnessed, so if I flip over the handlebars and break my neck this afternoon, you and the baby will still be able to lead very comfortable lives."

She turned away, but he caught a gleam of tears in her eyes and wondered if she'd really miss him. He reached for her hand. "I missed you last night. Let's not spend tonight apart."

"We won't have a choice if you're in the morgue."

He could almost see her mind work. She feared he'd die trying to catch René Charles, and she'd be left all alone. It hadn't been quite a year since Miguel Aragon had died. Maybe she feared he'd also be taken from her. It was too painful a thought to consider.

When they reached her condo, he walked her up to her door. "I'd like to call Montoya from here so you'll know the plan. Be careful opening the door—I brought the kittens home."

She peeked around her door. There was no sign of the cats. "All right, come in, but don't expect me to be part of this."

Fatima rushed up to them. "Did Lamoreaux admit he knew

anything about Jaime's death?"

"No, but we believe it was his chauffeur who killed him," Ana answered. The kittens were asleep on the sofa, and she sat down and gathered them into her lap. They yawned lazily, showing their pink mouths, and went back to sleep. "We don't actually know anything for a fact, but Alejandro is determined to solve the crime on his own."

Fatima swept him with an appreciative glance. "You look as though you could, but isn't it the police's job?"

"Thank you for reminding him of the obvious," Ana offered. "He's completely overlooked it."

"That's not good," Fatima replied.

Alejandro dropped into the wing chair and called Montoya. He explained he'd had an opportunity to let Lucien Lamoreaux know he planned to go riding again that afternoon.

"Where did you begin yesterday, from the Ortiz building or from your apartment?" the Lieutenant asked.

"I keep my bike at my studio." He gave Montoya the address, and they agreed upon a time.

"Begin there, but go a different route from yesterday. I'll station men on bicycles nearby, and they'll follow you at a distance. If René Charles appears and threatens to harm you in any way, they'll arrest him. Leave everything to us."

Alejandro ended the call. "It should work. We'll have a lot to talk about later. Do you want me to bring dinner tonight, or would you rather go out?"

Fatima returned to the kitchen, and Ana focused on the kittens. "This could get ugly, Alejandro."

"It could, but it won't. Charles may not show up, but if he does, he'll be the one being tracked. I'll call you later."

"Please do—and it better not be from the hospital."

He stood and wound his fingers in her beautiful hair to pull her close for a long, deep kiss. "I wouldn't jeopardize what we have, Ana. Trust me on this."

He left her with the cats and Fatima for company and hoped it wouldn't be the last time he saw them all.

There was no parking garage for Alejandro's studio. He parked on a side street and loosened his tie as he walked toward the corner. When he heard footsteps rapidly closing in behind him, he shot a glance over his shoulder. It was all he needed to recognize the burly man from the hospital. Rather than risk fighting such a muscular brute hand-to-hand, he had to move fast. While it had been years since he'd studied karate, he'd learned his lessons well. He jumped into a flying turn and sent a savage kick into the man's knee.

The man howled as he fell and struck his head hard on the concrete walk. Knocked out, he lay sprawled where he'd fallen, and his knife slipped from his grasp. Alejandro took a moment to catch his breath, and then pulled off his tie to secure the fallen man's hands behind his back. He picked up the knife with his handkerchief, surprised by its weight. Jungle Warrior was stamped on the nine inch black blade. The wicked weapon looked to be perfect for a jungle's hazards, if not a quiet Barcelona street. He'd relied on instinct and struck first. It had saved his life.

He called Montoya before anyone walking by on the main street noticed a man down. "I've got him, and he needs an ambulance." He gave his location and leaned against the ficus tree shading the sidewalk for support. He heard sirens in the distance and fought not to shake uncontrollably while he waited for the police to arrive. Rather than being frightened, however, he was enraged by how easily death could have overtaken him.

Montoya flew out of his car. Paramedics were working over the injured man and after ascertaining he was alive, Montoya crossed the sidewalk to Alejandro. "Clearly his plans didn't coincide with ours."

Alejandro handed him the knife. "Keep the handkerchief. He dropped this when I kicked him. He meant to attack me from behind. Fortunately, I heard him coming."

Montoya frowned as he studied Alejandro closely. "Do you have a black belt in karate, Mr. Vasquez?"

Still shaken, Alejandro wisely kept the tree at his back. "My father feared I'd get into trouble on the docks and insisted I learn to defend myself. I didn't earn a black belt, but mastered enough to survive today. If I'd been talking on my phone, or lost in thought, he'd have caught me."

"Probably meant to cut your throat," Montoya mused aloud. He called to a policeman to ask for the man's wallet, but no identification had been found in his pockets. The officer approached to hand Alejandro his tie.

"Thank you. This is one of my favorites." He rolled it up and shoved it into his pocket.

Montoya kept a firm hold on the knife. "He's most likely René Charles. We didn't release details on Jaime Campos's murder, but this matches the murder weapon. When Charles comes to, he may implicate Lamoreaux, but even if he doesn't, we'll have him for Jaime's murder and an attempt on your life."

"See if he'll tell you why he wanted me dead. There's no link between Jaime and me, or Lamoreaux, for that matter."

Montoya laughed softly. "How can you misunderstand? Miss Santillan is the link, but I try not to anticipate how a criminal will justify his misdeeds. You needn't remain here. I'll call you tomorrow, and we'll arrange a time for you to give us a written statement."

Alejandro glanced away. "Ana won't want to hear this was about her."

The lieutenant nodded thoughtfully. "True, but you tell her the truth, don't you?"

Alejandro sucked in a deep breath. "I'll wait until Charles, or whoever he actually is, tells his story."

"A delay might be wise. I'll speak with you tomorrow."

The paramedics were hoisting the unconscious man's stretcher into the ambulance. Satisfied he was no longer in danger, Alejandro struck off for home. As soon as he'd locked his door behind him, he called Ana.

"The police arrested the man they were after near my building, so there's no reason for you to worry. I'm fine, but I'd rather not go out to dinner. What would you like me to bring tonight?"

"You're sure you're fine?"

He'd not seen the knife before he'd kicked Charles with brutal force. Had he known what he'd intended, he might have aimed higher and broken the fool's neck. He'd never killed a man, and didn't wish to begin. Still, whatever damage he'd done had been self-defense, and

Montoya knew it.

"It hasn't been a pleasant afternoon, but I'm fine. There's not a mark on me. I promise. Montoya will let us know what he learns from René Charles, or whoever he is. Let's forget him. Do you know a place with really good squash?"

"Squash? Do you remember the first time we went to dinner? They have excellent squash. All their vegetables are good, and you could order a steak for yourself."

He didn't give a damn about squash—he'd simply wanted to steer the conversation away from that afternoon. "Yes, I remember where it is. I'll check the menu while I'm there." He told her good-bye and laid his phone on his worktable. He looked for the kittens before remembering he'd taken them home to Ana's. He stretched out on the futon and replayed his encounter with René. He'd reacted quickly, without wasting a second to think and thank God, it had worked. He'd thank his father for the foresight to send him to karate instruction, but the man was no longer alive to hear it.

Ana had changed from the outfit she'd worn that morning into her gold top and skirt. "Does it bother you when I say you're beautiful?" Alejandro asked. "Have I said it too often?" He carried the take-out bags into the kitchen and pulled plates from the cupboard.

She remained by the door. "I haven't heard it too often from you. Are you embarrassed when I compliment you?"

He swept her with a warm glance. "You don't do it often."

"I don't? I'm sorry, I should. You're a very handsome man, and you don't gloat the way Gian Carlo does over his looks. I wonder if he's still staying at Lourdes's place."

He glanced over his shoulder. "Do you care?"

She hopped up behind him, slid her arms around his waist and rested her cheek against his shoulders. He was deliciously solid. "No, not at all."

He took her hands as he turned. "I've never been jealous of another man until I met you. I'll work on it."

She leaned into him. "It's all right to have a few faults, Alejandro. I'm a long way from perfect."

"Not from where I stand. The restaurant gave me a taste of their squash soup, and it was so good I brought some along with the vegetable pasta and salad. Why don't you hop over to the table, and I'll serve."

"If you insist." She held the counter for balance and hopped away. "How long do you suppose Montoya will have to question René to get the whole story?"

He carried in the soup bowls and spoons and returned for the carton of soup and a ladle. "He may never get the truth, but we can leave it up to the courts. I noticed you had some sour cream. Would you like some on top?"

"Yes, that would be nice. Why don't you just say you don't want to talk about it?"

"I don't want to talk about it. There, will you stop asking me questions?"

"Curiosity is a plus, not a fault."

He looked around. "Speaking of curiosity, where are the kittens?"

"They're in the bathroom so they won't jump on the table while we eat."

"Shouldn't we be able to train them?" He gave her a spoonful of sour cream, and it floated atop the squash soup in a graceful swirl. "I'm too hungry to argue over where we're going to live, but please think about it. The board will expect me to spend more time working than I have been this last week, and I'll still want to see you."

She sipped her soup and murmured softly, "This is really good. If you'll be so busy, what does it matter where you'll live?"

"It matters to us, Ana. If there is an *us.* I don't want to push you where you don't want to go, but..."

She grasped his wrist. "Stop. Let's eat and talk later. This afternoon, I was terrified something horrible would happen to you, but you're fine, or pretend to be, and I'd like to enjoy it. It's probably only the calm before the next disastrous storm, but please, let's enjoy the moment."

"I enjoy every minute with you." He finished his soup first. "I'll bet there's always a market for tasteful nude photos. With my help, you wouldn't need Lamoreaux's backing. You could do the project on your own."

He looked so pleased with the idea, while she was appalled. "I'm thinking of how nice it is to be with you, and you're dreaming up business ventures?"

"The venture is all about you." He got up to serve the rest of their dinner. "Maybe you'd like to devote yourself to modeling maternity wear for the time being, and concentrate on photography after the baby comes. You could choose your own hours rather than having to follow a designer's schedule."

When he'd served her plate, she chose to focus on the meal rather than how annoyed she was with him. "The broccoli, carrots and asparagus are perfectly steamed and seasoned, and the pasta is warm and comforting. Please let me concentrate on my dinner."

"Do you think I'm too controlling?"

"You could be. No, I take it back. You most definitely have the tendency. You can say it's because you care for me, but you're also bent on pleasing yourself."

"That's harsh."

"We have a truce, remember? And I don't want to delve into the past. Let's just drop the subject."

"Should we save it for Tuesday?"

She shook her head. "Must we?"

"No, of course not. We should agree to only disagree on something if both of us wish to discuss it."

"That won't work," she pointed out. "Let's say I want a puppy, and you say no and won't discuss it. That wouldn't be good. Everything would end in a stalemate."

"You're right. Should I assume the puppy was merely an example rather than a desire to have one?"

"Yes. Two pets are more than enough for me. Why are you smirking? Do you want me to consider you as a pet?"

"If you'll be mine. I'll do better at reining in my thoughts. We're scattering my father's ashes on Saturday. Do you want to come with me? It won't be a long boat ride, but it would give you a chance to meet my stepmother and her sons. I forgot to tell you the best part—Rafael Mondragon is her son."

"El Gitano, *that* Rafael Mondragon?"

"Is there another? I suppose I should ask him if he'd like to go with us to support his mother. Apparently she hid the fact she had a son in his twenties, but my father knew all along."

"That's an awfully important secret to hide."

"She may have wanted to appear younger, although she must have been very young when Rafael was born. I never heard her mention she had Gypsy blood. Rafael is proud of it. The woman's odd. You needn't think of her as a possible mother-in-law. My mother would be the only one who matters."

Ana sat back and folded her hands in her lap. "I don't believe I've ever had such an unusual invitation, but I'd rather skip meeting your stepmother at such an unfortunate time. Once she's over the initial shock of her husband's death, we can get together. I have Maggie's number if you want to contact Rafael. He's rather difficult to get to know. Miguel thought highly of him, however. Whether or not he'd want to support his grieving mother, I don't know. If she hid his existence, things might not be particularly good between them."

"If you'll give me Maggie's number, I'll invite them. Things couldn't be any worse for Carlotta than they already are, and Rafael could help me raise the boys; they're half brothers to both of us."

"What do you plan to say when you scatter the ashes?"

He frowned, clearly perplexed. "Must I say something?"

"Isn't some sort of personal good-bye expected? Perhaps your stepmother has something planned."

"I'll be happy to give her the honor. Could we talk about something else?"

While she ate slowly, he went back to the kitchen for seconds. "The weather has been lovely," she remarked.

He laughed and leaned over to kiss her as he returned to his place. "We're avoiding every other subject, aren't we?"

"You avoid some, and I avoid others. Let's take things day by day and see how we get along."

He flashed a cocky grin. "And the nights?"

"We could live for the nights. We get along beautifully then. There, that's a compliment for you."

"Thank you."

"You're welcome." As soon as they'd finished dinner, she called Maggie Mondragon. "It's Ana Santillan. How are you?"

"I'm thrilled to be pregnant, but the mornings are wretched. Otherwise, we're both fine."

"How wonderful, congratulations. You and Rafael will make beautiful babies." Alejandro was pacing beside her, and while she smiled at him, she had no desire to disclose her own baby news. She explained why she was calling, and when Rafael took the phone, she handed it to Alejandro.

"I'm looking forward to meeting you," he began. "We share two half brothers. Your mother is heartbroken over my father's death, and I thought you and Maggie might want to come with us when we scatter his ashes on Saturday."

Rafael cursed softly. "I'd not come if you were scattering her ashes, and she knows why. Good-bye."

Alejandro returned the phone to Ana. "He sounds as though he doesn't need a cape and sword to get the better of a bull. Maybe I'll be better off not knowing him."

"He's had a difficult life, but Maggie adores him. I could invite them to come for dinner so you could meet him under better circumstances."

His gaze narrowed. "What about Libby and Santos? Would you invite them too?"

After a musical giggle, she apologized. "I shouldn't laugh, but he's simply not an issue. Please don't try and make him one. Did you bring some ice cream? I'd like to eat it off your abs, if you don't mind."

He caught her hands and pulled her to her feet. "I brought chocolate. Aren't you worried about staining the sheets?"

"I plan to lick up every drop. If I miss one, we can wash the sheets easily enough, and there's more than one set. Let me change while you get the ice cream."

Once in her bedroom, she looked for something new and took out her red wig. It was long and curly, nearly the same seductive shade as Valeria's. With a slinky black nightgown, she looked not only hot, but also like another woman entirely. She sprayed on a mist of a spicy perfume, turned off the lights and sat on the end of the bed to wait for him.

Alejandro flipped the light switch as he came through the door and nearly dropped the bowl of ice cream on his shoes. "My God, you're better than a chameleon at changing your look. That is you, isn't it, Ana?"

"Of course, it's me. I wouldn't share you with another woman. I'm going for a dangerous, sultry look tonight. What do you think?"

"You've succeeded." He set the bowl on her nightstand, stepped out of his loafers and peeled off his socks. His shirt came off with a quick tug and his pants followed. He remained in his black silk boxers and joined her on the bed. "I've never had a woman lick ice cream off me. Do you do it often?"

She eyed him with a provocative stare. "Are you incapable of thinking of me as your woman, rather than the mistress of millions?"

"I didn't mean that, and it couldn't have been millions," he argued. "You just made it sound fun."

She slid her finger under the waistband of his boxers. "You won't need these." She rolled them over his hips to brush his erection and tossed them to his pile of clothing. "Just lean back, and I'll do the rest."

He stretched out as ordered but flinched as she dropped a spoonful of ice cream into his navel. "That's cold."

"It's ice cream," she chided. She licked it off, blew her warm breath over the remaining cold spot and swished her curly wig over his chest. "Better?"

He grabbed the ends of her red hair to pull her up for a kiss. She licked his lips. "Do I taste like chocolate?"

"Hmm."

She spread ice cream over his nipples. "Tell me if you like this."

He pressed her close. "Do you plan to tease me all night?"

"Do you have an objection?" She danced her fingertips down his belly to encircle his cock and felt him grow even harder. "I don't feel one."

"Bastard never objects," he moaned.

She trailed her long curls over his hips. "Do you want him to?"

"No, never."

"Good, I don't want you to regret a moment of tonight." The cast on her leg forced her into inelegant poses, but she kept him too happy to notice. "Isn't this all a compliment?"

"Definitely." He arched his back as she drew his cock deep into her mouth.

Stretched along his thigh, she licked and sucked and fondled his balls with a gentle cupping. She loved the way his whole body reacted to each flick of her tongue and wasn't surprised when he yanked her into his arms. "Too much?" she asked coyly.

"It's never too much with you." He kissed her eyelids and earlobes before sending playful nibbles over her lips. "You have such a pretty mouth, perfect for kisses."

She caressed his chest and teased a nipple before savoring his compliment with a deep kiss that didn't end until he rolled her beneath him. She loved how easily he turned the night blistering hot. Wrapped in his heat, she reveled in his every thrust and gloried in a shuddering orgasm. Filled to overflowing with pleasure, she lay blissfully exhausted. She rested her head on his shoulder, and while she drifted on the edge of sleep, she could feel he was still wide awake.

"I don't want to do anything but this," she cooed against his chest.

"Are you calling me a boy toy?"

His voice held a deep, teasing rumble, but she rose up on her elbow to make certain he understood. "You're good for everything, but I'm talking about myself. I've worked twenty years, and I don't want to model maternity clothes or anything else for a while, or start a photography business. I only want to be with you and do nothing else—although I might learn to cook or sew and make some baby clothes. Call it an extended vacation, but please don't make any more suggestions for my career."

He responded with a skeptical snort. "You'll be happy trying recipes for squash soup and sleeping with me while we wait for the baby?"

"Hmm." She covered a wide yawn.

"Then you might as well marry me, Ana."

She was quiet a long moment. "Not until you propose properly."

"Diamond ring, flowers, live music?"

"Whatever you like, but it has to be a surprise, and please don't keep me waiting too long. The marvelous proposal you claimed couldn't be repeated didn't exist, did it?"

"I'm sorry, no." He hugged her tight. "But poetry can't be rushed."

She crawled over him and wiggled to rub his cock against her clit.

"Am I rushing you?" With a teasing kiss, she swallowed any objection he might have had. She'd fallen so unforgivably hard for him, but what she truly needed was the promise of love he'd never spoken, and she wouldn't beg for the sweet words, not now, not ever.

Chapter Twenty-One

Friday, Alejandro had to interrupt his proposal plans to see Lieutenant Montoya. The man looked even grimmer than usual. "What's wrong?" he asked.

The lieutenant escorted him into his office. Files were neatly stacked on the desk, and as soon as Alejandro was seated, he opened one. "You'll be relieved to learn René Charles wasn't seriously injured. That is the man's name. He's a Spaniard of French descent. He claims you jumped him without provocation, and that he carries a knife for his own protection."

Shocked by the absurdity of René's claim, Alejandro leaned forward. "You can't believe him."

"No, of course not. He's been arrested several times for assault after bar fights but never served any time. We found a trace of Mr. Campos's blood on his knife; obviously he'd not cleaned it as thoroughly as he'd imagined. When confronted with the blood evidence, he claimed he'd worked as a model for Mr. Campos but hadn't been paid. When he demanded the money he was owed, an argument ensued, and enraged, he killed the photographer. The brutality of the scene makes his story plausible. If he'd gone there intending to kill him, he'd have been quick about it, and there would have been no blood-splattered walls.

"He admits to working as a chauffeur for Mr. Lamoreaux, but swore the man had nothing to do with his argument with Campos. We have him for the murder but haven't found any proof Lamoreaux had anything to do with the attacks on you."

"René rented a car after I'd mentioned going riding to Lamoreaux. He didn't just drive down the street either—he came after me. Isn't that a clear link? He wasn't out for a stroll when he walked up behind me either."

"René claims he needed the car to run errands and had no interest in you, although he despises cyclists who take up too much of the road."

Alejandro fought to hang on to his temper. "This isn't right."

"I agree, but it's all we can prove. Now I need your written statement." He handed over a clipboard with the proper form.

Alejandro drew in a deep breath and sat back to scan the information required. "There isn't much to tell. He came up behind me, and I kicked his feet out from under him. What more should I say?"

Montoya rose and went to the window to adjust the blinds. "It's important to state you felt threatened. You didn't attack him without reason. Include that he's a large man and menacing in appearance. Perhaps you saw his knife?"

"I didn't, and I'm not going to add my lie to his." He wrote only the facts as he knew them, signed his name and handed Montoya the clipboard. "Thank you for doing what you could, even if there's no way to prove Lamoreaux is involved."

The lieutenant nodded. "It's my job, Mr. Vasquez, and I recommend you have nothing more to do with the Frenchman."

"I won't." Alejandro shook his hand and left.

He called Ana, stopped by her condo and made his point clear as he came through her door. "Even if there's no way to tie Lamoreaux to René Charles, I don't want you to ever see him again."

Ana had worn her hair down and flipped an errant curl away from her face. "Do I appear so lacking in intelligence I can't be allowed to make my own decisions?"

He saw Fatima shake her head and duck into the kitchen. "No, you're probably a lot smarter than I am, but..."

She interrupted him with a raised hand. "This is Friday, and we never argue on Fridays. If I call Lamoreaux and tell him I'm taking a lengthy vacation, will you be happy?"

He clamped his jaw shut rather than reply, but undeterred, she chose her usual place on the sofa and called the shoe designer.

"Lucien, Alejandro and I are having a baby, and I'm sorry, but I'm not accepting any new work. I plan to take off a year or two, perhaps three."

"I'm stunned," the designer responded. "You mentioned a complicated relationship, but you needn't stay with Vasquez unless you sincerely want to. Please meet me so we can talk. You might feel differently about your future after speaking with me."

She covered the phone and looked up at Alejandro. "Maybe I should see him."

"No!" he responded with hushed force.

"I'm not sure what I could say, Lucien, but thank you for being sympathetic. There are so many lovely models, you'll have no trouble replacing me."

"You're so beautiful, my dear, no one will ever replace you."

"Thank you, that's such a lovely thing to say. Why don't we meet for a drink in a hour or so?" She named a popular cafe along Las Ramblas. He agreed, and she ended the call.

"What are you doing?" Alejandro asked. "Do you think he'll confess? This is real life not some scripted TV show, and you shouldn't put yourself at risk."

She crossed her arms over her chest. "It's clear I'm involved whether I want to be or not. Why would Lamoreaux send René Charles after you unless he wants me for himself? He showered me with gifts, arranged for me to model for him, and when I mentioned photography, he offered a project to give me a whole new career. He's so anxious to draw me in, he'll probably talk for hours in an attempt to convince me to leave you. If I appear to give it some thought and then choose to stay with you, he may become angry enough to say something incriminating. You could be there, but just out of sight."

"You're damn right I'll be there, and I'm calling Montoya. He'll post undercover men, and I'm afraid we'll need them."

"We'll be out in the open, so Lucien can't behave too badly."

He responded with a particularly colorful oath he'd picked up along the docks.

Montoya was as exasperated as Alejandro, but he met them at the café. "What is it you're trying to accomplish, Miss Santillan?"

"It's a simple plan. I'll play on his emotions, and he might admit more than he means to. If not, all we've wasted is an hour."

"And man-hours from my budget," the lieutenant muttered under his breath. "Find an outside table and be ready for him."

Alejandro hadn't spoken to her since they'd left her condo, and she didn't expect him to wish her luck. He followed and took a table close to hers and hid behind an open newspaper. Her table could be viewed from all angles. Feeling safe, she ordered limeade and waited. Lucien walked up within minutes.

"What a charming place. Do you come here often?" he asked.

"Yes, I do. A waiter should come by soon."

Lucien moved his chair close to hers and regarded her with a knowing smile. "We won't be staying. You'll love my home outside Paris, and I'll make you far happier than Vasquez ever could. Young men have no idea how to really please a woman the way I do."

His blue eyes shone with an admiring warmth, and his seductive accent made his promise seem sincere, but she wasn't even tempted. Instead, she spoke up, hoping Alejandro would overhear. "I'm sorry if I gave you any such hope. You've been so kind, and I merely wished to say good-bye in person."

"How thoughtful." His voice took on a deep strident edge. "I'm a very successful man, and I'm always armed when I'm in Barcelona." He opened his jacket to provide a glimpse of his handgun. "Don't make me resort to force."

She sat up and twisted her hair over her shoulder. "Are you threatening me while we're surrounded by witnesses?" Two middle-aged women who had been passing the café stopped outside the ring of tables and pointed at her. She nodded and smiled, and, appearing flustered, they walked away.

Lucien whispered against her ear, "Nothing so crude as a threat. No one will see a thing. You're leaving with me. Stand, and I'll help you with your crutches."

The marble-topped table had a wrought iron base. She grabbed the edge and shoved hard to force the table over. He scrambled to get out of the way, but the edge of the marble slab slammed hard across his foot, and he howled in pain.

Alejandro, already half out of his chair, grabbed Lucien's arms and pulled him upright. He saw the gun before Lucien could reach for it and blocked the move. Montoya's men swarmed them, and Alejandro pulled Ana into his arms. "I heard enough to know you were in trouble. Did he threaten to shoot you?"

Trembling, she leaned against him. "Not quite, but I didn't expect things to go downhill so quickly. He meant to take me to Paris whether I wanted to go with him or not."

Alejandro hugged her tight. "This is the absolute end of it, Ana. Don't frighten me like this ever again. The car wreck wasn't your fault, but this stunt was deliberate, and you could have been badly hurt, or worse."

She saw more than one passerby raising a cell phone to take photos and knew they were in for another round of tabloid coverage. Certain Alejandro had only begun a lengthy tirade, she was grateful for an excuse to step out of his arms. "There are too many people watching for us to talk here."

He looked over his shoulder and stepped back to take her hand. "Maybe they'll believe we're filming a movie."

Ana had no such hope. Lamoreaux was quickly taken away, and Montoya joined them. "He has no permit for the handgun, and his foot appears to be broken—a terrible shame, of course. What prompted you to tip the table?"

A waiter had already set the table upright, and Ana retook her chair to describe her brief conversation with Lucien. "He tried to force me to go with him, and I objected. It has to be a crime to kidnap people off the street."

"As well as indoors," Montoya added. "When I tell René Charles Lamoreaux has been arrested, he may be more forthcoming. He may have been well paid for his silence, but if Lamoreaux isn't free, he won't get another euro from him."

"I'm glad you were able to make an arrest. Thank you for being here." She looked to Alejandro. "Let's go home."

He picked up her crutches. "Home?" he repeated. "Just where is that?"

She touched his sleeve. "Please—you know where I want to go."

Alejandro nodded to Montoya as they walked away, and the lieutenant shook his head. Whether it was in envy or sympathy, Ana couldn't tell.

"Send Fatima home early," Alejandro urged as he parked in front of her condo.

She'd seldom seen him looking so determined and assumed he meant to have it out. "I'm not going to fight with you, but if it's wild sex you want, come on in." She opened her door, and he circled his SUV to grasp her waist and set her down gently. "I would never have gone to meet Lamoreaux alone," she swore. "I was safe with you and Montoya's men there. Please drop it." She took her crutches and waited for him to open the condo's main doors.

He remained on the walk. "You couldn't count on being safe."

"Maybe not, but you were willing to ride your bike to trap René Charles, so you've no room to criticize me."

"I'll take all the room I need. Was today just a daredevil payback?"

"Not at all." She caught a breath, relieved no lurking paparazzi were in sight. "Would you please open the door? Or I'll wave to the guard to let me in."

He yanked open the door. "I'll be busy tomorrow with the burial at sea. I'll pick you up Sunday afternoon, and we'll do something fun for a change."

Coming from him, *fun* sounded like an obscenity, but she smiled as though it had been a pleasant invitation. "I'll look forward to it." She stepped through the door and waited to watch him drive away. If he were in as black a mood on Sunday, she'd stay home and read.

Henry nodded as she passed the desk. "He's going to regret leaving you before he gets home."

"I hope you're right." Fatima was waiting for her, and Ana gave her a quick rundown. "Alejandro has had enough of me for the day, but I'll see him on Sunday. Would you please make me a cup of tea?"

"In a minute, but first there's something you need to explain. I never deliberately eavesdrop on your conversations, but didn't I hear a mention of a baby?"

Her longtime housekeeper looked perplexed at best, and she deserved the truth. "Yes, you did. It's taken me a while to get used to the idea. I haven't even told my mother."

"Why not? She lives in France. Nothing shocks anyone there."

"I don't know if that's true, but she'll be surprised. I'd rather rest a while than worry about telling anyone else about the baby today."

"I understand, but it'll be very difficult to raise a child on your own."

Ann leaned her crutches against a dining room chair. "I grew up with a widowed mother, so I know that only too well. You needn't worry, Alejandro intends to be a good father and provide for our child."

The housekeeper rested her hands on her hips. "Then you'd be smart to marry him."

"That's what he says. Now may I have my tea?"

"Yes, and I baked some shortbread cookies."

"Thank you." It took a couple of cups of tea for her to realize Alejandro had been completely justified in his anger. She'd wanted a neat conclusion to the whole Lamoreaux affair, but their meeting could have easily ended tragically. She rubbed her arms to shake off a chill and ate another delicious cookie. More than one man had shot a woman who'd left him or threatened to leave, and she shouldn't have taken such a foolish risk with Lamoreaux when she barely knew him.

She reached for her phone, and then set it aside. Alejandro was probably still too angry with her to listen to an apology. Spending a couple of lonely nights would also improve her chances he'd be so happy to see her he'd accept any apology she cared to give.

"Fatima, is there any of your wonderful leek and potato soup in the freezer? I'm staying in tonight."

Saturday dawned bright with a cloudless sky. Alejandro followed Carlotta and her sons onto a fifty-foot cabin cruiser used for burials at sea. She'd invited a half-dozen of her late husband's friends, and many others who'd known or admired him followed in their own boats as the captain took them beyond the port to open water. Sailboats crossed on the horizon. It was a far more peaceful scene than Alejandro had anticipated. When the captain cut the engine, the sea lapped gently against the cruiser's hull. Squawking sea gulls flew overhead in a disrespectful chatter.

Carnation floral wreaths in the Ortiz Line's blue and white colors were ready for the boys to throw. Eager to get the ordeal over, Alejandro nodded to Carlotta, but she remained in her seat, tightly clutching the silver urn with her late husband's ashes.

Alejandro crossed to her. "Here, come with me." He circled her shoulders and led her to the rail. "Come on, boys. Let's do this together."

Rodrigo and Francisco joined them, faces solemn, and Alejandro wished he'd prepared something, anything to say. He had no favorite memories of the man who'd been more of a mentor than a father. He looked over his shoulder to his father's friends. "Would any of you care to say something?"

A bald, heavy-set man came forward, and Carlotta gave him a shaky smile. "I can't bear to tell him good-bye, Gael."

Gael Galvez took the urn from her hands and twisted off the lid. "A man who loved the sea with such great passion will be at home beneath the waves." He lowered the urn, and the ashes spilled in a fine line.

Alejandro watched the boys, who appeared more fascinated by the drifting ashes than sad. Only Carlotta wept. The boys threw the wreaths, and the flowers floated upon the sea in silent tribute. He waited until Carlotta looked up at him to signal the captain. The cruiser made a wide arc and returned to the dock.

Carlotta wiped her eyes on her handkerchief. "I know you've never liked me, but thank you for handling today. There are so many others who'll miss your father. I've invited them to a small reception at home. I really don't care if Orlando would object or not."

Alejandro took her arm to help her step onto the dock. "He won't know, so how can he care?"

She found a shaky smile. "Please come."

When she looked so vulnerable, he couldn't refuse. "I will."

The penthouse's stark furnishings and modern paintings gave it the appearance of an art gallery rather than a comfortable home, and Alejandro moved to a corner to stay out of the way. Gael had remained by Carlotta's side; the boys seemed to know him. His firm built components for their cruise ships. Alejandro had seen him often when he'd worked with his father before returning to the university. Gael had been widowed several years prior, but Alejandro thought it far too soon for him to hit on his stepmother. Maybe he was simply showing the abundant sympathy the woman craved.

Grateful Carlotta would be surrounded by sympathetic friends for the remainder of the day, he turned his attention to his brothers. The boys were in their room playing a video game. When he came to the open door, his gaze was immediately drawn to the poster of Santos Aragon on the wall above their desks. Santos was posed on his toes and twirling his cape as a mammoth Miura bull tore by him. The handsome matador had signed the poster, which made it all the more valuable to the boys.

Rodrigo won the round and jumped up to cheer. He looked surprised to find Alejandro at their door and tapped Francisco's shoulder so he'd notice. "Will you take us out on a boat again?"

"Yes, we'll do it soon." He left them each with his card. "Tape them to your desk. Call me if you need anything at all. Your mother and I will work out a schedule so I can see you more often, and we'll plan something you two really want to do."

The boys nodded and got back to their game. Alejandro wasn't certain what the boys might like to do—maybe take karate lessons—but he'd see they got to do it. His father couldn't have had much time for them, and they were too young to grow up without a father, or someone who'd willingly take his place.

Ana spent Saturday morning at her favorite spa. A massage, manicure, pedicure and a new hairstyle with abundant curls had melted the last of yesterday's lingering tension. She'd been home only a few minutes when Alejandro called, and he didn't give her a chance to apologize.

"Montoya wants to see us. Apparently there're some complications we didn't anticipate. Do you have time to come with me?"

"Yes, I'll wait for you downstairs."

He looked preoccupied when he came to the condo door, but he swept her with an appreciate glance and broke into a cocky grin. "That's just not fair."

She'd put on a short yellow dress with lime-green trim and a matching green jacket and looked down to see if something were wrong. "What do you mean?"

He helped her into his SUV, got in and just stared at her. "You look even more beautiful than usual. Did you just come in from a job?"

"No, I was at a spa. Maybe I'll go again on Monday if it dazzles you."

"You always dazzle me. I don't know what Montoya wants, but it didn't sound good, and I don't want to imagine what it might be."

She'd known he couldn't stay angry with her and apologized as soon as she'd buckled her seat belt. "You were right yesterday. My plan was foolish. While it may have succeeded in some respects, I shouldn't have risked meeting Lamoreaux when there was no way to accurately predict how he'd react."

He leaned over to kiss her. "You're forgiven, but I shouldn't have gotten so angry with you. I hadn't told you how René Charles was caught, and that was a major part of the problem."

She leaned against her window to search his expression. He'd grown so serious it frightened her. "Tell me now."

He gave her as brief an explanation as he'd written in his statement. "I'd wanted to lure Charles out so Montoya could arrest him, not fight him hand to hand. I was certain your plan could prove equally dangerous, and it did. I was mad at myself for not stopping you when you first thought of it."

"We really need to tell each other the truth, whether it's scary or not."

"I've nothing less to confess. Do you?"

She gave her lips a suggestive lick. "Give me a while to think, and maybe I can come up with something."

He caressed her cheek gently. "If it's forgotten, let it go."

Montoya met them at the front desk and escorted them to his office. Once they were seated, he leaned back in his chair. "While you're here, Miss Santillan, you can give us your statement. Unfortunately, René Charles wasn't fazed when he learned Lamoreaux had been arrested. It had been my hope he'd negotiate with whatever information he had about the man, but he's sticking to his original story, although now he blames steroids for causing the murderous rage that cost Campos his life.

"As for Lamoreaux, he claims he contacted Mr. Campos because he admired his fashion photography and hoped Jaime could convince you to pose in a collection of nudes. When Jaime told him you wouldn't even discuss being photographed in the nude, he says he had to be satisfied with hiring you for ads for his shoes. He was very pleased with them, by the way. He spent some time praising your beauty before I could convince him to focus on yesterday afternoon."

Ana sat forward. "Are you saying there's no way to tie Lamoreaux to Jaime's death if René Charles won't give you one?"

Montoya responded with a helpless shrug. "René says he'd worked as Lamoreaux's chauffeur when the designer was in Barcelona. He told us Lamoreaux owns a popular French BD/SM magazine; he models sometimes, and that's how they met."

"I'll bet Lamoreaux doesn't brag about that," Alejandro interjected.

Ana touched his knee. "He wouldn't dare, or it would ruin his reputation in high fashion."

Montoya nodded. "I'm also wondering what he would have done with the photos had you posed in the nude. He would probably have made the most of them. He might even have thought he could force you into a relationship with the promise he'd not publish them in his magazine."

"Now I feel sick," Ana said, growing pale. "Jaime talked about tasteful art photography. Lamoreaux had the audacity to ask me if I'd take over the project, but I refused."

"You were wise to avoid it," the lieutenant replied. "He's hired a well-known attorney and quickly posted bail. Even if he did use René for muscle, I doubt he'll come after you on his own."

"But you're not sure," Alejandro stated. He reached for Ana's hand and gave her fingers a loving squeeze.

"No one can be sure of anything, Mr. Vasquez. Lamoreaux presents himself as a responsible businessman who occasionally employed René Charles, and René's the one who confessed to murder. Lamoreaux does admit to being overly fond of you, Ana, and he believes you simply misunderstood what he describes as a gracious invitation to visit his Paris home."

Ana gasped. "You don't mean it?"

"I do," Montoya insisted. "He says you accepted gifts from him. Flowers, candy and kittens would be seen as romantic. You willingly posed in ads for his shoes and left his apartment on your last visit wearing a new diamond bangle bracelet. You invited him to meet you, reacted badly to his so-called invitation to visit Paris, overturned the table and broke his foot. Surely you can imagine how a skilled defense attorney could twist your testimony into a flirtation you'd encouraged until it ended badly. He appreciates your passionate nature, and while a broken foot is a great inconvenience, he asked me to assure you he'll not press charges."

"How generous of him. Does he still have his gun?" Alejandro asked.

"No, and he should behave well to ensure his chances of avoiding prosecution."

"Should?"

"I can't read minds, but his attorney has a high success rate with his clients. If we consider how your testimony would be twisted, Miss Santillan, all we can charge him with is lacking a permit for a handgun. That won't require a trial."

Alejandro nearly snorted. "So he'll continue designing women's shoes?"

"Probably. Scandal is always good for business. Now if you'll write your interpretation of your conversation with Lamoreaux yesterday, we'll be finished."

Ana took the clipboard, but she was so angry she could barely hold a pen. "I remember it word for word." She printed to make certain it was legible, then signed and dated the form. She laid the clipboard on his desk. "I should have worn a wire."

Montoya laughed. "He would never have admitted to having anything to do with Jaime's murder."

"I'm not so sure," Ana argued. "Is that all for today?"

"Yes." The lieutenant rose and escorted them through the station. "If we meet again, I hope it will be under better circumstances."

A fake smile flitted across Ana's lips. "So do I." She moved as quickly as she could on crutches and didn't draw a deep breath until they were seated in Alejandro's SUV.

"The paparazzi in Paris are even more rabid than they are here," she mused aloud. "If one were to learn Lamoreaux published porn, or however his magazines can be described, the clientele for his elegant heels might shrink dramatically."

"That's almost too good, Ana." Alejandro kept his eyes on the road, but his smile grew wide. "You wouldn't want anyone to tie you to the information, so a phone call is out. An unsigned letter to a tabloid editor couldn't be traced."

"True, and I can't think of any reason not to do it."

"We did pose for his ads," he reminded her.

"So what? If he's out of business, he'll have no reason to use them."

"Montoya is probably right and scandal would boost his business rather than destroy it, so let's think about it. I need to stop by my loft. Come in with me."

He hugged her close as the elevator rose. "I want to show you something new."

"More little houses?"

He unlocked his door and escorted her in. The worktable was a messy pile of scraps, but a beautiful model of a two-story Mediterranean-style home sat on his display table. Painted white with a red-tile roof, arched windows, balconies and a courtyard, it was as pretty a house as she'd ever seen. Behind the house, he'd made a sturdy tree out of gathered sticks, and placed a tree house in the branches.

"I love the tree house!" she exclaimed. "I'm surprised, though. I thought you were concentrating on the Ortiz Lines. When did you have time to do this?"

"I made the time. I want to build a home for us where we'll have plenty of room, and can even avoid each other if we need to. If you don't like this one, I'll design something else."

Touched, she braced herself against the table. "It's a lovely house, Alejandro. It's poetry in three dimensions, don't you think?"

He stepped close. "Are you giving me a star for the poetry element?"

"Yes, I am." His kiss was tender and light, sweet, when she longed for passion.

"Good. I've found another American comedy that's supposed to be even funnier than the last one we saw. Let's go today rather than wait for tomorrow. I've found a new place for dinner."

He appeared to be checking off a list and might propose under the moonlight, but her heart ached for so much more. "Could we stay here a little longer?"

"Of course. Do you want something to drink?"

"No, thank you. I'm fine." She focused on the beautifully constructed model and searched for the right words while unshed tears formed a painful knot in her throat. "I appreciate everything you do, but you don't love me, Alejandro, and some day you'll meet a woman who'll speak to your heart, and it won't matter how many delicious dinners we've shared or where we live. You'll choose her, and you'll feel less guilty then if we don't marry now."

He stepped close to press her palm to his chest. "Are you finished?"

She'd struggled for every word and sighed as she nodded. They would know each other forever, but she wanted to be so much more than the mother of his child.

He pulled her into his arms. "You're the only woman who's ever touched my heart. Can you feel it beating? I can't tell you the exact moment I fell in love, but I wouldn't use it for an excuse when I let you believe we were married. You'd have dismissed it as a pathetic ploy."

She raised her hand to slip her fingers through his glossy black hair. "You couldn't be pathetic if you tried. I fell in love with you when all you knew was my first name. It was so nice not to question your motives when you wanted to be with me."

He kissed her brow. "I let my father blow it apart, but you came after me."

"Because I didn't care about looking pathetic—but let's not keep track of our mistakes. I made them too. Let's cultivate the art of forgiveness."

He crossed to his desk and removed a small velvet box. "I planned to propose tomorrow. The restaurant has a beautiful view of the city and live musicians who play love songs until midnight. It would have been a perfect setting, but I can't wait. I miss you too much when we're apart, and you make every hour we're together a glimpse of paradise. I know I can be the man you deserve. Will you marry me?" He opened the box to show off a sparkling diamond solitaire.

It was a gorgeous ring, and his silvery gaze glowed with love. She rested her hands on his and took a deep breath. "This is really about you and me and not just the baby?"

"You and me," he assured her. "I want us to be a real family whether we have one baby or half a dozen. My father set such a poor example. I promise I'll do everything right and make you proud to be my wife." He hugged her and whispered in her ear, "The next time you offer hot sex, I won't leave. Will you please say yes so we won't be late for the movie?"

He'd already shown her how wonderful a husband he could be, and such a loving man would be the very best of fathers. She didn't care at all about going to the movies. "Won't it be playing tomorrow?"

"Sure, but please don't keep me waiting that long for your answer."

She wrapped her arms around his neck and placed a sloppy kiss in his ear. "Yes, I love you dearly, and I'll marry you. We'll make the best family ever."

Thrilled, he picked her up and turned with her in his arms. "Let's plan your dream wedding with the designer gown and your mother and stepfather and all your friends and my mother and the artist. Whatever you want to do, I'll be fine with it. I just want you to be happy."

"Let's wait until I'm able to walk down the aisle without needing crutches. But for now, there is one little thing."

He set her down and slipped the dazzling ring on her finger. "I'm almost afraid to ask what it is."

"You needn't worry. I was only wondering if you had any of the frosting left."

He responded with a wicked grin. "I do." He gathered her into his arms and muffled his laughter in her cascading curls.

About the Author

Always a passionate lover of books, this New York Times bestselling author first answered a call to write in 1980 and swiftly embarked on her own mythic journey. With more than seven million copies in print of her historical, contemporary and futuristic books written under her own name as well as her pseudonym, Cinnamon Burke, she is as enthusiastic as ever about writing.

A native Californian, Phoebe attended the University of Arizona and California State University at Los Angeles where she earned a BA in Art History and an MA in Education. Her books have won Romantic Times Reviewer's Choice Awards and a nomination for Storyteller of the Year. She is a member of Romance Writers of America, Novelists Inc., PEN, AWritersWork.com and Backlistebooks.com.

She is the proud mother of two grown sons and two adorable grandchildren, who love to have her read to them. She loves to hear from fans. Please contact her through her web site: PhoebeConn.com or her e-mail: phoebeconn@earthlink.net

Their affair is the main attraction...
and the distraction a killer has waited for.

Fierce Love
© 2012 Phoebe Conn

Magdalena Aragon never thought she'd answer the summons of a father she's never known. The world-famous, many-times-married matador has provided everything she needs—except his time. There's only one reason she packs her bags for Spain: what her psychologist calls "closure."

In spite of herself, she's drawn in by her father's charm, irresistible despite his desperate illness. Then there's his handsome protégé, a rising star in a sport she hates, yet he sets her passions on fire.

With a past as shadowy as his Gypsy heritage, Rafael Mondragon has always had to fight for what he wants. His freedom, his dream to become a star in the bull ring, and now his mentor's daughter, who stirs his every dark desire.

Certain she won't be staying long, Maggie escapes from the craziness of her newly discovered, fractured family to indulge in a red-hot fling. After all, Rafael is the last man she could ever love. Her heart has other ideas.

The heat from their affair captures the attention of the wrong people—the tabloids, and someone who has a twisted sense of honor. By the time Rafael realizes Maggie is the real target, it could be too late to save her.

Warning: Hot sex, dangerous secrets, men who challenge death for sport.

Available now in ebook and print from Samhain Publishing.

SAMHAIN
PUBLISHING

It's all about the story...

Romance

HORROR

Retro
ROMANCE

www.samhainpublishing.com